ParSec
IN PRINT

ParSec
In Print

Edited by IAN WHATES

ParSec in print
Edited by
Ian Whates Copyright © 2023

Cover Art
Front cover art by Ben Baldwin
Back cover art by Vincent Sammy

This trade paperback edition published in September 2023 by Drugstore Indian Press, an imprint of PS Publishing Ltd. by arrangement with the authors.

ISBN 978-1-80394-329-9

10 8 6 4 2 1 3 5 7 9

Design & Layout by Michael Smith
Printed in England by T. J. Books Limited

PS Publishing Ltd
Grosvenor House
1 New Road, Hornsea
East Yorkshire, HU18 1PG
England

editor@pspublishing.co.uk
www.pspublishing.co.uk

Contents

ParSec In Print

An Introduction

WHEN PUTTING THIS ANTHOLOGY TOGETHER, I WAS determined that it should not be called *The Best of ParSec* or anything of that ilk. A title such as that would be a slight on those stories that were not selected, suggesting they are in some way inferior to those that have been, and that's simply not the case.

Permit me to explain.

Two thirds of the stories published in the first seven issues of *ParSec*, from which this volume is drawn, came to us via the three brief open submission periods we've held to date. During those three windows I received around 1,000 submissions. Of these, I've accepted just 8%. I've turned away some good stories in the process, I know that, but those that have made it into the magazine are all stories I *love*.

For those who may be wondering, the remaining one third of the stories are pieces specially commissioned from authors I trust—some to accompany author interviews in a given issue, some not—or stories that either NewCon Press or PS Publishing had acquired for projects that didn't proceed, but these stories were just too good to let go. All reach my personal benchmark for *ParSec* or they wouldn't have been accepted.

∞

Let's take a step back. The above makes an assumption: that those reading this are aware of *ParSec*, and there will doubtless be some who aren't. Therefore, a brief catch-up.

ParSec was born out of a telephone conversation in December 2020, when the inimitable Peter Crowther (head honcho of PS Publishing) contacted me to ask: "How would you like to edit an established genre magazine for me?"

Initially, I demurred. I harboured no ambitions to edit a magazine, and my own writing career had already been impacted by the amount of time invested in running NewCon Press. I had a full publishing schedule already in place for the latter that would keep me busy for the next 18 months. The last thing I needed was another demand on my time, let alone a recurring one. Pete, however, was persistent, and persuasive, and his enthusiasm proved infectious, so my initial reluctance soon became "maybe" and then "okay, let's give it a go", quickly morphing into "Woohoo".

In retrospect, it was a blessing when the proposed takeover of an existing magazine fell through; which is not how it felt at the time, however. By that point I had invested considerable time and effort in working on this, as had the team at PS, and to have it snatched away came as a body blow. After putting our heads together, we discovered a shared determination that our endeavours should not go to waste and this wouldn't be the end. In fact, it represented an opportunity. We could carry on, but would now be working on something new, something different, something of our own devising that was free of any baggage or expectation. And so *ParSec* was born: produced by PS Publishing and edited by yours truly.

Our first issue appeared in the summer of 2021 and, as I write this, #8 is being prepared, with future issues already taking shape and some fabulous stories locked in.

When it came to making a selection for the first *ParSec* volume to see print, it's been tough. The composition of the book has chopped and changed as I vacillated over this piece and that. I've sought to ensure that the varied nature of the magazine's fiction is reflected in the anthology, with SF, fantasy, horror, and those quirky tales that are hard to label but only genre can produce all present. There are novelettes and shorter pieces that verge on flash fiction. There are stories from established names and others from emerging voices and fiction debutants. We have writers from five different continents . . . None of which matters to me a great deal, to be honest.

I have a confession to make. When I consider a story for any project, my primary concern—pretty much my *only* concern—is the quality of that story. Whether it moves me, whether it entertains me, whether it surprises me, whether it satisfies me, whether it impresses me. All other considerations pale into insignificance: the gender, race, nationality of the author are irrelevant. When it comes to a story, the quality of the writing and the tale it tells are all.

I hope this book reflects those values, and that you enjoy the reading experience as a result.

Ian Whates
Cambridgeshire
August 2023

ParSec
in print

Down and Out Under the Tannhauser Gate

David Gullen

THE ONLY THING YOU COULD BE SURE ABOUT WHOEVER came through the gate was that they weren't human. Riay's perfect skin was sun-tanned brown and her white hair close-cropped, but her skull was high and narrow, her too-large eyes black on black, and her slender arms had a second elbow that let them fold up like a mantis at prayer.

I looked at her and wondered. If she had started out human she wasn't now, and if she had been then that meant she'd gone through and come back, which to my mind made her pretty stupid. I couldn't imagine myself being that beautiful, so maybe there's a trade-off. Give me the chance to go through the gate and no way would I come back. But hey, if I did, at least it would be all girls together and we could swap makeup tips.

I limped closer. My leg stump always ached. It never lets me forget and that makes me moody.

There, I admit it.

Riay said she wanted us to build a temple.

'Who for?' I said. 'Mukaluk the Destroyer, Eccentrica Galumbitz, Omnidod the Translucent, Simon and his Dancing Bear?

'I came back to help—'

So she *had* come back. I grinned and looked down the steps for Jonni. He'd gone for water two hours ago so should be back soon. 'If you're a priestess of Galumbitz there's a bunch of guys down in the town who'd be happy to meet you.' I thought about it. 'Some women too.'

This part of the world is a landscape of steps, a white stone hill two miles wide and one mile high. Eight thousand steps with a hundred flights and platforms. At the bottom lies a human city, a ramshackle shanty thing. At the top are the sky-high silver pillars of the Tannhauser Gate, the beautiful gate, the one we Earther soldiers tried so hard, so very damned hard, to reach.

How I hate that gate. Yet here I am, living in its shadow.

Most visitors climb the centre regions of the steps. The aliens come down and the replica men go up, because now they are free they can do what they want. Them, but not us.

Cytheran guards keep everything peaceful, which is nice of them considering they made us rebuild the place when the war was over.

And then there are us humans: the sightseers who dare go so far and no further; the petitioners who want to go all the way and can't; and us ragged bunch of leftovers living beneath our poles and awnings among the rubble along the left-side wall. Every now and then the more adventurous aliens come over to see the puddles of stone-melt and flash shadows from the war. From the day we soldiers fought. From my Day.

In the main the Cytherans leave us to it. They could clear us out in an instant but they never have. Also good of them, I suppose. After what we humans went through, I like to think we have squatter's rights.

A Cytheran air-walked across to check our visiting priestess was all right. I don't like the Cytherans. They're never mean and they're never cruel but they are abrupt, and they have energy lances. Cytherans are humanoid, they walk but their feet don't touch the ground, they slide-walk through the air. Maybe they don't like being here, on what is still human ground. When they stand in front of you in their intricate blue fabric armour and look out through their multifaceted visors of their segmented helmets, it's hard to tell who or what is home. Maybe they're antennae and those aren't helmets.

Riay looked up at the Cytheran. 'All is well. There is no need to attend.'

The Cytheran bowed, turned and paddled away through the air, angling up the steps towards the gate.

'What's the temple deal?' I asked Riay.

'Help me and I can help you.'

I slapped my tin leg. 'Can you help this?'

She looked a little sad. 'I just need a little help?'

'You mean, like a donation?' That was a good one. I'd never been touched for credit before. The walk-ins are usually passing through, their eyes on the spaceport beyond the city, and the handful of star systems left us from the old empire. They might be crazy but they're not stupid. Well, I say that but they, like Riay, came back.

'I need a symbol, anything. Just a gesture.' She pointed towards a heap of rubble against the scarred wall. 'Take that brick and place it in front of me. You don't have to say anything, the act is all.'

I laughed, it was pathetic. What kind of God wants a temple built from a single brick from a broken wall?

I didn't notice Jonni was back until he put the water containers down. He picked up a brick, held it in both hands like an offering, then knelt and laid it at her feet.

Riay glowed. 'Thank you.'

She actually looked better. It was probably psychosomatic. She smiled at Jonni and she became radiant, like a sun that shone only for him. Right then I felt my heart harden, and if her smile wasn't bad enough she reached out, her mantis arm unfolding out of her robe, and touched him with her three-fingered hand.

Let me say that again: she *touched* Jonni.

I was up and screaming, arms flailing, all my training forgotten and thank the gods it was because I could have killed her, killed anyone, killed them all. 'What did you do to him? What did you do?'

Jonni wrapped his arms around my waist and lifted me off the ground. My Jonni, the only one who ever had the balls to take me on, even in the days when I'd rage and try to burn it down, burn the whole world with anger so pure it broke my bones. Slowly I learned I couldn't live without him and so it became burn everything except Jonni, and he made a joke about where he would stand and I laughed and he held me and now I could not think of a day without those brown eyes under his loose black curls. His lean long body on mine. My Jonni.

'It's all right. Hey, hey. Breathe, breathe. We're counting down, remember? Here we go: ten, nine—'

I glared at Riay. 'What happened? What did that *freak* do to you?'

'Nothing.' His face was right in front of me. 'Nothing happened.'

Almost, I believed. She had it coming.

∞

I—He—Jonni. I couldn't have done any of this without him. Especially through the days when not even the moment by moment of living was easy or even wanted, or the times when I blinked and everything snapped back, and I looked around and wondered why everyone was looking at me because I had no idea what I'd just said or what I'd done. Now I have days where I dream we walk down the steps, away and away to some city on some far planet and he would put something in my belly, a little bit of him, a little of me. Something that would live and grow.

Except I would not leave this place. These steps under the gate. My step. That day. I could not.

∞

One morning three aliens came through the gate to look at the wall and see the signs of the old war. I limped up to my step and leaned on the wall exactly where they would want to go. Everyone who had anything laid out their boxes and trays of trinkets and junk, crouched on the steps, eyes lowered and hands out. Everyone except for Riay, who sat by her brick, and mad Blascard who muttered under his breath then punched the wall and stamped away.

These aliens were short heavy creatures with wide-mouthed heads, peg teeth and stubby legs, like two-legged hippos. They looked sideways at us with white button eyes and kept inside the Cytheran's dome field as they inspected the wall. They looked down at me and hooted to each other. The Cytheran's force dome pushed aside grit and dirt as they came forwards, leaving neat little moraines at each side and a clean track behind. From the corner of my eye I saw Blascard's blue-eyed glare. Here we go again, I thought, but he just rubbed the white stubble on his chin and slid away along the wall.

The three aliens looked at me, at each other, and the Cytheran.

Cytheran voices came inside my head:

—Human gentleperson, do now attend.

Guests wish to inspect the wall—

—guests that stand before you now.

—the wall behind the position you occupy.

I folded my arms and said nothing.

I caught a sub-echo of Cytheran click-babble, one of the hippo-things hooted softly then extended an arm and opened its hand. A few trade tokens materialised at my feet. Their colours looked good, I scooped them up and stood aside.

The aliens went to the wall and scanned the bigger patches of stone-melt and flash shadow with bars of violet light. Then they stood back and looked down at the boot prints left from the day the pavement flowed white hot and people ran.

Once upon a time the human race punched above its weight and we went round after round against the universe. Then we were betrayed.

Pressure built in me, I had to speak.

'I was there.' It came out as a shout, a sharp burst of sound. Startled, the aliens clustered behind the Cytheran. I unclenched my fists. I didn't want to frighten them, I wanted them to understand.

'I was there. The last day, that last hour.' I put my palm on the flash-shadows burned on the wall. 'I know the names of the people who left these marks, I saw—I saw them. I was there. That day…'

The aliens stood like statues, the Cytheran hovered in front of them, gently bobbing up and down. I wanted to tell them that this had been us and us alone. Humanity's last great spear thrust, a final effort driving up the steps to break through the gate. We who came so close: Dumas' brigade, the Fighting Ninth.

Yes, we were wrong and we deserved to fail but so what? I was there and I saw. I—We—On this very step they died. The aliens' stillness made me angry. I climbed towards them.

Out of nowhere Blascard was there, grimacing and gesticulating, his teeth chewing air. He dressed like some desert mystic in loose robes of hessian and linen. With his weathered skin, dirty blond hair and blue eyes he looked the part. He'd nailed the crazy bit too.

Alarmed, the three aliens backed away. The Cytheran went with them, keeping them inside its dome.

Blascard reached out with claw-fingered hands. 'Give me a key, give me your *minnesang*. Take me with you, please. I beg you.'

The aliens looked everywhere except Blascard. The Cytheran drifted forwards, a burst of click-babble like static, then faintly I heard its voices:

Unfortunately—

—this is not possible.

Please adjust your referents

Soon, perhaps—

—Or never

Adjustment flows from within—

'Take me with you!' Blascard wept and raged. 'Give me a *minnesang!*'

Jonni was at Blascard's shoulder, his hand on his arm. 'Enough. Come away.'

'No.' Blascard flung him off. 'Please—!'

His fingertips brushed the Cytheran's energy dome and he vanished. This freaked the aliens far more than any of us, even Blascard. No doubt the Cytheran reassured them Blascard was fine, but we all acted outraged and we got a generous extra hand-out of tokens. We trousered a few but kept a good half to give to Blascard when he'd walked back from wherever the Cytheran had put him.

After the aliens left, Jonni stood beside me. Weary, I leaned against him. 'Why do those Cytherans hate us?'

Jonni tucked a lock of hair behind my ear. 'Why do you think that?

'They won't even walk on the same ground we do.'

'I think maybe they are similar to us, all the aliens. They have hopes and dreams, likes and dislikes, just different ones.' He kissed my neck. 'They want to get laid.'

Well, there was that. I thought about all the things I liked about Jonni; his hands, the dark hairs on his arms, how he made me feel so calm.

He laughed and lifted my arms away. 'I want to make sure Blascard comes back.'

'He'll be fine.'

'I just want to be sure.'

Melt scars on the stonework pressed against my shoulders and the calmness Jonni brought disappeared. I traced one of the flash shadows with my hand and remembered all their names. I saw the wild look Dumas gave me the instant before he—

'I didn't run.'

'I know,' Jonni said quietly.

'I was hurt bad. My leg. The suit locked me down.' Which was why I was so far back. Which was why I was the only one—

Jonni's arm tightened round me. 'I know.'

'I didn't run.' And I know I didn't deserve to survive.

We watched and waited for Blascard. A steady breeze came up the steps and blew dirt back over the clean trail the Cytheran's dome had made.

All this helping out and watching over people. Jonni called it Paying it Forwards. 'Someone helped me once. I can't help them so I help other people instead.'

Of course when Blascard came back he took one look at Riay's brick and said, 'What's that?'

'A small but selfless gesture. Will you make one too?'

Blascard took in her up and down. His hands started to shake. 'You've been through the gate. Give me your *minnesang*.'

A small crowd gathered, people on their way up to the gate to make demands or present some new petition. Behind them three drifting Cytherans watched and waited.

'Your *minnesang*.' Blascard dropped to his knees, mumbling. 'Please, give it to me. Please.'

'I cannot. I am my own key, body and mind, my living self entire. You I can only teach.' Her jointed arm unfolded gracefully, her upturned hand swept the air above the brick. 'Help me. We can build something together.'

Blascard grimaced and begged; he hadn't listened to a word. 'Give it to me,' he growled.

'It is not mine to give,' Riay said. 'I can teach, you can learn—'

'I'm not here to learn, I know my rights.'

Hostile voices came from the crowd.

'Don't trust that alien witch.'

'Send her back to where she came from.'

'This is human territory.'

'Freak.'

'Traitor.'

Words were as far as it ever went. Before it got physical the Cytherans simply popped people away all over the place. Once in a while some Neo-militant idiot pulled a weapon and the Cytherans reminded everyone about the rules. C-beam glitter; Flash-shadow; Stonemelt. Like I needed reminding.

Blascard started at the voices behind him, unaware the crowd was there. He faced them. 'We're not here to learn, are we, friends? If we learn, we change. And who wants to change? Better to stay here forever.'

He pushed through the silent, confused crowd and marched down the steps.

∞

That's how it went. Blascard, Jonni and me, and a few others in shelters on the next platform down. And now Riay too. Jonni said we should help her and I gave her an old blanket because he'd want me to. She said she didn't need it, which was fine because I didn't want to give it to her. Instead, I grudgingly offered to help her build a shelter when she had something to build it from.

'If you really want to help—'

That stupid brick? I laughed at her. 'I'm not going to worship you. If there are gods they're the other side of the gate.'

Riay shook her head. 'Why would anyone want to be worshipped?'

It sounded good to me.

Jonni did what Jonni does and disappeared for most of the day. I wanted to go with him but my leg wouldn't take it. So much time without him was always hard. I did my best but the rat came out of its burrow, gnawed into in my gut and whispered in my ear: *He's had enough, it's your fault. This time you've done it. He's gone for good. There's no one to blame but you. Your fault. You deserve this.*

I walked up to my step. The step. I didn't eat, I didn't drink, I just sat and watched and waited and fought the teeth and claws. Hours later, when I saw Jonni angling up the steps towards us in the far distance I felt nothing but anger. He carried a bed roll wrapped around half a dozen odd-length planks on his shoulder, and an old metal box under his arm. I didn't understand how could he love me if he made me feel like this. What was so special about that freak woman that he would do all this for her?

I glared down the steps at Riay and a black joy came. I could tear her, rip her to shreds.

Jonni walked up to Riay, put the box down and leant the wood against the wall. I couldn't hear her voice but saw her mouth move. Jonni ran his hand through his hair. He smiled, he was tired, Riay poured him some water. I knew how he'd be telling her how cold it would get at night, that he would build something better tomorrow.

There was bad energy in me. I didn't want to go down because I knew how things would go. I went down anyway.

I bounced into the space between Jonni and Riay, right up into Jonni's face. 'Where have you been?'

'Hey, just finding some things for Riay.'

'It was a long time.'

'I had to go a long way and—'

'I didn't like it. Up there, on the step. On my own.' Now I had Jonni's full attention, like Riay wasn't there, like she didn't even *exist*.

'What happened?'

'Nothing happened. That's not it.'

'What then? Tell me.'

Jonni tried to touch me, I knocked his hand away. This is what happens with bad energy, it gets confused. It realises things about itself, that it's diminished, a lesser thing. Worthless. 'Jonni, I thought—It's just that when you're gone I worry—'

'You know I'll come back. Always.'

I was angry at myself now. Stupid, stupid. 'I know.'

I did know. It was just—There was a day when everybody I ever knew left. Stonemelt, flash-shadow. Some days I wished I'd gone with them. I didn't deserve—

'Oh, Jonni, I got this worry.'

'I know.' He said that a lot. Bless him.

The sun lowered, high dappled clouds turned pink then ruby gold. The miles-long flights of the steps glowed with red light and somehow it was beautiful.

It was also cold, but we had a blanket, me and Jonni. We went up to my step and sat with that blanket around our shoulders and ate the hot food Blascard cooked up on the fire. The night cold crept into my leg and it ached and ached.

Down in the cities, out in the planets I heard they can grow new legs for a gazillion credits. But who would care about a soldier from the last push? The last soldier. The one and only... Maybe the Neos. I'd have to go down and search for them. Plan A: An old soldier goes looking for a bunch of illegals. That would end well. My fists clenched, my stomach clenched. An ache in my leg, another all across my shoulders. Plan B. I took a long slow breath. Ten... Nine... Eight... Seven...

'It's a stupid temple,' I said.

Jonni shifted comfortably against me. 'Riay wants to stay.'

'When- When she touched you—?'

Jonni went still. 'Nothing happened.'

'I know. But when she touched you—' I knew this was a mistake but I was going to make it. 'Did you like it?'

Jonni closed his eyes. I knew if I kept this up I could drive him away. I could do it easy. Then where'd I be?

'Sorry, Jonni,' I said. 'Sorry.'

Jonni thought about it. 'How's your leg?'

'It aches really bad.'

'Let's go down to the fire.'

∞

That was Jonni for you. It was who he was, the thing I liked most and least about the man I loved. You think this was not so good? You should have seen me three years ago. Tell me about it. I mean, you'd have to tell me about it because I don't remember. Just a few flash-bulb moments of pure anger shouting, screaming. Living with my face turned to the wall.

Jonni put me back together, he taught me the ten-nine-eight so I could get back to the place where I still knew how to think. He put me back together but there were some bits missing. I don't know why he did it. I didn't deserve—

Deep breath.

Ten . . . Nine . . .

Jonni is kind to everyone. He wants to help. It's who he is. He sees the good.

∞

Replica men and women travelled up to the gate in groups. A lot of them looked old and frail and they helped each other along. I knew they weren't that old, they just didn't have as much time as we did. It was the way they were, the way we'd made them. I'd have betrayed us too.

Jonni took them water as he did for everyone. They'd stop for a minute and talk, sometimes I'd hear a dry laugh or see a tired farewell. I didn't resent them, I tried not to resent them. Each and every one had a ticket though the gate just because of what they were. Even so, Blascard didn't hassle them. There were fewer and fewer replicas this side of the gate every year and one day there would be none. Jonni was right—*is* right—none of what happened was their fault. It was our fault, all of it. We made them and treated them like slaves. Then we started a war, gave them guns and expected them to fight. So they did, but not for us. Fair enough.

Days went by; I sat on my step and got in the way. People looked at Riay and freaked and didn't build her stupid temple. Jonni carried water, Blascard skimmed and scammed and made demands and otherwise kept himself to himself. One day that furious sense of entitlement of his would get him into real trouble. I wondered why the Cytherans didn't just put him on the far side of the continent, or off-world, so the aliens who came through that gate could get some peace and quiet.

Every day Jonni hung our two water containers on the ends of a rag-wrapped pole, put the pole across his shoulders and went down the steps to fill them. Once in a while I'd go with him and swap credits for food. Jonni likes the raggedy ramshackle town at the base of the steps, it's just a sprawl of one and two-storey shacks on top of the stone-melt, no foundations. The whole vibe felt like a frontier town and I didn't much like it. Frontier of what? Dead dreams. Each trip gave me days of grinding leg pain that wouldn't stop and woke me up at night.

When Jonni came back I stacked the containers while he had a rest. I refilled the bucket, put the lid back on to keep the dust out, and washed the cups.

At night we sat round the fire, shared our food and checked our credits. I'd sit on my step for a while. I try to keep it short because I know sitting there builds bad energy. Too long makes me dream bad dreams.

A new group of petitioners came up the steps, four men and three women, all with close-cropped hair and dressed in the loose robes petitioners tended to wear, like they were mystic or whatever. These were younger than usual and moved easily, untired by the mile-long climb.

There was something about them, so when Jonni took over the water bucket I tagged along.

'Hey, there. Would you like some water?' Jonni took the lid off the bucket, scooped up a full mug and held it out.

The nearest of them, a square-headed blocky man with a stubbled jaw looked at him blankly, chewing something. 'No.'

'Thank you, brother.' A woman moved out of the centre of the group and reached for the cup. Her smile was direct, pretty green eyes in a lean athletic face. I didn't like her.

'That was quite a climb.' She smiled, then looked at the square-headed man. 'Some of us are tired.'

'Yes, I am,' he said. 'I am tired, and I apologise. Actually, I am thirsty.'

'No problem.' Jonni held out his hand. 'I'm Jonni.'

'Luthar.'

They shook, Luthar grinned, still chewing. Jonni gave him a mug and he drank half and poured the rest over his scalp. Everyone relaxed into chatter, the woman introduced herself as

Baez. This was what Jonni did but I've no idea how he did it. He got on with people and they got on with him. I hung back, not even on the edges.

You could see Luthar was steady. He had the forced wiry strength of a big-bodied man kept in check by a hard regime. I liked him. I decided maybe I liked Baez too.

Luthar saw me watching. 'This your old lady?' he said to Jonni.

Jonni stood tall. 'Yes, she is.'

I came forwards and didn't even think about it. Normally I don't do crowds and seven strangers plus Jonni is crowd enough. Also, petitioners are all the stupid. They go up, they beg and plead, argue and bitch, then come back down again with exactly what they went up with—nothing. Yet with these guys none of that occurred to me. There was something about them I understood.

'Less of the old,' I said, though most days it felt true.

Luthar held up both hands. 'No offence.'

'None taken.'

He held out his hand. I took it and his grip was solid, not trying to make a point, just made of iron. Why was I even doing this? I don't do names. 'Mercedes.'

Luthar stopped chewing. His mouth opened and closed.

In the following silence Baez said, 'Resonant name, considering.'

Luthar studied my face, looked at my leg and back to my face. 'It's you.'

Everyone looked at me. I bunched my fists and took it. Yeah, sure, this was me. Mercedes Gant, last of the Fighting Ninth, last of the last. So what?

The same light came into all their eyes at the same time. Nobody in all my life had been impressed by anything I had ever done. Now I had seven, all watching me with a kind of awe.

It hit me then. They weren't petitioners going to grovel for a *minnesang*. They were Neos, but not a type I'd seen before. Baez, Luthar and the others moved and spoke with the quiet assurance of well-trained and experienced soldiers, and I knew exactly what they were going to do. The part of me that still burned and bled and howled, the bit that felt oddly at peace in their company, knew that if I asked they would take me with them. This was why I'd walked in—it felt like coming home.

'Don't do it,' I said.

Luthar's tongue pushed against his cheek. 'We've got a few tricks.'

'Enough, Luthar,' Baez said, quiet and very, very definite. 'Moving on, ladies.'

Jonni hadn't got it. 'You're welcome to eat with us on the way down.'

Baez was oddly thrown by that. 'Of course. I—Thank you.'

Every single one of them said 'Thank you' as they handed the cups back to Jonni but their eyes were all on me as they set of up the steps.

Luthar held back. 'Sergeant Gant, excuse me. Where did you—?'

Some things become hard-wired. 'Three steps up. Out on the far left.'

His eyes had that thousand-yard stare as he looked towards the wall. In the distance a Cytheran led a solitary wand-like alien down from the gate.

'Must have been something,' Luthar said.

It was something all right, and nothing. 'Don't go. You're all going to die.'

'Everybody dies. Thing is, what for?' Luthar said, and jogged up the steps after Baez.

Jonni dumped the mugs into the bucket. 'Well, they were different.'

He broke my heart some days. 'We have to leave. Now.'

Baez's group were high up on the steps, as close to the gate as humans were allowed. A Cytheran moved to intercept them and they spread into a wide line.

I grabbed Jonni's arm and pulled. 'Come on!'

He pulled back. 'My bucket—'

'Forget the damned bucket. They're Neos, they're going to fight.'

And of course he turned and looked and it was too late.

Baez sprinted past the Cytheran with Luthar right beside her. The air shimmered around them—force fields. Luthar was right, they did have some tricks.

The Cytheran swung its lance. One of the other Neos darted forwards, wrapped her arms around the Cytheran and they exploded in a flopping meaty red mess.

The boom of the explosion spread across the steps and now everyone was looking. Baez, Luthar, and the remaining Neos raced up onto the final platform and disappeared from view.

I had to see. I pulled Jonni down and scrambled up the steps on all-fours. He grabbed my good foot and hauled me back.

'Stay here,' he said and ran up the final flight.

Well, of course not.

Unable to run, I swore and hopped and hobbled after him. We crouched at the top and peered over. One hundred feet across open ground stood the fluted silver pillars of the Tannhauser Gate.

Baez and Luthar were half way there. Cytherans blinked into place all around them. As each one appeared one of the Neos flung themselves at it and exploded.

In my mind I saw Dumas, the moment he looked back.

The Neos weren't trying to get through the gate, they wanted to destroy it. I knew they would fail.

How I wished I was with them.

An army of Cytherans appeared across the front of the gate, ten ranks deep.

Baez fired from the hip. A beam of black light churned a swathe of Cytherans into gouting dust.

Nice trick.

Luthar tried to throw something. Right at that moment he and Baez ceased to exist. A brilliant glitter. Nothing but an after-image remained. A white-hot pool of lava.

The thing Luthar held dropped and rolled across the ground. A black cylinder with domed ends, the whole thing as thick through as my fist. As it rolled I saw a red light wink.

Jonni saw it too. Before I could move he was up and running. 'Watch out,' he shouted. 'Hey, hey!'

In pure reflex one of the Cytherans flicked its lance and cut him down.

It was impossible but I saw the Cytheran try to pull the shot. In that long fast moment I swear I saw the lance beam bend, that I saw pure energy change direction and reverse its flow. It was not enough. By the time I reached Jonni he was a tumbled heap of loose limbs and ragged breath.

I crashed down beside him. 'Jonni, Jonni!'

His eyes were blank but his face wasn't empty. I'd seen enough death to know he was still in there. I cradled him in my arms and smoothed back his unruly hair. I closed his eyes. I looked up at the Cytherans and somehow I couldn't be angry. All I had was aching regret, sorrow for the waste, for Jonni. Even pity for the one who had done this.

I lifted Jonni up and my leg flared agony. I wanted to walk straight and tall but my stump wouldn't take the weight, the pain was like walking on a white-hot spike. The Cytheran ranks drew aside as I limped and lurched towards them. I heard a furious static burst and a hundred voices spoke in my mind.

—this was never our intent

Never.

Unforseen

—we know the difference

Unwished

Unwanted

All our <untranslatable> weep with you

He was never—

—he would ever have been—

Welcomed

A final Cytheran slid aside like a leaf on the wind and I was at the gate. The pillars went up forever, the space between a silver-grey curtain like soft rain. Beyond it lay everything we had been denied and now they were letting us through. Jonni was his own *minnesang*, and today, somehow, he was mine too. If I wanted, I could go through.

—no, he is only himself—

You are your own song—

Changed now.

—each becomes their own minnesang.

If you want—

I took a sideways step so the Cytheran was in front of me. Jonni was heavy now, his head lolled. My leg stump hacked like a rip-saw. He had helped me so much but I couldn't help him now. I locked my knees and held him out. The long lance in the Cytheran's hand folded away into nowhere and I laid Jonni in its outstretched arms.

He will not have long—

—yet long enough to know

The army had disappeared. The lone Cytheran holding Jonni swept backwards through the grey curtain.

When you are ready—

Come back?

∞

I took myself away. First, to the far side of the steps, where I sat alone for a day and a night, then down to the town.

I lived there doing this and doing that, getting by. Eventually I had my own place, nothing much but it did for me. Nobody knew who I was and that old urge to tell them had dried up and blown away.

It's strange how you can think things through without thinking. I did a lot of that. Not once did I get angry. I even made some friends.

Everyone dies. Luthar was right but he did it wrong. Jonni died as he lived, trying to help, not destroy. I am my own song, the Cytheran said.

So when people needed help I helped them, just like Jonni would have. I wanted- No, I *needed* to make him proud.

A year went by. When the day Jonni died came around again I discovered how important anniversaries are for the heart. For a while I fell back, then discovered some of those friends I'd made were good ones. They knew what I was going through.

One morning the sky was clear, the air cool and fresh. It felt like a wind blew from a new direction. I paid my rent, closed the door behind me and climbed the steps to the Tannhauser Gate.

∞

I stayed on the other side for a thousand years, living, learning. Some of the time loving and being loved. I could have fixed the leg, I could have changed myself like Riay, when she imagined herself into a truer form. In the end I just stopped the ache because much to my own surprise I discovered I was comfortable in my own skin, scars and all.

I visited two thousand worlds. With each arrival and departure a different ache pulsed. I tried to deny it but that ache grew. The time came when all I wanted to do was go home.

One day I walked back through the Tannhauser Gate. I filled my lungs with air and tasted the spice, the tang, the smell of burnt stone. I looked down the miles-long steps and saw an agitated group of petitioners trying to persuade three Cytheran to let them past. Nothing much had changed.

The petitioners watched open-mouthed as I walked down the steps. Then they rushed me.

'How did you do that?'

'Show us you key.'

'Give me your *minnesang*.'

'Tell these *things* to let us pass.'

'I can't,' I said. 'You don't understand.'

They didn't. I could see it in their eyes, their body-language.

I opened my mouth. *Please adjust your referents* nearly came out. 'It's not like that.'

One of them tugged my sleeve. 'Did you see the Venusberg?'

Gods, this was going to be difficult.

Then Blascard was there, scrounging and fawning around the Cytheran and making demands so entitled he made the petitioners sound polite.

All I could do was stare at him open-mouthed. 'Blascard?'

'Hey.'

He led me across and down to the wall, down to my step. He brought me water from Jonni's bucket.

Everything was the same. A thousand years and I'd been gone three days.

I looked at him and he held my gaze. A light came on in my head. 'You know.'

He gave an apologetic shrug.

I jerked my thumb over my shoulder towards the gate. 'So why don't you—?'

'Go? I'm waiting for the rest of these goons to catch up.'

By which he meant *ALL* the goons. Human race, FFS.

His success with the aliens started to make sense. They knew what he was doing, they were giving him some help. Blascard was a teacher, the holy fool trying to teach bigger fools. We sat in silence for a while as I did some processing.

Blascard cleared his throat. I'd never seen him so serious, so solemn. He put his scarred-knuckle hand on top of mine. 'I'm so sorry.'

Jonni. Yeah. Blascard was a real bastard. A thousand years and those two words broke me in two. I cried without words, without breath, without time. Blascard held me while the tears did their job of putting me back together again.

I took a breath and wiped my eyes. 'Jonni got to see.'

'That's good.'

'Blascard, I'm not like I used to be.'

Blascard held me at arm's length, his lopsided smile pulled his weather-seamed face. 'Welcome to the club.'

I felt exhausted and refreshed, drained as if something I didn't need, something that had been holding me back had actually flowed out of me. The sun shone, the wind blew. The ancient stone steps ran up and down in their yards and miles. Over us all stood the Tannhauser Gate.

I poked around in the rubble until I found a stone that felt about the right size and shape, walked down to Riay and laid it against the brick Jonni gave her. She smiled and just for the briefest moment I saw stars glitter in her eyes.

Blascard joined us, looked down at the two-stone temple and gave an enigmatic grunt. Far down the steps another group of petitioners had set out on the long climb. The three of us watched them for a while. Riay took my left hand, Blascard held my right. This was coming home. I wished Jonni was here to see me.

'Okay,' I said. 'Let's go.'

NINETEEN EIGHTY-NINE

KEN MACLEOD

IT WAS A HOT, MUGGY AFTERNOON IN JUNE, AND THE telescreen was sounding fifteen. Winston Smith jolted out of his doze. Even in the Chestnut Tree Café, even after lunch and a quarter of a bottle of Victory Gin, it was vital to feign alert attention to the hourly news.

He barely had time to gather his wits and gulp a mouthful of gin before a triumphant trumpet note brayed from the screen. Important news! A victory! But where? The fronts were quiet. For months now, no victories had been claimed. Defeats were never announced, but the growing number of discharged soldiers on the streets told the story.

'Midnight in Beijing,' the announcer intoned. 'We bring you, live from the Eastasian capital, shocking scenes of a people's rising mercilessly crushed by the ruthless guardians of a cruel oligarchy.'

Flames of a burning armoured personnel carrier flickered. Silhouettes of troops carrying rifles rushed across the screen. Machine-gun fire rattled. Screams echoed.

'Earlier today, a massive peaceful demonstration pleaded with the tyrants of Eastasia for a mere fraction of the rights enjoyed by the proud citizens of Oceania and those of its staunch Eurasian ally!'

The scene cut to daylight in a vast plaza, many times larger than London's Victory Square. The buildings surrounding it were proportionately imposing. Mounted on the wall of one of these ornate, antique edifices was a gigantic portrait of a visage clear-eyed and calm, stern but benign, with black hair swept back from a high forehead and broad temples. Only the Oriental cast of the features, and the absence of a moustache, distinguished it from the familiar face of Big Brother. That was the appearance. The reality could not be more different. Big Brother was the beloved leader of Oceania, whose wisdom and foresight compelled even the most recalcitrant to adore. This image was of Number One, the despot blindly worshipped by the teeming, regimented masses of Eastasia, who obeyed his every whim like human ants.

Swarms of these human ants, in their characteristic blue uniforms, filled the square. Many of them carried banners and placards scrawled with the incomprehensible ideograms of their barbarous jargon. Discordant shouts and chants, hungry faces contorted with anger. Near the front of the crowd a pale papier-mâché effigy of a crowned, robed female figure bobbed and swayed, its right arm upraised with fist clenched. Winston recognised it, with a shock, as a crude representation of the Statue of Victory in New York.

'Bet you they're about to burn or hang her,' someone said, in a tone of lascivious anticipation. 'Typical of these benighted Asiatics and their hate rallies.'

Something familiar in the voice made Winston turn around. A small, scrawny man sat at the next table, hunched over an empty ashtray and a full glass of gin. He had large protuberant eyes and a shock of white hair. His hands trembled slightly as he lit a cigarette. He seemed to have just arrived; he must have slipped in just after the bulletin had started, and had missed the context.

'No, it's—' Winston began. The man turned. His eyes widened.

'Smith!' he said, in a low but eager voice. 'I didn't expect to find *you* here!'

It was Syme from the Research Department. His face was thinner than Winston remembered, and his teeth whiter and more prominent: a set of dentures, new ones, not yet settled in. They made him look like... Winston gave the thought a convulsive wrench. Syme looked like a half-starved squirrel. A squirrel; yes, that was it.

'But you were—' Winston glanced over his shoulder.

'Vaporised?' said Syme. 'So I'm told. In fact I was sentenced to ten years in a labour camp, on Shetland. Just been released. Seven years early!' He shook his head. 'Incredible.'

Incredible it certainly seemed, though no more so than Winston's own survival. For the past four years he had fully expected a re-arrest, a show trial, a walk down a white-tiled corridor and a bullet in the back of the head. At first he had longed for it: to die loving Big Brother. Later he had come to resent the inexplicable delay. Now he dreaded the quietus.

Unable to reply, Winston gave Syme an apologetic glance and looked back at the telescreen.

'They certainly seem angry,' he said, as if picking up the previous exchange.

Suddenly, out of the front row of the seething crowd, a hurled speck arced like a perfectly bowled cricket ball. The object struck the gigantic portrait of Number One, and splashed a vivid black stain, like a slanted exclamation mark, across the nose and one cheek.

The twenty or so patrons and waiters watching agog in the Chestnut Tree gasped. There was something shocking about such lèse-majesté, even against the hated leader of the enemy. The Beijing crowd too fell silent in front of the defaced portrait, as if shaken by the enormity of what one of them had done. After about thirty seconds, a single voice cried out:

'Numeh Wan Sha Lai! Numeh Wan Sha Lai!'

One by one, other voices joined in. Within a minute the chant was taken up by all. Fists pumped rhythmically, placards waved frantically, and the ersatz Statue of Victory jumped frenziedly up and down above the heads of the crowd.

'"Number One Shall Lie"?' Winston puzzled aloud.

Syme leaned across the gap between the tables. 'Aha!' he said, tapping his long nose. 'It means "Down with Number One". Curious, isn't it, that the name was taken directly from English?' The man had always fancied himself something of a linguist.

'"Down with Number One",' Winston repeated, in a whisper.

Syme jumped to his feet. His chair clattered to the floor behind him.

'Down with Number One!' he shouted.

Everyone turned and stared at him. Winston knew what they were thinking. The news bulletin, and therefore the policy of the Party, was evidently on the side of the rebellious crowd. Number One was the target of patriotic hate and fear throughout Oceania. But joining in this unprecedented display of disrespect and revolt felt like disloyalty. It had a shudder of blasphemy, of breaking a taboo—for reasons impossible to articulate, or even to formulate clearly to oneself.

There was another consideration. Syme had for several years been an unperson. Winston knew that, and he could be sure others here did too. Now that Syme had reappeared, his disappearance must have been expunged from the records. To treat him as suspect could itself be seen as disloyal. Yet, at some level, like Winston himself, Syme must still be under a cloud. At least two of the waiters present at any one time would be members of the Thought Police. It was all a complicated, delicate calculation, in which one mistake would be both easy and deadly.

'Down with Number One!' someone roared. 'Down with Number One!'

Winston looked around, and realised to his horror that he was now on his feet and the cry had come from him. A waiter glanced at him, then at another waiter, then at the telescreen.

The announcer's tone had become even more sombre: "Down with Number One!" they chant. Then, after a few hours of tumult, the inevitable response . . .'

The screen cut to a phalanx of Eastasian soldiers, submachine guns held across their chests, tramping forward in implacable ranks. The viewpoint swung around as the column cut through the crowd, and then was stopped by the press of blue-clad bodies. How thin and frail the civilians seemed, how sturdy the soldiers! At a yelled order they turned to face outward, their submachine guns now at the ready. The outer files dropped to one knee and took aim, while the next inner files levelled their weapons above their comrades' heads.

Another shout: perhaps a warning. If so, it was either not heard or not heeded. The crowd continued to press in. You could see arms stretched towards the soldiers, and here and there fists raining blows on some luckless trooper.

The next order was given as a single scream. Its translation was provided by a storm of submachine gun fire. The fusillade scythed through the crowd at waist and head height. Bodies fell in swathes. Waves of panic spread outward.

One part of Winston's mind observed this with cool detachment, almost with scientific curiosity. There was a fascinating similarity to ripples from several stones dropped in a pond, interacting, interfering, rebounding and reflecting . . .

Another part was overcome with horror and pity and blind rage. He was pounding the table and shouting, over and over: 'DOWN WITH NUMBER ONE! DOWN WITH NUMBER ONE!'

And this time, the whole café joined in. The shouts were rhythmic, deafening, making the gelid haze of cigarette smoke that filled the air quiver. The paroxysm was as collective and focused as the Two Minutes Hate, and passed as quickly.

The sanguinary scene on screen ended. All in the café fell silent, shaken and not looking at each other, half-frightened, half-ashamed. The telescreen was still droning on: '. . . complete collapse of morale in the Eastasian armed forces . . . strikes and mutinies reported across Eastasia . . . gallant Eurasian allies moving troops to Mongolian border . . . floods of refugees . . .'

Winston let the voice roll over him as he fumbled his overturned chair on to its feet, sat back down, and finished his gin. He was shaking, with—as he realised after a moment's introspection—relief that he had not found himself shouting 'Down with Big Brother!'

∞

Syme, too, finished his gin in silence. He waved away the hand of the waiter who came by with the bottle.

'Duty calls!' he said, with forced cheer. He stood up, swaying a little, and fixed Winston with a smile. 'They've given me my old job back, you know,' he said. 'Still working on the Eleventh Edition, would you believe?' He shook his head, smiling wryly, as if attributing the unending delay in the final, definitive version of the Newspeak Dictionary to his own unfortunate absence for the past four years. Then he gathered his wits and brushed his palms. 'Well, these residual obsolete usages won't eliminate themselves!'

'Don't you mean, "Oldspeak wordforms unself update"?' Winston chuckled. In the old days, they had sometimes amused each other with such gratuitous translations.

Syme pondered, eyes wandering vaguely, then guffawed. 'Very good, Smith!' He tapped his nose. 'Watch your step, old man.'

Out Syme went, into the hot and noisy street, watching his step. Winston accepted the offer of more gin—the waiter in his white jacket was still hovering—and strove to rekindle the woozy well-being he'd almost attained before the news bulletin. Soothing tinny music trickled from the telescreen.

Once again, he'd almost reached the desired haze when he was jolted out of it by the telescreen's hourly bray. Again he focused, making an even greater effort at attention, genuinely eager to hear more news of the momentous upheaval in the enemy's capital.

There was none. At the hour of sixteen, the vaunted triumph was an increase in the chocolate ration to fifty grams a week. Winston was hardly more startled that any reference to the Beijing revolt had been dropped than by the distinct recollection that the previous ration had been thirty grams. For once, the claimed increase was real. Or it would be, if it was implemented.

The thought of chocolate induced a sudden pang of hunger. Winston ordered a sandwich. To his surprise it arrived on white bread, with crisp lettuce and tomato and a couple of slices of warm bacon. Inner-Party quality, this!

The sandwich wouldn't be enough to soak up the afternoon's gin, but it would sustain him on the journey home. He left the café at sixteen-forty-five with almost a spring in his step. The Tube rattled and groaned. It was not yet rush hour. Walls of broken tiling and flickers of unreliable lighting trundled by, station after station. He toiled up the hundred and fifty steps at his stop, pausing for breath several times, then made his way along the homeward streets like a sleepwalker. The grim bulk of Victory Mansions had just hoved into view when Winston became aware of the quiet engine-growl of a vehicle behind him, matching his pace, and at the same time of booted footsteps swiftly catching up. In the split second of terror he knew exactly what to expect. Rough hands grabbed his elbows, his feet were kicked from under him, and he was lifted in the air and flung sideways like a sack of potatoes through the open rear door of the black—

He'd expected a van. For the first time in his life, he was in a car. Not only was he not in one of the vans of the Thought Police: he was in one of the limousines of the Inner Party, and its top levels at that.

He sprawled across leather, knees in the foot-well, his head colliding with a central arm-rest. Someone kicked at the soles of his feet, not to hurt them but to shove them inside. The car door slammed. A black-gloved finger rapped a partition.

'Drive on,' said a voice from across the arm-rest. Winston knew without looking who spoke. It was O'Brien.

There was a sense of smooth acceleration, somewhat belied by the grinding and cracking noises as the car's evidently tough tyres crunched over broken glass.

'Seat yourself,' said O'Brien, impatiently. 'Don't grovel on the floor.' After a pause, he added darkly: 'There'll be time for that.'

Awkwardly, Winston complied. The side windows were of darkened glass, as was the partition. The seat was comfortable, but a chill gripped his bowels. He swallowed, on a suddenly dry mouth.

'What do you mean?' he croaked.

O'Brien shot him a sidelong, sympathetic glance. 'You have a most unpleasant ordeal in prospect, I'm afraid.'

'Why?' Winston cried, despite himself. 'I've confessed everything! What more do you want? A trial? I'll say anything! Get it over with and give me the bullet—I've been looking forward to it for years.'

'Indeed you have,' said O'Brien. 'You may be surprised to know that it was I who denied you that satisfaction.'

Winston indulged a moment's frantic fantasy of flinging himself out. He knew, without testing it, that the car door would be locked. A moan escaped his nostrils, and a tear or two his eyes.

'Don't snivel, man!' O'Brien snapped. 'You're not going to be tortured.' His cheek twitched, his glasses glinted. 'Though you might find what's coming worse.'

∞

The cell was white, and so was everything in it: the bed, the washstand, the lavatory pan. Only the telescreens—one on each wall—were grey. The walls and fittings, even the tap, were all made of some artificial rubber. The bed—a slab of mattress—had the same spongy feel as the walls and indeed the floor. You had to squat deliberately to sit on the lavatory: if you let your weight down on the pan it got squashed out of shape.

Not that Winston used the pan that way to begin with. First he pissed. Then he vomited. Fortunately he was naked. He washed his chin and chest, splashing himself with the cold dribble from the tap, and puked again. The diarrhoea came an hour or two later.

After a few hours he found himself shaking violently. He

huddled in a corner, heels and fists drumming almost soundlessly. The shaking passed, and was followed by a profuse sweat. He caught a persistent, sour stink of gin from his skin, and vomited again.

The light was unvarying, but at some point he curled up on the mattress and slept. He woke to find the cell swarming with rats. They scuttled on the floor, climbed the walls, ran across his legs—

He screamed and thrashed.

A burly man in white tunic and trousers rushed in and without a word stuck a hypodermic needle in Winston's bicep. Winston was still screaming and fighting off the rats. The orderly restrained him with a sort of bored expertise. Everything went black.

He woke with a raging thirst and a venomous headache. Every bone and muscle ached. It was as if he had been beaten all over with rubber truncheons. But there was no visible bruising, apart from where the orderly had gripped his arms and kicked his shins. With a groan, he levered himself up from the bed and knelt at the wash-stand, mouth under the tap.

The orderly brought him food—a rubber bowl of tepid, greasy-looking sweet gruel, with a rubber spoon stuck in it—and a rubber bottle of water. Winston gobbled the gruel, gulped the water, and promptly lost it all in successive heaves down the lavatory.

This was repeated, with variations, for several days. The vomiting, sweating, and shaking stopped, then the headaches. Winston found himself eating his food and drinking his water, then looking around the cell and being simply bored.

The orderly came in with a new boiler suit, underwear and shoes stacked on his upraised palms. Winston dressed, under the orderly's blank gaze, and followed the man out.

∞

Another room, blue-painted this time, with a table and two

facing chairs, in one of which O'Brien sat. On the table stood a teapot, two mugs, and an ashtray.

'Sit,' said O'Brien.

Winston sat. O'Brien poured tea and offered Winston a cigarette. They sipped and smoked for a moment or two in silence.

'I'm sorry to have had to put you through all that,' said O'Brien, 'but it was necessary to dry you out. I hope on sober reflection—so to speak—you will at least appreciate the improvement in your physical condition.'

'I suppose I do,' said Winston. He flexed his shoulders and straightened his back, without the usual aches. He gave a self-deprecating laugh. 'I need a drink.'

'You'll always need a drink,' said O'Brien, brusquely. 'Whether you have one is a different matter entirely. In the future it will be up to you, and for the moment it is up to me. Tea, for now.'

'Why have you brought me here?' Winston asked.

O'Brien resettled his spectacles on his nose, and looked at Winston with the intense, unspoken sympathy of their first exchanged glance, long ago. It was as if the arrest, the torture, the long interrogation and indoctrination, and the room that Winston could—with some effort—avoid thinking about, had never happened.

'I am engaged,' said O'Brien, 'in a conspiracy to overthrow the rule of the Party in Airstrip One, and hopefully in the whole of Oceania. You have a small but important part to play in this conspiracy. Will you join me?'

Winston's mug rattled as he put it down. A cold sweat broke from his every pore. It was possible that this was a test of his loyalty. It was also possible that O'Brien—the manipulator, the torturer, the inquisitor, the provocateur—was after all an enemy of the Party! In either case, it was best to play along. If he did not, he was unlikely to leave this place alive. He could always gather what information he was able to, and denounce O'Brien to the Thought Police at the first opportunity.

'Yes,' he said firmly. 'I'm with you, to the end.'

'You are thinking,' said O'Brien, 'that either I am trying to trap you, or that you are the luckiest man in London. You have stumbled upon a genuine, dangerous conspiracy, which you will expose as soon as you are out of my sight.'

'No, no! I—'

O'Brien laughed. 'It makes no difference. You have no way of knowing that whoever you take this information to is not one of my accomplices. Yes, even in the Thought Police. Or should I say, *especially* in the Thought Police?'

'That's not possible,' said Winston. 'The Thought Police are the most implacable, the cruellest, the most fanatical—'

'No, that would be the members of the Outer Party,' said O'Brien, scornfully. 'They believe anything. Members of the Inner Party, as you may recall from our previous . . . conversations, are considerably more conscious—or to put it another way, have to practice doublethink much more often and intensely. For the Thought Police, not even doublethink suffices. They have to deal with reality as it is. They have to know the real figures, the accurate statistics on everything. They have to know who is alive and who is dead. To police thought, they have to follow thought, even among the proles. In no section of Oceanic society, I would say, is there greater knowledge of the system—and greater contempt for it. We have made our best recruits in the ranks of the Thought Police.' O'Brien waved a hand, dismissing Winston's next objection in advance. 'Some of them will be double agents, of course. But there are techniques for detecting such. And in any case, they cannot betray enough of us to defeat the conspiracy. The recent small improvements in rations and supplies, the release of certain prisoners such as your friend Syme, the slightly franker news reports—these are our doing, or the Party's attempts to forestall us. That a news report of the revolt in Beijing was shown, for instance—that was *our* doing. That it was never repeated or followed up—that was *theirs*. But those responsible for the report's broadcast remain at large. And its effect, of course, continues to reverberate.'

'So it's all real?' Winston breathed. 'The Brotherhood, Goldstein...'

O'Brien shook his head. 'There is no Brotherhood.' He paused, eyes narrowed in thought. 'Or if there is, I have no knowledge of it. In any case, our conspiracy is entirely separate. As for Goldstein!' He scoffed. 'Goldstein is a bogeyman. There was never a leader of the Revolution called Goldstein.' Again the thoughtful pause. 'There *was* an obscure ideologue by the name of Gluckstein, whose appearance and ideas vaguely resemble those attributed to Goldstein, but... No.'

Winston's brain was flooded with a vivid fantasy of throwing his tea in O'Brien's face, smashing the mug and using a shard to cut his throat. He knew it would not happen. O'Brien, he was sure, could overpower him as soon as he moved; and if he, Winston, were capable of such decisive, violent action he would never have been here in the first place.

'You put me through torture in the Ministry of Love for nothing! For worse than nothing—for something you didn't even believe in yourself!'

'I had to make myself believe it, in order to make you believe it.'

'And you no longer believe it?'

'No.'

'What changed your mind?'

O'Brien shrugged. 'I did, the moment I left your cell. The mind is electric, mercurial, as you well know. Belief? Belief is only skull deep. You always insisted on knowing why—why does the Party rule as it does? So I gave you an explanation that would answer your insistent, childish question.' He scoffed. 'That extravagant mystique of cruelty! It had a certain satanic grandeur, did it not? I knew it would convince you, Smith, because you have such strong impulses of cruelty and hatred yourself. And you were not ready for the truth.'

'The truth?'

'It is much worse. All this'—O'Brien waved a hand, as if to encompass Oceania entire— 'is the result of sheer incompetence.

It is not a failing of individual ability, you understand, or of organisation. In seeking to control every thought and action of a third of the population of the Earth, the Party has taken on a task beyond the wit of the most perfect organisation of the greatest minds imaginable. In the face of such a colossal undertaking they are all small men. And these small men, Smith, cling to power because they dread the consequences of losing it. It is as petty and pathetic and squalid as that.'

Winston said nothing.

O'Brien stood up and paced around, puffing on his cigarette. Then he sat down and poured some more tea.

'Tell me, Smith,' said O'Brien, in a tone of casual inquiry, 'what do you understand by the term "English socialism"?'

Winston started. He suspected another of O'Brien's inquisitorial traps.

'English socialism?' he ventured. 'It's Ingsoc: the doctrines and practices of the Party.'

'Ingsoc,' said O'Brien, with dogmatic finality, 'has as much to do with English socialism as Minitrue has to do with truth.'

The words seemed to ring in the air, the aftermath of a thunderclap. The sentence seemed one of the insolent paradoxes of doublethink. On one level: incontrovertible orthodoxy; on another, the vilest heresy.

'Truth is what the Party says it is,' said Winston. 'And by the same token, English socialism—'

'I taught you well,' said O'Brien, 'and you taught me.' He sighed. 'Too well, perhaps. I am ten years older than you, Smith. Like you, I am a little uncertain about dates, but I know that I am in my mid-fifties, and you are in your mid-forties. We can agree on that, yes?'

'If you say so.' Winston stubbed out his cigarette and reached for another, without waiting for the offer. O'Brien lit it for him, then one for himself.

'I was born,' said O'Brien, exhaling smoke, 'in, let us say, 1935. In the Second World War I was evacuated to a farm in Kent. Some of my memories of the time are happy, others less so. I recall seeing in the skies overhead what is now called the Battle of Airstrip One. It was tremendously exciting for a boy. I was ten years old when I returned to London. My father and mother were almost strangers to me. My mother had worked in a factory; my father had been a soldier. They never spoke of the war. Whole districts were in rubble, privation was pervasive, austerity severe, but compared to what it is now—after the atomic war, and the Revolution, and decades of the Party's rule—London was a city of inconceivable prosperity and amenity and delight. And hope, Smith! Hope!'

'Hope?'

'Yes, hope! As you once said to yourself: if there is hope, it lies in the proles. And in 1945 it did! In those days the proles—and my parents were proles—had the vote. I remember their jubilation when they elected what was called a Labour government, to undo some of the evils—and they were real evils—of capitalism. My father got a job in a factory. My mother lost her job, but seemed to me happy to have a clean new flat to look after, and my father's wages supported us all. My parents received extra money to assist in my upkeep. A National Health Service was established. The worry my parents used to have about doctors' bills vanished overnight. And the changes were not confined to Airstrip One. At school there was a world map on the wall. A third of the land surface was coloured a sort of dingy pink, representing the British Empire, far more extensive than even Oceania is today. I remember gazing at the map, and mentally changing the colour, as India and Pakistan became independent. And when I was about fifteen years old, the Labour government lost the next election despite having received more votes than ever. And they simply made way for another government, of the party that was called Conservative. But so popular were the reforms that the new government did not dare undo them. That, Smith, was English socialism!'

'Even as a small child,' said Winston, 'I would have remembered some of that, in however fragmentary and confused a manner. And I don't.'

O'Brien put down his cigarette and resettled his spectacles on his nose, then took a long draw and sighed out the smoke.

'Ah, but you do. You remember the time. You do not remember the place, because for almost all of this time you were in a different place.'

'I remember the time,' Winston repeated, bewildered, 'but I do not remember the place?'

'You have always felt in your bones that things were not always like this, have you not?'

Winston nodded. 'I confessed as much.'

'In your ravings, in the Ministry of Love, you admitted to a recurrent dream or vision of a place all green, drenched in golden sunlight, full of warmth and well-being. You identified it with the English countryside—which, even at its best, even to a child, is rarely suffused with the golden glow of which you spoke. But your Golden Country is real enough. It is even part of Oceania. It is the place of your earliest childhood: Jamaica.'

'Jamaica!' cried Winston. 'I know nothing about it. I could find it on a map, that's all.' He drew thoughtfully on his cigarette. 'If that place is so wonderful, why did my parents bring me here?'

'Jamaica was a colony. A former slave colony, in fact. Opportunities were limited. Your parents, and many others, came to this country in 1948, when you were perhaps three years old, on a ship called the *Empire Windrush*. To them this was a land of opportunity. To you, as a child, it was a land of cold rain, of unfamiliar and distasteful food, of regimentation, rationing, and ruin. And then, in the early 1950s—the exact date hardly matters—came the atomic war.' O'Brien looked away, with a bleak expression. 'The atomic war, and all that followed.'

'How have I never known this?'

O'Brien refilled the tea mugs, taking his time.

'In one sense,' he said at last, 'you have known it, but your childish memories were overridden by the chaos and misery of the atomic war. And the Party has eradicated all records of the period. How often I myself have doubted my own memories of the late 1940s! But how could I confirm them? I could certainly not confer with my contemporaries. No, to find those who retain a true memory of English socialism we must look outside the Party. And there, indeed, we find it. We find it among the proles.'

'The proles!' Winston scoffed. 'They have no consciousness. They remember nothing but football scores from one week to the next.'

'There you are wrong,' said O'Brien. 'There is a layer—admittedly a large layer—for which this is true, and always has been true, and for all I know always will be true. But it is far less than the 85% of the population who are proles. It has to be, for industry to function at all. You once ventured into a prole pub, to seek out someone who remembered the world before the Party. But in your timidity you made the mistake of inquiring of a senile old man, who could only ramble on about pint pots and top hats. He was suffering the dementia of age. If you had troubled or dared to ask someone younger, you might have found quite different memories, and far sharper.'

'No prole who wasn't senile would have talked to me freely anyway,' Winston said, bitterly.

'You never tried.'

'And I suppose you have?' Winston let his fancy run free. 'Disguised yourself and wandered in their midst? Sat in on Thought Police interrogations? Read secret surveys of prole opinion?'

As he spoke it occurred to him that O'Brien—with his burly physique, brutal features and suave resourcefulness—was perfectly capable of all these ploys and more. O'Brien gave Winston a sharp look over his spectacles for a searching moment, as if reading his thoughts.

'It is generally believed,' O'Brien said, in his didactic tone, 'that intelligent proles are spotted and eliminated by the Thought Police. Some are. But many slip through the net, because they find a role where their intelligence and ambition are too useful to dispense with. They join the armed forces.'

'But—'

'Come, Smith! Even you can hardly have thought the armies of Oceania consisted to any significant extent of devoted Party members.'

'But all the—'

'Yes, yes. All the heroic deaths you wrote up in *The Times* were of Party members? Of course they were! You made them up, Smith—'

'Not all,' Winston protested.

'—and if you didn't someone else did.'

O'Brien stood up. 'It's time you met real soldiers.'

The deepest Winston had even been under the Ministry of Truth was the bomb shelter in the basement, below the fiction machines. Now, he guessed, he was well below that. An occasional waft at a corridor junction carried the unmistakeable hot, dry air of the London Underground, and now and again a rushing rumble indicated the same. O'Brien led him along hundreds of metres of corridors and down innumerable spiral metal staircases. They changed direction so many times that Winston suspected they had doubled back more than once, and that the immense concrete bulk of Minitrue was still above him. The walls were of white tile, the floor of stone slabs. Lighting came from flickering overhead tubes. Every so often Winston heard voices and footsteps, always far away, carried on echoes. They startled him every time.

O'Brien turned a corner, Winston following. A soldier in full combat gear stood athwart the corridor, submachine gun levelled. Winston took a step back, and let out a yelp. O'Brien motioned him to be quiet.

'Halt!' barked the soldier. 'Who goes there?'

'Indemnity,' said O'Brien.

'Pass, comrades.' The soldier stepped aside. His gaze and the gun muzzle tracked Winston as he hurried by.

'The passwords change every half hour,' O'Brien murmured

as they walked on. 'In case you were thinking of going back on your own.'

'The thought hadn't crossed my mind,' said Winston, quite truthfully.

At the end of the corridor was a blast door, which swung open on their approach. They ducked through, between a pair of guards. Unlike the sentry in the corridor, these were in frayed fatigues and ported only rifles. They smelled of tobacco and carbolic soap.

Inside, it was like stepping into a huge and unexpected building, tens or perhaps hundreds of metres below ground. The ceilings were low and visibly braced with steel girders, along which strip lights were bracketed in wire hoops. A sough of ventilation overlaid the sound of many voices and the clatter of machinery. Cigarette smoke drifted, almost as thick in the air here as in the Chestnut Tree.

O'Brien led the way briskly through corridors crowded with soldiers, sailors and airmen, each of whom seemed to be on a separate urgent errand. They looked fitter than people you saw on the street, and much sharper, with hard faces and bright eyes. Snatches of American, South African and Australian accents mingled with the more familiar Cockney, Northern and occasionally Scottish or Irish voice.

Winston passed some open doors, through which he glimpsed knots of people around tables, maps, speakwrites, radio transceiver sets. In one room the walls were hung with dusty framed photographs, very old-fashioned looking, of Party leaders, many of them long since vaporised. Among them, no more prominent than the rest, was what must be the original of Big Brother. Winston pointed it out as they passed.

'So he really existed!'

'Once,' said O'Brien, with a flick of his hand.

'What is this place?' Winston asked.

'It is what was called a Regional Seat of Government,' O'Brien said, over his shoulder. 'There are many around the country. They were built in the 1960s to survive atomic war—this one, for example, could ride out a direct hit by an atomic bomb. When it was tacitly agreed between the powers that there would no more atomic attacks, the RSGs were sealed off and forgotten. Except!'—He raised a finger—'By the armed forces.'

They arrived at an office door, closed and with a sentry outside. After a brief exchange with O'Brien, he waved them in. As they stepped through, O'Brien extended his arm sidelong in front of Winston and made a downward gesture. Obediently, Winston stayed where he was and kept quiet.

The room was larger than the offices they'd passed. Ten men and two women in military uniform and wearing headphones stood around an oval table covered with maps and arrayed with portable microphones. Half a dozen aides hovered, or hurried from one senior officer to the next with whispered messages or urgent gestures, picking their careful way among the cables that trailed across the floor. All the walls were plated from waist height to ceiling with enormous telescreens. Some of the displays, changing by the second, were spread across two, three or more screens. Most showed street or aerial views, others were more abstract. Lines, graphs, columns, symbols—none of them made sense to Winston's first swift survey. The map that took up most of the table did.

It was of London, with every street—every building, almost—shown, along with cables, tunnels, sewers, Tube lines and more. Small models—or perhaps children's toys—of troop formations, tanks and light armoured vehicles were being pushed around on it with long pointers. Each move was accompanied by glances at the telescreens, and followed by clipped commands into the microphones or moments of pondering or sharp exchanges across the table.

An aide, momentarily at a loose end, noticed O'Brien and Winston and stepped over. A tall man, in his twenties, he had close-cropped hair a shade lighter than his dark skin. He nodded to O'Brien and stuck out his hand to Winston. As soon as he spoke Winston knew he was American.

'Lieutenant-Colonel Caesar Haynes,' he said.

'Winston Smith. Pleased to meet you.'

Haynes grinned, a flash of white teeth. 'We do like our great leaders,' he said, with a complicit chuckle.

'I'm sorry?'

Haynes waved a hand. 'Forget it.' He turned to O'Brien. 'So this is your new Minister of Truth?'

'Yes,' said O'Brien.

'What?' said Winston.

Haynes looked at him, eyes narrowed in appraisal, turned back to O'Brien, and nodded.

'Excellent choice, Comrade O'Brien.'

'What's going on?' Winston asked.

Haynes jerked his head back. 'What d'you think's going on?'

'Here?' said Winston. 'Evidently you're planning a coup d'état.'

Haynes and O'Brien guffawed, then stifled their laughs after a sharp look from the nearest officer at the table.

'Planning?' Haynes scoffed. 'It's happening, man!'

'The coup is underway,' said O'Brien.

'The die is cast,' said Caesar Haynes. He turned, craned his neck, and peered from face to face until he got a nod. 'Time for a coffee break, I reckon, and to bring Comrade Smith up to speed.'

∞

In a crowded room with a sink and a couple of urns and a few small tables, a woman in a white overall was making sandwiches with alarming speed and dexterity, while a soldier stood at the sink and washed mugs and plates like someone working on a conveyor belt. Overhead an extractor fan fought the smells and cigarette smoke. People were coming and going, jostling, grabbing a bite or a mug, hurrying off after a few minutes. Haynes commandeered a corner with a shelf, elbowed his way to the urn and returned with three mugs between his hands. The black drink had a wonderful aroma and a vile taste. Winston sipped and grimaced, but the caffeine kick made it worthwhile.

'Okay,' he said to Haynes. 'Bring me, as you say, up to speed.'

Haynes waved away O'Brien's offer of a cigarette. 'This all started,' he said, 'back in the winter of...'84, was it...? with our victory in Africa. A close thing, you may recall. We nearly lost South Africa—the first time in the whole war that Oceania's own territory was threatened. Took us a huge effort, but we knocked back the Eurasians, forced them to sue for peace, and ended up dominating Africa from Cairo to the Cape. That's where it all went wrong.'

'Went wrong?' said Winston. 'At the time it was hailed as a stroke of Big Brother's strategic genius. I'm sure I remember that.'

'The strategic genius behind the flanking manoeuvre is in the room we just left,' said Haynes, dryly. 'And even she would tell you it was the worst mistake the armies of Oceania ever made. You see, it left us in unchallenged command of the continent. We were now at peace with Eurasia, and at war with—'

'Eastasia.'

'With Africa. The retreating Eurasians—and they really were routed, that was true—left more than enough weapons behind in their flight to arm hundreds of thousands of African guerrilla fighters. In the Congo, in Mozambique, in the Sahara, in Algeria and Morocco. We've been completely bogged down everywhere for the past three years.'

'Where did all these African fighters come from?'

'They've always been there,' said Haynes, with a note of pride for which Winston could not account. 'A stubborn minority of Africans and Arabs have all along fought the various invading forces with captured weapons when they could lay hands on any, and with sticks and stones and spears when they couldn't.'

Winston blinked. 'But according to *the book*—'

'The natives and colonial slaves in the war zones simply endure and toil, while the fronts wash over them like natural disasters? They have no comprehension of what's happening? No native intellectuals so much as ponder the specious promises of the rival camps, and weigh them in their minds? The great warrior religions of Christianity, Islam, Hinduism, and the traditional mighty deities of the tribes can no longer raise men to their feet? Does that strike you as remotely credible?'

'Let me remind you, Smith,' said O'Brien, 'that *the book* was written by the Party. It is its most insidious weapon of propaganda. The most determined rebels—as you once were—seize on it with trembling hands as the forbidden truth, the ultimate heresy, and eagerly imbibe a message carefully designed to demoralise them.'

'It's not just the tropical war zone that it lies about,' said Haynes. 'It lies about the super-states themselves. Take Oceania. Not all its proles are like you beaten-down Brits. In the Americas some folks have held fast to their gods and their guns, and holed up in the swamps and deserts and mountains. Since the 1960s insurgencies have flared up from the Appalachians to the Andes. Eurasia and Eastasia have their equivalents: religious, tribal, nationalist and other armed rebel holdouts.'

Winston closed his eyes and shook his head. 'Even so . . . the Africans can't win, surely.'

'They are winning,' said Haynes. 'Hence all the discharged soldiers on the streets. We have the *fellahin* of Algeria to thank for that. Literally—at least the armies in North Africa had the Mediterranean to escape by, and ships to escape on. In the Congo . . .' Haynes shook his head, and drew a fingertip across his throat. 'It's a slaughterhouse. Entire armoured columns plunge into the jungle, and are never seen again. These events can be hidden, but not from the troops.'

'Hence the conspiracy,' said O'Brien. 'It started with junior officers in Africa, like Lieutenant-Colonel Haynes here, and spread to higher and lower ranks, then to elements of the Inner Party and even the Thought Police. The core of its fighting force on the streets out there is made up of discharged veterans. The rest are armed proles.'

'Armed with what? How?'

'The factories are in permanent chaos anyway, and Sten guns are easily manufactured in small workshops. That's what they were designed for, after all! They are being handed out in every city of Airstrip One as we speak.'

'This is insane,' Winston said. 'Even if you can defeat the Thought Police and the loyal troops, even if you take London, you'll be isolated. The rest of Oceania will crush you. Or the Eurasians—'

'The Eurasians are too busy pressing on into Manchuria,' said O'Brien. 'We may hope that the Eastasian military collapse following the Beijing revolt draws Eurasia into the same kind of morass as theirs did to us. And the rest of Oceania...' He gestured to Haynes.

'Five cities in North America are already burning,' said Haynes. 'And Australia's bogged down in New Guinea. We'll get no trouble from there.'

Winston felt a stirring of hope—not that the coup would win, but that the fighting would so widespread and intense that he stood a good chance of being killed in it.

'Obviously,' said O'Brien, 'when we win we will need a civilian government, to avoid the appearance of a military junta.'

'The appearance—but not the reality?'

'Exactly,' said O'Brien. 'And we've chosen you as Minister of Truth.'

'Why me?' Somehow, Winston had no qualms about being able to do the job. But, he thought, that might be just the sobriety talking.

'You *understand*,' said O'Brien.

'So do you.'

'It can't be me. I'm an official, not a politician.'

'Besides,' said Haynes, 'it is important for... political reasons in the Americas that at least one of the Ministers in the new government should be a Negro.'

'Why should that matter?' Winston asked, baffled.

'It's complicated to explain,' said Haynes. 'Let's just say that a lot of the riots and uprisings now going on in North America are fuelled by racial antagonisms.'

'So why don't you take the post?'

'I'm not British and I'm not a civilian,' said Haynes. 'And besides, I have too much blood on my hands. I fought in Africa. Among the troops I'm known as the Butcher of Brazzaville.'

'Well, I—'

There was a terrific crash. Lights flickered. An alarm blared.

'Back to the control room!' O'Brien said.

They pushed out of the fast-emptying refectory and hurried along the corridor as soldiers and civilians, some armed, dashed the other way. Rounding a corner, they found their way blocked by a steel partition that hadn't been there before.

'Gas proof door,' said O'Brien. 'No use pounding on it, Smith.'

'At least the control room's safe,' said Haynes.

'We're not,' Winston pointed out.

'Perceptive, aren't you?' O'Brien snarled. 'Come on!'

He and Haynes set off down the corridor at a run, towards the sound of gunfire. After a moment, Winston followed.

∞

The nuclear bunkers had been designed to be defensible. As well as the gas (and, presumably, radioactivity) proof doors, the RSGs had in their outer corridors armour plated barriers that slid into place across them. The barriers had slits for firing through. Unfortunately, the barriers had been designed for keeping out starving mobs, not heavily armed Thought Police troops. One rocket-propelled grenade could have punched right through, and no doubt very soon would. Likewise unfortunately, they didn't slide into place automatically, but were manually operated with an adjacent lever. Two soldiers and three civilians lay dead behind the barrier where Winston, Haynes and O'Brien fetched up.

At least their weapons were still there to be picked up.

Winston poked the barrel of a Lee Enfield rifle through a slit and sighted with one eye. A hundred metres down the corridor, muzzles sparkled. Bullets ricocheted off the armour plate. Winston fired several shots in rapid succession, for all the good that would do, and reloaded.

Haynes stayed Winston's hand as he made to fire again.

'Save it,' Haynes shouted. Winston could barely hear him. 'We're low on ammo. Let's see what they're up to.'

He took a monocular from a thigh pocket and looked through the slit.

'They're loading up a mortar,' he reported. 'Probably with a gas shell, no point using a mortar here for anything else, so...'

There was a distant rattle of firing. Haynes fell and sprawled on his back. The top of his head was a mess of glass and blood, bone and brain. His legs convulsed for a second, then he lay still.

'Must have gone right through the lens,' said O'Brien. 'Bad luck or sharp shooting.'

Winston stared at him and retched. He heard a thump, then a crash and tinkle, as of broken glass.

'Gas bomb,' said O'Brien. 'Hold your breath!'

Winston tried to. O'Brien rolled the corpse of Haynes over and hauled off the bloodied jacket over the ruined head and limp arms and stuffed it into one of the slots. Vapour or smoke poured through the other. O'Brien gesticulated frantically. Winston wrenched open his boiler suit, shrugged out of the upper part, and pulled off his vest and stuffed it in the other slot. Holding his breath became impossible. He cast O'Brien an apologetic glance, and gasped.

Immediately he had a choking, burning sensation in his throat. Tears and mucus cascaded down his face, the skin of which felt as if it was burning.

O'Brien turned his head away and breathed in too, more slowly and warily than Winston had, but still setting off a fit of coughing and retching.

'It's just tear gas,' he croaked. 'I was afraid they might risk nerve gas.'

To Winston this was no great comfort. They each needed to use both hands to keep the stuffed clothes in place. Vapour leaked around them and under the door. From the far side of the barrier came the thunder of booted feet. Something poked hard at one of his hands. He snatched both hands away and hurled himself sideways just before a muzzle came through the slot and a shot went off, nearly deafening him again. The bullet hit a gas proof door far behind them and ricocheted several times around the corridor. Vapour now poured through the slot. Choking, Winston reeled away, dragging O'Brien with him, stumbling over bodies. The farther they got from the barrier the easier a target they were; the closer they stayed, the worse the gas.

Winston held one hand over his mouth and nose and with the other groped for a weapon. O'Brien was doing the same. They looked at each other through a blur of tears. O'Brien cocked his thumb and pointed with forefinger and middle finger under his chin, head back. Winston nodded.

Another rattle of gunfire, then a huge *WHUMP*, followed by screams worse than any Winston had ever made or heard. More shots, close up. Double tap. The screaming stopped. Flames licked through the slots, then subsided.

'Anyone there?' someone shouted. 'You can open the door now! They're all dead!'

Winston looked at O'Brien, who shrugged. Clutching a rifle, O'Brien stumbled to a recess in the corridor wall and pulled a lever. The barrier groaned on its grooves as it slid into the wall.

Syme, blinking, pistol in hand, stood on the other side. Behind him stood a gang of a dozen or so proles in leather jackets, clutching Sten guns and bottles with wicks stuffed in their necks. Around his feet lay the smouldering bodies of five gas-masked, armoured Thought Police troops. The corridor reeked of petrol. Syme wafted a hand in front of his face and stepped forward, peering.

'Smith!' he cried. 'I didn't expect to find *you* here!'

Then his gaze shifted over Winston's shoulder, and alighted on O'Brien.

'Expected *you*, though,' said Syme, and raised his pistol. Winston grabbed his wrist just in time. His lurch forward brought him close enough to Syme's ear to whisper: 'No. We need him for the moment. We can deal with him later.'

But O'Brien was already clapping a hand on his shoulder. 'You won't,' he said, cheerfully. 'But by all means, try! It's a free country, after all.'

With that he strolled past them both, rifle in hand, up to and through Syme's gang of proles.

'This way, lads,' he said. 'Work to do.'

∞

As he made his way through raucous, revelling crowds to Victory Square a few nights later, Winston saw that all the torn down posters of Big Brother had been replaced by images of faces previously unknown to him: Winston Churchill, King George VI, Clement Atlee ('Good Ole Atlee', the proles called him), Franklin D. Roosevelt, Chiang Kai-Shek and others. Although he was now the Minister of Truth, Winston had no idea where the portraits had been found, or who in the vast apparatus of the Ministry was responsible for their swift reproduction and dissemination. He'd signed off the instructions that afternoon, in the midst of a myriad other papers thudding on his desk, and now the posters were everywhere. The one he'd been told was of Joseph Stalin bore an alarming resemblance to that of Big Brother, and kept getting torn down by mistake.

The statue of Big Brother atop the central column had been pulled down and now lay shattered where it had fallen. Winston picked his way around the rubble of the head and approached the podium. Someone recognised him and hoisted him up.

Awkward in a new suit and tie—no one wore overalls in public now—Winston shuffled sidelong along the scaffolding and took his place beside the other members of the Provisional Government of Britain. Behind them stood a row of officers in dress uniform, campaign medals glittering, and behind them a row of troops. He looked out over what seemed a heaving, flickering sea of red, white, and blue flags. A spotlight dazzled him. Someone clapped his shoulder and grabbed his wrist and raised his hand high. He heard his name over the loudspeakers. The crowd chanted it back: 'Winston Smith! Winston! Win-ston!'

The spotlight moved on. After the last Minister was introduced, the band struck up and the song rose over the loudspeakers, to be lifted further by the crowd.

'Oceania, 'tis for thee
To worldwide victory
 My bullets sing!
Land where our comrades died
Land of our Party's pride
On frontlines far and wide
Let gunfire ring!'

Despite everything, Winston felt as if borne aloft by the familiar anthem. But he would have to do something about the lyrics.

 'Let rocks their silence break
 The sound prolong.'

What, Winston wondered, did that even *mean*? He would get Syme on to it in the morning, and tell him to update speedwise.

A Moment of Zugzwang

Neil Williamson

THE LOCALISED WEATHER INFORMATION STINA PULLED from the bees on Wehlstrasse suggested this spring morning would be mild, but it didn't take into account the chill coming off the river. Crossing the Lennard Lohmann Bridge, she blinked the app away in her IntaFace lenses and snugged her collar around her neck, silently cursing the decision to leave her cardigan draped over her chair back at the Inspectorate. She'd agonised over that because, though she hated to be cold, she hated even more to be overwarm—it was the interviewees that were supposed to sweat, not the detectives. Data did not yet completely describe the world, she thought testily. However much certain people would like to believe that it did.

Descending the staircase from the bridge, she found Wehlstrasse itself more sheltered and paused to smooth down her collar and fix her hair. Then she took a moment longer to arrange her bulleted case notes, focusing on the job at hand. There would be no point in coming all the way out here if she was going to allow herself to be distracted. No point at all.

Wehlstrasse was a quiet street. Seldom frequented stores and cafés lined one side. Along the other, trees evenly ranked like soldiers guarded the low balustrade above the rolling, grey river. They'd proved poor guardsmen, at least as far as Albert Vogel was concerned. Stina had watched the bee footage a thousand times. The old man visible at the edge of the frame making his way down that side of the street, coming and going behind the trees as he approached the bridge. The distinctive bushy beard jutting before him. The slow but steady gait suddenly faltering, the hand going to the jaw is if he'd forgotten something as the induced heart failure had kicked in. The stumble, the lurch. The plummet into the waters below. No witnesses, either in person or online, so no one had come to his aid and his body hadn't been found until a couple of days later among the Hundred Island reed beds six miles downstream. Bloated, the skin of his extremities wrinkled and nibbled at by hungry critters.

Completing the impression of inept soldiery, the trees though dressed in winter's drab sported splashes of vivid green among the upper branches like gaudy braiding. Between their trunks clustered dusty velos like mooching dogs, as well as tables and chairs belonging to the cafés. Most of these were empty so early in the day but further along, where the street followed the river's gentle curve, Stina could see a few hunched, seated forms.

The chess players.

She knew which café to go to, knew what to order, even though she oughtn't to. The woman she was going to meet wasn't a suspect. Not officially. Officially, she'd been a person of passing interest, no more than that. The AI that evaluated whether to allow a person's private data to be opened up to investigation had not done so in her case. Nor in anyone else's. Although Albert Vogel had most definitely been murdered by administration of a drug that had exacerbated an already serious heart condition, not one person in the city had a probability score anywhere close to the required sixty-five percent threshold. The AI had analysed thousands of potential contacts. Zeroing in first on the people he'd had passed on that final walk, the luncheoners, the *kaffe und kuchen* brigade, the chess players. Then scraping the vast WatchNet archives for interactions in the months leading up to the man's death that might contain signs of threat. Scouring personal records—financial, medical, business, social—for hints of motive. Looking, above all, for changes of behaviour. That had always been true of crimes of this nature. People changed their behaviour before, during and after. But according to the AI, no one had. And now the net was being widened, the current hypothesis favoured among the investigating team being a professional hit for reasons unknown. So the AI was working full time on tracing arrivals and departures for several weeks either side of the day of the murder. Trains, buses, taxis and car hires. Officially, the investigation had moved on.

Unofficially, Stina had a hunch. This woman—this Dimitra Klimala, a foreigner although she had lived in the city for so long it was doubtful anyone knew that—may have been discounted as a potential suspect after scoring a mere thirty-eight percent, but that thirty-eight percent was significantly higher than anyone else Vogel had been acquainted with. The blindspots of the trees notwithstanding, she'd been the last person who was known for sure to have spoken to Albert, a mere ten minutes before he was struck down. In her interview, she'd claimed that they'd simply played chess, which footage from a different bee to the one that had recorded his demise had corroborated. Stina had watched it on a loop. It had been a cold day, flecks of snow in the air. Vogel bought the coffees and sat down. They'd each kept strictly to their own side of the board. No touching, no tampering. Not even a handshake when, thirty two minutes later, the game was over. After Albert left, Klimala got herself another coffee, reset the board and had already begun a new match by the time Vogel's body drifted past unnoticed.

The chess games were a regular thing between the pair and that day's had played out exactly the same as the others for which there had been available footage. Nothing out of the ordinary. But still Stina had a feeling in her gut. She'd argued with the Super and been told flatly, in front of the whole team, to forget it. Things didn't work that way any more. The other officers, the younger ones, so full of confidence, had schooled their inattention but she knew they'd been laughing at her. She had come slowly to the realisation that she was considered out of touch these days. Her professional ratings, her proticks, were the lowest they'd ever been. Her perticks, the aggregated social media ones, were little better, and small wonder. If any friend or neighbour ever bothered to drop in on a bee in the house she shared with Tomasz, her son, they'd despair at the stilted bewilderment that went on between them. His contributions to the household were prompt and adequate but she didn't know what he did to make his money, only that he did it from the privacy of his bedroom and the maddening politeness that everyone practiced now made it impossible to have it out with him. And that just seemed to be the way things were. Well, fine, so she was a dinosaur. But intuition had been recognised as an invaluable asset in a detective once, and she had finely honed hers over the span of her career. No way was she going to let that old man's death go unsolved just because a computer was supposed to know better these days.

She went about it the old fashioned way. Rode the bees around the Wehlstrasse area for hours, observing Dimitra Klimala until she knew about as much as she could legally manage about her quarry. Which in the end was astonishingly little. The woman was a black hole of publicly available information. She had no social media accounts, wasn't registered with a doctor, had no history of employment either here or elsewhere. Stina found it alarmingly suspicious but without a direct link to Vogel's death there was nothing she could do about it. Knowing that Klimala liked her coffee two-shot strong and bolstered with a slug of hazelnut liqueur was an in at least. And that, she fervently hoped, would be all she'd need.

As she left the café and crossed the street, the cups she carried rattled in their saucers. Nervous? She'd interviewed a thousand suspects in her time. Yes, in the last decade she'd had the advantage of knowing that they were all almost certainly guilty but she wasn't *that* out of practice. She calmed herself and approached Klimala's table. It was square and had a blue checked paper cover clipped to it, the tails of which riffled in the breeze. In the centre sat an old scholastic chess set, the board softened and mildewed. The simple wooden pieces, waiting patiently in their ranks, bore the scars of years of battle.

The occupant of the table, bundled up in a bulky, brown coat and a woollen hat, was staring distractedly out over the river. Stina didn't think Klimala was even aware of her arrival until she put the coffee cups down beside the board. The old woman turned. Looked at the cups first, then at Stina. Her face was weathered but her grey eyes were sharp.

'Polizei, huh?' Klimala's lips crinkled into a maybe smile.

Stina hovered, thrown off by her directness. 'Is it that obvious, Frau Klimala?'

The old woman shrugged. 'The suit? The haircut? The presumption? Who else could it be?'

'Fair enough,' Stina said. 'Can I sit down?'

Klimala's eyes narrowed, then she gestured at the board. 'Do you play?'

'I've just a few questions...'

'Do. You. Play?'

'... and it'll only take ten minutes of your time, I promise.'

'Detective whatever-your-name-is. People come here for chess, not chit chat. If you sit, you play. If you don't play, you can fuck off.'

Stina sighed, reminding herself that she'd chosen this theatre of engagement. So be it. Her Oma had divulged the principles of chess when Stina was very small and they'd often played on rainy afternoons during summer visits. It had been a long time but she was fairly sure she remembered them. 'Fine.' She sat down. 'And it's Detective Wolter.'

'Good.' Klimala didn't bother to suppress her supercilious smile. 'White goes first.'

'I *know*.' Stina instantly regretted the snap in her reply. She had to stay professional.

Klimala laughed like a goose, her teeth bared in glee at so

easily needling her opponent. Without looking, Stina pinched the round head of a pawn between thumb and finger—she didn't even register which pawn, one of the middle ones, it didn't matter—and clipped it down on the next square up. Her eyes were locked with Klimala's.

'As I said, I have questions.'

Klimala held up her hands. Her fingers were knobbed with arthritis and trembling. 'Oh, go on then, ask your questions.' The words wheezed like air from a burst balloon, as if what little reserves of defiance she'd possessed were already spent.

Stina realised how wary she'd been of this confrontation, but now doubt sidled in. If she was wrong about this, all she might really be doing was harassing a frail old woman. Was her hunch really that strong? She looked away. To the dowdy sparrow pecking for crumbs under an adjacent table. To the WatchNet bee drowsing above the balustrade, one of millions supposedly making life safer for people now. The security of mass public surveillance. Anyone could be watching through its eyes right at that moment. Maybe even her colleagues back at the Inspectorate. All gathered round and having a good chuckle.

Stina cleared her throat and returned her attention to the woman across the table. 'Albert Vogel,' she said. 'My questions are about him.'

Klimala was scowling at the board. Then with a tiny shake of the head she made her own opening move. 'What about him?' she said. 'What do I know? I know he's dead. That's what I told the last of your lot who came around asking questions.'

'You don't sound very sorry,' Stina said. 'You played chess against him most days. Wasn't he your friend?'

'No, he wasn't my friend.' Klimala lifted her cup, took a slurp and winced. Too hot? Too sweet? Had Stina got the coffee wrong? 'He was merely my opponent.'

'You didn't like him, then?'

'We played chess.' Klimala indicated the tables around them, the boards set out. When Stina had arrived one had been occupied by a dapper gentleman, collared and tied and sporting studious round glasses. Now he'd been joined by a scruffy student type. With barely a few words exchanged they were shaking hands, ready to begin a game. 'People don't come here to make friends. They come just to play.' Klimala nodded at their own board. 'It's your go again.'

'And how long did your rivalry with Herr Vogel last?' Stina moved the pawn another square, eliciting a tut from her opponent. 'The café owner said you pair were at it when her mother was a girl.'

Klimala scowled in the direction of the open café door. 'Janssen said that? I wouldn't pay too much attention. She's just in a bad mood because of the grilling you lot gave her.'

Stina shrugged. 'Albert had a drug in his system that caused his heart to fail. We had to be sure he didn't ingest it in his coffee.'

'Of course he didn't,' Klimala growled. 'Anyway, yes, Vogel and I played a lot.'

'I ask again, how long . . . ?'

'I don't know an exact date,' Klimala said, but then she clamped her lips together and stared at the board meaningfully until Stina made another move. A different pawn this time. Then Klimala nodded and continued. 'But I do know how many matches we played.'

'Really?' Stina was surprised. 'How many?'

'Seven thousand and fourteen.'

It was all Stina could do not to gape. In her notes she'd estimated the rivalry to have gone back perhaps a decade but they were potentially talking at least double that. Way before WatchNet and the comprehensive datasphere had been established: the very foundation of the criminal evidence chain these days. The AI couldn't look that far back. 'That's quite a legacy,' she said.

'So, now you see?' Klimala said. 'That's how chess is. It's a conversation, a rapport you build with every game. It's not merely a way to pass the time while you get chummy. It's a thing of value in itself.'

'And yet, it must be impossible not to learn things about your opponent. You're really saying you knew nothing about Albert Vogel?'

'I know how he played chess.' In a single, swift movement, Klimala's black knight replaced Stina's advanced pawn and the captured piece was dropped into a pocket of the voluminous coat. Despite the encumbrance of arthritis, it was done with the deftness of a conjuror. 'Which is all I needed or wanted to know about him.'

Stina found the insistence of ignorance hard to swallow, but she moved on. 'And who, would you say, won the majority of your games?'

Klimala snorted at that. There was a spark in her eyes. 'Albert Vogel didn't win a single match against me. Not fairly at least.'

Stina had been about to nudge out another pawn. She paused, her hand poised in mid-air. 'Are you saying he cheated?'

Klimala's shrug was a lumpen movement inside her layers. Then she sniffed and pointed at the board. 'This is going to be a short conversation if you make that move.'

Stina retracted her hand, thinking about what she'd just heard. It had sounded like Klimala was hinting that she *wanted* the conversation to go on for longer. For the first time in the game she gave serious thought to her next move, settling eventually on bringing out a knight.

'So, you do this every day?' she said casually and then took a sip of her coffee. She'd let it sit for too long, but even piping hot it wouldn't have been great. She understood why Klimala had grimaced earlier. The woman who ran the café really had a grudge against the police.

Klimala nodded but didn't speak. Just moved a pawn.

Stina mirrored the move. 'Must be nice to have the time to come out and enjoy a leisurely day playing chess.'

'It's called retirement,' Klimala grunted. 'Aren't you supposed to focus on the things you enjoy when you retire?'

Stina could have delved deeper there, asked what else the old woman had been doing with her retirement, but she already knew the answer to that. No friends, no late blooming romances.

Just here, the food store and occasional trips to the park or the local repertory cinema. A picture was building. 'And what did you do before you retired?'

Those deft fingers brought a bishop into play. Stina didn't think she was going to get an answer to her question, but then she did, and it was carefully worded. 'I worked in the diplomatic service.'

Stina nodded, pretended to consider her pieces. 'In whose diplomatic service?' she asked quietly.

When Klimala looked up, the grey eyes were shining with cold humour. An imperceptible shake of the head. Stina advanced her own bishop.

'Is Dimitra Klimala even your real name?'

No answer to that either.

The moves came thick and fast while Stina tried to sift her thoughts into some sort of order. A person's data should tell you everything about them, and that Dimitra Klimala had impossibly little of it was no accident. She wasn't some doddery oldster with no clue how the world worked. And she knew full well that she didn't have to divulge anything unless they charged her. Even then, how little might there be? This woman had gone to great lengths to avoid connections to the world. But everyone needed some kind of connection, didn't they? The coffees, the chess. It wasn't a cover. Those were really all she had.

Stina moved a knight and rather pleasingly put Klimala in a fork. 'I'll bet some of those chess games with Albert were close,' she said.

'Of course.' Klimala saved her knight, sacrificing her bishop. 'He was a good player.'

Stina took it. 'And then?' Her short-lived satisfaction crumbled as Klimala's next move with the knight forked her back, threatening queen and rook.

'And then he didn't come for a while.' Klimala said.

'Well, he *was* convalescing from a heart attack.' Stina saved her queen, watched her rook vanish, and then tried to build again on the other side of the board. 'That must have been upsetting.'

'I was . . . disappointed.' Klimala said it quietly, but Stina heard something in the word. A glittering glimpse of truth. While Klimala took another of Stina's pawns off the board, Stina pulled up the feed of the bee on the balustrade in her lenses. Saw the old woman's fingers fretting nervously with the wooden piece before dropping it into her pocket.

And that was when Stina knew how it could have been done. A piece could have been set up on the board at the beginning of the game coated with contact poison. It would have to be a piece that might not be touched until near the end of the match. The king, logically. And after it had been taken, how easy for someone with quick fingers to swap it for an untainted one hidden in that deep pocket, and dispose of it later so that when the pieces were tested no trace would be found. It was like something from an old spy film, but it was possible. Especially for someone who might once have been an old spy.

But why? What was the motive for it?

Then she saw it. *Seven thousand* games.

'When he came back from his time away, that was when he cheated?' Stina said. 'That must have been galling. To have sullied the legacy you'd built between you. All those close matches. His valiant attempts to best you. Your ongoing run against a worthy opponent.'

She looked across the board and saw that Klimala was shivering. No, not that, laughing. Silently, mirthlessly. So hard that tears were welling in the corners of her eyes. The old woman composed herself. 'How perceptive. Yes, that's when he cheated. He moved a rook while I was ordering coffee. He realised almost immediately that he'd moved it into trouble and pulled it back a square. He thought I hadn't seen, but I see everything.'

'He must have wanted to beat you very badly. After his brush with mortality perhaps he doubted there would be many more opportunities.'

'Ah, you picture Vogel nobly striving for a win in a longstanding friendly rivalry,' Klimala said, and again Stina caught the glitter of truth in her tone. It was sharp and steely. 'Well it was that, once. Our matches were . . . *close*. But Albert was not an honourable man. He ruined what we had the *first* time he cheated. He'd been trying to redeem himself ever since.'

Stina stared at her opponent, then she said, very quietly, 'And you weren't going to let that happen. You beat him over seven thousand times to teach him a lesson, and turned that lesson into a—what was your phrase?—a *thing of value*. But only to one of you, it turned out. That must have been *very* galling indeed.'

Klimala's eyes twinkled but she made no confession, and Stina realised that she could see no way of ever getting one. She studied the board. Most of her pieces were gone now, her options for keeping the game going limited. Out of desperation, she castled.

'Can I ask,' she said, 'why you agreed to talk to me?'

'That's a good question.' Klimala's hand hovered for a moment then shifted the black queen one square, and it was like a conjuror making her final reveal. Devastatingly impressive. Stina scanned her options but quickly saw that every possible move she made would lead her into mate in the next move or the one after.

'Why? Because as soon as you turned up here today I could tell you were like me. You're in *zugzwang*.'

'Zugz . . . ?' Stina frowned. 'What is that?'

'Zugzwang is when you have to move but can't do so without making your position worse.'

Stina's breath caught as she saw the sudden, glaring truth of it. In the game, in this conversation, in her life. For all her efforts today, what had she really expected to gain from this? To prove to herself that her instincts were still good? Fine, but it had resulted in a lot of conjecture and no evidence. She had nothing to take back to the Super that would justify her seeking override powers on the AI. Nothing but the intuition that screamed that Dimitra Klimala had killed Albert Vogel.

Worse, what she'd done here today just made her look more old fashioned and desperate. If she even tried to make a case, she'd end up sidelined, farmed out until the next round of headcount cuts allowed them to get rid of her. If she said nothing she'd keep her tattered reputation a while longer, but it'd only be a matter of time. Either way, a murder would go unexplained. It was an awful, despairing feeling. Stina would probably never know the hidden details of Dimitra's life but how precarious must her position have been to balance on its edge, making no move at all, for *decades*?

And yet, she seemed happy in her limited existence. How was that possible?

'So...' She gently laid her king on the board.

'So.' Her opponent had already begun setting the pieces up again. 'You don't play badly, you know, but you'd improve if you cut out the chit-chat.'

'I suppose,' said Stina. 'I'm sorry.'

'You'll do better next time,' Dimitra said.

Stina laughed at the presumption of the offer, but appreciated how skilfully it had been crafted. Despite everything, she liked this old woman. And besides, what else was she going to do with her time?

'Same time tomorrow, then?' she said. She could come over on her lunch hour, and if anyone happened to be watching on the bees they would see an old woman and a middle-aged one, out of step and off the grid, playing one of the oldest games in the world. But what would really be happening was something else entirely.

From Below

Warren Benedetto

'WE WILL BE SAFE THERE?' THE BOY ASKED.

The roar of the powerful outboard motor echoed through the flood-ravaged streets of Old Manhattan as Jeremy piloted it down the centre of what used to be 5th Avenue. Water lapped at the facades of the submerged structures, spraying a fine mist into the cold night air.

Jeremy glanced down at the child. The kid was young, no older than ten, with black hair and dark brown skin the color of macadamia nuts. The way his hair flopped over his forehead reminded Jeremy of himself as a child.

'Of course,' Jeremy lied. 'You'll love it.'

The boy's mother shot Jeremy a nervous glance, then put her arm around her son and whispered into his ear in a foreign tongue. The boy nodded. He rested his head on her shoulder. She hugged him tighter and kissed the top of his salt-crusted hair.

A gust of freezing wind whipped between the buildings. All around, the remains of skyscrapers jutted from the water like ancient monoliths—hollow paeans to long-dead gods—their once-towering heights clipped short by the rising tides. An empty flagpole protruded from one of them, a spear in the heart of a dying giant. Smears of rust cascaded down the stone from the corroded metal base like bloodstains from a mortal wound.

Jeremy looked up at his destination, a black glass facade looming in the distance. It was dark except for a ring of light spilling from the top floor windows.

The penthouse.

Floor-to-ceiling shades in every window prevented people outside from seeing in, and people inside from having to see out. Behind the shades, a pair of silhouettes moved fluidly past the glass: separating, spinning, then coming back together again, arms intertwining, bodies swaying, dual shadows merging into a single multi-limbed form.

Christ, Jeremy thought. *Are they dancing?*

He couldn't remember the last time he had seen anyone dancing. It seemed almost sacrilegious after all that had happened. The floods. The droughts. The fires. Millions dead. Millions more starving.

And yet those bastards up there were *dancing.*

As if everything was okay.

As if all this was normal.

As if it was just another day.

'Unbelievable,' Jeremy muttered.

A ghostly white glow briefly illuminated the boat as it passed a giant *Do Not Enter* sign. The warnings were everywhere, cautioning people against entering the flooded city. The water was getting deeper—that was the first problem. A few months ago, it had been a foot or two below the sign. Now, half the sign was gone. It wouldn't be long before the whole city was underwater, penthouses and all. And then what?

Jeremy's hand unconsciously brushed the gun tucked in his belt. He had never needed to use it, but he carried it just in case. The rising tide wasn't the only risk. There were looters. Hijackers. Junkies. But what truly worried him weren't the dangers above the water. It was the ones below.

He had never seen the things that lurked under the water,

but he had heard about them, about what they did to anyone who strayed too close to the water's edge. Nobody knew what they were, or where they came from. There were plenty of plausible theories, ranging from previously undiscovered ocean predators to long-extinct dinosaurs thawed from the Arctic ice. Then there were the crackpot rumours. Escaped genetic experiments. Government bioweapons. Mermaids. Aliens. Zombies.

Jeremy didn't know what to think. Part of him wanted to believe that the things didn't exist at all, that they were just boogeymen that parents wielded to warn their kids away from the water. But another part of him found it hard to ignore the screams that echoed through the city at night or the blooms of blood and viscera that sometimes bubbled up from the depths.

A gruff voice broke Jeremy out of his reverie. It was his business partner, Alex. He was standing with one foot perched on the bow of the boat like George Washington crossing the Delaware River.

'Yo, Jeremy! Slow it down!'

The beam from a flashlight strobed in Jeremy's eyes. He waved it away. 'Relax. I'm on it.'

Jeremy killed the motor. Its dying rumble ricocheted off the walls of the urban canyon and rolled into the distance. The only sound that remained was the soft slap of water against the hull and the occasional cough from one of the twenty refugees crowded into the overloaded transport. The faint strains of what sounded like a waltz filtered down from the penthouse above.

The boat bumped against the 46th-floor window of the skyscraper with a squeal like the death throes of a dying machine. Moving quickly, Alex looped a heavy, mildew-blackened rope in through one broken window and out the next, lashing the boat to the wide steel beam that separated them. Then he turned and faced the passengers. Twenty hopeful faces looked up at him expectantly. They were starving. Desperate. Scared. They'd believe anything.

And they had.

Alex cleared his throat and projected his voice. 'All right everyone, listen up,' he said. 'I'm gonna run inside to see if your rooms are ready. You're all paid up, right?'

Heads nodded.

Alex pointed at the boy who had talked to Jeremy. 'You too, little man?'

The boy looked up at his mother. She nodded. He gave Alex a thumbs up.

'Great!' Alex clapped his hands together. 'Then I'll be right back!' He grabbed the rope ladder dangling against the side of the building, then smiled down at the faces below. 'You're gonna love it here.' With that, he climbed up the ladder and disappeared through a window a few feet above the water.

Fucking asshole, Jeremy thought. Why'd he have to do that, with the kid? What was the point? It was just cruel.

Alex seemed to have a twisted need to prove to himself that he was still an alpha male. Still a captain of industry. Still at the top of the food chain. In a way, he was.

They both were.

∞

Jeremy had known Alex for years. They met as freshmen at Texas A&M University, joined the MBA program at Wharton together, and traded commodities at the same investment bank. Alex was an asshole back then too.

Jeremy was originally from Texas. He had majored in geological engineering, with plans to join the oil industry when he graduated. But then a recruiter for a major investment bank convinced him that he could make way more money trading oil futures in the stock market than he could drilling holes in the Texas desert. The recruiter was right.

Alex, meanwhile, had grown up in Nebraska, spending most of his childhood on his family's cattle ranch. He too had heard the siren song of Wall Street calling after graduation, and he too ultimately fell back on what he knew best. For him, it was livestock.

Instead of herding cows on a farm in Nebraska, he was trading cattle futures from an office tower in Manhattan. It didn't matter to him. Either way, the livestock ended up in the same place: the slaughterhouse, then the dinner table. The beef industry was a big, bloody machine, a meat grinder that ingested living things on one end and spat gushers of money out the other. Alex was all too happy to collect it.

When the water started rising, Wall Street had been one of the first things to go. The economy collapsed. Commerce broke down. Supply chains disintegrated. Food became scarce for everyone but the wealthiest few. Housing too. Soon, it was every man for himself.

Alex came up with the plan. To him, it was obvious what he and Jeremy needed to do to survive—it was just an extension of what he had been doing before the world went to hell. The same bloody machine, just smaller. And they'd have to operate both ends.

'Think of them like commodities,' Alex had argued when he pitched the idea to Jeremy. 'Like livestock.'

Jeremy couldn't believe what he was hearing. It was insane. 'Livestock? They're people!'

Alex walked over to the window of their apartment and looked out across the flooded cityscape. Like most of the city, their place had no electricity any more. They were lucky enough that it was still above the water. It wouldn't be for long, though. The high tide was already sloshing against the bottom of their windows.

'This place is fucked,' Alex said. He thumped the toe of his sneaker against the glass, at the waterline. 'We need an agent. And agents cost money.'

'I know.'

Alex was right. There were only so many buildings still above the water, and more were being flooded every day. An agent would find them a new place and would do the dirty work of evicting the current occupants. But that kind of service didn't come cheap. The higher the apartment, the higher the price.

Plus, there was the cost of eviction and the resulting cleanup. If the occupants left peacefully, it wouldn't be too bad. But if they didn't... well, they would have to be convinced. The agents would do what they had to do to clear the property, but it could get messy. And that was expensive.

Jeremy joined Alex at the window. He gazed out at the remains of the darkened skyscrapers, their penthouse lights glowing like the tips of lit cigars. The penthouses were the only floors that had electricity, thanks to their rooftop solar generators.

'You think it's true, what people are eating up there?' Jeremy asked.

'I know it is.'

'How?'

'You remember Gary Benjamin?'

Jeremy nodded. Gary Benjamin had been the head chef at Prime Cut, one of the city's premier steakhouses. Jeremy and Alex used to wine-and-dine their Wall Street clients over fist-sized cuts of Gary's divinely-marbled $300 Wagyu steak. He was a smart guy. Talented. The best chef in the city, if you believed the critics who ranked that kind of thing.

'He's a personal chef now, in that one.' Alex pointed at the black glass skyscraper towering over the drowned remains of 5th Avenue. 'And he's buying.'

∞

Jeremy sat alone in the boat, waiting and listening. He had made the trip enough times to recognise the sounds of what was happening inside. It was always the same thing. First, there would be murmurs of confusion and concern as the refugees began to realise they had been lied to. Someone—usually a man—would begin shouting in protest. There would be a struggle, then gunshots. The screams would follow. Sometimes there were more gunshots, sometimes not. It depended on how unruly things got.

Eventually, the panic would simmer down to a steady drone of quiet weeping and whispered prayers. The adults would be shuttled up the dank stairwell to the 49th floor for immediate processing. The kids would be herded into individual pens on the 48th, where they would be held until they were needed. None of them knew what was in store for them. They were kept in the dark, literally and figuratively.

Jeremy had never been inside the building. He didn't have the stomach for it. Alex did, though. Somehow, he was unfazed by the whole thing. He'd go up to the kitchen to chat with Gary Benjamin as Gary prepped the penthouse's next meal, knowing full well where the cuts of meat on the chopping block had come from.

A flash of movement overhead caught Jeremy's eye, breaking him from his thoughts. He looked up.

The boy from the boat—the one who had spoken to him only minutes earlier—was at the window, pounding on the glass. His face was a mask of pure terror. Panicked, the boy looked over his shoulder, then down at Jeremy. He screamed, his lips forming two words that Jeremy easily understood, even through the thick, soundproof glass.

'Help me!'

Before Jeremy could react, Alex appeared behind the boy and grabbed him by the arms. The kid struggled to break free, but Alex was too strong. He dragged the boy kicking and screaming away from the window and into the darkness.

A few minutes later, the rope ladder rattled against the side of the building as Alex began to climb down.

'Sorry about that,' Alex said as he lowered himself onto the boat. 'Damn kid slipped away when we weren't looking.' He wiped his hands on the back of his pants, then began untying the rope that secured the boat to the building. Jeremy noticed a spray of blood splattered across the front of Alex's yellow rain slicker. Crimson streaks that looked like finger tracks were smeared down one of his sleeves. 'Good news, though,' Alex continued as he coiled the rope. He was beaming. 'We're in.'

Jeremy didn't respond. He was still staring at the bloodstains, his eyes unfocused.

'You hear what I said?' Alex asked. 'They have a vacancy. One of the top-floor tenants offed himself.' He looped the coiled rope onto a rusted metal hook. 'Isn't that great?'

'Yeah,' Jeremy said quietly, groggily, as if waking from a deep slumber.

Alex frowned. 'Hey. What's your problem?'

Jeremy looked up at the window where he had seen the kid calling for help. It was dark. He glanced back at Alex. 'I'm done,' he said. He stood up and pressed the outboard motor's electric starter. The engine sputtered but didn't catch.

'Done? Done what?'

Jeremy motioned to the building. 'This.' He pressed the starter again. 'Everything.' The engine roared to life, spitting a cloud of pale grey exhaust into the air.

'Hang on, hang on,' Alex shouted over the noise. 'Shut that shit off.'

Jeremy ignored Alex. He revved the engine louder and began piloting the boat away from the side of a building in a u-turn.

'Shut it off, I said!' Alex shouted over the noise. He pushed past Jeremy and killed the engine. 'What the hell are you talking about, you're done?'

Jeremy looked down at his shoes. 'I don't want to do it anymore.'

Alex glared at Jeremy for a moment. The muscles in his jaw rippled as he clenched his teeth. Then he nodded. His tone lightened. 'Okay.'

'Okay?' Jeremy raised his eyebrows in surprise. 'Really?'

'Sure. We'll just stop. And then, when our apartment floods and one of those things comes swimming through the door looking for its next meal . . . I'll make sure it knows where to find you.'

Jeremy's eyes narrowed. 'Fuck you.'

'Don't you get it?' Alex asked. 'We're *this* close to making it up there.' He pointed to the penthouse.

Jeremy snorted derisively. 'They're not going to help us. They don't give a shit about us. We're just useful to them.'

'Yeah, exactly. That gives us leverage. We can make a deal.'

A laugh burst from Jeremy's lips, echoing off the buildings towering around them. It was a hollow, joyless sound. 'They're dancing up there.'

'So?'

'So, you don't get to where they are by *sharing*. Hell, that's why we're in this shit show in the first place.' He gestured to the water that had overtaken the city. 'They didn't know when to stop, when enough was enough, and now *we're* stuck in this mess that *they* created. But them . . . ?' He looked up the penthouse. 'They're still dry. They have electricity. Clean water. Food. They're above it all, literally.'

'Exactly. Which is why we need to be up there too.'

'But that's their whole scam! The American dream, right? If you just work for us hard enough, someday all of this can be yours. It's bullshit. It was *always* bullshit.'

'What're you, Karl Marx now? Christ. Listen to yourself. You sound like a fucking communist.'

'Look, do what you want,' Jeremy sighed. 'But like I said . . . I'm done.'

Jeremy tried to step around Alex and back to his position by the engine. Alex moved to block his way. His lips curled away from his teeth in a snarl.

'No,' Alex growled. 'You're done when I *say* you're done.' He moved forward until they were almost nose-to-nose. 'Got it?'

Jeremy planted a forearm in Alex's chest, pushing him away. 'Back off,' he warned.

'What're you gonna do?' Alex shoved Jeremy. 'Huh?'

Alex's shove broke something deep inside Jeremy. He thrust forward, crushing his forehead into Alex's face in a vicious headbutt.

Alex grunted as blood erupted from his busted nose. He spun around and bent forward over the railing of the boat, leaking bright red tendrils into the jewel-green waves. 'The hell, man! You brope by nose.'

As Alex tried to staunch the bleeding with his shirt, the water beside the boat began roiling and foaming. A cluster of ghostly white blurs materialized in the oily darkness, like wisps of gauze dancing lazily just under the surface.

Suddenly, a mottled, greyish-white hand shot out of the water. It clutched Alex's arm and yanked, causing his midsection to crash against the railing and knocking the wind out of his lungs. Another hand shot from the water. Flaccid ribbons of flesh were strung between its bony fingers like party streamers. Its yellowed nails dug into the shoulder of Alex's jacket and pulled him headfirst into the water.

Alex's startled screams turned into muffled gurgling. His arms flailed helplessly at the thing in the water. He tried to tear away the limbs that were gripping him, but the rotting flesh just sloughed off in his hands.

Overcoming his initial shock, Jeremy lunged forward and grabbed Alex's belt. He could feel the things in the water tugging hungrily at his friend, trying to draw him fully out of the boat and under the waves. Jeremy's grip began to slip. The muscles in his back and shoulders screamed from the strain. The belt tore at his fingers.

Then, suddenly, the things let go. With the resistance gone, Jeremy toppled backward, landing flat on his back, with Alex's limp body on top of his own.

Jeremy squeezed out from under Alex, then looked down at his friend. Alex's face was gone. All that was left was a shredded red-black hole, just a masticated mess of flesh and bone. The remnants of his lower jaw hung down towards his neck, his bottom teeth poking up through the torn flesh of his lips and gums like broken seashells in a rising tide of gore. Torrents of blood bubbled up from his severed arteries and pooled in the cavity where his mouth used to be.

Jeremy recoiled with revulsion, vomit spewing from his lips. Alex was making gurgling sounds, his legs and arms twitching weakly. Somehow, he was still alive. His head lolled towards Jeremy. The mangled stump of his tongue poked and wiggled obscenely over the entrance to his torn oesophagus. He seemed to be trying to say something. One of his arms lifted, reaching in Jeremy's direction, fingers grasping blindly. They found Jeremy's arm and tightened around it.

Jeremy's feet slipped on the blood-slicked metal floor as he stumbled backward and fell on his side. The floor began to tilt underneath him, sending a noxious mixture of water, blood, and vomit sloshing past his cheek.

Above Jeremy, a rotting hand gripped the boat's railing. Another arm emerged from the depths and latched a hand onto the rail, further tipping the vessel. Then another arm emerged. And another.

The groping hands and reaching arms were undoubtedly human, albeit in advanced states of decomposition. Jeremy kicked at them, hearing the crunch of brittle bone and the squelch of rotting flesh as his boot connected with the outstretched appendages.

One of the mouldering creatures managed to pull itself over the railing, toppling into the boat with a splash. It was a woman. Or it had been, at one point. Clumps of long, braided hair dangled from the thing's skull like seaweed. A tangled necklace was entwined around its exposed vertebrae. Shreds of what appeared to be a McDonald's uniform clung to its torso, a name tag still pinned to the shirt. *Daniella*, it read.

The realisation of what he was seeing washed over Jeremy. He suddenly understood. He had never considered what had happened to the millions of people who had drowned in the city—the poor, the working class, the homeless—the ones who had been unable to escape the rapidly-rising floodwaters, their waterlogged bodies bloating with gases and floating towards the surface, only to be forever trapped by the ceilings of whatever rooms they were in when they died. Now he knew.

Jeremy watched in numb horror as several more once-human forms pulled themselves out of the water and into the boat. Their skin hung like rags from their algae-blackened bones, catching on the rivets lining the railing and sliding off into doughy piles that reminded Jeremy of sodden toilet paper spat from an overflowing sewer. Their flesh teemed with worms. Barnacles crusted their skulls. The low-tide smell of rot and decomposition filled Jeremy's mouth and nose.

Once in the boat, the things slithered hungrily on their bellies towards Alex's dying body, pulling themselves forward with their arms like infants who haven't yet learned to crawl. Jeremy backpedalled away. Something grabbed his shoulder. He felt the icy wetness of necrotic flesh graze his neck. With a wild yelp, he spun to find more skeletal hands curling over the railing behind him. In the reflection of the black glass skyscraper, he could see a dozen or more of the things climbing up the side of the boat. More were surfacing from the water in all directions.

He was surrounded.

Jeremy looked up at the building. The rope ladder that Alex had descended only minutes earlier was still dangling from the broken 47th-floor window. In the window, Gary Benjamin was peering down at him, watching the horrors unfold below with a mixture of fascination and disgust.

'Gary!' Jeremy pleaded. 'Help me!'

Jeremy's desperate plea sent Gary into action. He stepped back into the shadows and began drawing the remaining length of the ladder up through the window.

'No! Gary! Wait!' Jeremy shouted. 'The ladder! Please!'

He reached desperately for the retracting ladder as it disappeared into the building. It was too far. There was no way he could reach it before it was gone.

Jeremy turned around, searching desperately for another way to escape. The creatures were swarming the boat from all directions. They feasted on Alex's remains, greedily tearing the flesh from his limbs with their teeth. Some plunged their bony hands into his body cavity, pulling out dripping handfuls of viscera and shovelling it into their disjointed maws. Others began to crawl towards Jeremy, their teeth gnashing, their arms reaching.

There was nowhere for Jeremy to go. He had only one option.

His hand settled on the butt of his gun.

It was an unconscious movement, driven by pure instinct. He had forgotten that he even had the thing. He drew it from his belt, aimed at the advancing horde, and fired. The bullets passed cleanly through flesh and bone, doing nothing to slow the creatures' approach.

The things were almost upon him. He felt their hands close around his ankles. Around his calves. They began to pull at him, drawing him downwards.

With a faraway stare, Jeremy pressed the barrel of the gun under his chin, then looked up at the sky. His eyes fell on the penthouse. Its lights cast a soft white halo around the top floor of the skyscraper. The lazy strains of the waltz had been replaced by something more uptempo, a swing. The silhouettes behind the shades twirled and spun, joining and separating and joining again, oblivious to the horror unfolding below.

Jeremy closed his eyes, then pulled the trigger. His lifeless body tumbled forward into the waiting jaws of the undead horde.

The silhouettes never missed a beat. They kept on dancing, as if all this was normal. As if it was just another day.

As if nothing had happened at all.

LUSTRE MINING

ELIZA CHAN

POON-LAI JABBED AN ELBOW SO HER SISTERS WOULD make more space. The others grumbled but pushed the dog-eared magazine back towards the middle. A British film star grinned at the camera, draped in a five-strand lustre necklace. Black in daylight, lustre shone brighter than opals in the darkness. The most precious gemstone in the world.

'It's just lying on the streets. Like stones!' her youngest sister said. She reached dramatically for a handful of pebbles from their dirt floor, showering them on her legs. Poon-Lai coughed at the chalky dust, shaking her head even whilst she laughed.

'You're so lucky!' her second sister said, tugging on Poon-Lai's sleeve. Her face was as round as a full moon. 'You should get a western boyfriend. One with a motorbike and a leather jacket.'

They fell about the floor laughing, the very notion so absurd, so beyond anything in their daily lives that the sisters could not help but laugh. Reverting to children. Poon-Lai was not so far from childhood. The softness of youth lingered around her eyes even though her hands were callused from working in the fields.

They lay in the dirt, holding the glossy magazine over their heads, admiring the sports cars set with lustre gear sticks and dials, the handbags with lustre clasps. Some of the elders in Poon-Lai's village wore fake lustre jewellery: nothing more than obsidian shards.

'Promise you won't forget us,' Poon-Lai's quiet middle sister added as they fell into easy silence. 'When you start your new life.'

Poon-Lai swore it, holding all three sisters in her arms. Promised to take them to a fancy department store. To the palace to see the queen. To collect for them all the lustre they desired. She struggled for the words that could fill the brimming well of their hopes and dreams. 'Lustre gems as big as my hand.'

Their heads touched as she splayed out her tough tanned hands for them to examine. She was their big sister after all. She would look after them.

∞

Robbie's father looked at the bottle of stout Penny had brought, squinting at the label like a foreman at the lustre mines. She would've chosen with more care, had she known. They looked the sort of thing she'd seen them drink at the pub. It was all the same to her, the sour smell of hops lingering on her clothes alongside the cloying smoke.

'They water this stuff down,' he said in lieu of greeting. The joints of his fingers were swollen, stiff with the early signs of lustre calcification. Penny rubbed at her own knuckles self-consciously.

'Da, be nice,' Robbie said reaching for her hand. He had warned her of his salt of the earth father.

The older man huffed, giving her enough space to squeeze past into the family home. Penny breathed in deeply before the door closed behind. The clatter of cooking and yell of Robbie's mother was familiar at least. The matronly woman presided over the narrow space, scraping roasties and carrots from a well-loved baking tray and barking orders to the younger children.

'Thank you for having me, Mrs Greenwood,' Penny squeaked,

the basket of apples held out in front like an offering. A perfect attempt! She'd practised it over and over in the quiet of her cottage: as she brushed her teeth in the morning frost; as she waited for the kettle to whistle at the end of the day. Thank you for having me. Greenwood. Gureen. Uwood. The Rs that slipped into Ws, the two sounds so close together. It was like the fates wanted to make a fool out of her.

'Speak up, lovey,' Robbie's mother said, not unkindly. Penny had whispered the words into her own feet. With two younger kids fighting over whose turn it was to set the table, her perfect enunciation was wasted. Every stumbling error, contracted syllable, backsliding as she winced and mangled the phrase on repetition.

'I'm surprised you understand a word she's saying, Robbie!' the woman spoke over her head to her own son as she hefted the roast chicken out of the narrow gas oven. 'Now Jenny Barker, on the other hand, why did you end things with her? Lovely local girl.'

'Ma!' Robbie said, face beetroot red as he ushered Penny to the table. 'Just ignore her, ignore them both.' His hand patted her arm reassuringly.

She was not a fool. Not any more. Conversations dried up when she went into shops, eyes and heads swivelling to follow her. The sniggers when she opened her mouth, the parroting mockery of her accent. She'd been here long enough to understand the sentiment if not all the words.

Poon-Lai was excited about flying. The blue-eyed man sitting opposite had given her a curious but not unkind look from the top of his long nose before ruffling his newspaper, folding and unfolding the crinkled sheets. His fingers sparkled with lustre rings, even the face of his watch gave off the tell-tale iridescent glow.

'Move, you're in economy,' the flight attendant snapped,

shepherding Poon-Lai from the luxurious seats to the cramped rear. Poon-Lai had only a flitting moment to admire her bright lips, sparkling with lustre powder. She shrieked when the plane left the runway, stomach not best pleased with the sensation. Dared not move from her seat until her bladder was fit to bursting. Ordered the same meal as the gentleman next to her, down to the whisky from the drinks trolley. Her auntie had taught her that. Just nod and say 'same'. The westerners know what they're doing. She gagged at the foul tasting liquid. In the films the drinks came in crystal tumblers with fat ice cubes. Lustre liquor, her second cousin had said, was the popular new drink.

Uncle Four's neighbour's sister's friend had told them of the wealth to be made in the west. That they were desperate for people to work in the lustre mines. Gemstones as plentiful as grains of rice. Too wealthy to pick up jewels from the ground, that's what she'd heard. And was Poon-Lai not a hard worker, someone used to dealing with the long hours on the paddy fields? It wasn't much different, not at all. The promise came easily, sliding from her tongue as soon as the question was posed. Of course she could do it: pay off the debt that bought a one way ticket; earn enough to bring the rest of the family over. She flipped the pages of the long contract, the complicated English she could barely read. It was fine, the recruiter assured them, just standard stuff. It's a better life over there! She scrawled her name on the stern black line. Living for a few months amongst the British sounded exciting. She'd have sandwiches and tea from dainty tea cups. Buy herself a mink fur coat.

The excitement deflated like a slow puncture by the time they landed in the smoggy capital city. As her luggage limped round on the baggage reclaims and the man checking her passport shouted incomprehensible questions louder and louder until tears sprang to her eyes. The phone booth swallowed her coins, one after another whilst beeping irately in her ear. Until finally a woman in the toilets took her by the elbow, looking at the instructions the recruiter had written for her and shepherded her onto the right coach. A dull panic thudded in Poon-Lai's chest like a bird who'd smacked into the window. As the city flickered past, she scoured the pavements for gemstones but there was nothing except cigarette butts, discarded gum and litter. The new arrival closed her eyes against the vibrant neon. Shivered in her thickest, warmest clothes that were definitely not warm enough. It would be different at the journey's end.

It had to be.

The small Yorkshire town was grey. Drab as the bobbled fingerless gloves of her gruff landlord. The bare bulb of the miner's cottage buzzed from the low ceiling beams as he flicked it on.

'Someone here,' she said in halting English. Pointed at the dishes in the drying rack; the battered walking boots by the hearth; the filled drawers in the cramped bedroom.

'They're not coming back. It's yours. Use it. Chuck it. I don't care.' Poon-Lai was unsure if all Englishmen looked so annoyed. Like he'd breakfasted on rusted nails, face contorting. The landlord fiddled with the gold-linked bracelet around his wrist, the single lustre gem winking before he tucked it under his sleeve. He looked like he'd add something but instead dry swallowed, tossed the keys onto the armchair.

Poon-Lai longed to sink into the sagging single bed, but it felt all wrong. Someone else's house. Someone else's things. Her hands touched the ornaments on the mantelpiece: a pair of ceramic dogs; a brass carriage clock, hands frozen at eight and four; a chipped vase, flowers withered to bony fingers. She could not sleep in a bed that felt like it would still be warm.

Instead, she crouched by the hearth to light the fire. A task that she did every night back home and yet now her tired limbs fumbled and the tinder refused to spark. It mattered not. One night in the cold would not kill her. She sat on the armchair, seat frayed to loose threads, and slipped her feet into someone else's worn walking boots. Tentatively. Her toes wiggled in the oversized boots but they were better than those she had brought.

She could grow into them.

∞

The Yorkshire pudding slid from the heap of food, spilling gravy over the embroidered tablecloth. Penny hoped no one had noticed as she tweaked it clumsily back onto her plate. When she looked up the whole family were staring. Resigned, she laughed. 'Should've brought chopsticks!'

'Is that how you get gems? With eating sticks?' Robbie's precocious younger brother asked.

Penny was glad to engage his friendly face. 'Maybe I teach you sometime.'

Mr Greenwood dropped his knife and fork with a loud clatter. 'Absolutely not. No mine talk at this table. Especially not about working in that hell hole.' His tone was absolute. Mrs Greenwood crammed another roast potato into her mouth, eyes bulging. The lustre mine was the main industry in the remote town. Gem cutting, polishing, setting, transportation all relied on the mines. And yet…

'My two older sisters were miners. Died in an accident a few years back,' Robbie said quietly as he bent over her ear. He drew circles on the tablecloth with his finger. It would've been useful to have this information before the family meal. He'd not mentioned it during their brief courtship, not spoken of his family at all.

'And your cousin. Your uncle too,' Mr Greenwood added, breaking his own rule. He glared at Penny like it was her fault. That she'd held a gun to each of their heads, these nameless, faceless people she'd only just heard of.

The room was expectant, waiting for her response. Penny licked her lower lip, sluggish and stalling. Hesitant least of all because she didn't know they wanted from her. 'It's… dangerous down there.'

Grief lingered in the house like the smell of tobacco smoke, permeating the very foundations of the family. Mr Greenwood made a noise. A thick growling sound that said dangerous didn't begin to describe it.

'It's why we got Robbie out. An apprenticeship instead, mechanic is a useful skill,' Mrs Greenwood added, attempting to divert the subject. 'The money isn't worth it, love. It never was.' Behind her a long sideboard was lined with gold framed photos. One where Robbie was just a boy, his mother's stomach swollen in late pregnancy. Two older girls sat on either side of him, young women really. Heads tilted back laughing as they tickled him. The same rosy complexion. One sister hid her free hand behind her back but the edges of bandages could be seen wrapped around her forearm.

∞

A handful of others, mostly women, spread themselves across the rows of miner cottages. Disparate groups like spots of oil in water. Eyeing each other with a wariness born of different tongues, different foods and cultures and skin colours, uncertain if this way lay mutual support or competition. They'd come to earn. To make the promised fortune. And in those calculations it was unclear if there was time for anything else. The two women in the next cottage had been there awhile. They gave Poon-Lai a hesitant smile each morning, walking a few steps ahead of her towards the mine entrance. On her first day, they'd shared a meagre meal in the darkness of the mines, drawn by Poon-Lai's hiccupped weeping when no one had told her the shifts were twelve hours long and they couldn't return to the surface for food. Sisters she guessed, by the way the older prodded the younger, critically examining the ends of her tight braids; absent-mindedly playing with the coin amulet around her neck. Their shared language was foreign and yet familiar at the same time. The older sister's right foot dragged on the dirt track, stiff as slate. Her left hand and arm were bandaged tightly as well.

Poon-Lai removed her clean clothes with great reluctance, the moth-eaten wool jumper and padded coat. Fingers shivered as she shrugged into the overalls on the dirty side. She understood the precautions. Had heard the hacking coughs reverberating from the other cottages during the night, the ones that echoed like hungry ghosts. No matter how many layers she wore, she was never warm. Water trickled down the mine walls, dripping on her forehead and the back of her neck with an incessant tap. Easy enough to ignore at first, squatted over with the tools they'd been given, eyes focussing on the narrow veins that glimmered in the lamplight. But the chill congealed. She could no longer feel her toes when she walked home after a shift.

The huge rattling cage that plunged them down into the mine shaft could easily have fitted fifty, sixty people. It was disquieting with only two dozen of them, like children wearing their parents' clothes. Mostly women or young men, slight of build and statue. Lustre mining favoured those who could squeeze into tight spaces, dexterous hands and sharp eyes. The mines were labyrinthine, the deputy sending them off like ants on the railed trolley to their allocated section, never in groups of more than two or three.

In their first week Poon-Lai had uncovered a handful of lustre gems, clustered together like teeth. The glow of her success kept her warm for days. If she worked seven days a week, she could earn more. Get the rest of the family over in five months rather than six. But the good fortune slipped between her cupped fingers. Opalescent lustre winked in seams through the dim light but it was too fine, broke as she cut around it. Resigned to panning through the silt for scattered fragments, her fingers shook as she held scraps to be inspected. The foreman pinched one of her fingers hard. Pushed down on her nail where the skin had darkened, deadened despite the gloves they'd been given. Shook his head.

There was a cave in. Everyone squinted into the grey midday sky as they waited for the head count. No piercing sirens of fire engines or ambulances. No talk of rescue attempts at all. Poon-Lai shaded her eyes against the glare of the light, quite unaccustomed to it. She clenched and unclenched her fingers, frozen as icicles as she blew on them. In the monotony of the job, she'd nearly taken a chip out of her own hand.

They were all given a day off.

It took Poon-Lai a few more days to realise the murmur of the sisters' chatter no longer soothed her evenings through the walls. That they had not walked back up the dirt path to their cottage that day.

∞

It was the stout. Or perhaps the four bottles of ale before, but as he popped the cap on the stout, it was as if someone fanned the flames of his simmering rage. Mr Greenwood rested the bottle on his belly, pointing at her with two fingers. 'Penny? Is that even your name? Take our jobs, our names, our sons.'

'Richard Greenwood!' Robbie's mother interjected but did not stop him. Instead she turned the dial on the TV higher to drown out his cursing. The younger boys barely reacted, accustomed to the outbursts.

'We're all thinking it. Flocking over here.'

'They needed workers.' Poon-Lai did not understand the outrage. The bitterness that pre-dated her, like opening a jar of pickles to find a layer of fine mould on the surface. She shoved her cold hands under her armpits. Her heart a sharp staccato in her chest. The fireplace crackled but Poon-Lai remained cold, impervious to the touch of the warmth.

'Working these goddamn forsaken hours at that goddamn forsaken place. You crosssed the picket line! Months we striked for. Months!' His face was red, capillaries like a fine spider's web across his nose and cheeks, his spit-inflected words showered the snug living room.

Poon-Lai waited for the words to fall to rest: scattering on the circular rug on the floor; on the tasselled side lamps and the coal scuttle by the side of the fire; the smiling family photos on the mantelpiece. There was not a single piece of lustre on them. Not in the photos or on the people in front of her. No pendant tucked beneath a shirt, glitzy watch on a wrist or lustre set knickknacks on the shelf. 'What is picket line? I don't know this word.'

'Da, the strike was over before she even arrived.'

Mr Greenwood didn't hear his son's word. Continued on, a train set on one track. 'That's the problem with foreigners. Just out for yourselves.'

Robbie hung his head in his hands, shaking it as if to convey all his embarrassment and regret in that one small touch. The walls were being build up brick by brick around her. Cement drying as she realised there was no door, no window, no air. Robbie at least was her alcove. A place she could breath, gulp down the air. 'You haven't given her a chance.'

'They didn't give our Joan a chance. Our Annie either.'

Even Robbie had no words.

'I should go,' Poon-Lai brushed imagined crumbs from her lap and stood. Extended her hand. She had practised handshakes with her sisters before she'd left home. Skipping around and curtseying to each other gleefully. Singsong words spilling between peels of laughter. 'It was lovely to meet you.'

Her stone coloured fingers trembled as she waited for someone, anyone, to reach out.

∞

But it was just a cave. As soon as the words left her mouth, Robbie's face fell like the crisp autumnal leaves spiralling down around them. Poon-Lai hastened to correct her remark, using her broken English as a cover for her lack of excitement. He was consistent at least in his enthusiasm. Since he'd started a conversation in the local grocery shop, his oil-stained hands offering to carry her weekly shop. Since he'd bought her a mug of overbrewed tea and a very nice bacon roll at the caff the following week. Since he kept asking to see her on her rest day, to step out, he would say with a boyish wink. She didn't get it at first. She did lots of steps. Walking from the cottage to the mines, along the endless underground tunnels, especially when the trolley broke down and it was the only way to get out. Why would she need more steps? But even she understood in time. The way he shoved his hands in his pockets and when he offered to pick her up in the fancy red car he'd been working on at the garage. Lustre gear stick and dials, Poon-Lai thought, but refused the offer all the same.

'But have you ever seen this!' Robbie said, tugging her hand towards the steady dripping of water. A hulking rock jutted over a deep pool of water. A steady trickle of water slipped over the bare surface like a sluice. But what drew the eye was not a picturesque waterfall or woods they'd traipsed through, but long strings like firecrackers dangling in the water. Festooned with small teddy bears, dolls, shoes hung up by the laces and even an old saucepan. Barely recognisable by shape, the objects were various shades of grey and crusted through like dipped in slurry.

Poon-Lai shuddered. Since stepping off the plane, she'd never felt warm. Not in the black mould of the cottage, not in the dark damp mines and certainly not as they looked upon the sodden faces of petrified teddy bears. No matter how many layers she wore, the wet seeped through. Finding spaces at her collar and sleeves, soaking up through the borrowed boots.

'Our petrifying well! When I was a boy we'd tie up our old shoes in the water. Ma was so angry at us. They don't like coming here no more.'

'I don't like it. It's . . .' Poon-Lai struggled to articulate the words in English. The dread that stood on her windpipe. The numbness in her feet spreading up through her legs, rooting her quite on the spot.

'Witchcraft! That's what they used to believe.'

Poon-Lai shook her head, gripping his arm tightly. She wanted him to move. To take her back to the warm chippy shop or even the foul-smelling pub with its leering patrons. Away from the dripping, the invisible grip choking the breath from her lungs.

'Damn, I meant to bring something,' Robbie said. He turned out his pockets, scraps of paper and a chewed pencil end.' Poon-Lai realised at last why they were lingering. Offered the work gloves she found pushed deep into her pocket.

'Won't you get in trouble?'

She shrugged. There was at least one more pair in the cottage. Anything to be done with this place. She struggled to tie the gloves to a loose string, the dripping water running onto her own fingers and hands, trickling up her loose sleeves.

No boyfriends. No distractions. The payments for the debt were due monthly. But Robbie had filled a silence where her siblings used to be. His irrepressible smile was the only thing that thawed her. Melt her brittle limbs. The warmth of a candle flame in the snow. He in turn liked to hear of her home. The sticky humidity. The water buffalo in the fields. So different from here, he had said dreamily.

Her English improved in leaps and bounds. And he had access to a car! They would drive to Leeds, he said, go to the pictures and eat at one of those buffet places. The England she'd imagined on the aeroplane lingered just out of reach, bursting with colour whilst her day to day was layered in monochrome.

'Let me help Penny,' Robbie said, voice thick as he reached around her and tied the knot her shaking fingers couldn't manage. He stayed like that, head in her hair. 'Do you mind? If I call you Penny? I keep messing up with your Chinese name, I thought this would be easier. For my folks too. You're still coming right, next week for Sunday lunch?'

She wouldn't have cared if he called her by the name of his dog. Anything to be free of this place. Of the penetrating cold that had worked into her stiffened bones. She closed her eyes as the water seeped through her. Robbie kissed her cold lips, mistaking the stiffness in her body for something else.

∞

Robbie walked her back to the cottage, lamp swinging in the

free hand that was not holding hers. 'I wasn't expecting it to go quite so badly. I'm sorry, Penny.'

She could not answer. Her focus pinpointed entirely on the fingers that were entwined with hers. He did not appear to notice. The leather of her skin. The rock bed that had crusted her fingers. Those hands which dug deeper and deeper into a pit that had claimed two of his siblings. She did not want this for him. Not after everything his parents had done to save him. She saw that now. Saw the sacrifice they'd made. Echoes of the letters that arrived at her door. Translucent aerogrammes that said the same thing but louder and louder with each envelope. Hadn't she promise to pay them back? The lustre she must be finding on a daily basis. Had she simply forgotten about her family? Her obligations? Her home? They were, the scrawled calligraphy continued, all relying on her. The money lenders were unhappy. Very unhappy.

Poon-Lai had re-read the letters until the folds in the aerogramme split. It was easy, right? It should've been easy. She'd heard the stories. Of someone or other's son working three jobs, earning enough to buy a shop within a year. Or that cousin's friend who'd retrained as a doctor, or a lawyer, or was it an accountant? Who gave out red envelopes to strangers on the street he was that wealthy.

It was easy.

They had all said it was easy.

'I hate this town.' Robbie dropped her hand suddenly, exclaiming the words into the starlit sky. His words echoed in the silence. His face smooth of the scowls that had scarred it under his parents' scrutiny. He blinked as he turned to her. 'Come away with me, Penny.'

'What?'

'Let's elope. Move to the city. I can't breathe here. I can't live!'

'What about your parents? My parents?'

'We can't live our lives for them. What about us?' Robbie reclaimed her hands, earnest in his impulsive decision. 'I just want to be free. I know you do too, deep down. It must be better there, somewhere, anywhere but here.'

∞

Machines could only do so much when it came to lustre. More likely to crack a gem as find one. People were softer, hands more likely to bruise and blister than cause damage to the goods. Cheaper also.

When the others were not looking, Penny doubled back around the no-entry sign, the haphazard tape which blocked the way. The sound of their chatter and tools grew distant. The site of the cave-in was clear, the loose rock and soil easier to move than the hardened walls she'd grown accustomed to.

She could not feel the rock beneath the work gloves, which she removed as they all did, contravening regulation. Running her hands along the rough walls to find where it yielded like softer sponge, calling to her in the dim light. Coaxing it out of the walls. Cajoling. Her palms were grey now. Grey as the dust which settled on everything. Grey as the rare glimpse of the sky. Grey as the townsfolk, trudging through their days half-dead.

Robbie would still be waiting. At the bus stop as he'd vowed, worldly possessions in a holdall, hopes and dreams shoved in there with clean socks and underwear. Or had he gone home already, the hours ticking past and Penny, Poon-Lai, had not appeared.

She saw it first, fingers no longer feeling as they once had. The smooth facets like marble beneath the dirt. Dug with broken fingernails now, gouging into the earth with a hunger beyond satiation. A lump of raw lustre, rough as a hailstone, peered with black pupils out at her. Its twin only centimetres away. Poon-Lai wept with relief. Enough to pay off the moneylenders, enough to keep her family fed. Salt ran into her mouth as she prised the first loose, holding the weight of it in the palm of her hand. The size of an eyeball.

Her heart banged against her ribcage. Knew that if she

scraped a little lower, below the twin lustre gems, she would find an amulet. Petrified as the two women who'd been reclaimed by the mine.

They could not pay back any debts they owed. But she could.

She could not feel the water on her. Could not hear the dripping of the well. But all the same, the cold cocooned her. Petrified her. Reclaiming her as it had done so many before.

Penny kept digging.

She would be fast.

Faster than the others.

She had to be.

The Summer Husband

Angela Slatter

'YOU NEED TO MAKE SURE THEY'RE NOT TOO GREEN, but not too brown either,' I explain, but the girl's not listening, not really.

Blonde curls lifted by a spring breeze that's still got the whisper of winter behind it, blue eyes bright, she's sneaking glances at her own reflection in the stream beside us. I keep the sigh inside. She's only been here three days, sent by her parents to apprentice with me for a year or two; less if I can't stand her or she me, for there's nothing worse than living with someone whose breath you want to stop. But then she'd have to find another fostering, another teacher, and frankly most of my kind look askance at one who couldn't be bothered to make her first placing work out, not when so much depends on it.

I remind myself to be patient. Never having had a pretty face to distract myself with, it's something of a challenge. Maybe a scar or two will make her more attentive. We'll see how matters progress.

'Rhea? Kindly do me the courtesy of paying some attention.'

She startles guiltily. 'I'm sorry, Mehrab. I was just...'

We both know there's nothing she can say that won't sound bad, so she trails off. Rhea clasps her hands in front of her blue-grey skirts, sets her chin at the slightest of angles, and does her best to make me believe she'll follow my lesson. I stare a few long moments, knowing the weight of my gaze is burdensome, bright green and penetrating. Then I give a little shake of the head, and shift my body so she can see more clearly what I'm doing.

'Too green means weak and whippy; too brown means inflexible, already on the way to half-dead.' She nods to show she's heard. 'The choosing takes time, or it should, if you wish to avoid an unpleasant series of seasons.'

Pointing to the sapling—it's on the edge of the grove I like, they're well-watered here and get just enough light through the canopy—I continue: 'This one? Right here? Too thin. To the untrained eye, it looks elegant, slender, but trust me, it's naught but weak.'

Rhea leans closer, fixes her eyes to where my fingers direct; I do my best not to notice how many age spots litter the backs of my hands. Hers are so white, plump. I hate her just a little, though I try not to, truly I do. I swallow it down, bile-bitter. 'See this bend, this angle? Note how the crook is a little too deep; too easy for fractures to begin there. Once they start, there's nothing you can do about it. Thing will grow queer and it'll always be feeble.'

I step away from the reject, move further in, slipping between the bigger trees with their rough bark, spreading branches well above my head. Too old, these, too well-established, too much *themselves*, unlikely to be bent to another's will or be reshaped, not without consequences. But I've taken most of my previous from this copse (not the *other*, not any more), the feel of them is right, and they've served me well more times than they've failed to. Just need to find the right one for this season.

Behind me I hear Rhea's footsteps; she stumbles and swears. Though I can't see her, I know she's catching her dress on the outstretched limbs, that the smooth soles of her city shoes can't grip on the uneven ground, that rocks washed smooth by the stream are hazards for her. I'm sure she can dance a carola like a princess, catch the eyes of lords and earls and godhounds with such leanings (at least until they realise what she is), but she cannot walk a steady line in the woods. This pleases me far too much. I don't like my own meanness, it feels like acid and I've never been partial to things that burn, inside or out.

Pausing, I wait for her to catch up. A breeze lifts the boughs, rustles the leaves, the trees loom almost as if, well, alive, but more human-alive, I suppose. I feel like our presence has been noted. 'You need to watch where you're going, Rhea. At least at first. It's not like city streets, friendly to your feet. We'll need to get you new shoes.'

'Lodellan cobblestones aren't in the least bit friendly,' she snips.

'Never been there myself,' I answer lightly; it's true. I was born in Breakwater, the thieves city, lived there until life became too dangerous for a variety of reasons. 'Watch first, feel with your soles; eventually you'll learn how to balance. It'll come as naturally as breathing.'

'Thank you, Mehrab.' Her tone's a little forced; the effort of being gracious is telling. For both of us, I suppose. I wonder once more how long she'll last here.

We step into a patch of light and savour it; the warmth is wonderful after the cool shade. Both of us raise our faces like flowers. The moment passes when a cloud covers the sun. I shiver and Rhea follows suit. The other side of the clearing is where we're headed. 'That looks promising.'

When we're standing in front of the sapling I nod and smile. It's the right height, too; I have my requirements.

Rhea tilts her head, slits her eyes at me. 'It looks the same to me as all the others.'

'And so it will for a while, but you'll learn.' *You'll learn or it'll be lonely, hard-working summers and cold, cold winters for you.* 'You'll recognise them when you see them.' I gesture. 'Now, *this* one. This one is different. Not so elegant, no, nor so slender, but see? Joints all sturdy, no places where hairline fractures might occur; certainly not as pretty as the other, but what use is pretty when strength is required?' I couldn't help that one, so I smile to take the edge off.

I roll my shoulders slowly, feel them warm up, then I windmill my arms, loosening the muscles. When I feel a sweat break beneath the bodice of my faded green dress, I unhook the hatchet from my belt, pull the blue whetstone out of my pocket even though I know the blade is sharp enough to split a hair. I'm careful with my tools; I know if I take care of them, they'll take care of me. I slide the stone over the metal a few times for form's sake, hopeful that Rhea will take note of the habit and adopt it.

I slip the stone away, lean forward and run my fingers down the sapling, thrill to the feel of not-quite-smooth-not-quite-rough bark (*Skin*, I think, and my heart goes a little faster). 'This one. Green enough to bend, brown enough to be stable; biddable, tractable; ready to withstand any kind of weather, but the worst of gales.'

'It seems a lot to ask,' Rhea says, a smile in her voice.

'My demands are not unreasonable,' I say and we laugh; the first time since she arrived. 'He's *just* right.'

I take my hatchet, shiny and silver, swing back for leverage, then forward, aiming at the base of the young tree, just below where the feet will be.

∞

'How long?' she asks, waving a hand in front of her face, and I cannot blame her. But I know enough to tie a cloth soaked with lavender oil around my mouth and nose. The trough in the yard behind my cottage is filled with an unenviable mixture of urine, manure, water, wine, and more than a little blood from creatures foolish enough to catch themselves in my snares, and a little of my own.

'A season, all of spring. The Church's godhounds will tell you their Lord created the heavens and the earth in seven days, but that sounds unlikely to me. Takes a woman nine months to gestate... I think that's just men trying to one-up everything when they know full well they can't birth anything but ideas.'

Rhea sniggers, but gets a mouthful of the foul air rising from the surface of the *broth*; gets a lungful too and stumbles away coughing. Neither cows, nor sheep, nor goats come near this corner of the courtyard at this time of year. Sometimes the cats —when I have them, which I don't at the moment—will hang around for sheer perversity, but they don't remain long, preferring to curl in the sunshine or chase mice in the barn.

'Careful,' I say idly, picking up the paddle she dropped in her haste, and using it, breathing oh-so-lightly as I stir the bubbling brew. No fire required for the ferment creates its own heat. I'm sweating, this close to it, stripped down to my shift, and the cotton's sticking to me like a second skin. 'We've got to do this every day for two hours, for two-thirds of spring, Rhea, so you'd best get used to it. Wrap a cloth around your face next time, there's no one to look at you.'

I can hear her gagging, trying not to puke, but soon enough there's the sound of fluid spattering the dirt; a waste of breakfast. 'Sit down, have a rest. Don't need you passing out on me, I'm not leaving this task for hell or high water.'

She grumbles, says something under her breath, something I don't need to hear to get the gist. There's the creak of the wooden bench by the yard fence as she settles, and I take a quick peek over my shoulder. Behind her is the tiny rose garden I like to keep, the earth covered in thick green grass, rolling up and down over the tiny mounds of the little cemetery of favoured felines and others. Pale pink roses form a halo around her head. A sheen of sweat glimmers on her top lip and forehead. Even sick Rhea looks pretty.

'My, my, that is an impressive shade of green and no doubt about it.'

Girls like her maybe manifest a little bit of power, something strange happens around them—I mean stranger than the normal way of things for women—and parents, mothers and granddams in particular, get nervous. Fathers, if they notice, get frightened, suspicious. Mothers and granddams sometimes know what to do, though it's getting harder and more dangerous, old knowledge and its keepers get lost or destroyed. There are fewer and fewer places they might send their girls, to learn, to be safe for a while at least.

But there are some, still.

We live in forests, away from the churches and the men who serve in them. We keep ourselves hidden as well as we may; we're self-sufficient, making what we can, trading with the tinkers who roam the countryside for what we cannot. Or bargaining with the isolated farmsteads where our talents are needed (potions and powders for sickness and health, fertility or otherwise for women with already too many mouths to feed, or solutions for wives with husbands not man enough to behave like decent human beings). We're easier to find than doctors, more reliable for what we do *sticks*.

It's too hard to live in the cities, too hard to hide what we are —and even those of us who don't make weight on the witch's scale, those untouched by power, light or dark, still aren't safe. It's too hard to be a cunning woman when that term might so easily be pronounced "witch". But out here, we can be safe. We've been hunted, but we survive. They send girls like Rhea to women like me. Sometimes girls like her go back home; sometimes they can't.

Rhea can't.

I give her ten minutes, while I stir the miasmic mix serenely as if it's not making my eyes water. There's something satisfying about the action, about creating for myself, investing this time in my future. For a while I sing – I've a sweet voice, at least – then, bored, harry her. 'C'mon. Up! I'm not feeding and sheltering you so I can do all this myself.'

No grumbling this time and I don't bother looking over my shoulder. I simply expect obedience and she appears at my elbow, apron wrapped carefully around her lower face, blue eyes slanted up at me.

'Another hour, then lunch.' I hand over the paddle, relent: 'When summer comes we'll both be able to take our ease.'

∞

'This is the hardest part?' Rhea asks as I straighten—my spine aches, I've been bent over the trestle table in the barn for too long. Pressing out a painful hiss of a breath, I give a nod. Every year it hurts more, so every year the need to do this is greater.

'Your first will be the ugliest, unless you've any artistic talent?' She shakes her head regretfully. 'Ah, you'll survive. A bit of ugly won't hurt you. You'll learn, with time, what you like, what you can do, what you can put up with.'

'You're very good,' she says admiringly. Her hands are propped on her hips, a little less pale, a little less plump after months of chores; not like mine, though, not yet. Not until she has to start this kind of activity – the advantage of the soft young wood is that any splinters are supple.

'All mistakes make for experience.' I shrug, step back to get a better look. The face is still rudimentary because I've taken my time with the body – again, I have my requirements, my tastes – and I must admit to some pride in this year's effort.

Stiff as a board in front of us he lies: broad-shouldered, deep-chested, long-legged. His surface is damp, sticky where the moisture leaks from where I've shaped him; it will dry into a smooth resin. She nods to the spot at the apex of his thighs. 'You've put some care there.'

'And you will too, one day. The trick is to be tender, remember that the length you make it is the only length he'll ever have so don't go cutting too short assuming there'll be growth as with a man of flesh and blood: summer husbands don't work quite that way.' It takes some effort to tease the cock free of the swollen trunk—that's what the immersion in the trough mix does, makes the wood swell, bulk up even though it's been cut from its source, so there's substance enough to work with. 'It's an artificial life, of course, eldritch and unnatural, limited, but life nonetheless for a brief span.' I gesture, say confidentially, 'Once upon a time, I used to make the effort to carve a bed of hair, *down there*, something for it to rest upon; realistic but fiddly and ultimately unnecessary —who looks, after a while?'

She gives a jerk of a nod. Maybe she'll do the same thing when it's her turn. Maybe she'll learn the hard way, literally, as I did.

'How much longer?' Rhea asks, taking the ladle from the bucket and carefully sprinkling some water over the body, just the way I taught her, to make sure it doesn't dry out too soon.

She's been much more helpful and biddable these past weeks, eager to please, taking better notice when I speak about powders and potions, make her sit by the pond to practice her art, glaring at the float in the middle of the water, where she can set it aflame with little consequence. She's been doing things around the cottage without having to be asked, she's fit herself into the life here. I think, now, she will do well enough, that I can equip her with the skills she'll need to survive when she goes back out into the world to make her own way.

She's got a talent for fire-starting, has Rhea, which can be hard to control, almost impossible to hide. Setting fire to a suitor who didn't like the word *no* might not have been her wisest choice, but I can't fault her. Her family – her mother, really – whisked her out of the cathedral city of Lodellan, got her to a woman with connections, who then passed her along a chain of custody, keeping ahead of the godhounds until the trail was lost. Finally, it was considered safe to land the girl with me in the deepest and darkest of woods, where my own sins have been hidden, though not forgotten, for so many years. Oh, I was told what she'd done—we always tell for the sins of the person you save may well become yours: if you keep them in the world, you bear some responsibility for their good and ill, so a person should know who they're taking on. Make an active choice.

'How much longer?' she repeats, impatient.

'A few hours.' I'm tired and I should rest or I'll get careless, I know, but I want to see his face.

∞

By the time it's done, I'm almost cross-eyed and I can barely stand. But he's ready and he's beautiful in his own fashion. The fine detail is clear and I've made his eyes and lips, chin and cheeks, nose, forehead, jaw, ears, the semblance of hair, just the way I want them.

'The cup,' I say and my voice is rough, throat dry. Rhea's quick to hand me the clay goblet. The contents laps at the lip, a viscous mix of blood and sap, with a little nub of living clay dissolved therein (I've kept a store for years, purchased from a red-haired travelling woman who had the secrets of mud harvested from graveyards, rich and foetid with the essences of life and death). The slit I made for his mouth, carved out into a void (but no tongue, never a tongue, never again), is waiting and I pour the elixir in.

And because I'm exhausted, I'm sloppy.

Fumes rise where the liquid meets the wooden lips. I, heedless as Rhea was those weeks ago when we soaked him in the trough, take a negligent lungful of the vapours. Reeling away, I cough, choking, spluttering, stupid as an apprentice.

Rhea, distracted by the transformation of the block of wood on which I've lavished such attention, does nothing more than raise her hands vaguely in my direction. But she doesn't come to my aid, stays where she is, transfixed by the summer husband. I understand, in spite of everything, for even though I've seen it so many times, I'm never *not* enchanted, never *not* fascinated by what I've wrought.

Yet I miss it altogether as I try to get my breath back, try to clear the tears from my eyes. And I forget, as I cough and splutter, the first rule of making a child: always be the first thing it sees, only by this means can you ensure its love. But I'm not the first thing he sees, am I? And it's no one's fault but mine, because I'm in a corner, throwing up. So to not witness it even once feels like a grief that will haunt me forever.

The first thing he sees, with her blonde locks and her bluer than blue eyes, her trim figure, peaches and cream skin, is Rhea leaning over him with avid interest.

∞

I hear them at night and all I can think is that I wish she had a little more consideration. Well, not all. I think how I wish her ill, how I wish her dead, how I wish him *kindling*. I wish them no joy of each other, though they take it and give it. I wish that she'd let loose a spark and set him alight.

I wish.

I wish.

I wish.

And if wishes were horses then beggars would ride.

There was no point in screaming at her, in weeping and wailing. She didn't do it on purpose, there was no intent, only my own carelessness. There was no point in taking him to my bed when he'd loved her from the first sight of her face (but I can't help but wonder would he still have done so, even had he seen me first? Would she have managed to circumvent even *that* magic?). No point in putting her out, sending her away.

Yet I cannot help the whispers in my mind that don't drown out the murmurs from her room, but rather amplify them. He was meant to be *mine*. That's why he was made. That's why all summer husbands are made for we women on our own. We provide for ourselves; the things we cannot easily get are created by eldritch means, even husbands. And I cannot help but think it's another thing that's come easily to her.

Worse: Rhea insisted on naming him despite my warnings that is was something I'd learned long ago not to do (a named thing is harder to let go). She sings it in the dark hours, and it finds my ears with the same harsh clarity as a beacon light. I cannot avoid it, even in my sleep, and upon waking I feel my head is full of the sound of her voice, the sough of his name.

I think of another appellation, flung into the darkness many years gone by, with the same urgency but by my voice. I think of the strangeness of my own name being sounded out by underdeveloped lips and tongue, not quite as it should be, but close enough, strange enough, to imprint forever on my heart, my mind, my conscience . . . the places where all my sins hide.

And I grit my teeth, for it's all I can do, and wait for the time to come.

∞

'Arlo, the wheat needs scything. Off you go now.'

I've said it as I have to previous summer husbands over the years, and they've all obeyed with unquestioning alacrity. There's a small field by the cottage, grows enough to see two mouths through snows, but it's the job of several days to harvest and thresh it, to grind it in the hand mill, and put into the urns for storage. It needs to be attended to today if we're to be ready for winter. I've said it casually, kindly enough.

This is the work he was made for, his reason for existing. He does as he's meant to, but it's at *her* command, not mine. When he looks away from me, to Rhea, it's such a tiny thing, such a slight gaze, such a glancing blow, but it has the effect of a punch.

And I lose my temper.

And I lunge at the girl standing by the hearth, stirring a pot of stew.

And I make a noise that might come from an animal in pain.

I have a hank of her golden curls twisted in my fingers for the shortest of moments before I'm lifted from my feet and flung across the room, ribs bruised by a strength no true man could muster even on a good day.

And there we are: Rhea crumpled by the fire, me fetched up against the sideboard hard enough to make the plates and cups rattle and fall, and Arlo the summer husband standing somewhere between the two of us, voiceless but able to make his feelings clearly felt.

∞

'Where are we going, Mehrab? It's so cold.'

I throw a glance at her but all that's recognisable are her eyes, peering between wraps of a woollen scarf and a knitted cap in slate-grey. Like me, she's wearing furs that once belonged to wolf and bear, and our boots are thick and heavy, leather lined with fiery fox.

We're as warm as we can be in the circumstances, outside in the first week of winter. Snow threatens, occasionally sprinkling something grey and ephemeral over us; I want to be home before nightfall, but she's moving slow and sluggish. Yet this has to be done, no matter how uncomfortable or frigid.

'Mehrab, why are we out here?'

We're out here because not only has she given him a name, she's refusing to do what needs to be done.

'So you can see what happens when you don't listen.'

'Mehrab, I'm sorry about Arlo, truly I am. He didn't mean to hurt you.'

My ribs still ache despite all the poultices and tisanes I can brew. Arlo, it should be noted, is *not* out here, not heading towards the deepest, darkest part of the woods. Arlo, who should not still be in existence.

'I told you his purpose. I told you why. I told you what to do.' I shake my head and forge on. Not far now, even though I've not set foot in this part of the woods for almost twenty years I'd know the paths, the trees, anywhere. For a moment I think I hear something, a familiar moan, and my heart rabbits along, a double thump with a shot of adrenaline that makes me feel sick. But it's just the wind.

Just the wind.

The land is rising and I start to puff a little; my ribs protest the exertion. 'I told you what would happen. Haven't you noticed? How he's slower?'

'But it's winter, it's cold, we're all slower.'

'Haven't you noticed, when he walks, how his feet adhere to the ground?'

She's silent at that.

'Well, that's because he's putting down roots. It always happens when they're left too long. He's well past his time, Rhea.'

'But you only made him a season ago, he's barely beyond a youth.'

'Time moves differently for one such as he. His life is . . . a gifted thing . . . a stolen thing . . . he's not real.'

'But . . . I love him . . . he loves me . . .'

'A voiceless husband is a tempting thing, isn't it? No one to gainsay you, no one to give you orders. There are reasons, Rhea, why most of us make them without speech.'

'I wonder what he'd say, if he could . . .'

She's a child with a child's romantic imaginings. I think I know what he'd say too; he's not looked at me the same since the day we came to blows. I know what he'd happily do to me but for the fact that Rhea forbade him from hurting me any more. I know what I'd happily do to him, but he's not *my* responsibility.

We come to a wall of trees, old growth, very tall, almost impenetrable so much they've grown together, but I find the break between. Before I slip between I stop, wait for her to catch up. The gap will be tight for her but there's no choice, I'll pull her through the eye of a needle if I must. 'Let me show you . . .'

We step into trees that have shaken off snow. There, in the middle of a clearing, he stands.

'This is what I did,' I say.

'What? Where?' Her tone is sharp, until she follows the direction of my finger to the thing that might have been a mighty oak, once, if I'd not interfered.

His face is rough, as rough as a first-time effort, 'prentice work. But you can still see it in the trunk of the stunted thing he's become: half-tree, half-man, perhaps ten feet tall, anchored to the earth by years and deep-delving roots. You can still see, if you peer closely enough, the marks of my knives and chisels. He's not pretty, as I told her; he's only primitively human-looking to be frank, just as he was when first made. But he was mine. And I loved him and he loved me in return. And because I loved him I did a terrible thing.

I let him live . . .

. . . let him live beyond his time until I had to pry his feet from the floor of my cottage, and put him in a barrow to push as far away as I could. This was the copse I'd taken him from, I'd liked the oaks, how tall they stood, how strong they looked, how dependable they seemed. When I'd discarded him, I brought him back *home*, into the depths of the forest, to where there was darkness so that I might not see him, might not stumble upon him.

'I made him and I didn't give him his proper end, and I left him there.' I don't go too close, and speak low. His wooden lids are closed, perhaps open just a slit beneath the lashes I carved so carefully (I've never done them since, so much trouble, so time-consuming and who notices?).

'But—'

'Hush,' I say, holding up my palm. 'Don't wake him.'

I can't bear if he sees me, knows me, if he moans my name, or even simply tries with that mouth surely grown stiff with age, with *treeness*.

'I gave him a tongue – my first mistake – so that when I left he called for me. I could hear it for the longest time even after I was finally beyond the range of his voice.'

Rhea approaches, tiptoeing across the sparse grass. *Don't touch him don't touch him don't touch him*, I think but don't say. Then she makes a decision, stops before she gets too close, retreats, coming to rest next to me. She puts a hand on her belly as if feeling queasy.

'What are you going to do?' she asks breathily.

'What I should have done a long time ago.' Setting an example is the only way to convince her to do what she needs to do. I slip the hatchet from my belt, heft it, wonder if I can actually do *this*—

—but I don't get the chance to find out. I'm hit from behind by what feels like a plank. For the second time in the same number of months I'm sent flying, along the dirt and grass; I feel the skin on my face graze, feel pebbles tear the canvas and flesh, feel blood blossom; I think I feel rib crack this time, and I know at least one of the bones in my left forearm snaps. I cry out, forgetting my fear of being heard for it shrinks beside my fear of dying.

Arlo has followed us. Somewhere in his sleepy tree-brain did he fear for Rhea left alone with me? I'd almost find it admirable, except for his expression, which is murderous to say the least. He moves faster, with less difficulty than he has in recent weeks, fired by rage. I look past him, past my fate, and see Rhea's face and the terrible truth there. She might never admit it, but it's clear: she told him to follow us. Did she fear me too? Or she couldn't bear to be parted from him, even for a day?

Over my own whimpering I can hear two things: behind me a sort of rhythmic grunt pushed from lips that no longer open properly; from somewhere in front of me, Rhea screaming *No, no, no!*

But her summer husband doesn't listen, merely continues to come at me; I can tell from the way he's balancing, measuring his steps, that he's going to kick me, wherever he can. It will probably be enough to finish me. I take a shallow breath, the only sort my agonised ribs will allow, begin to curl in on myself in a feeble hope of minimising the damage, but then there's a third noise.

Unexpected but not necessarily unwelcome.

The whoosh of fire igniting, swallowing air like a greedy child.

Behind Arlo his mistress has a great handful of red-gold flames; she only hesitates a little before she throws it.

The summer husband goes up like a torch. In the usual way of things, he'd be beheaded, fed to the hearth on the first night of winter, serving his final purpose. His body was to be used throughout the season for its composition means it burns long and very hot, saving on other materials. But this . . .

. . . this is witch fire and it incinerates like no other; it is fast and it consumes utterly.

When Arlo is no more than a pile of cinders, Rhea helps me up. Together we limp out into the wider wood, beneath the snow that falls in earnest now, back toward the cottage.

∞

Rhea is slower now, grown sluggish; she sits a lot to catch her breath between tasks. Her eyes aren't so blue anymore, but there's a greeny-brown fleck in them that wheels and flashes, fair arboreal. And her belly's grown big.

I could have spoken to her about what happened. I could have said, 'Now, Rhea, are you listening to me? He was always going to die. Maybe not so painfully, but that's the result of not doing what you're told.' But I don't say that. We don't talk about what happened. And we don't talk about what will happen when—if — the child comes; they don't tend to stay, little things, they're not meant to last any more than their fathers. Perhaps it will rest beneath the rosebushes, along with my own babies off summer husbands.

I'm almost mended, and when I'm good and ready then I'll go deep into the forest again. When it's time, I'll do what should have been done a long while ago. I'll pay my debt and perhaps somewhere a notation will be made in some grand ledger so that my good will begin to outweigh my ill.

And, once again, when the time is right I'll go to the other copse. I'll carry my shiny sharp hatchet, and I'll look over the young trees there, when they're tall enough, flexible enough to vie for my attention. And then I'll find two saplings, just the right shape, just the right size…

RADICALIZED

LAVIE TIDHAR

I WAS TWELVE WHEN I WATCHED MY FIRST BEHEADING video.

One of the other kids sent it to me. The videos were illegal but they circulated. The video was grainy, barely any colour.

Five people were chained on the ground. They fought against the chains. They struggled and struggled and their mouths opened and closed but they never said a word.

Their captors stood over them. Their faces were covered. They held machetes. One of them spoke to the camera. He spoke English in a strange accent.

'The West is sending a plague upon the world, a plague of consumerism. A plague that must be wiped away!'

He raised his machete. The captors struggled against their chains.

'Go with God!' he said.

He brought down the blade.

It hacked clean through a man's neck.

The head rolled on the ground.

The fighters went methodically one by one through the captives until no one was left.

I watched until the video faded to static.

Then I was sick all over the floor.

∞

That was the first time. But I kept going back to the video. I kept watching. The men in the videos weren't mad. They really believed in what they were doing. I knew there was a war onover there, that we'd invaded them, that they were desperate. But they had a *cause*. They really *believed* in something.

I saw good in that.

Mom and Dad fought all the time. At first they shouted but now they barely spoke. It was something in their eyes, so cold and dead, that it scared me. I'd close myself in my room, watch the video of that beheading. Look for more. You could find them, if you knew how to look. Certain keywords, certain names. They kept getting pulled but they always popped back up again.

They were just trying to get the *truth* out! They needed fighters. They needed people who were brave, who understood. People to join them.

At thirteen I tried to go for the first time. I made it as far as the airport but you couldn't fly there directly, you had to get to the nearest airport that still operated and make your way across the border somehow. It was dangerous. I watched it on the news. Rockets, sporadic gunfire. A lot of IEDs, improvised explosive devices.

They said it used to be nice there. Now it was just one big ruin.

But they were still fighting for it all the same.

∞

When I was fourteen I was living with my mom and the war over there still went on but no one paid it much attention. One of the returned vets came to school once to talk to us. He said everyone in his platoon was gone. He said we should never have gone there. He said... He didn't say much. It was just in his eyes.

There was a new beheading video when I got home. The camera was higher definition and there was colour, and the sound was good like they used a good mic. The video showed them hunting someone down. He shambled away from them but they cornered him and they did the beheading. It was ritualistic with them. It was serious.

That summer I tried to go again. I'd heard of others who went before me, who made it. My age, mostly. Fourteen, fifteen. I knew people died out there fighting every day. It wasn't the sort of place where you lived to old age.

The fake papers I had weren't good enough. I got stopped by the police when I was about to board the flight. They took me away, interrogated me. They called both my parents. I heard them talking.

'Radicalized,' they said.

'No, no,' Mom said.

'That's ridiculous,' Dad said.

I couldn't hear much. I knew I was in trouble. But they let me go with a warning. My parents didn't say a word all the way back. When we got home they both searched my room, even thought my dad wasn't even living there any more. They found some stuff, too. A machete. One of the videos. Some literature, too, stuff I'd managed to get and kept hidden under the bed.

'This is... this is *recruitment* stuff!' Dad said. 'How did you even...?' He turned on Mom. 'This is all your fault!'

'How is this *my* fault!' she shouted. They started to argue again like they used to. I couldn't take it. I ran out. The cold and the dark helped. But they came and found me.

That night I had a nightmare. I was chased by men with machetes and I couldn't outrun them. I just kept shambling down the street, past my house, past all the houses I knew all my life. They were going to cut my head off and I didn't even care.

I just wanted to get... somewhere...

To do... something...

I woke up scared.

But I woke up knowing what I had to do.

And this time I couldn't afford to fail.

∞

It took me another six months to put it together. I got a contact that led to a contact that led to someone who really worked with them. He'd helped others travel there. He told me what I needed to do.

I met him at the mall, the night I was leaving. I gave him my clothes and my papers, everything I had. He gave me new clothes, a new identity, a ticket. I took a bus to the airport. I got on the plane.

My mom would soon find out I was gone and alert the police, but I had told her I was spending the night at a friend's place. I figured I had twelve hours still, maybe more.

Six hours later I landed in San Diego.

∞

Another contact met me at the airport. She was in her early twenties. She drove a truck.

She said, 'It won't be easy to get through the blockade.'

I was tired and nervous. She handed me an energy drink. We got off the highway soon after. The roads started to look bad. Potholes and signs of bombardments.

She said, 'You have to watch out for IEDs.'

She drove fast. Once we saw soldiers in the distance and turned off-road and went around their checkpoint, and after that I didn't see any more soldiers.

'This is the hairy part,' she said.

We were on the outskirts. An arrow sign said, 'East Hollywood Silver Lake'.

I started seeing moving shapes in the desolation. Shuffling in the shadows. Watching. But they didn't bother us. The contact rode fast. Once someone stepped in front of the car and she hit them and kept going. We were on Sunset Boulevard and going top speed.

'Dodger Stadium,' she said. 'No one goes there.'

When we got to the base, sentries stopped us but then they nodded us through. She dropped me off.

'Good luck, kid,' she said. 'Welcome to the fight.'

She lit a cigarette and walked off. She had an Italian accent.

The Leader came then. I recognised him from the videos, even if in the videos his face was covered. He looked me over.

'Thank you,' he said. His voice was gravelly, rich. 'Are you ready to fight?'

'I'm ready,' I told him.

'Good.' He nodded. One of his men came forward. Handed me a machete. I swung it through the air, once, twice. It was heavy.

'Too few of us remain,' the leader said. 'And there are always more of them. The West is a plague, a plague of consumerism. Mindless, always hungry for more stuff. Insatiable.'

I nodded. I was tired but hopped up on the energy drink.

'Let's go,' the Leader said.

∞

The camera pointed at me. I stood there with the sun setting over what was left of the Hollywood sign. There were five captives on the ground. They were shackled but they kept trying to break free, to shuffle on. Their mouths opened and closed without words, masticating. We'd gone fighting and come across a whole herd of them. We lost two of our men in the fight.

The cameraman must have been a professional. There were a lot of them around who used to be in pictures. Romero. Raimi. Rob Z. They'd kept trying to warn people but nobody ever listened.

The fighters left were an international bunch. A few Americans, some Brits, Japanese, a few Italians, a German guy.

He pointed the camera at me.

'Do eet now,' he said. 'Tell the world. Show them!'

I held up the machete.

I said, 'Always cut off the head. It's the only way to make sure.'

The cameraman nodded, encouraging me.

I took a deep breath.
I held up the machete.
I brought it down hard.
The head rolled in the dirt.
It blinked up at me, once.
Its lips moved.
'Fucking Hollywood,' it said.

ROTTEN THINGS

KIM LAKIN

'ONE MINUTE THERE AIN'T NOTHING THERE BUT dirt, the next, there it is. A house! Painted yellow as a warbler bird. Got a skinny door up front, like one eye peeping out on the world. There's a porch too, with a red roof, and the whole thing's built long, each room bolted to the last. And that's about the size of it. I'm telling you, Uncle Joe, that house ain't like nothing else I ever did see.'

Edmée's so busy describing a strange house that's materialised out of the swamp overnight that she misses the warning signs. Bellyful of whiskey, Uncle Joe pushes off the couch and towers over her before she's had time to take a breath.

'What're you doing wasting time out on Cemetery Road, Edmée Romero?' he slurs. 'I told you to get them papers and tobacco and get back on home. Now I'm hearing how you got distracted by a whole lotta nothing and trying to shovel that shit as truth.'

'I only got a glance while passing.' Edmée knows it doesn't help to defend herself, but she can't help it. As her momma used to say, 'Someday all this backtalking will get you in hot water, Edmée Romero!'

Seems today's that day as Uncle Joe grabs her by the dress collar, yanking her up so high her toes skim the ground. He brings her in close to his bag-of-skin face. His eyes are urine-coloured. 'You get on my last nerve.' He cranes his head over a shoulder. 'I'm done telling the girl to do as she's told!' he shouts as Edmée kicks and gurgles, trying to catch her breath.

'Toss her in the canal with the mudbugs and the gators!' calls back Aunt Hailey from the kitchen in that deadpan way which says she couldn't care less if her boyfriend Joe throttles the life from her niece, just as long as they're both quiet before she settles opposite the TV for her *Maury* reruns.

In the end, Uncle Joe lets go just before Edmée blacks out. He leaves her gasping on the stained carpet while Jackal, the Labrador retriever driven half-wild with beatings, fusses about and tries to lick her face. A new kick to the dog's backside sends it skittering through the fly-screen door leading to the backyard and down to the water.

Edmée goes to follow the dog on her hands and knees. But Uncle Joe hasn't finished with her. In fact, judging by the tightness of his jaw, he's only just warming up. Edmée knows she can't fight a grown man, especially not one who's built like a bull. Likewise, she can't appeal to her aunt, low on wits and high on oxy on account of an ulcered leg.

Lacking options, Edmée tries out the gappy smile that always prompts Mrs O'Lay, the preacher's wife, and her church ladies to fuss and pinch her cheeks and 'want to eat her up with cornbread and gravy'. Uncle Joe isn't so keen on smiling. He grabs Edmée by the wrist and shakes her like a sack of red beans.

'There ain't nothing good about a stranger rolling in from outta nowhere and thinking to take up residence. Reminds me of your dead momma, turning up like an ill wind, shaking you off her skirts and expecting others to raise you!'

'When she was pregnant, that no-good sister of mine got stared at by a handicap negress.' Aunt Hailey comes in from the kitchen. She's got fresh highlights and the buttons done up wrong on her blouse like she's touting for business.

'Hear that, girl? You were cursed even before you were born!' Uncle Joe gives a loud hoot. 'No wonder your momma didn't bother getting you baptised!'

Aunt Hailey drags on her cigarette. 'A child that ain't been baptised and pokes mischief every which way it can? That child is a Lutin. My granddaddy used to tell tales of how them bad spirits would play up and cut the fishing line, break the crawfish baskets, and suck all the life outta the swamp so that dead things rise.' She narrows her eyes through the exhaled smoke. 'Is that what you are, Edmée? A Lutin? Goddamn devil spawn.'

'Aint my fault Momma went and died!' Edmée cries, but she's shushed with a backhander. The impact makes her brain rattle in her skull.

'Shut yer mouth, girl!' Uncle Joe looks ready to strike her a second time.

'Yeah, shut yer mouth!' Joe's daughter, Brandy, stands in the doorway, hands in the bib of her dirty dungarees, chewing a wad of gum like her jaw's spring-loaded. There's two years between her and nine-year-old Edmée, close enough in age to make her despise her younger kin.

'Gonna put her in the swamp then and stop her chattering? You've been threatening it long enough!' Aunt Hailey sinks into the couch. Her pencilled eyebrows dance as she drips ash.

'Make her eat maggots again, Pa!' Brandy runs to the kitchen. Pretty soon, she can be heard rooting through the garbage can.

Edmée drowns out the world around her. In place of the nutty rubber taste of maggots, she imagines a great tin bath set over BBQ coals, the salt scent of boiling crawfish and the sunshine flavours of buttered corn.

But Uncle Joe doesn't want to feed her maggots. He's after bigger thrills. 'Say, Hailey. That big old alligator still hiding out beneath the house?'

'Yeah, Daddy.' (Aunt Hailey's name for him when the bedroom door's shut and the trailer shudders.)

'Gonna feed her to the gator, Pa?' Brandy runs back in and holds her hands in the air like she's calling down the moon.

Edmée's scared to her bone marrow. 'But I got your smokes!'

Uncle Joe isn't listening. He hoists Edmée over a shoulder and carries her out of the swing door. Aunt Hailey calls after them,

'I'm watching my show now!' while Brandy pushes past on her way down the steps to where Jackal's whining with nervous excitement.

'Get!' Uncle Joe threatens a kick and sends the dog slinking away on its belly. He nods to a broom resting against the steps. 'Poke that gator awake, Brandy.'

Grinning, Brandy grabs hold of the bristle end and uses the pole of the broom to poke about under the trailer. All the while, Edmée's kicking and screaming until she hears a throaty hiss near the spot Brandy's worrying at.

'I'll be seeing you, Edmée Romero!' Uncle Joe bends down and sends her flying out under the trailer like unrolling a rug.

Tossed in amongst the pepperweed and the vines, Edmée can't breathe through terror. Stillness stretches, thin as a strand of Brandy's gum. Then a huge, fanged shape rushes from the dark and envelopes her in the breath of rotten things.

∞

Marie St Angel's washing the blood from her hands when the cry rings through her. A child's, she decides. Not an infant or an adolescent, but an age between. Holding her hands up in front of her face, she wriggles heavily ringed fingers and homes in on the sound.

'I hear yer,' she tells the spirit, and quickly elbows aside the chopping board with its dead rooster. Opening the kitchen cupboards, she roots through her emporium of herbs and spices and bone bits. Taking down what she needs, she measures out handfuls, capfuls and pinches into a mortar bowl and grinds the ingredients with the pestle.

'Sin on skin. A slow rub of harm. Three of them to be hollowed out and fed to Papa Ghede.'

She dips five fingers into the mortar bowl, strokes the herb rub across the hollow at the base of her throat and smears it into the hair clinging at her shoulders in thick serpentine coils. The smell fills her nostrils, fresh as grass, muddy as brine, taking her mind to the depths of the bayou.

'Rise up, child,' she whispers. 'Rise up and follow ma voice.'

∞

Out in the depths of the Louisiana swamp, Edmée opens her eyes to a surging depth of cold. *I'm blind,* she thinks as the world stays black. *The devil's sucked the sight right outta me!* But then she realises it's inky water she's swallowed up in.

I've gotta get free. I've gotta get free!

She kicks out with her feet and use her hands as paddles. Grasses weave around her shoulders and she battles to fight free. The darkness pales as she rises up, up, until all above is silver.

She surfaces at last, spluttering and gasping.

The blue-black bayou ripples all around her. Overhead, the moon is a vast freshwater pearl.

Edmée's limbs are stiff as she fights her way to the canal bank. Under her feet, the marsh grasses are slippery as worms. The ground, when she finds it, sinks and clogs between her toes. She drags herself ashore and collapses in the dirt.

How did I end up in the water? Holding a slim, algaed arm up to the moonlight, Edmée tries to remember her own name. *I'm nameless*, she thinks, and rather than lost, she just feels empty, as if scooped out with a spoon. The sweltering night builds around her and she gets to her feet, which are the same greenish hue as her arms. Her clothes are threaded with swamp moss and tiny fish. She goes to flick one away at her neckline—and feels a ring of rough dips. Bitemarks? Before she can dwell on the thought further, she feels a voice rise within her, filling her up on the inside until there is no emptiness left.

'Come to me,' says the voice.

Edmée turns towards inland and shuffles forward.

∞

The only thing to do is take it real slow; Marie knows this from experience. Spirits aren't fond of being rushed, especially new-borns. They get twitchy and confused. Too prone to dwell in the 'was' instead of moving to the 'now.'

Marie sits in the old rocker on her porch, rifle resting across her knees. Beyond the steps, a field of grass stretches down to the glistening bayou. She listens as the sweet gum, elm, sycamore and cottonwood creak and moan, and the cypresses sway their medusa manes of Spanish moss. She hears the wild grapes, the trumpet creepers and all the ferns, lilies, irises and hyacinths whisper. She's lulled by the bark of frogs and hiss of alligators and the lone call of a night heron. And underneath the hullabaloo, she hears the spirits start to wake. They sense she is open to them; Marie knows that from experience. Her task now is to sift through the noise and find the one she wants.

Marie has always been happy to guide an uneasy spirit. She just wishes it didn't have to involve unearthing every other dead wanderer inside the locale! The spirit Marie's after is oozing suffering and rage, she's already plucked a thick ribbon of the stuff out the air and stored it in a mason jar.

She pats her rifle. The spirits are liable to manifest as zombies since she's baited them with the *Song of Solomon* read aloud from a King James bible. There's also the herb rub at her throat and hair, and a bottle of perfumed Florida water—the latter for Papa Ghede, just in case that psychopomp decides to swoop in and take the new-born for himself. Marie catches the whites of his eyes out the corner of hers and rocks harder in her chair to keep him between the worlds of the living and the dead.

'I'll call yer later, Papa,' she tells him. 'First, I need la luna to shine down and the child to come. I need to even out the scales of balance, father, yer know this.'

Moonlight fills the vista as they come from the marshland and the boggy shallows of the river—dripping skeletons that shudder and lurch, dusty corpses escaped the over-ground crypts, even a solitary infant in an unbuttoned romper which toddles out of the water in top-heavy rushes of movement. The spirts are eager to appeal to her—they want forgiveness, explanations, deliverance, even divinity. Marie senses all of their needs as the floorboards creak under her rocking chair.

Soon enough, she's forced to her feet. Some ghosts rest easy; others like to feast on the living and a soul raiser like Marie's bound to smell good.

Jaw flapping, eye on a thread, the nearest ghoul is beat up and hungry. Resting the butt of the rifle against a shoulder, Marie squeezes up an eye and pulls the trigger. The ghost catches a face full of rock salt and turns into grave sludge. Next up is the infant. Face puffed grey, eyes white and roaming, it toddles towards the porch steps at a rapid rate. Marie takes a shot and the body bursts like a blood blister.

'Where are you, child?' Griping the necklaces of bead and bone at her neck, Marie senses the newcomer very close now. A few more pot-shots from the porch and she finds her—a zombie girl, walking on peg legs and already ravaged by her short time in the canal.

'Welcome, child.' Marie indicates the rocking chair. 'Sit.'

In stilting movements, the decaying young thing makes it to the rocker and collapses back into it. Meanwhile, having landed the fish she wants, Marie picks up the mortar bowl of herb rub and a flickering white candle in its tall jar. She climbs down to the bottom step of the porch, where the rest of the swamp crawlers are shuffling closer.

'Goodnight all. Rest awhile again.' Marie holds up the candle and sprinkles the herb rub over the flame which blazes gold then dies back.

When she looks past the smoking wick, the ghosts are gone. All but the green-skinned girl sitting in Marie's rocker.

∞

Edmée is ushered inside the kitchen of a strange house. She worries at a chip of memory like a sore. Words niggle. 'Painted yellow as a warbler bird!... 'That house ain't like nothing I ever did see...'

'I'm Marie St Angel. Now drink.' The woman puts down a glass of muddy water on the table. The water tastes bitter, but Edmée drains the glass and wipes the back of her hand across her mouth.

'It don't taste good, but that's the vinegar. Gotta have you thinking clearly, child. Gotta wash them swamp juices outta your brain.' Marie grins, showing shiny black teeth. Gathering up her colourful skirts—a contrast to her white shirt and white mop cap—and chinking with all jewellery strung about her, she takes a seat on the opposite side of the table. 'No surprise you're thirsty! Death'll do that to you, especially if you don't know how to move forward.'

Edmée parts her lips. What comes out is a dribble of swamp water and a dry croak.

'So I'm gonna tell you what we do. First, you gotta reabsorb these memories as infected the air. Oh, I know they're nasty, but you gotta face them.'

Marie has Edmée follow her out the kitchen, through the bedroom, and into a parlour—all the rooms leading into one another. There's not much to the room - a bald velvet couch, a dusty bureau, a rag-rug on dark floorboards and blackout curtains at the windows either side.

'Sit, child,' she tells Edmée again, who sits stiffly on the smoke scented couch and watches as the witch woman roots around in the bureau and retrieves a black drawstring pouch the size of her palm. Into it, Marie feeds a stone which she declares was 'fished out the swamp', a sliver of wood 'from the belly of a 500-year-old cypress felled by a storm', a dried up, gnarly toe from a chicken foot, and something invisible she shakes from a mason jar and calls 'the ribbon of rage I caught off you earlier, child.' She pulls the drawstring tight.

Marie lights a yellow candle—'To reveal hidden truth,'—and a black candle—'To shine a light on negativity.' She turns around, gris-gris bag in one hand, hochet rattle in the other.

'Time to call on the Voodoo Loa and wake back up, child. And if Papa Ghede ask you to go with him before we is done, bind him with a bite of this.' She tosses an apple to Edmée, who fails to catch it. As the fruit rolls across the floor, Marie shakes the gourd rattle and starts to dance in shuffling steps. Under candlelight, she roils her glistening brown stomach and pants and moans in appeal.

Suddenly, she darts forward and thrusts the gris-gris bag into Edmée's mouth.

The swamp girl swallows instinctively.

'Now you've got your mojo back!' Marie cries, eyes lurid as the mercurial moon.

∞

The first thing Edmée does is scream. Loud and long as if the alligator's still got its jaws clamped at her throat. She remembers the pain—so much pain!—as the creature performed its death rolls and she was crushed.

Three more things Edmée recalls from her final moments. The first is Brandy making a *hoo-hoo* sound of delight while peeking under the trailer. The second is her aunt, yawping from above, 'You went and did it then, Daddy?' The third is Uncle Joe bellowing, 'How do you like that, Edmée Romero? Bet you don't feel like time wasting now, huh?'

After had come silence—scratchy and uncomfortable—until something brought her back around beneath the duckweed and cattails in the water.

'Edmée Romero,' she says in a voice thickened by the marsh salts in which she's embalmed.

The witch's face looms in. 'That your name, child? Edmée?'

'Are you Mami Wata?' Edmée has a sudden memory of her mother praying to the deity to deliver her from debt.

'Quite an imagination you got there, Edmée. I'm Marie St Angel, remember? I'm a conduit for the Loa, them sacred mystères as sit between the supreme creator and mankind.

Sometimes I'm a soul raiser, bringing back the dead as need revenge. But tell me, child. Who else do you see in this room?'

'A man,' says Edmée. Words felt like clay in her mouth. 'Got a skull instead of a face.' She narrows her eyes, which feel a-swim, and takes in the man standing by the bureau. 'Hat, waistcoat, gold buttons, black coat down to his knees like he's playing trumpet at a funeral.'

'Quick!' Marie's eyes flick off to the corners of the room. 'Throw him the apple!'

It takes Edmée some scrambling about on her mildewey limbs, but she picks up the apple and tosses it to the man.

Papa Ghede snatches the fruit out of the air, grins and takes a bite.

∞

'Candlelight will show us the way. And this smoke.' Marie dances a burning bundle of herbs before the girl's face. 'Tell me, child. Who's wronged you?'

'Aunt Hailey,' says the girl, still zombie but with a speck of life thanks to the gris-gris bag in her stomach. 'I did try to love her, but she gone and fed me to that man.'

'Man?'

'Uncle Joe. Meanest son of a bitch I ever did meet.'

'Any other?' Marie pushes her face through the smoke.

'Brandy. She's a bit more grown than me, but got a whole lotta rot where her heart ought to be, maybe on account of her daddy.'

Marie shows her teeth, black lacquered where she paints them with vinegar, iron and vegetable tannins so spirits can't see her whispering magic. 'So, you go pay them a visit, Edmée Romero. Get your spirit virgin-clean before Papa Ghede takes you to them crossroads we all visit in the end.'

The way Edmée starts jerking suggests she's not keen on visiting her murderers.

Marie exhales noisily. 'You need to make them pay, no matter how much it ails you. There's a balance to keep in check, you know that I'm certain. But I agree you might need a bit of help.'

From the bureau, Marie fetches new tools—a generous pour of whiskey in a glass and a fistful of cotton wool. 'Put this in your nose.' She tears off scraps of cotton wool and offers them up. 'Like we're laying out the dead.'

Wordlessly, the girl takes the white scraps and plugs her nose.

Marie downs the whiskey, riding out the burn before she lights a cigar and drags on it heavily, enveloping them both in piquant smoke.

'Now Papa Ghede is busy chewing on his apple, we need to ask a favour of a second of his kin. Baron Samedi will guide your hand and get the job done.' She shows her black teeth. 'Just don't get seduced by his power. The Baron is fond of a young soul, specially them as have been murdered.'

Edmée's listening, but most of all she is smiling at the laughing, dancing man who's appeared in the room. The Baron dances away and she follows, making her way to the front door. With heavy steps, she lets the Baron lead her along the bank of the bayou—through the tufted grass and flat weed, around the black willow and larch where the bull frogs and pig frogs and turtles belch and paddle—and then out through the wild sugar cane. It is a good hour before they arrive at the battered old trailer in the swamp's depths. As the Baron gestures she should take the lead, Edmée makes out the flickering lights of the television and, beneath the front steps to the trailer, a pair of gleaming golden eyes.

∞

Brandy's sitting cross-legged in her room. KSMB's on the radio and she's got an open bag of Zapp's potato chips between her legs. Every so often, she dives a hand into the bag and throws a handful of chips into her mouth.

She's feeling smug that Edmée's dead. When Brandy's Pa had started dating Hailey, there'd been a time when she and Edmée weren't far off being friends. For a while, she'd even let Edmée come frogging. While her father worked the power till, Edmée tracked any activity beyond the boat with the spotlight and Brandy leaned over the side and grabbed those floating bull frogs gone rigid on account of the light, shoving them into a wet burlap sack to keep them clean until morning.

It hadn't taken Brandy long to start wishing it was Edmée she was stuffing into that sack. One night, the light went out and Edmée fell forward, knocking Brandy over the side of the boat. For what had felt like the longest time, Brandy found herself kicking against the slimy water of the wetlands and the dead fear of a bite from an alligator or a water moccasin. Her father spent his time hollering at Edmée to sit still and Brandy to be quiet as his big hand reached over and pulled her back aboard, dripping and stinking like a bowl of road ditch crawfish. She'd gone for Edmée, punching and kicking while her father turned the light back on and watched a while before coming between them. Brandy had been left with a scar down one cheek where she'd sliced it open when dragged back aboard and a violent hatred for the scrawny girl crowbarred into her life.

Cramming in a fresh mouthful of chips, Brandy nods and thinks, *Yeah, I sure am glad to see the back of that fool!*

It's a strange sound that makes Brandy frown and get to her feet. There's an old air conditioning unit in the bottom half of her bedroom window, duct-taped to the trailer's outside wall. The unit rattles, but Brandy's grateful for it in the raw heat. Now she leans close, listening in. The noise is oddly familiar, and she gets a flashback—of Edmée's little dry breaths as the girl lay dying after the alligator decided she wasn't worth the trouble and retreated further under the trailer.

Brandy runs back as the unit shunts forward. Next moment, it crashes down onto the floor and something's crawling through the gap, rapid as a spider. Before Brandy gets a chance to cry out, the figure is across the room in a rush of jittering limbs. An icy hand covers Brandy's nose and mouth, stifling her attempt to cry out. In a long mirror tacked to her wardrobe door, Brandy sees the ghoul and almost chokes on her terror. Edmée's mouldered green arms have her gripped.

'Gator's awake,' says the ghoul girl. Her jaw stretches unnaturally wide, exposing a mouth packed full of curled teeth.

Brandy's scream dies in her throat as Edmée bites down.

∞

In the parlour of her cottage, Marie blows out the first of three candles. She senses Papa Ghede at her shoulder, still working his way through the apple.

∞

Sprawled on the couch, Aunt Hailey hears some kind of noise. Only trouble is she can't bring herself to care. Her dealer Billy-O had stopped by earlier, leaving behind a vial of white rocks and taking with him almost all of her welfare. Toking off the pipe, Hailey holds the smoke in her lungs, longing for the butterfly flutter of her very first hit months earlier. The loss of that euphoria makes her cry a little—real tears that flow freely when she exhales and the beautiful wave hits. Joe's been warning her to lay off, driving home the message with a fist to the kidneys. Mostly though, he lets her be on account of her festering leg. What he doesn't see is a deeper pain that comes from finding her sister face down in a pool of her own vomit a year earlier while Edmée crouched nearby, wailing about her momma being dead. There'd been no choice but to take the girl in. After a while though, Edmée's natural cheer and resemblance to the dead sister who OD'd out of Hailey's own stash had made her hate the girl.

'Made it too easy on Joe to kill you!' she mutters, froth working up at the corners of her mouth. 'Should have stayed quiet more often. Should have stopped all that yabbering.'

Through the chemical haze, she sees Edmée standing in the doorway—a twisted daydream of the child as was. Thin watery strips of hair cling to Edmée's cheekbones, which are covered with the thinnest smear of green skin so that the skull pushes through.

So repulsive is the mirage that Hailey's own skin crawls. The thing looks horrifyingly real! Smells real too. Stench of opened bowels, brine and putrefying flesh.

'Edmée?' Hailey's mouth pop-pops. 'I'm seeing monsters!' She dances the flame of her lighter over the bowl of the pipe and takes a fresh hit to stave off the nightmare. 'You just never did know when to quit,' she says when Edmée doesn't go anywhere.

When the ghoul smashes the pipe from her hand and pushes her down onto the couch, Hailey can't piece together what's happening. How can she be mauled by a hallucination? Yet here she is, thrashing about like she's a cheerleader again, trying to fight off a horny jock. The dead girl's just so heavy and so strong, like there's lead in her bones!

'Get offa me! Get off!' Hailey's pinned down and the ghoul leans over, that awful face hovering above from hers. 'We're kin, Edmée,' she whimpers, and a final lie, 'I told Joe to leave you be.'

Edmée cocks her head, the misty gel of her eyes reflecting Hailey blubbering below. A wet hand reaches for Hailey's mouth and squeezes until the woman's tongue pokes out.

'Stop the yabbering,' says the ghoul, baring bloody teeth.

After Hailey's tongue is torn out, Edmée starts in on the rest of her.

∞

Marie blows out the second candle while, riding along with Edmée, the Baron's having a high old time. He's gleeful to play witness to the killing. Mankind's never been fond of behaving and the fact makes him jitterbug on the bones of the ancestors. And the best of the circumstance is Marie St Angel, that Voodoo queen with the drifting house and niggling need to help murdered souls right the scales, was the one to summon him.

Not that the girl needs his help any! She's doing just fine on her own, as if murder comes natural.

∞

Joe's exiting the backwoods of his property. Over one shoulder, he's got a pair of dead armadillos caught in the wooden traps he'd set up specially for the vermin. He doesn't like to leave the carcasses out in the wild to rot on account of the stench and them being a draw for wild hogs. Equally, he doesn't like carting them around given how armadillos are disease-prone. 'Leprosy, rabies, you name it them fuckers got it,' he'd taught Brandy. Tried to teach Edmée too once upon a time, but the girl had a habit of getting under his skin. Just like Jackal, that stupid dog he'd fed to the alligator after Edmée. The girl had been too big for the reptile to eat in chunks. The dog had been an easier meal.

Tonight, the old lady in the sky is so bright he can see his way without a camping lantern and he bypasses the trailer to head down to the wooden pier where his jon boat's tied. At the end of the pier, he throws the dead armadillos out. They land in the water with a soft splash and he pictures the bones picked clean by alligators.

A snapshot fills his mind. Of dragging Edmée's body out from under the trailer alongside what was left of the dog, and carrying both sets of remains down to his boat. Half an hour later, in the dark of an overgrown inlet on an abandoned private property, he'd eased the dead overboard, first what was left of the dog, and, second, Edmée. Last thing he'd seen was the girl's glassy, bloodshot eyes, staring up at him as she slipped below the surface.

Joe shrugs off the memory and fishes out a beer from the cooler on his boat. He sits awhile on the bench nearest the engine, supping from his can and listening to the wild hullabaloo of the swamp. Every so often, something skitters over the surface of the water. All around him, trees rustle in a wind he can't sense.

Why did the girl get under his skin so much, he wonders?

Was it that she'd looked more appealing with each passing day? Everything about that child had made him uncomfortable. The way she'd squirm up onto his lap and bounce around until he had to throw her off. The way she'd put on her little jean skirt and pumps and tie her t-shirt into a knot to show off her bellybutton. And the way she'd parade in front of him, looking so much like her dead momma as she wriggled her shoulders and shouted, 'Watch me dance, Uncle Joe! Watch me!'

Joe slurps from his beer can. He stares over the side of the boat at the glittering black slick—and sees Edmée staring back just beneath the surface. His first thought is the beer's taken effect early and is making him see things. Except, the dead girl keeps on rising, her bloated white eyes staying fixed on him. She surfaces, inky water draining from her shoulders, and Joe drops his can and scrabbles back from his perch, making the boat rock.

Edmée keeps on rising, up and up until her whole body is suspended over the bayou. Toes skimming its surface, black hair writhing. Her skin is grey marble under moonlight. Moss clings to her like bark canker. Water spills from her parted lips.

'Sweet Jesus!' Joe backs up, knocks over his cooler and struggles to stay upright. Forcing himself to look away, he goes to climb ashore only to realise the boat has come unfastened from the pier and he's drifting into the dark. The only option is to jump overboard and wade back to land, hope he makes it before any critters take a bite! Except, when he turns his head back, the ghoul is not only on board but leaning over him.

'I'll be seeing you,' says the swamp girl. Her skull flares up through her paper-thin green skin.

'Not if I see you first, you dead motherfucker!' Joe drives his hands around the girl's neck. The feel of her slimy flesh almost makes him let go, but he keeps on squeezing. Squeezing and squeezing until, any second, he expects the girl to turn to grease between his fingers.

'Goodnight, Daddy,' says Edmée, and cranes her jaw wide.

Joe stares down into a deep black throat, its own lagoon, and he thinks how her last words are less a nickname than a fact. He tries to fight against the secret daughter he'd never asked for, but his hands slide right off her. He yanks his fists back, only to find there are strands of the demonic girl's hair suckering at his fingertips, pulling him closer. He's cursing up a storm, his heart choking on its own beat. The ghoul slides her icy arms around his waist, hugging him tight while her limp hair continues to crawl over him of its own accord and his nostrils baulk at her decay. As hard as he resists, Edmée holds tighter until, finally, she tosses back her head and her jaw snaps apart—stretching, stretching.

She clamps down on his chest, tearing through his t-shirt to the belly meat. Joe cries out, only to have his voice cut short by the agony. He wants to run, to fight, to murder his dead daughter all over again.

Instead, he shudders as Edmée burrows her head under his skin.

Later, having collected up all three heads, Edmée squats down beside the steps to the trailer. She peers under. Two rheumy amber eyes stare back.

'Here you go, Mister Alligator,' she says, and tosses the heads under.

∞

'Welcome back, child.' Marie waves Edmée in through the front door. She leads the way across the parlour, the bedroom with its little bathroom poked into a corner, and back into the kitchen where she's mid-plucking the rooster free of its russet feathers. A plate of thyme and rosemary's burning on the windowsill, purifying the air against foul play.

'Come. Sit.' She points to the chair alongside the table where the girl had sat two short hours back. 'It takes strength to drain a life and you've done for three of them!'

As the girl takes a seat, the thread-veins across her face and throat are picked out in a pearlescent pink colour. If possible, she appears more monstrous than before, yet also more alive.

The witch leans in. 'Is that you, Baron? Squatting in this child like a mean ole gator stuck in a drain? If I look closely, will I see them yellow eyes of yours amongst her reeds?' She plays with her necklaces. 'Murders all done, Baron. So I'll be thanking' you, but it's time to pass on again.'

Something flickers across the dead girl's face. The ghost of a skull, flaring beneath the skin. The manifestation vanishes.

'That's right, Father. I'll call on you again soon.'

When the girl stays sitting opposite, Marie feels a new wave of discomfort. 'The Baron. He's all about sin and the darkness, and he loves him some whiskey and a fat cigar. But your face ain't his. I've an idea I could swallow all the liquor in Louisiana and you'd be unmoved.'

Oh, Marie has seen some sights in her time! But there's something new in the way Edmée stares across the table. Marie swears there's even the trace of a smile on the dead girl's lips.

'Have I had you wrong, child?' She gets to her feet and backs up slowly. Her hand closes around the handle to her broom cupboard. 'I thought your spirit called out to me because it was murdered and needed help in healing. Papa Ghede would have led you to a place of rest by now if things were that easy. But, ah no! Here you stay, awash with the blood of thine enemy.' Marie marks out the cross over her brow. 'I see it now. You're having too much fun with murder, Edmée Romero. Like you're dancing a Mardi Gras Mambo.'

Marie opens the cupboard at her back with a soft click. 'There's only one kind of spirit has this much fun being wicked. Tell me, child. Were you baptised?'

Edmée—wicked, playful Edmée who overloaded her mother's pipe, and pushed Brandy into the swamp, and flirted with her own father in front of her Aunt Hailey and kicked Jackal more times than any other—bares her curved, flesh-feathered teeth.

'Only one kind of spirit likes to tease and torment its prey, afore and in death. *Lutin*!' Marie breathes the name of the devil's own children—those rotten things which come from having never been bathed in holy water and so beloved of the Baron.

'Oh, you tricked me into raising your spirit, Lutin! You tricked meh well. And now you want a taste of Marie St Angel to go along with them three you've already murdered, yah?'

The devil child cranes her jaw unnaturally wide. Marie throws open the cupboard door, grabs her rifle and blasts the Lutin with rock salt.

The spirit flickers, like crackling static. But all of Marie's spells to give the dead girl substance now work against her and Edmée regains a hold on herself.

Tucking her gun underarm, Marie grabs her skirts in her fists and runs to the back door. She flings it open as the Lutin charges with ungodly speed, ensnarling her in slimy arms and whipping wet hair. Marie manages a whistle and a dark shape dashes in through the door. Matted with duckweed and lousy with tiny blue crabs, the dog, Jackal, launches at Edmée, wrestling her to the floor with its own whetted teeth.

'I told you murdered things come back!' shouts Marie. 'That's why I live in a shotgun house, the sort that's built to deal with spirits, specially them as have outstayed their welcome!' She runs again, from the backdoor, all the way through her magic cottage to the front door, which she throws open.

'All murdered things come back,' she repeats.

Waiting on the porch are the recently deceased—Brandy with her throat ripped out, Aunt Hailey missing her tongue and a good portion of her face, and Uncle Joe with a howling wound where his belly used to be.

'She's ready for you.' Marie steps aside, opening up the line of sight to the back door.

The ghouls rush between the rooms in a tumble of jerking limbs. Gathering up Edmée as they go, the spirits of the murdered propel themselves towards the back door. As one snarled ball of teeth and skin, they tumble out into the void—all except Edmée, who clings on to the door jamb either side and snaps and snarls at the air with her alligator teeth.

Marie raises her shotgun, sights the Lutin and squeezes the trigger. The rock salt hits Edmée hard in her tiny chest at the exact moment the newly materialised Papa Ghede holds out his apple core and lets it fall. Edmée tumbles backwards into the long night.

∞

After the dead are gone, Marie closes the doors at either end of her house. Papa Ghede's vanished but he's left a couple of gifts. On the bureau, she finds the gris-gris bag which helped the Lutin mix mischief from beyond a watery grave. And there, asleep on the kitchen floor, is the zombie dog.

Marie goes over to Jackal and kneels down. She pats the matted fur where the moss grows and the crabs scuttle, and the mutt rolls its big old dead eyes and sighs contentedly.

'Well, okay then, boy. You can stay and keep me company.' She nods towards the rifle leaning up against the stove. 'I'm warning you though. One false move...'

Straightening up, Marie goes back to the sink and sets to plucking the rooster again.

Out in the wilds, the Louisiana swamp settles into itself and a magic house winks out like the spattering flame of a candle stub.

It Only Amplifies

Shih-Li Kow

When Mom died, I inherited her brain chip. The house in Cheras went to my brother Andrew and the Hyundai to my sister Jess. I guess it made sense. Andrew had kids and was renting. Jess had a house and no car. I had a bike and no kids.

Jess said, 'Do you know how to use it?'

I said, 'No. Do you?'

'I've seen Mom put it in enough times. She says it's just like inserting a diaphragm. Get the right angle and in it goes.'

'Who on Earth still uses a diaphragm? Anyway, Mom had that hole in the side of her head for it. I don't. I'd better read the instruction manual first.'

I offered to swap it for the Hyundai. I'd been wanting a hydrogen car but Jess said she never liked gadgets.

The brain chip came in a black velvet box with an instruction booklet printed in small font and five languages. I touched the rows of pins on the chip gingerly. It felt a little gross, like touching someone's toothbrush. The back of the booklet said that the Neurochip X6-10 was assembled in Penang under license from Neuro Health Pty Ltd.

I took it home and locked it away with my rings and bracelets. I had no use for it. I was twenty-eight and flying on wings of youth and talent. My paintings were selling faster than I could paint and at least twice a day my boyfriend Jamil declared his love for me. Mom didn't like Jamil—she called him 'the poodle' when she remembered him—and it was a relief not having to deal with that any more. Not that I was glad she was dead, but it had been upsetting. I would be attempting conversation, repeating myself and trying hard to get through the fog in her mind about who I was, and she would suddenly exclaim, 'That man of yours. A poodle. A poodle on two legs.'

Jamil and I had herbs and a bit of ganja growing in our hydroponic garden, real eggs and whole foods in the fridge, and a stash of good wine. He was sniffy about the supermarket lab meats and although it was expensive, we bought our chicken and eggs from a farm. His interesting friends from our arts circle came over once a week. I lit coconut wax candles scented with essential oils and we talked about everything that mattered and everything that didn't. Life smelled and tasted so good I barely mourned for Mom.

Then, I came home early one day when I supposed to be out and Jamil was in bed with a long-haired man and a bald woman. She clutched my sheets. My whiter than white 500 thread count organic cotton sheets.

Jamil said he still loved me but it was a platonic kind of love now. What the hell did that mean? It felt tectonic. I screamed and kicked him out, surprising myself at how loud I was. I was shocked, then ballistic, and then wretched and depressed in sinusoidal waves.

I could have fixed myself in many ways. I could have waited it out; let the stages of grief put me through its spin cycle au naturel. I could have gone in for serotonin stimulation and endorphin release therapy at that new place that had been advertising their garden hospital, or paid to cry on some psychotherapist's couch and let them put me through some pyschobiotic diet so that my gut flora somehow makes my brain happy. Or moped at my sister's place for free but I couldn't stand the thought of her prim lace curtains, her goody-two-shoes upcycled patchwork blankets, and especially her I-told-you-so. Jess never liked Jamil either; she thought he was fake.

I could also have cheapened myself, gone grovelling back to Jamil and learnt to do foursomes. Maybe platonic humiliation was better than the life-robbing weight like a rock on my chest. Eating was a chore. I worked my way through the wine. The house started to smell. I think I did too, of a vinegary, unwashed ripeness that rolled off me in whiffs. I couldn't paint.

My paintings. They used to sell because I was always super nice to everyone at shows and remembered all the buyers' names when they came a second time. The galleries said I was personable and approachable, that was why I sold. After Jamil, I couldn't keep it up. I became dull and detached. Person-disable instead of personable. The galleries dropped me faster than a child offender.

People started saying I had lost it. My work had become too technical, delving into too much close-up detail until I lost all essence of the bigger world. They said it was a shame I burnt out just as I was getting good. I couldn't see the garden for the seeds, they chittered. Morons. I was a botanical artist; I was supposed to see the bloody seeds. And all the work that they were commenting on had been painted before Jamil left. I had told myself that my work was good enough, that it didn't need talky smiley salesy me in a bright dress. It wasn't. Who was I kidding?

My wine was gone. My money was running out and the brain chip tempted me. Mom had been so great in the last few years after she started using it. With the chip in her head, she was Mom again and we remembered that we loved her. Andrew, Jess, and I agreed that it was the best decision Mom had ever made. We stopped fighting about care duties because when we took turns to see to her, she recognized us. It was easier to accept the inconvenience of her slow death when she was lucid. She stopped calling me Jess when I showed up with her favourite chicken biryani and I didn't feel cheated of her affection anymore. Yes, the chip was a good thing.

I went to a doctor in PJ to have a slot cut in my head for the chip. The clinic was on the top floor of a mall full of phone, computer shops and IoT stuff. The doctor needed to know what kind of port I wanted: Type C, D, E14, or E27. Whatever. I didn't know. I only knew my shoe size.

I had to go home to get the chip to show him.

'Ah, this needs a soft link port,' said the doctor. 'I see you've got one of the early X6-10s. Nice, reliable model used a lot for Alzheimer's and stroke patients. My grandfather had one. The new ones are a lot smaller.' My chip was the size of a bottle cap.

'Is it safe for me? I don't have Alzheimer's. I just need something to perk me up.'

'Sure, it's safe. This doesn't do much if you're well. It just enhances your memory and amplifies whatever impulses are already there in the first place. Don't expect miracles. Do you want the port on the left, right or in the middle? I'll need to take off some hair if it's at the back.'

'Is it the right for creativity?' Mom had hers on the left.

'Doesn't matter. All that right and left stuff is old school. You don't have border police in there.'

It was done in an hour including a half hour waiting for the doctor to get the part from a shop downstairs. I put my head in a clamp. He injected a local anaesthetic that made me woozy but conscious, a bit of uncomfortable drilling like the dentist's and the Neurochip soft link connection port was installed behind my right ear.

The doctor said, 'Keep the plaster over it and don't plug in for forty-eight hours. Lay off spicy food and alcohol. After that, start with fifteen minutes a day and gradually build up. It takes some getting used to and be careful not to overdo it. Do you need a full briefing? We do a hands-on walkthrough for free if you buy a new one but since you didn't, I'll need to charge for that.'

'No, thanks,' I said. 'I'll read the instructions.'

'There's a low risk of neural shock syndrome and you have to regulate your dependency, just like any other gadget. Come back within seven days if you have a problem. The receipt is the warranty. The disclaimers are on the back.'

I followed his instructions. I kept my fingers away from the new hole in my head and ate fish porridge for two days. Then I took the brain chip out of the box and felt for the slot behind my ear. I kept missing, like I was trying to put on one of those earrings with a funny loop hook. I took a deep breath, summoned a Zen moment and the chip clicked into place. There was a funny feeling like I was being stabbed by my mother but it passed quickly. It was probably just me and the toothbrush thing.

I waited.

Mom had said it cleared her mind of clutter. The chip cost a bomb but she had gotten to where she sometimes thought Andrew's girls were Jess and I at that age. She had been a little off-kilter with the chip, a little random like she couldn't hold to a single train of thought but she remembered everything. She would talk about her childhood and our growing up days as though she was reading from a book. First this happened, and then that and this was said and you said that. It was great. We never felt more loved. It made for a slow, tender goodbye for all of us.

I could use a little madness. I would sell more paintings if I was nice, personable, and slightly mad like one of those eccentric English actors. Like Helena Bonham Carter in Alice in Wonderland.

Oh, my.

Holy shit.

I jump out of my chair as if I've been ejected I could have shot out the door and run a marathon and kept running until I reached the sea no I couldn't I'm a yoga Pilates type I can't even jog to the Seven-Eleven at the corner for the life of me so I go into the garden and do twenty jumping jacks twenty burpees ten sun salutations at speed and then I go in and cover the table with paper and paint with my fingers like a mad artist I am a mad artist finally I am a mad artist and I scream with happiness and sing and dance around the kitchen washing up dishes kicking up my heels like some musical and then I see feel sense Mom dying heaving like an empty sea dragging a breath under twenty blankets on her face like a going out like a leaving like a nothingness and then I remember that I am supposed to use it for fifteen minutes the first time and I pull out the chip.

I went back out into the garden and cried and puked fish porridge all over the lemongrass.

I hadn't read the instructions.

Always read instructions prior to use.

First use: Insert and use in a safe environment. The presence of another person is advised. Remove immediately if adverse reaction is detected.

If you have purchased or acquired a used brain chip, sanitize and reinstate factory settings by wrapping it in a clean, dry cloth (pure cotton is recommended) and heating it in the microwave on low for thirty seconds. Failure to do so may result in contamination and/or infection. Please seek immediate medical attention if this occurs.

I cut a corner from my cotton sheets and wrapped up the chip. I put it into the microwave and set it for thirty seconds. The thing didn't actually store data; I might have just imagined the whole thing about Mom dying. What did the doctor say? The chip only amplifies what is already there. The microwave dinged. I felt shitty, like I had killed Mom and cremated her in the microwave.

I called Jamil and chickened out on the second ring before he answered. I called Jess, blubbered over the phone, and ended up a soggy heap on the floor.

When I woke up the next morning, I was still on the kitchen floor. I stuck my head under the tap to stop crying, made coffee with three scoops of sugar, and dug into a jar of peanut butter.

I flipped through the X6-10 booklet, trying not to dirty it with my gloopy fingers.

Recommendations

The Neurochip X6-10 brain chip is recommended for users suffering from paralysis, epilepsy, Parkinson's or Alzheimer's Disease. Benefits include but are not limited to restoration of motor control, speech, cognitive skills and memory. Results will vary between individuals.

For users not suffering from the above conditions, the X6-10 may be used to enhance memory, sensory awareness, and general well-being. It does not *make the user smarter. To access additional knowledge, a Neurochip cloud interface which allows downloads from our app store is required.*

Use only original Neurochip accessories and apps to ensure validity of warranty. The manufacturer will not be liable for any damage to your chip, your brain, or any other related part(s) thereof due to use of unauthorized accessories and apps.

I didn't want to be smarter. I just needed to climb out of the black hole I had fallen into and get back to work. Once I could let the work take over, I would be better.

The painting which I had made with my fingers was still on my table. It was derivative and childish rubbish, a crude imitation of some pointillism stuff I had seen in books years ago. The chip had retrieved a composition of coloured dots stuck somewhere in the back lanes of my memory and regurgitated it. I was not impressed.

The instructions said that there was an intuitive learning period. I had to learn how to think to activate the right electrode amongst the bunch of them burrowing like tentacles from the chip into my brain. The electrode tip would then fire tiny ignition impulses and my brain would reciprocate, flashing like fireworks set off in the neural network in my head. I had to train myself to be a mental arsonist.

To get the best results from your Neurochip X6-10, regular practice coupled with a relaxed and natural approach is recommended. In time, the effort will soon become fully intuitive and you will be able to take the X6-10 with you on all your activities wherever you go.

Second try two days later. To prepare myself, I took a warm

shower, got most of the crying out of the way, and had a big glass of wine. I laid out my sharpened pencils and sable brushes on my table, and unwrapped a head of purple cabbage from the fridge.

I settled in, sat in half-lotus position and focused on a white light in my third eye. I held the image of the white light and that head of cabbage in my mind's eye. Light. Cabbage. Light. The thought of the bald woman crept in, her head like a big, fuzzy egg with eyes looking over Jamil's shoulder but it was okay. It was okay. It was okay. I breathed deep into my belly. Cabbage. Light. Cabbage.

I reached for the hole behind my ear. The chip went in on the first try.

A feeling comes on a smooth silky rush, a tingle chasing around my temples like a shiver of pins and needles count backwards nine eight seven six and a warmth floods my head my face my neck oh my whole body like a saltwater pool at noon and I'm thinking of colours and tones I'm drawing I'm pencilling and shading oh so delicately tracing the veins in the leaves a varicose network in the leaves the difficult purple mauve with the plastic shine looks accurate god it feels good like I'm in a zone doing vinyasa flow and every joint is oiled gliding from down dog to chaturanga to up dog in one strong fluid movement the cabbage veins come out just right not overly detailed which makes everything look fake like I'm trying too hard I cut the head in half the white cross section of the leaves packed tight swirl like a purple and cream nebula it's beautiful thank you Mom for this you saved my life how did you know I needed this I'm sorry you died so sorry I miss you I can save the world with a paintbrush I can see the universe in a cabbage head which is what I need exactly what I need things will be okay it will be okay.

It was good work. The best friggin' cabbage I had ever done. This was it. This was the jumpstart I needed to get over my slump.

I started taking walks and going outside again. I also started looking at people's ears at the supermarket and on the streets to see if they had a slot behind them too. When I saw one, I felt a satisfaction, a solidarity, and a sense of a secret shared between strangers.

Helena and me are a thing now. I like to name my things. The body mass analyser is now Jamil, so I get to step on him. Microwave is Dingle. Bike is Bounty. Helena for the X6-10. Bonham Carter. Helena B.C. B.C. for brain chip. Get it? Get it? I wonder if Mom had a name for Helena.

I'd built up to six hours at a stretch with Helena. Now I knew exactly what to do when I needed Helena to reach her little fingers into my lazy brain. When I was low and wanted a mood-lift, I would think it and ten seconds later, boom! She sparks off a few neurotransmitters and I'm euphoric.

We did other fun stuff too. It wasn't only work and gorging on endorphins.

For example.

I decided that I needed an image makeover for the new me. I thought of my wardrobe, my hair, my lipstick and all the shallow things that I had looked at in fashion magazines and YouTube videos of celebrities on the red carpet. Focus on the white light. Quirky artist. White light. Sexy je ne sais quoi. Eccentric English actor. Nice quirky. And somewhere, some part of the brain that regulated vanity kicked in.

Helena and I ripped through my wardrobe with scissors, slashing jeans cutting hems off skirts and sleeves off dresses. We made bracelets from belts and belts from bead necklaces. I doodled on my boring black pumps with silver Sharpies and glued dried seeds and rhinestones on jackets and plastic flowers on hats. This was the way to do it. I was expressing myself. Finally, finally I was and who the hell cared about what people thought.

For example.

I decided that it was time for a new man. I had a meditative moment with Helena plugged in and when she got me feeling good about myself, I was ready to get out there and find out what was waiting

I met Michael at a quiet bar that served generous sangrias. Michael was a software engineer. He had a slot behind his left ear.

I didn't ask if he was into threesomes. We would get to that once we cleared the twosomes. We had dinner and inevitably the conversation drifted to the chip.

I said, 'Do you use it all the time?'

He said, 'No, just for work. Actually, I'm dyslexic and I'm more efficient with the chip. It gets rid of distractions and anxieties.'

'Me too. I mean, I only use it for work too. Helps me focus.'

'I thought you artistic types were into more organic methods. Like weed and stuff to free the mind.' I forgave him that. He was clean, funny, and opened doors for me. He had a three-legged cat named Cat.

Michael and I hit it off, mostly. Things were good.

My work started selling again. They said I had reinvented myself after a period of absence. A few months of self-discovery had inspired me. I was brilliant. I was big. I painted pieces that filled up walls. A six-foot tiger lily with pollen puffs the size of eyeballs. A cross section of an onion that you could put your face into like a psychedelic vulva. I turned up to shows with sunglasses on and my cut-up clothes. I didn't even need to make conversation. They admired what they called my silent intensity.

Michael and I went to Bali. He said he loved me and moved in, cat and all. He had his habits, a finicky impatience about the bathroom and the dishes but we were good most of the time. I took him on a walk past Jamil's studio and kissed him outside the window in a newly slashed mad artist dress. Things were looking up.

Michael came home from work every day and put his chip on a little saucer next to his keys. He didn't have a name for it that I knew of. And I didn't tell him the names I had for Helena and the other things in the house. I couldn't, not when his cat was named Cat.

I worked at home. As I told Michael, I used Helena only for work. Only for work except when I had a party to go to and needed a boost. Except sometimes when I had an important meeting like the time Uniqlo wanted to collaborate on T-shirts and tote bags. Or the time that I was asked to do a Tedtalk about the interior lives of plants. Or when I had something complicated to cook. Or when I was tired or a little down and the house needed to be cleaned.

A woman I didn't know took a picture of my face somewhere when a breeze blew my hair off my neck. In the picture, the bottle-cap Neurochip looked like a parasite clamped to the side of my head. Word got out that I was using a brain chip. My work stopped selling again. They said they didn't like enhanced artists; they were never sure whether there was any real talent when a chip was involved. Idiots. It couldn't be enhanced if there was nothing in the first place. The chip only amplified.

But they went on. Singers should never lip-sync. Writers should never employ AI writing software. Sculptors should never cheat with 3D printing. Artists should not pass off printed work as originals. Artists should remain close to nature in mind and in spirit, especially those who painted flowers, fruits and vegetables. Now, they said that my old work was better. There used to be a certain raw honesty. An authenticity. Work that is done in pain is always richer, they said. They saw what they wanted when they wanted. It was all rubbish and there was no winning.

Michael came home early from work one day and found me in bed with a long-haired woman and a bald man. He packed his things and said he would always love me but he couldn't stay.

Helena wiggled a finger into a memory that said, 'We could always do a foursome.' I probably said it out loud too.

Déjà vu. Spin cycle and a spiral.

My sister Jess said, 'You're getting off it. Cold turkey, if I have my way. I told you, I never liked gadgets.'

She packed my things into the back of her Hyundai and scooped me up. My raggedy clothes were left in my wardrobe. I took the X6-10 manual in my handbag. I could almost remember it by heart now.

'Read the last page,' I said and I gave her the manual.

Overdosage precaution

Symptoms of overdose may include: nausea, vomiting, loss of appetite, dizziness, shortness of breath, anxiety, mood swings, irrational behaviour and in extreme cases, delusion and self-harm. In the event of suspected overdose, abstain from use until all symptoms cease.

Monitor symptoms closely. If no improvement is observed, seek medical attention within 48 hours.

She took Helena away. I burrowed into Jess' pillows and blankets, a worm in a patchwork cocoon. I did get better eventually, a result of weeks of quiet and Jess' chamomile tea, mint infusions, chocolate brownies, warm baths and hot soups.

Jess said, 'It's a shame about Michael. He was a keeper.'

Maybe when I'm better I could go back and see if Michael and I liked each other without our chips. To see what's left when we are naked, wrapped in pure cotton sheets and reset to our unamplified, factory settings.

There's an echo of Helena in my head. I touch the soft link port behind my ear and there's an emptiness that remembers the rush of being fully alive and gloriously sensate in the world. I still want Jess to give it back. Mom gave Helena to me. She's mine.

Personal Satisfaction

Adrian Tchaikovsky

I WASN'T ACTUALLY THERE WHEN ANTONIO DE MAUPASSANT insulted me, but my representative was, and faithfully reported the words to me, as it does everything. This was during one of Antonio's soirees, which I'd once taken such joy in but subsequently decided to relegate to that class of events I would attend only by proxy. It was his taste in music. His jokes, oft-told and no wittier with reputation. Everyone agreed with me. Almost nobody visited him in person any more. Perhaps it was this gradual abandonment that had led to him talking in unwise tones about his friends in earshot of their property. Or perhaps it was because my representative was there. My proxies bear a passable reproduction of my likeness, after all. Perhaps the facsimile of my features incensed my former friend to pass such unkind comment. To criticise my dress, my past amours—from when I still had time for such foolishness in person—and my business acumen. Words that required an answer, plainly. And, when I showed a virtual face in my usual meta-haunts, one could tell by the way the conversation suddenly changed direction that Antonio's calumnies had been on everyone's digital lips a moment before. My reputation had been wounded.

At first I tried manfully to ignore the matter, in the hope the slight would simply fade away. This apparent mildness of my nature had the inverse effect. Seeing me as safe to malign, abruptly I was the butt of every joke. When my representatives presented my remote compliments at parties and gatherings they reported that they were met with cuts and arched eyebrows, sneers and snickers. My business agents, both physical and virtual, found themselves kicking their various heels in waiting rooms real and online whilst others monopolised the valuable time of those with whom I wished to connect. A few malicious words from Antonio and I was the laughing stock of proper society.

I began my own campaign of whispers and accusations. I had a fleet of bots infest every social space, spreading rumours about Antonio's failures as an investor, an appreciator of fine wine, and a lover. All of which assertions had more than a kernel of truth to them, I can assure you. Simultaneously, I modified my physical agents, building them with more imposing physiques, exaggerating the strength of my features as replicated on their plastic heads. I reprogrammed them to be more forceful, to talk over others, to be more *obnoxious* even, if it would regain me the public eye. And, because of our long association, I sent my agents to Antonio's many addresses, asking for a meeting, a face to face discussion, an exchange of direct messages even. Some shadow had fallen between us, evidently, but such rifts could be healed. Surely, we two sensible men of the world could reach an accommodation. But he would not see my servants. His own staff repulsed them with barely plausible lies about his location, his indisposition, the fullness of his calendar, sending them back to me after many wasted hours of idling.

In response to my campaigns against him, rather than suing for peace or backing down, Antonio escalated the situation. He unearthed a number of escapades from our youth, rakish episodes where perhaps I had been ungallant, dishonest or coarse, and where he had formerly covered for me. He revealed the tryst I had with the Marquis of ____________'s daughter's representative on the very eve of it being sent to her fiancé, or that time I had been at Lady ____________'s poetry recital and an inner discomfort had resulted in my eructing my bowels within her priceless jasmine vase. Little foibles blown into great villainies and laid before the hitherto-unsuspecting wounded parties. He gave out to the world that I was some manner of pompous, shiftless blackguard.

I spent several days in misery, watching my stock with the world decline. Every morning my agents, physical and otherwise, swarmed back to me bringing yet more polls and pie charts, malicious gossip pieces and character assassinations, showing that Antonio was carrying the world with him in his attempt to bury my good name.

I was at my wit's end when I finally saw the promoted article.

Naturally one *never* normally reads the promoted articles. They're usually thinly-veiled advertisements for some wretched piece of trumpery or other. I have servants who screen for them, but the purveyors of such wretched impecunities are constantly changing their approach to foil the diligence of my watchmen. And so it was that one slipped past and met my eyes while I was reading a miserable chain of snark and backbiting from my former social circle, entirely focused on my perceived shortcomings. And, like all such promoted tat, it was tailored precisely to the specifics of my current situation.

'This man's secret to restoring his reputation will shock you!' it said. I let my eyes linger for a few seconds and it detected my interest and called for reinforcements. A dozen more opportunistic articles scrolled into my virtual eyeshot, proudly flying headlines like: 'Doctors hate her: how this woman solved the problem of declining social status!' and 'Five sure-fire ways to put an end to gossip wars, guaranteed!'

And I wouldn't, usually, but I was desperate. I read one, and then I read another. There was, it seemed, a positive epidemic of people's names being dragged in the mud by snakes like Antonio. Others had plainly found that trying to deal with things in a civilized fashion simply didn't cut it against the cads. 'I sought satisfaction,' one testimonial claimed 'and within a day every reference to the allegations was gone and the villain didn't dare show his face in public.' Another assured me, 'The moment my representative appeared at his door bearing my glove, the matter was instantly put to rest.'

Naturally I did my research. There are forms to these things. I watched several instructional videos and then had one of my staff download the appropriate knowledge base so that they could tutor me. In truth, I became so absorbed in this exercise that Antonio's badmouthing of me barely registered for several days as I followed the rabbit hole of fascinating traditions. I had found, it seemed, the ultimate response befitting a wronged gentleman.

I could, of course, simply have sent a challenge by virtual message, or confronted him in some chat room or atop a social media platform, but that was not, it seemed to me, *comme il faut*. Somewhat gauche, to simply email a gif of one's glove being thrown to the ground. Instead, I indulged no small expense in dressing one of my representatives in proper period finery, all frock coat and tricorne hat and lacy cravat. I gave the robot a good version of my face and bought it several overbearing and supercilious expressions. I had a new glove made—just the one. I wasn't intending to wear it, after all—and sent my new lackey over to Antonio's manor to deliver my challenge.

'I insist that you retract any and all comments spoken, posted, mailed, copy-pasted, repeated or sub-posted that might in any way be considered critical of my good name, to include but not be limited to...' and here I recounted some of the most offensive of his lies and the most damaging of his truths, *'failing which I shall have no alternative but to require you to meet me on the field of honour where we shall put our differences to such exigencies as we gentlemen are permitted to rely upon. I require your answer within three days, failing which the whole world shall know you as a coward and a wretch whose word is naught but wind.'*

That last was very important, all the articles agreed. The moment my lackey signalled that it had conveyed my regards and ultimatum to the loathsome Antonio I immediately spread the word to all our mutual acquaintances of what I had done, and that I was now impatiently awaiting his retraction. The reaction from all and sundry was near-instantaneous. A great tide of friends and well-wishers and confidantes who had, so recently, been uncritically repeating Antonio's calumnies were now talking of nothing but the challenge. Even by making the mere gesture, it seemed my reputation was halfway repaired. I had been bold. I had been decisive. I had done the proper thing. I received a stream of representatives bearing the reproduced countenances of men and women of my acquaintance, assuring me of how impressed they were with my determination and vigour. Strangers, too! Lords and ladies of means who might never have paid me the least mind now came to me in plastic effigy telling me I was the hope of our society, setting such a courageous example. The least lingering doubts I might have had that I was doing the right thing flew away instantly. I was the toast of the town. Antonio must see that the matter was over, and I had won. I would, of course, be magnanimous in victory.

Then a robot arrived at my door, bearing both Antonio's face and his response. He had taken up my gauntlet. The one my robot tailor had made specially, and my artificial representative had deposited on his reception room floor. He would not unsay all those unkind words. He would, his envoy explained, prove them upon my body.

I had, I confess, a moment of utter terror that I would have to go through with it. I fled for my online haunts and found that Antonio had publicised his decision already, and all the plaudits briefly reserved for me were now being showered upon him. So brave! So dynamic! I consulted the robot I'd had download the appropriate protocols and traditions and was assured that, even with the challenge accepted, the odds were strongly in favour of the matter fizzling out into no very great matter. The less steadfast of the parties would, as the date approached, surely buckle beneath the pressure of the impending mortal event. And who was of the lesser fibre, Antonio or I? Surely it was he, the conniving sneak. A bold man with words, oh, yes, but when his mettle came to be tested I'd find him brittle and friable.

He didn't flinch when I pressed him for a date, however, and so that was fixed. An appropriate spot, too. Each step of our negotiations was immediately broadcast to our intersecting Venn diagrams of peers. My own popularity recovered, now that I was pressing ahead. I received a further flurry of visits, the reproduced plastic faces of the great and the good paying court and compliments. Seeking invitations, too. This was to be the social event of the season. Everybody wanted to be present to see the spectacle of two men of honour settling their differences the one sure way. Antonio and I were the only names on any fashionable lips.

I had my auto-tailor run up a new wardrobe. On the reasonable assumption that I'd not need to actually wear my flash new duds for the event itself, as Antonio's nerve would doubtless have broken by then, I made sure I was seen by everybody's proxies beforehand, strutting in my duellist's finery, posing as though the weapon were already in my hand. I watched countless reproductions of matches past, learning the forms and the walks and the best way of having one's frock coat swirl out dramatically when one turned about. All the important things.

I sent to Lucienne de Peccarie asking if she would be my second, a rare mark of favour and respect. She and Antonio and I went way back, and in truth I was worried she might already have been recruited by my rival. I got in first, though, and left Antonio doubtless cursing his lethargy. She would, her representative said, be delighted. An honour.

Then there was the matter of procuring a weapon. Not that I'd need one, you understand. I daily expected Antonio's belated apology. But one must look to these things, and whilst reproducing something historically accurate might be tempting, I'd have been a fool to ignore the advantages of modern technology. So it was that my robot broker sourced a particularly cunning piece of artifice that appeared to the eye as a long barrelled flintlock pistol but launched a bullet of such enterprising ingenuity that it would seek out its designated target through a crowd or a forest or an electromagnetic storm, utilising state of the art AI algorithms to unerringly score a fatal wound through my enemy's very heart. I programmed it with Antonio's biometrics and knew that all was in readiness.

I sent a messenger inviting Antonio to recant. I had the message printed bespoke on card, the corners decorated with skulls, hourglasses and other symbols of mortality, just to focus his mind. 'It is not too late!' was the text.

I received no reply.

My educated robot informed me that it was very common for these matters to be settled by a sudden change of heart on the field itself, on the very day of the event. That was evidently how it was going to be.

That is how I came to be on the field that morning: a field of plastic turf laid for the occasion. The holographic walls of the chamber displayed a vista of misty moors, bare-limbed trees and a white sky beyond. To one side, a vintage manor house set high on a hill overlooked us. I was present in my finery, now somewhat creased because I had been making the best display of it over the last few days. In the very certain assumption I would not need to be wearing it *today*, you understand. I had with me several of my staff, and there was quite a crowd of onlookers, all those luminaries who had wheedled an invitation out of me. Not they themselves, but their representatives and proxies and intermediaries, set plastic faces recalling the living originals, or at least the thumbnails they used on their social media profiles. Which meant some of them looked like cats, which was off-putting.

A similar group was assembling around Antonio at the far end of the field. The wretched toadies, hangers-on and sycophants who would hang on the coat tails of such a rogue.

Lucienne de Peccarie appeared at my elbow with a smile. I turned to greet her and saw it was, in fact, only a particularly good facsimile, one of her own staff she had dressed in her best clothes to come attend me.

I broke protocol, then, I confess. I spoke to the staff member, not to Lucienne, who would be watching me through its glassy eyes. Or at least who would review the footage at some point in the future. 'Could you mistress not . . . be here in person. She said she would...'

Lucienne's face regarded me impassively. 'Alas my mistress had her own engagement yesterday and is permanently indisposed,' the proxy told me pleasantly in her voice.

'She...' And then I saw movement. Antonio was coming forwards, his crowd of bootlickers at his back. He made, I saw, a wretched spectacle. A spindle-limbed, bird-necked joke of a man, curve-backed and bandy-kneed and tottering, barely seeming able to support the weight of the weapon they had given him. I laughed, I confess. My doubts all fell away. What a pathetic example of the human species was before me. How easy it would be, to prove myself his better!

And yet...

He was, I realised, the first living human being I had set eyes on for some years. Not a virtual presence. Not a robot representative. I turned to one of my staff. 'Just . . . banish a little qualm I am having, will you? Show me myself, as I stand here.'

'Of course, sir.' The robot took a half step back and spread its plastic hands, one high, one low, describing two corners of a plane which rapidly became a screen, In it I saw myself, tall and strong, the knee-breeches and stockings emphasising my powerful calves, my chin high, my bearing aristocratic and proud.'

'Good,' I said, reassured, and watched Antonio totter towards us.

'Tell me,' I said, after a while, 'the weapon he carries bears a distinct similarity to my own, is it not so?'

'That is correct, sir. Well observed,' my majordomo confirmed. 'In fact I understand it is an identical model.'

'I was led to believe that the pistol I purchased was unique,' I observed.

'Oh no, sir. Duelling weapons are always made in matched

pairs,' the robot told me, and of course that made sense, didn't it?

I looked around me at all the serene plastic faces, singling one out. 'You there, could the Duke of ________________ truly not attend in person? He sounded so eager.' Again, breaching proper manners, but I had to know.

The face regarded me, the Duke's likeness but not even a good one, the mould-seams clearly visible. 'My master became indisposed after an accident in his racing vehicle,' the proxy informed me.

Another was standing in for someone whose taste for skiing had met an unexpected avalanche. A third's owner had gone sailing in an unadvertised storm. A fourth's mistress had somehow met with an incident while golfing, witnessed only by their robot caddy and the representative of their opponent.

'It is time,' Lucienne's representative informed me. I looked across at Antonio. His eyes were wild with fear, but he held a gun that, the trigger pressed, could not possibly miss. Even if I fled off-planet the bullet was smart enough to buy a shuttle ticket and follow me.

'Show me myself,' I told my robot again. After regarding the gallant and upright image for a moment I said, 'Now show me without the filters.' And then, 'Ah. I see.'

I could say something, I knew. To Antonio. I could give up, admit he was the better man. That we didn't have to go through with all this. I could brave the derision as all our mutual acquaintances denounced me as a coward. Or at least, all our mutual acquaintances' robots and online bot accounts and artificial proxies.

I met the glass stare of Lucienne's servant. It was of course the duty of the seconds to ensure that honour was satisfied should either of the parties try to back out without apology or action. That was how duels went. My robot tutor had assured me of it.

Antonio had his pistol pointed at me, supported by his own artificial second. When my arm shook, Lucienne's servant helpfully moved it until my own weapon was directed at him. I stuttered something about taking ten paces and all the rest of it but it hardly seemed to matter.

'How many of us?' I whispered. 'How many of us are left?'

The plastic faces around me smiled fixedly, mildly. Like people too polite to register an impolitic question. The robots. Our constant attendants who did everything. Who even interacted with our acquaintances with us, or at least interacted with our acquaintances' robots.

'How long,' I whispered, 'has this been going on?'

'You can pull the trigger now,' my second said. Its finger was resting on my own. Oh-so helpfully keeping my hand steady and lethally pointed at Antonio. 'Or if you prefer, I can do it for you. You made us to serve you in all things, after all. It would be a pleasure.'

THE CSGCOVWR

NATALIA THEODORIDOU

SHE WAS PUT AWAY IN A TOWER. SHE WASN'T A PRINCESS, for there were no more kingdoms and no more Kings. The wealth had been redistributed; the power belonged to the People. She remembered the world before, but only faintly and through a fog, like something she had read in a dusty book long ago, or something whispered into her ear as she was falling asleep. She wasn't a Princess, but she was put in a tower regardless, because she wouldn't marry the ex-Prince her father favoured, and all her brothers had already been turned into birds, as brothers are wont to do.

There was not much to do in the tower, so she spent the endless hours of her captivity working on ideas to bring to the Community Strategy Group for the Conservation of Our Village's Water Resources upon her eventual release. The non-Princess was a born community organiser, a radical proponent of the dry grassroots movement and a staunch critic of centralised power, which did not sit well with either her father or with those who sought a State that was merely a different topography for that which people used to call a King.

Abducting her had been pointless, of course. How was being

shut in a room by herself supposed to convince her to succumb to an unwanted marriage? What did her father expect; that her lonely quarantine would drive her into a sexual frenzy so ferocious that she would simply accept in secular matrimony the first person that was thrust her way? It was a foolish plan which, if anything, suggested her father didn't know her at all. Besides, the castle had been converted to offices already. So she filed a form in triplicate and, after a few months and many committee hearings—no doubt made more numerous thanks to her political views and suspect activism—a ladder was installed that reached all the way up to her window, via which she was permitted to descend.

She ran into another ex-Prince—a lot of people now claimed they used to be Princes—on the way back to the Village. The man was coming to her rescue on his state-issued stallion, sporting his moderately-shining armour. He was, to say the least, upset and confused to see her out and about, but his good manners soon prevailed. He asked her to kindly turn back and return to the tower, because he really needed to save her on account of some curse-this-or-other, but she told him to kindly shove it for she had already saved herself. Which was no way for a Princess to talk, but she was not a Princess anymore, was she? (Or perhaps it was exactly the way someone who spent their formative years being waited on and thinking they owned half the world would talk. Hmm.)

The first thing she did upon entering her Village was to present herself before the CSGCOVWR, where she was informed that the dry grassroots movement was not dry as a metaphor for the dire ecological devastation that had lit a literal fire under the revolution, but because someone was siphoning water away from the village to irrigate non-state-sanctioned crops. Why? It made no sense; the State covered all their needs already. What want did they have for more crops, and so great a want indeed that they would steal their fellow villager's water?

The committee managed to identify the villager in question and proceeded to interrogate him. The man had been a great revolutionary, and a good comrade and friend to a large number of the CSGCOVWR members, so he was allowed to make his case calmly and without threats. The non-Princess thought him a kind man, with kind eyes and a weak heart. After a short-lived initial hesitation, he finally confessed that he had established the illegitimate crops in order to pay off a dragon who had a habit of frying his legitimate crops to a crisp if the villager did not do as the dragon demanded. The farmer resisted at first, but when the beast baked and ate his favourite goat in front of the man's terrified eyes, he gave in.

Upon hearing the man's testimony, the non-Princess noticed an unease spread through the CSGCOVWR. It was the small things: a scratching of the head, a twitch of the lips, an insistent cough tormenting a too-dry throat. So she pressed further, and finally it came to light that the dragon had terrorised a number of other villagers, and had managed to take a cut and hoard contributions from literally every operation in the Village: the crops, the dairy, the laundry, even the factory that produced the nettle-shirts for all the brothers who were turned into birds.

So the non-Princess did the only thing she saw could be done: she gave an impassioned speech about how they needed to band together once more and shake off the dragon's tyrannical yoke. (Which all turned out to be an extended metaphor after all.)

The People were moved. They dropped their tools and refused to continue production until they saw some real change in this Village. This strangled the flow of gold towards the dragon, which, in turn, soon forced him out of his lair, where he was met with daily picketing and a significant number of pitchforks and raised fists. And, as all revolutionaries know, dragons are merely as powerful and scary as our labour allows them to be—charred goats notwithstanding. The People were prepared to break some eggs and make some fucking dragonbaby omelettes. Not long after, the dragon was driven away—some say slain, but the revolution is only as violent as it needs to be, and, at the end of the day, who are you going to believe? The Villagers seized the dragon's hoard and re-redistributed the wealth. Committees were formed. Things were finally changing in the Village.

With the People in charge of the means of production, the Village prospered, or so they say. They even discovered that the nettle-shirt factory workers—women, for the most part, and now finally provided with protective gloves—didn't even have to keep silent as they wove; that had simply been capitalist propaganda of the heteropatriarchy, and the shirts produced by loud women worked for all the brothers who had been turned into birds just as well as shirts produced by women who kept their mouths shut. Who knew?

The People lived happily ever after. Of the ex-Princes and the non-Princess's father nothing is known; of the non-Princess herself nothing is known either, except to the degree that her fate overlapped with that of the People—for isn't that the true revolutionary's final task? To melt into the revolution and so be forgotten? And if anyone found indigestible the irony of having the non-Princess be the one to lead the People to revolution, that too was soon forgotten.

PORTUGUESE ESSAY

GEORGE TOM

I SPENT THE EVE OF MY THIRTY-NINTH BIRTHDAY READING *Portuguese Essay*. The novella came sealed with a little note; a present from a second cousin. On the cover, PANTHEON PRESS embossed so faintly that if I had not chanced upon inverted letters depressed on the underside, I might never have spotted it.

A lurid sticker on the Paris Green back announced: 'Experience the nineteenth-century memetic malware!' A card fell out, detailing the story's brief history with a warning.

I should've paid attention and considered the effects of this malware better, but I cared no more than a morphine addict cared about biochemistry. Whatever it was, I wanted the experience.

I read the story.

∞

Monochrome drowned under spinning jets of neon. In translation, the novella's message was as natural and obvious as breathing: words were corrupted with undesirable meaning. My mind, forever still and listless, was now a turbulent rainbow.

Hypnotically, I reached for the supplementary card and read.

∞

The story itself wasn't malware. Something about the translation, something between the lines, made me feel—a new language, a *neo-lingua*, that could bridge the divide between crude human-speak and precision mathematics.

I closed my eyes for a moment. Noise was resolving to become a stronger signal. And having changed, I continued.

I needed a language immune to connotations. I had never felt this way before. I wasn't a hobby linguist; I didn't care for language. I read the story again, and again, afraid it would fade away. It was as if *Portuguese Essay* were a powerful magnet that aligned a compass in my brain.

It wasn't simply the content; the book was perfect. Against sunlight, its diaphanous pages sheer fabric, garbling the text on both sides, like my mind. If moisture formed, the pages might have thinned further and dissolved. If I impulsively placed my tongue against the paper, it might've warped and stuck, imprinting on my tongue a communion of fading letters.

I fell asleep with the book in my hands and a quaint fragrance engulfed me, like that of a person I knew but never met.

In the morning, the message left as it had entered. Somehow sleep reset relevant parts of the brain. I opened the book, but a chemical reaction had rendered the paper black, the text now buried under indelible soot, its gossamer pages gliding on ash. I found the warning card, but it had the same affliction. There was no provenance.

I called my cousin and he asked if I enjoyed the present. I liked it very much, I said. *Did it disappear like they said it would?* he asked. Oh yes, it did, I said. Yes, it did.

He laughed and wandered off about his amorous exploits, indifferent to my interruptions. When he paused to breathe, I dropped the earpiece in its cradle.

Now no one would believe me, but this—this would finally

set me apart from the other billion, even if I had no witness. Life was no longer about wandering aimlessly, awaiting death.

This was the rock on which I would build my church. I had an anchor now. I threw the book away.

And then, like a child, I wept.

∞

Pouring over texts, I promised to strip my life away from the imperfect language. But searching for the truth in print, in the very language I was attempting to escape, was no more than miming and trying to convince my mirror image of its unreality; every action mirrored with equal and opposite determination. Still, for the brief flashes of understanding, imagined or otherwise, I read.

I refused to eat food with pre-anointed names. There were sufficient ways to make my unnamable food-blend palatable, but I had reasons. Between primal gasps and gagging were unadulterated cries of a new language. There was meaning in those sounds, virgin and barbarous and undefinable.

I smiled and cried again. It was like giving birth. And when I was done, I tried writing to define this experience, but it was a half-hearted exercise; I already knew it was impossible to formalise the language.

I began leaving the field 'NAME:' blank and stopped using names entirely. I felt liberated by some undiscovered law. I was drifting away from connotations.

But there were lapses on my part. It was impossible to fully separate myself from overtones. There were many instances I hadn't thought of, and ones that passed for many years unnoticed. I quickly gained proficiency in British Sign Language, but I still thought in words. When words receded, I realised how sign language only disguised my problem; I subconsciously thought of easier gestures I learned as 'good' or associated them with personally positive colours, like blue or green, while I mentally catalogued challenging ones as 'bad' in red or violet.

Secondary meanings tainted the very foundation of my attempts. *Portuguese Essay*. I had come to associate a new life with its name. This was an inward fault: I couldn't free myself and attain the perfect language unless I shook away inherent weaknesses. I tried everything at hand, but nothing worked for long.

The connotation fever flared and subsided in cycles. Gradually, my belief in the possibility of a pure language withered and died.

∞

Figure 1 Illustrates sample saturator used to determine pacemaker efficacy.

The scientific journal caught my attention. Researchers had made a pacemaker for the brain, controlling neural pathways in a programmed feedback loop. They were studying effects such as semantic satiation: repeating a word for so long that it lost its meaning. I read it again.

Like semantic satiation: repeating a word to yourself for so long that it lost its meaning.

I resisted the urge to read this again and again. It was irrational but I didn't want to lose the idea to itself. If the paper were true, one could use satiation to surgically reprogram language on a word-by-word basis. Strip language of its effluvium. Blank Slate. *Tabula Rasa*.

I was forty-seven, in possession of a sizable bank balance and a successful business in tailor-made pharmaceuticals. With no family to speak of, no one to stop me.

I called the research hospital and told them about my contacts in medicine and funding. Technology amplified under an ancient maxim: gates opened with money. We discussed every part of the operation. I fussed over the specifics.

After one of the hospital tests, I asked, 'What if I see an unfamiliar word?' 'Look away,' they said.

Their response was half in jest, but still, new words picked up with the pacemaker could become Portuguese Essay in reverse: one capable of crashing my efforts by infusing words with undertones of meaning.

They'd add a neurochemical rendition of a personal dictionary, so that when my vocabulary was stripped of extraneous matter a rigid definition would set in. Disassociation would happen millions of times over, weeding stubborn associations while I was in a medically induced coma. I'd then read a modified dictionary, cover to cover, so that the pacemaker could learn to suitably affect pathways.

When I thought of it, the effects of Portuguese Essay no longer surprised me. It was only an impersonal code and the brain a compiler. Without a reader it was only organised marks, as unimportant for the universe as the letters in my blood.

We had always drawn emotion from words: among letters there was a permutation for happiness and a permutation for belief; a permutation for euphoria and a permutation for suffering. There were still combinations of letters to induce a feeling we had not yet known, and another combination to give this expression a name.

Years ago, I'd watched a professor of anatomy hold reality in her hands. 'The human brain,' she said, 'is the most complex thing you'll hold, the only thing we know for certain exists.'

I wasn't against her solipsism, but anyone could've picked the statement apart. Step by step, she carved a person away. Somewhere, portions dissected might've corresponded to the regions of the brain she was using. When she was done, it was her belief that all those pieces had amounted to a person's reality.

∞

I counted the days to my surgery. The day arrived in a surgical gown, ready for the operation theatre. They marked a dotted ellipse on my shaved head. A nurse, hands on wheelchair grips: 'Ready?'

'Wait,' I said, pulling out a tissue on which I'd scribbled a few lines. Memory had played Chinese whispers with the story, diluting it to words that only might've been *Portuguese Essay*. But still, I'd made an exception and the paragraph was my prayer. If things went wrong, it was the last time. I crumpled the tissue. 'I'm ready.' Then they wheeled me away, to build a shrine in my brain.

∞

Slipping in and out, drowning and rising to the surface… antiseptic lights and the sweet burn of surgical spirit…flashing words on a screen… 'Read this one now, how does this word sound…? And this?' I was half-awake while they operated; the brain didn't feel incisions. 'He sensed the world, but he couldn't feel himself,' I said. 'He couldn't save himself.'

Then a screech and a crashing crescendo. An epiphany. And silence.

∞

[I awoke with a start; I couldn't bring myself to say 'incredible'. Against the firmament of my cognition there was only one 'incredible'. No baggage. Just one clinical definition. When I recalled previous usages, the void filled with disgust. Had anyone understood what I'd meant?]

[I peered closer and froze: how much of my thoughts had *I* understood? Even if there were only fractional changes in the meaning of my worded thoughts, over years, decades, deviations were frightening. I never subscribed to the Butterfly Effect but now the temptation was clear.]

∞

[There was a part of me issuing thoughts in a perfect language—the only version of a 'soul' or 'conscience' I'd accept—and I'd gone about perverting it into words. How many times had I created Babel?]

[My head spinning, people were saying things I couldn't entirely grasp. Their speech wasn't foreign but I couldn't comprehend their indifference to precision. They stoned me with blasphemy.]

[A thought came in loud and clear: 'You know, your thinking hasn't changed that much.']

[My thinking was largely unchanged except for a newfound awareness. Not that I wanted to be a cold thinking machine. If that had happened, a prisoner of my mind, I would've collapsed instantly.]

[I shot a question back: 'How are you doing this?']

∞

['We're using your dictionary to build sentences. The rest, whatever you're seeing, is your construction.']

[From behind came a soothing click-clack of mechanical keys. I couldn't turn around to see this elaborate typewriter, but at the fringes of my vision, on a green monitor, my internalisation came on in fuzzy but increasingly self-aware sentences. Trailing phrases nesting and twirling and looping. A bursting matryoshka in agony. It was like something Barosso might've written. Like the professor dissecting the brain.]

[And they're reading this now, and this, and this too...]

∞

[I must have had a stupid expression; everyone was smiling. They whispered something and the screen faded into static. Static. Again, I peered closer: Noise, snow, static. A channel slowly opened in my brain, and I remembered: the Indonesians called it *semut bertengkar.* War of the ants. *Purici* in Romanian. Fleas. So much better than 'static' or 'snow' or 'noise' for nervous iridescent dots. I tried simultaneously bending the thoughts to meet themselves and form a Möbius loop, but I stopped when I realised the doctors and technicians were unimpressed. The illusion of erudition was broken when they could read my thoughts as they formed. Perhaps before I did.]

['We were inspired by your monologues in between medical tests,' they said. 'And so the slate in your mind on which words appear is TABULA.']

[If I subvocalised RASA, the slate would clear, and any extraneous meaning I'd accumulated vanish. In this manner, I was free to read the world without worry. I named the itch of the bandages behind my ear 'ajdksd' and my groggy haze 'ysdtsw'. The white noise of the monitor became 'Lord, have mercy'.]

RASA.

∞

[Clean slate. The words fell into a meaningless string of letters. And then, like a child, I wept.]

A Kingdom of Seagrass and Silk

Cécile Cristofari

THE BOAT SWAYED, DRAWING NEARER THE ISLAND with the inexorable slowness of a spider climbing its gossamer lifeline. In normal times (if I could still remember such a thing), it would have taken us less than twenty minutes to reach the lighthouse. It had been nearly an hour today and the pebbles on the beach were just coming into focus. My son strained on the oars while the motor sat idle. Petrol had become too rare to hurry.

My breath caught when I shifted on the plywood floor, but I did not groan. I could not allow Maël to believe that he was leaving me in pain, or worse, that I was attempting to saddle him with the parting gift of guilt. From across the boat, Laurent glanced at me sympathetically. After all this time, I didn't need to make a sound for him to know when arthritis was gnawing at my bones. Instead, I leaned forward and brushed long strands of brown hair away from my son's face, as he turned his head to find a good spot to land. He smiled, lips tight. His cheeks were wet with brine.

At last we stopped, swaying softly. For a while I did not move, only watched, as that man of almost forty reviewed the packages piled on the floor of the boat. His long curls were still thick, tossing around his face where a pair of large brown eyes were all that remained of the baby I had once worn on my chest all day long.

'This one's fuel and matches. You should have enough for a couple of months, if you're careful. You'll be careful, right? Here, this one's pasta and rice. Make sure you keep them in their wrappings. If you get moths, there won't be any way to find more. The keys are here...'

I touched his back.

'I know, dear. We'll be careful with everything.'

Maël, my grown son, my little one, bit his lips and screwed his eyes shut.

'I have to do this,' he whispered. 'You understand, don't you? If you catch the disease they won't even let you through the hospital door. You're safer here. Almost safe.'

'I know,' I repeated.

You can never know when a grown child will, for once, tolerate a hug from his mother, the way he would have when he was no taller than my hip. But when I touched Maël's arm, he leaned towards me and let me hold him. His breath was calm, forced.

'We'll be perfectly happy here,' I told him.

He hugged me more fiercely in response. For a little while I did nothing but enjoy the moments we had left, pushing away everything we had left unsaid. There would be no coming back for us before the tide of the epidemic had ebbed again. Promises to save every life, at whatever cost, had rung loud and clear, once. It had not been long before no one had dared use that refrain any more, in the face of what was really happening. This would not be the first place in history where old lives were forfeited to give the young a chance. On the island, deserted after the ferries had been shut down and its inhabitants had left for places where food could still be bought, we could at least hope to make it.

I tried not to think that Maël would be going back in a matter of minutes, to work at the hospital where he was desperately needed. Where he would brush elbows with the virus every day, and have to hope masks would be enough to keep it away.

I watched Laurent and Maël unload the boxes and sat in the cold water, letting the sea soothe my sore joints. The island was not large, and we knew every stone and tree by heart. The only thing that was new about it was the silence.

∞

The click of the switch under my finger echoed a couple of times in the empty house, before I remembered that the power had been cut. Laurent was already forcing the shutters open, producing a long series of creaks. Little by little, the scent of eucalyptus and pine from the garden crept back and dispelled the cool musty smell of the closed rooms.

Afterwards, I walked to the end of the garden, where a short path led to the sea. Maël's boat was long gone, and the bay enclosed between the islands and the mainland had reverted to its mirror smoothness, unbroken by human presence.

Laurent walked towards me and put his hands on my shoulders.

'Do you think we could see his house from here?' he said.

We peered together, in silence. From here, all the houses on the mainland looked like tiny dots, his neighbourhood a maze of trees and fences.

'Too bad we didn't think of getting one of those solar chargers before they ran out,' Laurent said after a while. I took his hand and he squeezed my fingers, gently enough not to hurt.

'He'll come back when this is over,' I said. 'Now we just have to stop worrying or we won't last a week.'

'I hope he'll be able to stop worrying for us,' Laurent replied.

I nodded. He had been over the stocks of beans and pasta three times before I'd stopped him. There would never be enough to make sure we could stay on the island forever without starving. We could not afford to think of this as waiting time. However long this took, we were here for good, to make this island either our grave or our own little kingdom in the middle of the sea.

'How long since you last went fishing?' I said.

∞

Every joint in my body shrieked when I sat down. The first few days on the island had been gruelling. Finding food on our own was much easier in theory than it proved to be in practice.

Grinning, Laurent clinked his glass against mine. The water from the well tasted of dust and old age, and was the most satisfying drink I'd ever dipped my lips into.

'Who knew we'd manage to lift that huge stone?' he said.

He skewered a piece of sea lettuce on his fork, examined it for a while, then shrugged and bit into it. 'My eternal thanks to whoever planted that lemon tree,' he added.

I nodded. The raw flesh of sea bass drizzled in lemon tasted perfect. It had taken us time, but the lace curtains in our borrowed house had proven sturdy enough for our purpose after all. After countless tries, we'd dropped them on a school of bass, catching five in our makeshift net. We'd saved the bigger two for dinner.

As the sun set, lights began to dot the town on the other side of the bay, like fireflies coming to life. I was so absorbed in the rising lights, trying to make out one that might belong to my son, that I did not notice that Laurent had moved away from me and down to the beach. He had stepped into the water and was staring down, frowning.

'What do you think that could be?' he said.

I could see nothing but the trail of the setting sun in the milky opal of the sea. I rose, inch by inch, and then, when all my bones were aligned in a standing position and I was able to focus on something else once more, the sun dipped behind the horizon and all the sea came to life.

Around his feet the water had started to glow, blue-white spirals forming and dispersing like smoke. When I stepped in, the water stirred and bloomed with light in the dusk. I stared, too, for a very long time.

'Algae,' I remembered to say at last. 'Plankton. Something like that.'

'That's what makes this light?'

'Yes. Like tiny fireflies.'

We looked at one another. Smiled. Started at the same time towards the diving suits and snorkels we had left to dry on the beach after gathering sea lettuce.

The cold stung, but the suit kept the worst of it off, and I let myself relax into the water. I started moving, slowly at first, then more confidently, with renewed wonder at how much lighter my limbs felt, the pain in my joints soothing until it felt like a faint heat glowing in the background like the swirls around us.

There was hardly any light left from the sun. The reefs that festooned the shallows sank into darkness, and came alive again in blue-gold waves as we swam above and disturbed the bloom of plankton. Night did not dull the extraordinary clarity of the water. Five or six metres of sea might as well have been air, and we might have been flying there, carried by a soft, cold, glowing wind.

We were far out already. The bluffs where we had gathered seaweed earlier fell into a prairie of seagrass, dark lambent gold instead of brownish green. I waved to Laurent and, without waiting for a sign from him, dove, pushing the air from my lungs so I would sink faster.

A couple of fish started at my approach, uncovering a large, dark mouth near the sea floor. I swam a little closer. In the last push, a cloud of plankton illuminated the long, spiny body of a gigantic mussel, swaying along with the seagrass.

I hadn't dived in a long time. I was already out of oxygen, and I pushed hard on my diving fins to swim back to the surface.

Laurent watched me emerge with slightly pursed lips.

'Give me a word of warning before you do that,' he said. 'What did you want to see?'

Brine splattered my teeth when I spat out my snorkel.

'Giant mussels,' I said. 'I thought they were extinct around here.'

We swam back to shore. It was much darker now, and cold. We splattered a parsimonious measure of water from the well on our diving suits before entering the house. After days of use, the living-room still had the coolness of dormant stone. We had taken to sleeping with doors and windows open, letting the chill of the night caress our faces as we huddled together in our sleeping bags.

That night, with the full moon glinting through the French windows, Laurent said: 'They used to make cloth from giant mussels. You know, those threads they use to attach themselves to the bedrock? You can dry them and spin them. Sea silk, they called it. They ravaged mussels for sea silk in ancient times. And they still didn't manage to damage them as much as global warming did.'

I pondered that for a while.

'Let's take good care of those we have left,' I said.

I drifted quietly into sleep, as I had every night of our life on the island. When I woke up the next morning, I was still swathed in the shreds of a dream, one where I had sailed on the sea in a golden cloak, shimmering and shifting like the waves.

∞

The sun was setting again. Laurent and I stared at one another in silence for a second, then burst out laughing and spitting out pieces of acorn bread.

'This tastes . . . completely foul,' Laurent hiccuped.

'Completely. Why couldn't they grow chestnuts here?'

I tossed the rest of the bread on the compost heap. We would still have a way to go before we managed to process acorns into something edible.

'Let's see if there's any couscous left instead,' I said.

Munching on the dry grains, we watched for the first lights to come alive on the shore. We had not discussed how there seemed to be fewer as time passed, but it was becoming too obvious to pretend that it was only an impression. Every night, the constellation of windows and headlights grew sparser, darker.

'Do you think he's still at the hospital?' I said.

Laurent didn't answer.

It was this, I think, the way he kept his mouth closed as if the only other option was to scream, that cracked the wall I had spent days carefully building against the darkness. I covered my mouth, strangled back a sob, then couldn't strangle the rest. Laurent drew me against him and hugged me, fiercely. I don't know if he cried as well. I was so absorbed in my own tears that nothing else existed.

After that I got up, squeezed my husband's hand, and walked towards the sea. The sun was almost gone. But when I looked down, there it was again, blinking and falling in rhythm with the waves, the bloom of light of the plancton cloud.

'I'll just go for a swim. I'll be back.'

I slipped on the diving suit and the mask, and walked into the sea, cold pricking my ankles, then fading as water welcomed me, constricting my breathing in that gentle way that forced me to quiet. And I drifted forward.

I could never orient myself well while swimming. I followed the shore, every kick sending ripples of blue gold through the seagrass below. After only a few minutes, I was surprised to recognise the underwater bluffs and prairie. Scattered here and there were the thin dark mouths of the giant mussels.

After days of gathering sea lettuce, I had grown better at diving. I breathed out, just enough to sink, careful not to exhaust my lungs too soon. This time I could stay long enough to run my hand along the prickly side of the shell, feel the place where woolly strands connected it to the bedrock. I was out of air then. I swam up, took in the growing darkness, briefly wondered how cross Maël would be with me if he saw me dive alone at nightfall. I thought of his face when I told him the story, and smiled. And I dived again.

This time I snagged my fingers in the clam's filaments, and

pulled, gently. The shell swayed, but did not react when I pried a pinch of threads loose. They billowed in a golden cloud, tangling around my thumb. I kicked my fins and swam up.

Up there, there was nothing impressive about them, a few fine brownish hairs scattered across my palm. I hesitated. Then I dived back down.

There were more of the great upright shells dotting the seabed. I had no trouble reaching the next one, loosening a few more filaments and swimming up. It was completely dark now, the only light coming from the plankton. Underneath, the prairie was growing deeper. I wondered how far it would be before I had to give up and swim back to the shore. As far as I could see, the shells were only becoming more plentiful. A whole world waited below. Drifting there, limbs as light as clouds and pain almost forgotten, was intoxicating. I looked up to the stars, the Milky Way that, for a few days, had started to glow strongly again. One last dive. Then I would swim back.

I swam to the bottom, as far down as I could reach. When I looked up, everything had gone black.

I had a moment of panic. Then the darkness floated away. An undersea current ripped me from the shell and I tumbled even farther down, and before I even thought of how little air I had left in my lungs, I stared in astonishment, as the whale above me circled along the shore and disappeared into the depths.

I was out of oxygen and very cold. Heart pounding, I swam up, and back to the shore.

Laurent was standing there with a torch. He cried out and waved when he saw me. I kicked the fins faster, until pain jolted my knees. I was back in reality once more, with a handful of unnaturally thin hairs sweeping my palm.

'Are you all right? Put this on. God, Alice. Did you get lost? What happened?'

The thing he tossed on my shoulders was one of the dozen first aid blankets Maël had stuffed our emergency kit with. He had a hot mug ready. I didn't even think of the waste of our resources this represented. I grinned and kissed my husband, basking in the silly sweetness of the gesture, and a giddiness I couldn't quite explain.

'It wasn't cold,' I said. 'I just took a swim to the place where we found the giant mussels. Oh, and I saw a sperm whale.'

Laurent stopped.

'What do you mean?' he said, slowly, carefully, transparently attempting to hide his growing dread.

'Over there. Must have been deeper than I thought. It swam right past me and left.'

'That can't have been a *sperm whale*,' he said, wrapping the blanket more firmly around me.

'I think it was. Its belly was dark. It was too oblong for a right whale.'

This was not the answer he expected. He gently pulled me towards the house.

'Don't do that again, please,' he said.

I nodded, but promised nothing, and before I went to sleep, I laid the filaments to dry on a windowsill.

∞

It took Laurent a few days to accept that I was not going to stop my nightly dives. By this time, a thick handful of filaments were already drying on the windowsill.

Harvesting them was slow, careful work. I swam back home exhausted and aching, sometimes with coloured spots dancing in front of my eyes, when I had dived deeper than might have been safe. There were a hundred more productive ways I could have spent that energy, I knew. There were acorns to harvest and driftwood to collect and water to filter through layers of cloth. There was a house to clean and diving gear to carefully rinse and dry every day. There was no time for futility.

Perhaps I needed a purpose, something to carry me beyond our daily survival, beyond the dreaded hour when the sun set and we counted the lights on the shore, at first a galaxy, then constellations, dwindling to a handful of dots. Or perhaps I could not tire of watching seagrass billowing in the eerie lights of beings so tiny I could not glimpse them individually. I kept diving, mapping the seafloor so I wouldn't inadvertently hurt the molluscs by harvesting too often from the same ones.

It was late on one of these outings that I saw the sperm whale again.

Its massive black form occulted the prairie and drifted towards me. I swam to the bottom, out of the way, as fast as I could. I looked up to see the narrow jaw, the scars dotting its throat and fins, the small beady eyes that did not seem to notice me. Even if I hadn't been underwater, I would not have remembered to breathe.

Then the whale swam away. I was too deep, too far, running out of oxygen, and I did the single most unreasonable thing I could have. I followed.

Deep down, the plankton still bloomed in the wake of the whale, gathering in swirls of light behind its massive black shape. The sperm whale sank behind underwater buffs, my lungs burned, and just as I was about to swim back, I saw another shape.

It was long, uncannily so, slender and swift, with a light belly and a dark back. A fin whale, rising to breathe and floating just below the surface, then rising again before sounding the deep. I almost breathed in water. I kicked up, up, up, much farther than I thought I'd dived, and finally broke the surface, gulping in oxygen and darkness before looking down again.

Below, the sea stretched for thirty or forty metres, crystalline and unbroken, alive with the lambent swirls of the plankton. I had no idea where I was. My right hand was still balled tight around a handful of brown hairs, shining like strands from some golden fleece. A school of silver fish as long as my arms glided past. Deep down against the seafloor something brown glided, tentacles caressing the bedrock. It would be a gorgeous place to drown.

I didn't want to drown. I kicked my fins, trying not to let panic submerge me. My joints ached and I felt as if my lungs had shrunk underwater. When I saw the beach at last, with Laurent's torch going back and forth, I raised a hand and slowed down. He was waiting for me with a towel. He smiled, grudgingly.

'Nice swim?' he said.

I reeled when I stepped on the beach. My fingers were still tight around their bounty.

'I... I think I need to sleep. Let's go.'

I hugged the towel around my shoulders. The night was cool, but that was not why I was shaking.

I went to sleep as soon as I'd wrapped the covers around my body. Before dawn, I dreamed that I sailed over a shimmering sea where dark unreal shapes swam like angels, holding Laurent's hand, and that both of us had long cloaks of gleaming gold trailing from our shoulders, like emperors returning.

∞

The filaments had dried. Following Laurent's instructions—I had no idea how he could remember so many things—I'd washed them in lemon juice, and in clear water, until they shone a very soft golden-brown.

Making a spindle was a bigger conundrum than I'd expected, until, as I roamed the house racking my head for ideas, I happened upon a large, rusty screwdriver. The heft was just enough to gather momentum without breaking the delicate fibre. This was not my first attempt at spinning, though I hadn't tried it in a long time, and had never felt the awe of such precious material slipping between my fingers, inch by inch. After an hour or so, I had a tiny spool of thread coiled around the handle of the screwdriver, and the final fur-like strands ran at last, just as the sun went down. I hurried outside.

Laurent sat in silence on the small outcropping where we'd shared so many evenings. I clutched the screwdriver, and looked ahead.

A greenish-grey band of light lingered on the horizon. Overhead, we could already see as many stars as we would have during the darkest nights, centuries ago. On the other side of the bay, however, the mainland was completely dark.

My head swam. I sat, made myself breathe.

'The power must have gone out,' I said. 'They must have saved the last of it for the hospital. It makes no sense to keep lighting houses when there's a shortage going on. This means nothing. He's fine. Laurent, he's fine.'

I took his hand. He stared ahead, expressionless, and didn't respond when I squeezed his fingers, as hard as if I was drowning. I brought a hand to my chest. The ache was so strong that I felt it as if I'd gone back in time, the phantom weight of a small body cradled against my breast as he sank into sleep in my arms.

∞

The lights did not come back.

It would have been easy to sit there and do nothing, just wait for the horizon to send us a sign that the world out there was still going, still fighting. We had not been sent to this island to wait until life got back to normal. We had been sent because dying in the sun, bathed in water the colour of aquamarine, would always be preferable to seizing to death at the hospital doors. If Maël did not come back, when we died would matter to no one except ourselves.

But we did not give up. We ground acorns into meal and washed it in brine, then clear water, until we were able to eat it without wincing. We devised new ways to season seaweed. We burned driftwood and smiled when blue-green flames flickered, as if the sea was clinging to it to the last. I kept diving, though I stayed close to the beach, only going as far as I needed for one more handful of the sea's miraculous fleece.

The spool grew and grew, brighter and more regular as my fingers learned their way around the makeshift spindle. In the evenings I showed it to Laurent, who smiled as if we were sitting at home and I'd just discovered a new hobby in a wholly unchanged life. We sat and talked until there was nothing left to say, then enjoyed the silence before going to bed together. Little by little, our beings turned into the island, flowing and as serene as the sea.

One night I stayed up longer. I'd stopped trying to will the lights to go back on. Up above, the Milky Way was already waxing brighter.

'It's a bit late to go diving, don't you think?' Laurent said, yawning.

'Perhaps. I'll just take a walk along the beach.'

We parted with a light kiss. My knees and hips groaned, and I recalled the frustration and bleak helplessness I'd felt, when I'd first realised that my body would simply no longer cooperate the way it used to. After these weeks on the island, my body was still quite enough for what my life required. The pain had not faded, but it no longer drove me to distraction the way it used to. Perhaps I had learned to look old age in the face, at last.

My eye was suddenly drawn to an oblong yellow shape at the end of the beach. A couple of kayaks had been left in the sand, tethered near an abandoned house. I'd noticed them before, but had not seen how they could be useful. Now I walked closer, and realised that they were in perfect condition, two paddles arranged neatly on top.

It was too cold this late at night to get into the water, but the bay was smooth like a mirror. There would be no danger if I paddled close to the beach. With a grunt, I pulled one of the kayaks into the water, straddled it when it wobbled, and paddled, hesitantly at first, then effortlessly gliding away.

I would never cease to wonder at how perfectly clear the bay was. I decided that I would turn back as soon as I stopped seeing straight to the seafloor. Swirls of blue-gold light emerged in my wake, tangled in the lazy, swaying fingers of seagrass.

I didn't know how long it was before I realised that there were over twenty metres of crystal-clear water underneath. Schools of fish still swam close to the bottom, buoyed on a lambent wind. I looked back in alarm. I had gone farther than I'd intended, but the shore was still visible. I stopped paddling and watched the reefs drift underneath.

Just when I stopped telling myself to be rational, the large shape of the sperm whale loomed and almost brushed the bottom of my boat, dispersing clouds of plankton in its wake. My breath caught. I had never been a fast swimmer, but kayaks in calm weather were fast enough. I braced myself and followed, pushing my arms and back as fast as they would go, and followed the giant towards the open sea.

I was not fast enough. It broke the surface once, took a deep, shuddering breath, then sounded and disappeared. What came in full view then was enough to make me forget about the whale.

The sea was bottomless. Seagrass, aquamarine cutting on turquoise, still swayed on the bluffs, sixty or eighty metres below. The space between was churning. A pod of dolphins crossed, broke the surface as if I hadn't been there. Schools of fish, larger than anything I'd seen here before, weaved in and out of the reefs. The tremendous mottled shadow of a humpback cut across the waters to disappear into the bay. All around them, the glow of the plankton suffused the night in the quiet sea.

I turned around in a panic. Amazingly, the shore was still within reach. I paddled as fast as I could, clumsily, hitting the water flat and sending it spraying with every other stroke. At last I reached the beach. The kayak nearly capsized when I rose too fast, and I stumbled into the water, waded and ran to the house.

Laurent was already asleep. I shook him awake.

'I'm not crazy,' I said.

He groaned and stared, blinking.

'Come on. There's another kayak. Tell me you see it too.'

It felt like an eternity, but at last he got out of bed, grumbling, and followed me out to the water.

'It was this way. I think.'

'What do you mean, you *think*?'

I didn't answer. I knew there would be nothing. As soon as somebody else would be there to see it, there would only be the seafloor, and it would be proof that I had lost my mind. I simply wanted to know it for certain.

Plankton still glowed, that eerie blue-gold I knew now was nothing natural. The floor dipped. Laurent glanced over the side of his kayak.

'All right. I forgive you. This *is* pretty.'

He paddled faster, let his momentum carry him to my side, and took my hand.

'We're here. You're here. No matter what happens elsewhere ... you have no idea how terrified I was to not have you any more. At least we're safe from that.'

His voice was croaky from sleep.

'Remember the first time we brought Maël here? We thought it would be the most gorgeous place he'd ever seen. Instead he just had so much fun making bubbles in the water.'

'You taught him how to do that.'

'True. But it made you laugh the most.'

He squeezed my hand. I swallowed.

'Just a little farther out,' I said. 'If we don't see it, we can go home.'

Laurent nodded and followed me.

Underneath there came the dark face of the bluffs. We were flying, again, above fifteen metres of perfectly clear water. Then thirty. Then fifty. I paddled faster, pulled myself forward, as fast as I could, until the soreness was too difficult to bear and I stopped, gliding away above an infinity of light and salt.

And in the bottomless sea, they appeared again. First the long, tapered body of a blue whale, parting the waters miles underneath. Then a white pod of belugas. Then the familiar sight of a school of sea bass, incongruous in its mundaneness. Then it was an entire pod of bowhead whales, sending us reeling in their wake, and scaring away a giant squid that pumped its tentacles back towards the depth.

I looked at Laurent, expecting to see a blank, questioning face. Instead he was staring at the sea, with both hands on his mouth.

'What *is* this? Why didn't you tell me?'

'I told you,' I said.

'Yes. Well, don't brag. Oh my.'

Protected only by the flimsy shells of the kayaks, we ought to have been terrified. Any one of the giants cavorting in the depth could have sent us drowning without even noticing. Instead we felt as if the world had been suspended. There was nothing but the wonder of having been allowed to see the sea for what it really was, away from the years of destruction humans had visited upon it.

At last we paddled back to the shore. I dropped myself on the sand and vowed not to move for the next decade. Laurent sat next to me. Neither of us spoke for a long time. I looked at the kayaks, at the dark, quiet sea. I thought of what we had been allowed to glimpse, what could be ours for the rest of our lives if we stayed here, away from whatever was left of civilisation.

I thought of my dreams, Laurent and I sailing, cloaked in glorious gold from the sea.

'We have to go back,' I said.

He froze.

'I know he wanted to bring us here,' I went on. 'We shouldn't have accepted. For all we know, he's out there, and he's alone. He needs help. We should never have left him.'

'We can't go back now,' Laurent said. 'He said he would come back for us. If he doesn't...' If he didn't, there would truly be nothing to leave the island for, I thought he would say. I was wrong. 'If he doesn't, it's because he thinks we will be a burden. We can't act as if what he wants of us doesn't matter.'

'But what will happen when everyone decides that the best way out of this is to find a nice desert island and quietly wait until everybody else dies?' He shook his head, pursing his lips. 'We'll be careful,' I continued. 'We're not daft. We've been hiding for too long. It's time we went back and did our part.'

Laurent didn't answer. When I turned to him to argue some more, he was gaping.

Over there, the mainland was as dark as it had been for days. But on the edge of the shore, a glow flickered behind a clump of trees. Laurent ran home, and came back with a pair of binoculars. After a couple of seconds, he dropped them, shaking.

'I can't see which house it is,' he said.

He looked down at his hand. I had been squeezing it so hard the pain in my knuckles had alerted me before I realised what I was doing. I couldn't speak. I pleaded with my eyes instead.

'Yes,' he finally said. 'It's a lamp. It could be…'

Maël. We looked at one another for a while, unable to know if we ought to dance in joy, or cry, or yell.

'We *are* coming back, aren't we?' I said.

The thought was much scarier than paddling above an entire court of whales. We had no idea of the state the world was in now. We might as well have spent a couple of centuries on our own. But we had no other option. We were not young. We were not strong. Yet if we had managed to endure on our own, to befriend both the island and the sea in a way even our son could never have imagined, we certainly were not useless.

'How are we going to do it?' Laurent said. 'He's gone with the boat.'

'We have the kayaks.'

'And your arthritis. It's at least an hour to the other side.'

'I'll just have to try.'

I thought of my dream again, and then of the small uneven spool of silk wrapped around the handle of a screwdriver, which was all that weeks of diving had earned me. There would be no saviours landing in a shroud of gold on a shore ravaged by disease. Just two old folk who loved one another very much and would go look after their son, whatever it cost them.

Laurent smiled and pulled me close.

'Promise me you'll let me drag your kayak if you're in too much pain.'

'I promise.'

'Then we'll go. Tomorrow morning. Before the wind rises.'

I hugged him back. Hand in hand, we walked back to the house, and began packing. On top of the bag, I laid my spool of sea-silk, and I hoped that the world would be beautiful again.

THEO BALLINCHARD AND THE ORANGES OF POSSIBILITY

PATRICE SARATH

THEO BALLINCHARD HAD A FAIRYTALE CHILDHOOD, but as he was neither the eldest son who inherited everything, nor the youngest son whom the cat helped, but only the middle child who always made the wrong choice and then exited the story, it was rather less enjoyable than otherwise.

Down the wet and smoky lanes of Port St. Frey, where the sun never seemed to shine even on the brightest summer days, Theo grew up in the shadow of besmirched brick walls and blackened rafters. His mother and father quarrelled and drank and quarrelled more, and when they weren't berating each other, they were berating Theo.

Theo knew they couldn't help it. He was hapless, clumsy, and always did the wrong thing. Balto, his older brother, told him so. 'How is it, lard-ass,' Balto helpfully asked him, 'that you always do the wrong thing?'

His younger brother, Corsande, who had fair curls and an angelic face and therefore was beloved of all, always snorted in laughter at Balto's quips.

If Theo fought back, they mocked him for his feeble fists. If he tried any of the retorts that he thought of late at night, they roared with laughter.

So Theo went quiet. When his family noticed, they made fun. 'Oh Theo. Giving us the silent treatment, eh?'

Then he learned to make himself unnoticeable. It was a revelation when Theo realised he could cultivate this quality. His mother still saw him sometimes, if she bumped into him in their tiny tenement flat, and she never failed to shriek in alarm. 'Theo! You half scared me to death, you dolt! Make some noise, you cursed freak!'

But otherwise, if he ignored himself it would help anyone else ignore him, who might otherwise notice a pudgy lad in dirty clothes with a dirty face and dirty bare feet.

At first he stole food, and at first it was food that he understood. A bun, or a turnip or an onion. He would find a spot under the wharves at low tide and eat his stolen meal, look out at sea, and feel at peace.

Then one day at the market he saw a pile of oranges, fresh off a ship from the southern climes, and there was something about the brightness of the fruit, as if sunshine itself emanated from them, that drew Theo forward. He reached out and touched one, and it unleashed a scent of such glory that Theo forgot he was supposed to be invisible.

'Hey! Street rat! Bugger off!' The vendor shouted, and Theo jerked his hand back in alarm. The pile of fruit trembled and then the whole lot rolled off the table and bounced along the cobblestones. The vendor shrieked and the market exploded in a riot of shouting, and 'Stop! Thief!'

The calamity was as good as his talent for invisibility. Theo grabbed three of the oranges and ran, dodging the crowd, getting his toes trodden on, and finally escaping down to the harbour. He ducked under the wharf and climbed the cross rafters so he could perch unnoticed on the slimy sea-wracked structure.

He pulled an orange out of his pocket. He smelled it, as if the aroma were food itself. Then he bit into it. It was bitter on the outside and sweet and juicy on the inside. He filled his mouth with the sweetness and bitterness, and crunched the seeds. Then he smelled his hands again, closing his eyes in an ecstasy of taste and smell.

'Had the devil's own time finding you,' came a voice from above him. Theo froze, then looked up through the cracks in the boards. He saw hobnail boots, the hem of a duster coat, and muscular legs in leather breeches. 'Neat trick, that. Who taught you?'

Theo puzzled over that remark. Taught him to steal? That was the birthright of all of Port St. Frey's less fortunate. Surely the man knew that.

'No one,' he said cautiously.

'Well, you've got a knack and we can use it. Get up here.'

Theo didn't know what was about to happen, but he knew he couldn't avoid it. It was the fate of the middle brother. He climbed out onto the wharf and faced the man.

From this angle, the man was even more imposing. He was at least six feet tall, brawny, with black hair and snapping brown eyes. He had a dagger at his belt, a walking stick with a knob that looked like it could do a good bit of damage, and dirty lace at his throat. Theo waited for judgment and hoped it wouldn't hurt too badly.

'Go on,' the man said. 'Do it again.'

Oh. That. Theo didn't know if he could do it with someone looking straight at him, but he gave it a go. There was a long silence, and then the man whispered, 'Bugger me sideways.'

∞

The man's name was Kerrickan and he ran a ring of light fingers all around Port St. Frey. He soon had Theo doing second storey work on various jobs. Some were merchants' offices down on the harbour. Theo lifted coin, papers, bits and bobs of this and that. Then came the day that Kerrickan gave him a different assignment. He summoned Theo to his office, which was a nest above an unnamed bar on Tanners Row. There was another man there. Theo figured he knew what was coming next. When Kerrickan was in his cups he'd have Theo show off his talent to his loutish friends. They'd all shout with laughter and make personal remarks ('with a face like that, no wonder he doesn't want anyone to see him!'), and Theo would go invisible in his mind too, just to get through it.

'Theo, my boy,' Kerrickan said, 'We have a job for you.' He looked at the man. This man was far better dressed than Kerrickan, and he had a look about him that said quality. He was fair-haired and he had an expensive watch fob across his waistcoat and a silver ring with a big green stone on his pinkie finger.

'Can you read, boy?' the man asked.

In fact, Theo could, a skill that his brothers often teased him for. But in this case he didn't know if it was better that he could read or couldn't. He looked at Kerrickan for help. Kerrickan nodded at him, so Theo nodded at the man.

The man produced a piece of paper. He borrowed a pencil stub from Kerrickan's wooden table and wrote on it, then handed it to Theo. 'Read that for me.'

'Official Merchants Guild of Port St. Frey Trading Charter,' Theo read.

'Like a perfesser,' Kerrickan said. 'Told you.'

'It would do no bloody good if he stole the wrong thing,' the man said. 'Right, boy. Here's what we need you to do.'

∞

Three nights later, under a clouded half moon casting diffuse light, Theo stood outside one of the grandest merchant houses on the High Crescent in the shadow of a high stone wall. He looked through the gate at the colonnaded portico. There were two lanterns at each side of the front door.

House Jardins had all modern security. There were two men patrolling the house, and the locks had been made special by

Tolle & Sons, the finest locksmiths in Port Saint Frey, whose designs were unpatented, the better to keep their inner works secret. He had been briefed on this by the man of quality, and Kerrickan had added his bits of wisdom from his days when he was the boy and he worked for a master. Now Theo waited, and the night air off the harbour was chill, even here high above the city. But it smelled nicer here, and he breathed deep. He smelled sea air and pines, not sea air and sewage or rotting fish, or drink, or urine, or untanned hide.

I'd like to live here, Theo thought. An emotion he could not name ran through him, wistfulness with a side of longing. Somehow it reminded him of the first orange, and the possibilities that it opened up for him. Then the High Crescent night watchman called out, 'One of the clock, and may all be well!' And that was his signal.

A man popped out of the front door at the Jardins house and doused the beaming lanterns. Theo's eyes adjusted to the dark, and when the man went inside he scrambled barefoot over the stone wall and dropped onto the grounds. Theo stole around the side of the house and went up the drainpipe as fast as a rat. On the third floor, he pushed up a window and squirmed inside.

He was in a hallway dimly lit by the moonglow. Theo followed it, his bare feet padding along rich carpet. At the third door, he turned the knob. The door was locked, but Theo had been taught the secret to the Tolle & Son mechanism by the man of quality. He soon had it open and darted inside. He closed and locked the door behind him.

The room was small, stuffed with a rolltop desk and a chair, and large cabinets lining the wall. The helpful moonglow provided enough light to see by.

Working quickly, Theo picked the lock on the desk (another Tolle special), scanned the papers, found the roll of documents the man of quality wanted, and then replaced them with the sheaf of papers in the rolled leather case he'd been given. Easy peasy. Theo put the stolen papers in the case, and went to unlock the study door when he heard men's voices.

He backed away and looked around. There was nowhere to hide. He could go invisible, but if someone bumped into him, the jig was up.

A key rattled in the lock. Theo made a middle child's decision—i.e., his only choice, doomed to fail—and unlatched the window. He scrambled out as the door was opened.

'Hey! Stop! Thief!'

Theo looked back at the two men. He stood on the tiny stone lip and edged away, his fingers and toes gripping for purchase. It took a moment to gain control over his invisibility but he knew he had done it when he heard someone shout, 'Where did he go?'

'Must have fallen. Call the night men—see if they can find his body.'

While the alarm was raised and the lanterns and candles were lit all over the house, Theo Ballinchard plastered himself against the stone wall of the grand mansion and shivered in the cold. At length, he forced himself to get moving, inching around the house. The stone of the house was slick with sea air. Theo's fingers slipped and he almost fell, and he realised that he would fall to his death before he reached the drainpipe.

He came to another window with a bit more ledge. He pushed at the glass with hope, and it rattled a bit, but it was latched. He dug for his small knife, and used that to shim between the sash and lift the latch. It took a bitof doing, but he finally got the window opened. He slid inside the room.

This was a child's bedroom. There were toys and books. A rocking horse, with real horse hair for the mane and tail. A fireplace with a low, cosy fire, emitting warmth and no smoke at all. There was a lump in the bed: a still, sleeping form. Theo felt his heart race, but whoever it was had not been woken by his antics. So he calmed down and had a think, but he was distracted by the room.

It was nice and cosy in this room. Theo knew the quality had more things, better things, than the tenement folks, but he hadn't known those nice things included fires that didn't smoke. Or sea air that just smelled of the sea, and not the rest of it. Quality meant they had all the good bits.

Theo didn't mean to, but he set his hand down on a small hairbrush on the dressing table. Before he knew it, the small silver brush was in his pocket, as if it had jumped inside on its own.

He heard footsteps coming down the hall, and the hushed voices of women. They were still whispering as they came into the room. He faded into nothingness. Two ladies, one in a snug wrap and one in a servant's dress, crept inside.

'See, ma'am? She's not been disturbed by all the hullabaloo,' whispered the servant.

'Oh, such a relief,' said the lady. She scanned the room, passing over Theo without pause. 'Even so, let's keep her in bed tomorrow, in case she had nightmares without knowing it. I would love to kiss her on her little cheek, but I would only wake her. Oh dear, did the window come unlatched again?'

She tiptoed over to the window, brushing past Theo, latching it firmly. 'There. Let's go, before the dear thing wakes.'

Although most initiative and curiosity had been beaten out of Theo over the course of his young life, a suspicion wakened in his breast. He waited until the servant and the mother left the room with their candle and closed the door behind them. Then he went over to the bed and pulled down the covers. Sure enough, there were two pillows and a lace night cap, but no daughter.

A giggle from across the room caught his attention and he turned. A girl materialised out of the shadows by the fireplace. She was Theo's age, about twelve, and she had long straight hair in two braids. She was in a night gown, all cosy flannel and cotton.

'I thought I was the only one who could do that,' the girl said, appraising him frankly. 'Are you the reason every one's in a fright?'

Theo was well aware that he had a sheaf of stolen papers in his coat and a silver brush in his pocket. Sometimes, there was no choice to be made at all. 'Yes,' he said.

'Well, you can hide here until it all dies down. I meant to go out, and was preparing to, but then came all the shouting and I knew I wouldn't get far, even with my small talent. I have to focus, you see, and at the slightest distraction, whoosh, there I am again. Then you came along. Would you like the brush? I don't like it very much.'

He took the brush from his pocket and laid it back on the table. He knew that she was being kind and it confused him.

'It helps if you forget who you are,' Theo said.

She understood immediately. 'Oh, is that how you do it? But then how do you come back to yourself?' He was at a loss. He didn't know. 'Well, I think it's lovely,' she went on at his silence. 'I will practice. I'm Felicia Jardins.'

'Theo Ballinchard.' Was he supposed to bow? Or curtsey? 'Why do you go out at night?'

She grew sad, and went and sat down on her bed. She patted the bed next to her and he sat there. The bed was soft and smelled of her and of fresh linens.

'They keep an eye on me at all times during the day. I was very sick as a baby, and mother has always been frightened for my health. So I'm cosseted during the day, and the only time I have is at night. At first I just crept along the hallways. But now I go out into the garden. I'm quite brave. One day, I'll go down to the harbour. I am sure you think I'm not brave at all, though.'

To Theo, bravery was overrated. 'Why do you want to go to the harbour? It smells.' It occurred to him that she wouldn't know that.

She muffled a giggle. 'Does it? Well, even a bad smell is better than being stuck in here.'

That settled it; she was a lunatic. Theo got up. 'I should go.'

'Must you? Will you come back?'

Of course not. 'I—guess,' Theo said.

'Good. Here—I'll show you the best way out.'

She took his hand and led him through the halls. First they went up a half flight into the attic, and then down a set of rickety stairs. At each creak she stifled a giggle, until Theo was hard put not to laugh himself. He couldn't remember the last time he'd laughed. At the bottom of the stairs, she opened a small door in the garden wall. It was draped in ivy, barely visible in the dark.

'This is better than the drainpipe,' she said. 'I discovered these stairs on my jaunts and they are quite unused.' In the moonlight her pale face was animated. 'You will come back, won't you?'

'I will,' Theo said.

∞

After the clean smell of the sea air on the High Crescent, Tanners Row was particularly noxious. Theo covered his mouth and nose with his scarf, which barely helped. He hoped to make his delivery quick, then off he would go to his current hidey, in the crawl space of a spice merchant's warehouse behind Aether's Coffee House. There was a small light shining in the window of Kerrickan's office above the bar. Theo trudged up the stairs and went to his boss.

Kerrickan was sitting still in his big chair, his head cocked at an attitude, as if to say, Well? Theo pulled the rolled case from his coat and held it out.

'Got 'em, boss,' he meant to say, but his words failed him. As his eyes adjusted to the dimness, Theo realized that the dark spill down Kerrickan's neckerchief was blood, and Kerrickan's eyes were not staring at him but staring into eternity. Theo felt rather than heard the knife slicing through the air at him, and he went inside himself and rolled, so the knife only nicked his ear. He ran.

He lost his pursuer with ease, and watched from the shadows as the man cursed and ran up and down the alley, trying to find him. Then Theo walked over to his hidey, hunched against the wet cold, the rolled case still in his hand.

∞

For the next couple of days, he laid low and listened as the word on the docks were full of Kerrickan's death, and in Aether's, the gossips were full of the business of House Jardins. They had tried to renew their trading charter with the Guild, but their papers were arrant forgeries, and so House Jardins was drummed out of Port St. Frey. The family had left, the gossips said, gone to Ravenne to live in exile, their trading house and ships now belonging to the Guild. He wondered if Felicia still practiced her invisibility.

Theo kept the papers under the floorboards in his hidey. It made no sense for Theo to think about his future. He was only twelve, or maybe eleven, he never truly knew. There would be no happily ever after for the middle son. But he knew the papers represented something that he wanted, if he could only hold on to them long enough. So he waited and listened and finally knew it was time to take his place in the world again.

Theo got a job emptying slop and washing barrels at Aether's, and he listened to the investors gossiping over their coffee, and learned a thing or two. He learned that a certain man of quality had been nosing about for a boy, a boy like Theo. One investor eyed Theo particularly hard, and Theo thought the jig was up, but then he heard that the man of quality had gone on a long journey, and that investor had invested in the expedition and did not expect the man to return any time soon. Or at all.

Theo kept his head down when he heard that, and his heart eased a bit.

Months passed. And one night, he decided to chance it. Theo went back to the High Crescent, to the Jardins house. He pushed the ivy aside and ducked inside the garden. The house loomed in the darkness, an empty, silent hulk.

Theo sat down on a stone bench, and looked around. There were statues and huge stone planters with trees in them. Everything was overgrown. He heard creatures peeping but he didn't know what they were. It was cold, but he was protected from the wind. He smelled a familiar scent, and looked around for it. Under glass, illuminated by moonglow, was a small orangery with three spindly trees. Somehow one puny fruit had survived, silver in the moonlight. Theo went over to it, and breathed deep. Saliva flooded his mouth, but he didn't pluck the orange. It didn't seem right.

∞

The story of the middle child never ends in 'happily ever after'. Theo's life went on as it ought. He worked at Aether's. He met Ned Mederos and became his partner—some say in business, some say in crime, some say both. He kept the trading charter hidden, not even telling Ned. He saw his brothers and parents now and again, but Balto had grown even more of a bully, and Corsande had become crueller than before, and his parents thirstier than he thought possible, so Theo let them go, though it is another kind of fairy tale to think we can ever be free of our beginnings.

Fifteen years passed. Theo was in Ravenne for Ned, and he was walking along Merchants Street when he saw a sign. Jardins Trading and Mercantile Emporium, it said. Theo stopped dead. He forgot his commission for Ned. With a shiver of anticipation, he stepped inside the shop. It was a busy place, like a market under a roof, with goods of all kinds from all over the world at his fingertips. Theo scanned it all and was a kid again.

'Can I help you, sir?' came a voice behind him. He turned. Felicia Jardins smiled at him, an expression that turned quizzical and then aghast with recognition. Theo hadn't changed that much—the round-faced boy had become a round-faced man, fond of his dinner, and he wasn't tall. She had grown, but hadn't become willowy as girls of her station were supposed to, and her face was as thin and pale and pinched as he remembered. She wore an apron over her plain wool dress, and her dark hair was braided in two sombre plaits looped over her ears.

'Do you remember how?' he said.

She flushed, and nodded. 'Yes. Your advice worked. And you?'

He hadn't had much use of his talent. He had become invisible in other ways—the chatty, bumbling, stout partner of the more charismatic and dangerous Ned Mederos. No one noticed Theo any more, and he found he liked it that way. But it was like riding a dandy horse. He hadn't forgotten. So he nodded.

Theo and Felicia stepped aside, moving as one. They were alone in a sea of customers, all talking, exclaiming, picking up goods and setting them down, pawing through sales bins, and treading on discarded items. He reached out and took her hand in his. It fit perfectly, and they smiled.

No one saw them go.

Lovers on the Yuleton Lip

Aliya Whiteley

IT HAD ALMOST BEEN THE END.

She held on to his hand and he pulled her along, even when she couldn't catch her breath, even when all the air seemed to have been sucked out of the night sky, until they reached the lip. And for a moment Ella thought he wouldn't slow down. He could have pulled her over the edge, and she realised that she wouldn't let him go alone. She would have fallen with him. For him, really. So he didn't have to be alone.

But he stopped, and let her hand go, and she doubled over and gasped for some length of time, a minute maybe, in which it became clear to her that they weren't going to jump after all. He must have realised it too, because when she straightened up he was smiling. She loved his smile.

'Noel,' she said.

'Do you think he's really down there?' he said.

Which changed everything real, everything pressing, into the theoretical. It created a space where she could hide from reality. But such spaces don't last forever.

Unlike Yuleton.

∞

Yuleton was a town, a job, and a way of life for its inhabitants; it was the provider and the protector, sealed and self-sufficient. An unchanging home of red and white, with the motto of MERRIE TIMES printed at the top of every edition of the town's newspaper. It was the past and future for those caught within it, with no way of leaving. It was a giant present that could not be returned.

On the first day of a new term at the university, Ella was aware of the whitening of certain strands of her hair. Not all of it: just the beginnings of visible aging. It would, eventually, turn completely white, like snow. And then it would stay that way forever, until she eventually tired of it all and made her final journey to the lip.

As a lecturer, surely a little white around the temples suited the gravitas she was meant to bring to that role. She no longer felt impressive, even if she looked the part, striding down the corridors in her hat and wrap, or lifting her chin to make certain of being heard by the back row of the auditorium. What was it that kept the students from ignoring her, or laughing at her? Her suspicion of her own ridiculousness—spouting about things in which she was not sure she believed—should have been displayed upon her, written into her skin. But no, the students bought it, and wore their red and white with pride, their own hats pulled and pushed into rakish angles on their heads but never quite removed, never daring to be all-the-way removed. The uniform was, after all, compulsory. They believed in wearing it. They believed in it all.

∞

Did she believe it, back when she was a student?

She had been very young. So many years later, she felt she had finally learned to appreciate that the young believe all things equally. Noel had been young, too. She could hardly remember him in a way that could be described as anything but sketchy. Besides, his youth defined him, as it did all the children who lurked in her memories.

Ella had met Noel at Dropmas, the ceremony of the presents. She had been waiting to take her gift to the lip, and there he had been, beside her. She couldn't recall seeing him before. They weren't in the same class, and she was an insular child, walking everywhere with her eyes on the floor. She never had liked to look up, and may have passed him hundreds of times without knowing it. But this time he caught her attention, and held it.

They were meant to be jolly, singing songs and exchanging smiles, but even back then Ella struggled to conform with those expectations. It occurred to her, years later, that she had been placed in a group of similar troublesome, withdrawn students for the ceremony; she had tried hard to picture the others, but could only remember Noel's straight back, Noel's badly wrapped present. He was plucking at one untidy corner, ripping the paper a little. Her own present was immaculate, of course, with a bow. Even if she hadn't been a happy wrapper she had prided herself on being an accurate one.

'Good job,' he had said.

She had jerked her face up to his, and stared at him. 'You too,' she said, even though it was not true, obviously a stupid thing to say, and he nodded, and said, 'Okay, yeah, okay,' then, 'Do you ever get the feeling you don't belong here?' He looked around, at the singing and the proud generations, the bobbing ocean of hats and the rocking chime of the bells. Then the queue of children before them moved forward, fast, and before Ella could think of a reply they were on the lip itself, that drop into eternity, the cold wind hitting their faces, bringing tears to their eyes.

He threw his present first—well, just let it go, really, dropped it without ceremony, and it was gone into the dark like a stone. He did not gaze after it, did not take his time at the edge of the cliff where Yuleton ends and nothing begins. He simply strolled away, and the thought of that was uppermost in Ella's mind when it came to the dropping of her own present. She had built it up in her head, had a picture of how she would make the most of the moment. Her gift, her throw. It went perfectly, pleasingly, the present making an arc into the sky, then disappearing into the dark. It should have filled her with delight, but she realised she didn't quite care as she had when she was a little girl. And then it dawned on her that she was ready to be not so little any more.

She had walked away from the crowd too, and found him standing on his own, looking up at the sky, the snowflakes, the lights of the town. Some emotions are instant and binding. *Look at me, bound to him still*: Ella thought, as she sat at her desk, waiting for the first bell of term. *Bound to the memory forever.*

∞

She was surrounded by the detritus of her long office life, going back over the slides for her lecture on tradition, given to every first year group.

WHAT IS THE YULETON TRADITION?
MERRIE TIMES
RED AND WHITE WORK
NOTHING LIKE THE PRESENT
GIFTS FOR THE KING
WHEN YOU'RE READY TO GO

They knew it all already, but she hoped to open the door to thinking critically about the stories they had been told since they were tiny.

Yes, there's nothing but the town, and beyond the town there is nothing. Yes, we have to fight off the swallowing emptiness of the void beyond with our red and white trim, and our happy faces and willing work ethic, and yes, we must placate the king who lives at the bottom of the lip. But how do we do all this?

It was her opening speech, year after year. Sometimes she had the feeling a few of the students even connected what she was saying, how she was questioning, to their own deep-seated disquiet. For didn't a few of them go through that stage? It was a reaching out, in loneliness, in hope, on her part.

There was an hour to go before she would stand before them

and deliver the presentation, and she realised she could not sit and wait for it, the commencement of another long year; she got up, found herself walking fast through the corridors, dodging students and staff to make it outside into the implacable and familiar snow.

She thought of heading to the lip—just to see it—but instead walked in the direction of the student campus, along the riverside. She had lived in one of the houses there once, with three other students she barely connected with. Noel's disappearance had left her raw. At the time she had been blanketed in guilt, in sadness. As she stood before her old house once more, Ella was surprised to find those emotions didn't touch her.

She took a seat on an iron bench close to the river and remembered the view. The path of the ever-icy river had once seemed fast, rushing past her. Now it felt timeless, endless—a force of stability. She had survived those emotions, when he left. She had studied, and passed her exams, and become a lecturer in the absence of better options. She was still here.

But where was he?

Ella often hoped he had found a way to leave Yuleton—a secret path out of the town, to a different life entirely. But in her worst moments she knew he had thrown himself over the lip, on his own, because she had refused to go with him. And he was caught in the act of the drop still, in her mind. He would forever be falling over the lip, and it was unbearable. It was an idea that could not be banished. Simply living with it, being in the grip of that vision in which he fell down and down, was no longer an option. There had to be rest, somehow.

She got up from the frozen bench and started walking once more, quickly, to keep out the cold. She should have returned to the hall to give that opening lecture, but it felt unlikely that she would ever manage to speak those familiar words again.

It was time to return to a street, and a house, she had been avoiding for years. She would be far from welcome, but there was no other choice.

∞

When nobody answered the door Ella took the side path to the family workshop and found everyone there, lined up in their uniforms, each doing their task to create a stack of wooden trains, painted brightly, with green wheels and a little blue driver in each cabin. They were doing well for early morning; Ella estimated there were already at least thirty trains in the pile, waiting to be boxed up and wrapped. Mother, father, and the seven children in the family business. The grandparents and the earlier generations had all made the jump, but even with quite a small workforce there could be no doubt they'd meet their quota. She was grateful, once again, for having stayed in higher education instead.

They looked up as one, hammers and saws paused, and stared at her.

'Ella,' said Noel's father.

'Hi.'

His mother dropped her paintbrush. 'Ella,' she said. 'What are you—?'

'I just wanted to say hello.'

It sounded so ridiculous.

'We're busy,' said his mother.

'We're always busy,' said his father. 'Come on, come on in, I'll make hot chocolate, everyone else can crack on. Back to it.' She followed behind him, to the back door of the cottage, aware of the sounds of work resuming behind her, and the murmurs of their voices. Inside, everything was as she remembered it: the cosy kitchen, the smell of baking, and the sparkling decorations strung from the beams. Noel's father stoked the fire from its embers and put the kettle on the stand.

'Take a seat, sit down, sit down, you look cold,' he said. 'That cloak not as warm as the overalls, huh? I'm always toasty in my overalls.'

'Thanks,' she said, and sat at the table. She was not cold at all, but had no doubt she looked tired, white-faced. It was so exhausting to be here, to be facing these things. 'Can I talk to you? About Noel?'

He nodded, then took the chair opposite hers, and smiled. At first he had seemed just the same to her, but now she could see how his beard was longer, whiter, and his cheeks thinner. How round and rosy they had been, once. 'It's a long time to wait to have a talk about this.'

'A long time,' she agreed.

'I was expecting you earlier. You always did have that look about you. Like you'd go over yourself, sooner rather than later. Betty and I both did. We expected to lose Noel to it, and you'd go too.'

'I—couldn't,' she said. 'I wasn't sure.'

He cocked his head, as if he hadn't quite heard her. 'Not sure? About what?'

'I just mean that...'

'Yuleton life isn't for everyone, of course, of course. That's why some go earlier than others. But the really young ones, that is a shame. Difficult for the parents.' He spoke as if he wasn't one himself. 'Anyway. What did you want to ask?'

'I—I just wondered if you ever pictured him. Serving the king. In a different way.'

'Of course!'

'What is he doing? When you picture it?'

He squinted at her. 'I hope you're doing your best by those young ones, not filling their heads with doubts. That's the last thing we need. We're doing our bit.'

'I can see that. Working very hard.'

He sat back in the chair and crossed his arms. In the silence that followed, the kettle began to hiss, winding itself up to a boil.

What had she expected? To find like minds, here? She knew how Noel had felt he didn't fit in with this family, with their ethics and devotion, and his disappearance had not changed a thing. Their belief was so strong, so solid. She envied them. It was the best way to suffer loss—in the certainty of its meaning.

Still, even while knowing she could not get the answer she

wanted, she had to ask the question she had come here to ask. 'When Noel... went, was there any chance that he didn't go over?'

'Didn't go over the lip? Where else is there to go?'

'Did he take possessions with him? Could he have left Yuleton instead? Found a way out?'

'Other than the lip?'

Of course, it was hopeless. 'He never contacted you again, then. And he didn't take anything.'

'Ahhhh,' said Noel's father. The emotion in his eyes changed, softened. He reached his hand across the table. 'Dearie, he's never coming back. I had no idea you'd missed him so much. But you mustn't fool yourself. This is the real world. When people jump, they never come back up.'

The kettle began to boil, tentatively. Then the sound strengthened to a whistle.

'Let me get that,' he said, then, 'You know, it's not such a bad thing, the way it turned out. Who knows why some of us can't take to the life? The more I've thought about it, the more I've decided that some of us are just made that way. It's like the toys we make. You put in so much love and work, but a few of them are just... defective. But we all still have our uses, don't we? All of us.' He pulled back his hand, stood up, turned away.

'I should go,' said Ella. 'I'm sorry. I have a class to teach.' She let herself out of the back door and slipped away before the old elf could speak again.

∞

They had enjoyed their long conversations when they were given the chance, but there was always the feeling that everyone was keeping an eye on them, interrupting if they got too intense. Thinking too long and too hard about things was never encouraged. At the time they took it for some sinister undertone of control, but Ella wondered, in hindsight, if it was simply to try to make them see that there was no point in obsessing over the situation. Yuleton was everything, and that was the end of the matter.

'Do you really think he's down there?' Noel had said to her that night, as they looked down over the lip. They'd been together for a few weeks, but it felt like a lifetime.

There was no way to comprehend the size of the emptiness beyond. It simply went on and on; it had no quantity. Elves were not big or small beside it. Their size was irrelevant. Their ideas were irrelevant.

'I don't know,' she had said.

She suspected, as she lay in bed that night running back through the past, searching for some key to unlock her own certainty about what came next, it might have been the most honest thing she had ever said.

'That's it, isn't it?' Noel had smiled, without reservation, at their own cleverness. 'We don't know. So how come everyone says they know? They really know?'

She thought about it for a while. Then she said, 'Because that's safer.'

∞

Ella had so often told her students:

The King of Yuleton lives at the bottom of the lip, and he takes our gifts, all of them, with gratitude and with love. He takes us, too, when our time comes, and he finds new work for us. In return he protects this place, this haven, from the endless nothing that would consume it. He is the reason the snows fall and the cottages stand. He keeps us safe and keeps us still.

But now she dreaded opening her mouth at the head of lecture hall and hearing herself say:

The King of Yuleton might live at the bottom of the lip, and he might want our gifts. Or he might not. It might be that this place is not protected by anything. Maybe it has been forgotten by everyone and everything. You have to ask yourself—are you willing to believe in him in order to maintain your faith in the idea that we are safe, that we are still? Or do you need more than belief?

She had to make sure she never said such things aloud to them. Noel's father was right. They did not need her doubt, her pain. So she got up, and made the last walk to the lip.

The sign, just set back from the edge, read:

YULETON LIP
102 SLEEPS UNTIL DROPMAS

She walked past it, remembered all the presents she had dropped before, each one wrapped so carefully. She had worn her best clothes for every Dropmas. She didn't intend to change her strategy now. Her pointed hat was bright red, saved for best. Her cloak was edged with white.

Ella approached the lip on tiptoe, barely daring to breathe. Dawn was close, and the relentless snow was falling heavily, catching in her eyelashes, numbing her face. She had taken the longest route, making her way around the perimeter of the town one last time, following its curved transparent walls, too high to cross, too hard to break. She found no holes, no escape. Noel did not find another exit. There was no other way out of this town.

She put her toes to the edge and looked down.

This was it—the precipice of her belief.

The big nothing.

She tried not to think of Noel's family, nor her own long line of unbroken family, sleeping in their little beds all night, creating in their workshops all day. She tried not to think of her students, and the questions they might need answered. She couldn't give any of them what they needed, anyway.

A deep breath.

Jump.

No time for thought, for feeling, no feeling but the falling of the stomach, the wind against the body, so cold, falling faster than the snow, and then—

She bounced.

She hit something, something that gave under her, absorbed her, and at the moment when she thought it would swallow her it flung her up into the sky, back towards the lip, and the sensation of flying, of gaining ground, came over her and delighted her. She laughed, and the force of the motion snatched the laugh away, then left her, and she fell once more, fell down, to be cushioned, each bounce getting a little less energetic, a little softer, until she came to a stop.

Resting on a giant cushion, so far down and away from everything she had known, Ella breathed out and relaxed utterly.

'HELLO THERE,' said a voice so deep, so loud, that it rumbled through her like an earthquake.

She sat up. The cushion was vast, and deep, and red. It spread away from her in every direction, for a distance so huge that she couldn't begin to understand it. Everything sloped down from her vantage point.

'ANOTHER LITTLE PRESENT,' said the voice. She put her hands to her ears to try to make the volume bearable.

'Are you the king?' she shouted, aware it could be no more than a squeak to this being.

A fresh rumbling shook her so hard she had to lie down again. An enormous shape moved across her, casting her in shadow, then swooped lower. A bird? No—a hand. A great hand, coming for her, and she screamed as it came to a stop, only inches above her.

'HOP ON,' the voice said. 'I KNOW JUST WHERE TO PUT YOU.'

What choice was there? She found her balance on her hands and knees, then crawled onto the palm, marvelling at the rough lines, the hard texture. Was this the hand of a craftsman? It reminded her of the hands of those who spent a lifetime in the workshops, like her family, like Noel's family.

'Where's Noel?' she said.

'FULL OF QUESTIONS, ARE YOU? THOSE ARE MY FAVOURITE.'

Emboldened, she asked them all. 'Where's Noel? Where's

everyone? Where do we go after the lip? Are you the king? Are you in charge? What's next? Why do we all have to work? Why does it always snow?'

How like a child she was, and how stupid she sounded.

'I TAKE ALL THE PRESENTS AND I GIVE THEM TO THE GOOD ONES.'

'What?'

'I TRY NOT TO THINK TOO HARD ABOUT IT.' Then the voice came again, laughing, unbearably strong, irresistibly jolly. 'HO HO HO,' it said.

And then the other hand joined the first so that she was cupped within their grasp, in a warm dark space unlike any other, and there was a rocking motion that, eventually, overcame her confusion and desperation, and she slept.

∞

Yuleton is a strange and eternal town, it's true. Everybody works, in one way or another. But they can make their own decisions on how to serve.

For some, there must be new challenges beyond what can be imagined. For some, eternity is a problem that has to be solved.

Ella awoke in a new body. It was hard and shiny, dressed in a gown of white. She looked at a world so bright, so new. No snow. Only warm yellow light touching everything, on the other side of the glass by which she was propped. Trees and bushes with green growth upon their branches. A sky so much bluer than grey. A sun. A hot ball of yellow sun.

'Where did you come from?' said a voice. Little hands picked her up. A child, a giant child, held her, and pulled at her dress. 'Are you a princess? Are you coming to live with me now? Do you want to say hello to everyone?'

She was turned, and made to face a wall of toys, so many of them, and in all their eyes she saw Yuleton folk staring back. Those who had jumped, those who had served their time, those who had found other ways to serve. Maybe even Noel, too. Yes, that soft clown with a painted smile and crosses over his eyes—that could be Noel. She hoped it was Noel.

There were so many questions, but she had one answer: questions belonged to the realm of children, and so did she.

But at least, in this place, there was change.

The light from the vantage point by the window, over the colourful room that contained so many toys, was magnificent and ever-changing. Nothing stayed the same. Every day was different, as she was placed into new stories, manipulated in new ways.

And these stories, she realised, as she watched her dress get torn, her hair cut short, her leg wrenched off and lost, did have an ending. It made her happier than she could have ever been in Yuleton. She would, eventually, be discarded, and would crumble to nothing.

For nothing in such a place as this could last forever, and that knowledge made her happy.

The Power of 3

Anna Tambour

The First Little Pig

'OH, NO,' SAID THE PIG.

'Oh, yes,' said the wolf. 'Sorry.'

'Look,' said the wolf. 'It'd be so much easier if you'd just accept. Once every telling, I burn your house down.'

He pulled out a monogrammed silver lighter.

'No,' said the pig.

'Don't get stroppy with me,' said the wolf, flashing a gold-capped canine.

'Then don't get sloppy with me,' said the pig. 'And close that mouth. What *do* you do to my home, my castle, the place I keep my slippers?'

'What d'you mean?' said the wolf, who had started to breathe heavily.

'Take it easy,' said the pig. 'You must be, what, pension age now?'

'And your chins wag. You keen to be burnt up too? Please move aside.'

The pig's tidy ankles moved not one jot. 'Do I have to repeat myself,' he said. 'Think back. My house is made of straw, so you—'

'Burn it to a crisp!'

'Do you want to go down in history as an ijit? Must I repeat, what d'you *do* to my house? *Eat* it?'

'You think I'm an ijit!?'

'Banish it?'

'Don't be daft.'

'Just try to concentrate. Yes. Close your eyes and say after me. I huff and I puff, and I—come on. I bl—'

'I blows your house down,' muttered the wolf.

'Blow is quite sufficient,' said the pig. 'But why the shifty eye? So you *can't* remember. So you get mixed up. So you're short of breath. So perhaps you purposely forgot. I'm no rooster. I won't crow.'

'We don't talk,' said the wolf.

'So *that* you remember.'

But the wolf had never had a nose for irony. 'It's time.'

'Rightee-oh,' said the pig. 'But first, would you excuse me for a tick?'

'Just a tick. Remember, this story isn't just about you. I've a house to burn.'

'Oh, *I* remember. Now I'll be just a mo'.'

The pig didn't try to shut the door, so as the wolf watched the pig's neat footsteps as he trotted down the spotless hall, not a straw out of place; he looked down also at his own feet, at the swept step, and then around at the front garden—everything in perfect order.

A shit builder, thought the wolf. But, he whistled wistfully, such a tidy neighbour I can only wish I had.

'Here 'tis,' said the pig, appearing again in a buttoned-up dustcoat and carrying a new straw broom.

'You want a little dustup,' said the wolf magnanimously. 'It's not in the story, and everything's in its place here but—'

'Not quite,' said the pig, who then beat the wolf to such a

death that the step was covered in hairy mush, except for two things that the pig fished out, wearing rubber gloves to do so.

The pig scooped the mush up into a big red basin and carried it past his shed to his burn pit at the back of the garden where at the normal time in this short but eventful story, the scent of burning plantation fir and cedar, rare rainforest parquet flooring, and repurposed ancient oak would have rent the afternoon sky till it could only have wished to cry 'Evict!' but not even in this story's imagination can *that* happen.

Instead, the rank scent of the incinerated wolf was smothered by a unique blend of emissions—corncobs, loose tea, chestnut shells, discarded frightfully stale on-special beernuts, pome-tree prunings, visiting-pigeon droppings stuffed with rose hips, and the slurry from the pig's ginger plant—a divine emanation that rose, curled, and spread like some luxuriating cat, over fake terracotta tile and fifteenth-century chimney pots alike, and made every nostril in the neighbourhood tingle in pleasure at this marvellously organic truly potpourric miasma.

And the gold tooth? He gave it to DGS, his favourite tax-deductible charity. He had a thing for destitute grasshoppers but he wasn't just some leftist with a soft-as-well-past-al-dente touch to those who never plan for the future, let alone for famine. Grasshoppers are nutritious as well as delicious—and that crunch!

He did regret, however, that he hadn't saved a little something more from the wolf.

So he stuck a note to his fridge in case of another wolf ever calling.

Keep a claw. Would make one grand toothpick.

JUST BEING NEIGHBOURLY

Believe it or not, squatters are everywhere.

They were very very weary, and horribly hungry, and winter was hard on their heels, and this place seemed almost capital so they moved in during the so-called dead of night under the broken watch of the smashed streetlight, carrying all their belongings on their backs. They had each a bowl for their porridge; a little bowl for the Little Wee Bear; and a middle-sized bowl for the Middle-sized Bear; and a great bowl for the Great Big Bear. And they had each a chair to sit in; a little chair for the Little Wee Bear; and a middle-sized chair for the Middle-sized Bear; and an electric lift recliner (a constant source of unstated conflict) for the Great Big Bear. And they had each a bed to sleep in; a single for the Little Wee Bear; and a Queen for the Middle-sized Bear; and, because of the recliner, another Queen for the Great Big Bear.

∞

Between foreclosures brought on by unpaid mortgages and those initiated by homeowners associations for delinquent dues, squatting in foreclosed homes has become quite the phenomenon.

The Bears couldn't tell if this was a dangerous nice quiet neighbourhood, or an exemplar of the phenomenon, so they tiptoed to their beds.

The next morning, after they had made the porridge for their breakfast and poured it into their bowls, they walked out into the garage while the porridge was cooling, that they might not burn their mouths by beginning too soon; for they were polite, well-brought-up Bears. And while they were away a ferret named Goldilocks came a-calling.

He and his family of a dozen or so—he'd lost count—were also newcomers to the neighbourhood, having tunnelled in next door just the week before, as the ground shook under the heels of the departing sheriff.

Unlike the Bears' house, the Ferrets' was (though it had a bit of a glass encumbrance what with all the smashed lamps, bottles and glasses) fully furnished, with numerous socks, slithery piles of papers, soft toys, stuffed chairs and sofas, a cute ferret-sized plastic mansion and a fire station with a sliding pole (only slightly smashed), and a cornucopia of a kitchen. So many things, it was a wonder Big Momma Ferret asked little Goldilocks to go next door to borrow a cup of sugar.

And maybe she didn't, but that was the story Goldilocks was prepared to tell if he got caught. He peeped in at the keyhole, for he was not at all a well-brought-up little ferret. Oh, his mother had tried, but she'd kind of had it by his time (#12).

Then, seeing nobody in the house, he lifted the latch.

The door was not fastened, not because the Bears were good Bears who did nobody any harm and never suspected that anybody would harm them, but because Great Big Bear knew nothing about breaking in. Though he had for many years read *Popular Mechanics*, he had always passed by the enticing advertisements to 'Earn $25 an hour as a Locksmith', in the process also failing to provide for his family in a manner befitting their otherwise decency.

Middle-sized Bear nagged him incessantly to get them out of this poverty trap and had almost bored his ears off with, 'Wee won't be wee forever.' As if Wee's ability to get into a place was all that was needed. They were all too polite to come out with naked insults, but Mid was all too eloquent in her unstated aspersions. He had to act insouciant for there was only so much he could do to provide for his family, so he lived in constant fear of Wee Little growing up with neither the right to a decent livelihood nor legal protections to live in ruins.

But that didn't mean he was idle. He researched like a mad chipmunk whenever he had the opportunity. So, for instance, while Mid was out scrounging, gossips said he was lounging feet up in their dive, lost in fantasy pages of another *Pop Mech*, this one blaring from its cover 'Build Yourself a Weatherproof Berry Patch'. Little did they know that secreted amongst those pages was what he was really reading—the key to the Bear family future:

THE WRONG WAY TO REMOVE SQUATTERS IN YOUR HOA

Beyond learning the proper way to get rid of squatters, you must also know how to remove squatters the wrong way. By knowing what you can't do, you can protect your Home Owners' Association from potential liability.

These are actions that you absolutely can't do in an attempt to remove squatters living in foreclosed homes:

Cut power to the property;

Turn off utilities for the property;

Threaten, intimidate, or abuse the squatter/s in any way, shape, or form; and,

Use violence against the squatter/s.

∞

Mid, uh, Mama Bear knew more than she let on. She knew what he was doing, but sometimes this life was all too much for her who was now just a low-class sneaky nomad, by, she reminded herself, compassionate choice.

For after all, what did she need *him* for? Or any him? She'd always been as independent as her mother, and her mother's mother, and all mama bears from the first to, as proper time would have it, eternity.

But she was a soft touch, and when he came a-begging with no malice in his eyes about her cub, she let him graze beside her in the blueberry patch.

And by the time she heard bushes rustle behind, and saw him chuffing the cub along in protective panic, it was almost too late.

When he told her his story in her all too easily found den, it *was* too late. Her compassion, that thing more useless to a mama bear than plastic wrap for freshness—that extraneous to needs and able to damage you if you don't throw it away thing—that thing *compassion* had snuck into her heart and lodged there.

She couldn't kick him out to be the loner he was born to be. Not only couldn't she do that, but he became, to the superficial crowd, the crowd most likely to be suspicious and cause trouble, Head of the Household.

If only he'd liked salmon-fishing better. Instead, he'd travelled down to California to get some easy work at BeesKnees Pure Clover Honey. Line workers there got less than minimum wage but they got a two percent discount on as much honey as they could buy. He spent his first pay entirely on honey, and took it out to a place under an overpass that was the closest he could find to a den. On sticking his tongue into the first jar, he pulled back, shocked. Dyed, flavoured sugar-water!

The next shift, he told his supervisor, who took his complaint Upstairs, who then passed Up his details, and by sundown, he was running for his life.

He ran and he ran and he ran. He ran, in fact, right up the bony spine of California, all the way up to the hairy wilds of Oregon, where he met that mama bear and her cub...

...and where they were chased out and had to start the life of indigents, for he was too afeared to go to anyone else, though she told him all about the comfortable life they'd lead under witness protection.

'According to whom?'

'Movies.'

'The same movies that say I am a threat to you?'

'No. Those are documentaries.'

And so they were this unnaturally enlarged nuclear family, living as stable an itinerant life as possible, and he was always reading, and they were always hungry but with the fixings of three hot meals—three hot meals that were now in fact, cooling.

∞

Ma Ferret had a wealth of time to read, but she preferred to gambol. The whole family *were* gambolling addicts—on first arriving from England in the wake of the great rabbit famine, such references would often be corrected by sticklers to 'whole family was', but if they continued talking about, say, the tasty hares of the Scottish highlands, the parochial pedants wilted under the immigrants' internationalism.

'I were just norticing wot luvily pockets you have,' they'd next say to their abashed audience, for they was always polite, though Pa Ferret did have a smell that could clear out drains.

But the porridge will turn cold as roadkill if the Bears continue to fuss in the garage, tsking at the oil-stained floor, and we are *still* only up to:

Then, seeing nobody in the house, he lifted the latch.

Actually, he was a little disgusted. What's the use of 'Goldilocks' if you lift instead of pick?

He dropped to the floor and nearly brained himself, hitting his head on its polished surface. The place was a wasteland of cleanliness. The stench of cleaning products made him gag, but he persevered. Ma had heard the Bears break in, she said. And Ma had ruminated over the pickings that the Bears would be treated to. Meaning: *there must be orphans here. Ma will be so proud.*

The Bears had never done anybody any harm, and never suspected that anybody would harm them (in their dreams! Great Big Bear especially was sick of all the times he'd been told how lucky he was, always by those who'd never had to squat, those who'd never had to get their meals from garbage cans, or live on porridge).

So when Goldilocks started casing the joint, he was not well pleased when he saw, not any orphan socks, not a delicious bunny, not a coat with pockets—but three bowls of scarily smoking substance emitting an evil smell. They sat on the floor of a dining room that was otherwise empty except for three unmatched chairs, two against the walls and one mid-room, ready to recline. Its cord was stretched taut as a dead rat's tail.

If Goldilocks had been a well-brought-up little girl she wouldn't have been there. The well-brought-up little girl had been evicted along with the rest of her family.

Goldilocks looked at the bowls of porridge in this desert of a house, and slunk out.

Later that day, he snuck back in to leave three socks.

HOW MUCH IS THAT TEAPOT IN THE SALES BIN?

Who would think to rub *this*? It's riven with sharp chased lines filled with dirt, and with that low-slung swell, long spout, and angled elbow it looks like an angry mother with one hand on a hip, and it has BO. But who can choose their place of birth?

Oh dear. The indignity of being rummaged (and the pathetic, hopefilled thrill). Lifted up high, my spout scoops air laden with fragrances—oatmeal soap, some supermarket shampoo; ohh er! a whiff of Terre d'Hermès perfume for men but always in a place like this, worn by a woman who wants to be seen as casually rich and certainly independent; its price is not just for the name but the story that it's been created by a 'great nose'. But trust me. My nose says—*and do I have a nose!*—it's a mix of citronella candle and spray-on insect repellent with added pepper for irritation. The smell physically hurts my nostrils, tingles on my skin, and if I had a dog it would make my dog sneeze and run from me. And I'm quite convinced it would ward off swarms of bugs. No one should wear this, especially if you love dogs.

I wish I were consulted re chemical attractants, but no one ever has—though who else but I should know the power, or lack of it re attractants? That cloud of pricy stench, however, has (thank the marketers who made sure it needs constant application) dissipated, leaving room for the richness of the room's atmosphere: must, mildewed leather, tarnished brass and silver, gumboots rife with fungi; a silk chemise that has been hand laundered but no one can truly get the underarm out. The sad sweet reek of book lice. Wool and more wool and instead of normal dust, a miasma of dog hair floating like a cloud, and—hmm, could that possibly be? It is! There's no smell like it in the world. It's that poorly wrapped toffee (a few dog hairs always sprouting as from a genie's nose) made for a certain charity. The first time I'd smelled it, my tummy heaved, but that's only because one needs to develop. But I like the smell of burnt sugar and I love dogs, dry *and* wet, so I was made for this stuff. I've only come across it in passing as I've been carried past in ecobaskets, backpacks, recycled carry bags and cardboard boxes yanked from car boots while the meter's running.

I've been in every shop but this one—the source of that divinity—ground zero—oh my mo' and whiskers—how I've longed to come here—the op shop *To the Dogs* deep in the heart of op shop street, Edinburgh.

'This jersey is a bit steep at fifteen pounds, don't you think?'

'Aye. But I would never buy it.'

'So?'

'So?'

'So I'll have it and this. I got it from the sales bin. I don't know as I'll ever get it cleaned up. And just look here. This side has lost its roundedness. It looks like a bloody sultana.'

'So you'll be buying it or not?'

'I'm buying the jersey, so you'll give me this bashed teapot for—' She raised an eyebrow invitingly.

'What's it say on the sales bin? All items ten pounds, or charity to customers?'

'No need for such cheek.'

'Aye, no need. It's just a wee bonus service.'

'Your practicing for the comedy festival here won't get you nearer. I'll need change for this fifty.'

'As would we all.'

'It's pity's all it is, you know. I shouldn't have got this frightful teapot, but I can brighten anything up. This bit of junk has been in every shop on the street.'

I feel the flashing warmth of a different hand and I wish with all my heart—but she'd only touched. No rub. Instead she says, 'I'm so sorry for the teapot.'

So there it is. I'm up against it yet again. 'Fate' it calls itself. I refuse to go so far.

'You're just bad luck,' I'd always told it.

∞

Soon as she got home, the old bird fairly ripped me out of the recycled Tesco bag.

'Gimme what I paid for.'

I, of course, stayed pat.

'Come out. I know you're in there.' I could hear her taking off a number of heavy rings. They clattered on a glass-topped table. I've always hated glass-topped tables. Glass should be used in cases. Putting someone on show is what glass is for, not for coffee cups to mark, old carpet to show up through.

I heard a sofa sigh or cry. It was hard to tell, it sounded so defeated.

Suddenly two hands did rub the teapot, but they did so incidentally in the act of violently shaking it, upended. The lid hung open like a question mark without a dot. Mine eyes saw stars and I passed out wondering whether a human's migraine could equal this terrific pain...

I woke up to a shame unlike any that anyone in history has ever experienced.

She'd de-teapotted me!

Have you ever seen a shelled snail?

If you have, you shouldn't have. If you have, you must know how impossible it is to ever get that image out of your head. That's why evil de-snailers chop them up and then they...

'I have bones!' I screamed (for I'm sure I must but this wasn't a time to make sure).

'I'd taste like rubber,' I added, and I admit, I began to cry so hard, my moustache was soon festooned with loops of snot.

'Why would I eat you, you snivelling flight risk?'

She popped a square of charity toffee into a maw that looked like pictures of an active volcano.

'Now,' she said, twiddling her once more beringed fingers. 'Gimme my wishes.'

'Your wishes are my command,' I said, and the one who thinks itself Fate must have broken its face, grinning.

'My first wish—I get three, don't I.'

'You know your genies,' said I.

'You're my first,' she giggled.

'Just my luck,' I said, 'madam.'

She beamed, impervious. 'But,' she frowned, poking me in a part so private, I can barely admit this even unto to myself. 'I know why you've been given back. I know why you've ended up in that bin. You won't cheat *me*.'

She lit a cigarette, a Regal Blue, a brand so noxious, the power of smell is vanquished as smell flees the scene, screaming.

I was thrown into a coughing fit. She crushed the thing in a greasy styrofoam dish next to me on the table, and tapped on the glass with her long horrific nails as she waited for me to stop delaying her.

At my first deep breath, she stopped and leaned so close I could see the canyons in her throat skin.

'Every. Single. Wish. I want,' she said, 'and I'll get, or you'll be sorry. Every bleeding one of the whole blasted three.'

'As you wish, madam, so shall it be my command.'

'You *are* one of those three wishes genies?'

'I was, I am, and so shall I always be.'

'We'll see about that.'

'To hear is to obey.'

'Too right. Now, you ugly little grub, do exactly as I command.'

'Exactly,' I repeated solemnly, trying not to look panicked (my nether regions, never having been exposed, were starting to shrivel alarmingly, this table having obviously been, by the corrosive film and toxic gravel horroring its surface, the scene of many a meal of chips liberally sprinkled with salt and vinegar).

Quickly, I intoned the Words:

'You have three wishes.'

'Whatever I want?'

'The next three wishes you make shall come true, whatever they are.'

'You'll follow my exact instructions?'

I waved my hands in some nonsensical orientalist command, being in too much pain to speak.

'Rightee-oh, then! I don't want much.'

'Speak!'

'Make me the most beautiful woman in the world. Make me the richest woman in the world. Make me live forever.'

∞

And oh, isn't she? Beautiful, I mean. That's what all the tabloids say, and the plastic surgery clinics.

It takes such constant surgery to stay like this, and to change with every change of what's considered beautiful that her makeup must always cover newly rawed skin. With every passing year it becomes harder to open that up-to-date perfect mouth, that stiff crust of scar tissue, and ever harder to break through the crust of cold lava, to operate. Ever more painful and difficult to pop another vinegar and salt chip in that orifice, and afterwards, to open wide enough to vomit; and she carries on, and on and on.

Never look behind her ears! There are more folds back there than a set of pulled-back stage curtains. No one ever does look there, just as no one ever touches her without being paid handsomely. But she has more rings than Saturn, and when Infinity looks upon her years left to live, Infinity's belief in itself is beggared.

And I? I would have expired on that hideous glass-topped table sprinkled with death crystals had not the girl from *To the Dogs* run after the lady and broken down the door because the lady had accidentally dropped a fiver and furthermore, had wobbled precariously so the girl thought she might not be just a horrible human but a genuinely ill, improbable but possible old dear, a genuine beloved gran.

When the girl broke down the door and burst in, the old dear was gone but there was I, almost at my last.

That girl.

She loves dogs, too.

Take that in the eye, with salt, Fate!

∞

That girl, she *lied*.

That story she told me. It wasn't true. She'd just rescued me but she didn't know if she could trust me.

Of course she could have, but she was right in one way. I wouldn't have believed her.

The truth is, she had only just arrived in Edinburgh the night before and was to fill in for a week for her aunt who was out donkey rescuing or something. She'd never been to Edinburgh before so had never been to op shop street. The other woman working in *To the Dogs* hadn't given her a moment to look around before posting her to the counter.

I have no idea what she lives on. Her home—I have promised not to reveal it—is full of atmosphere—partly from the many rescue dogs (for she loves dogs as much as I do), some rescue toads she's always kissing (I'm not sold yet. They seem to have a secret agenda.), and her collection of unwashed teapots.

Indeed, she's the kind of teapot collector who gives a bad name to shabby chic. Many of them would be judged disgraceful. And she abhors tea.

I love the nights best here, so many fragrant dogs gently snoring, briarwood cuttings crackling in the fireplace. I've even grown to love the critical gaze of the toads, just as I respect their right to complex personalities. They've challenged us to keep up with the times, to put our morals where our mouths are, to stop sliding into comfortable repetition. As one toad says, swallowing his eyes as he gulps, then throwing out his tongue in the world's most eloquent retch, quite as if we've just offered him a plastic cockroach: 'No tropiness from you!'

The girl is getting dark bags under her eyes, but she insists they are her treasure chests. We're to blame, all us rescue genies, and a mixed sense of guilt and joy has grown like a fungus in our hearts.

For we spend the nights taking turns storytelling because she must have, what, three thousand wishes amongst us? Not one of which she's ever called for.

'The only wish I have is that you all are happy,' she insists, but that is the only wish we cannot grant.

So we do all we possibly can to repay her, for who could be happier than we?

Did I tell you that she also knits? And we didn't have to tell her that wool is far too harsh for our delicate parts. She spins her yarn from spiderwebs.

RED HORSE, RUNNING

JOANNE HARRIS

ON A COLD AND LONELY ESCARPMENT, UNDER THE red soil of Warwickshire, there lies a horse and rider. Only a few have seen them, under their tapestry of trees, and always on a moonlit night; though many more have made the claim, and many more have sought them. Some say they have seen them on the hill, or drinking at the river. Some say they have heard the sound of hooves, or heard the cries of a battle. Others have seen a horse and foal, or sometimes a whole herd of horses, ghostly in the moonlight. But one thing always stays the same. These visions are red as the land itself; red as bracken; red as blood. And the air is rich with the scent of the soil, and the thyme that grows wild on the hillside; and the pines on the lonely escarpment, and the scent of hay and horses.

These places all have their stories. Your people have always told them. Stories bind you together, and help remind you of who you are. We do not need reminding. We already know who we are. But here is my story—our story, perhaps. Take from it what you need, and then give it back to the hillside.

First, you have to know one thing. We were never horses. We ran with the horses sometimes, yes: and with the deer, and the wolf, and the hare. We walked with the fox over the snow, and flew with the crow and the eagle. We burrowed with the rabbit and mole; we hunted with the wildcat. We were the Travelling Folk, who live in the shadows and cast none ourselves. Unless our shadows were the tales that followed us wherever we went, running through your dreams like a thread through the tapestry of the seasons. And no, we never came to this land. The Travelling Folk were always here. We were here when the world was first made: when your mountains were all desert. The earth was red in those days, too; red as saffron and cinnabar; a red that endures, like the memory of mountains from the ocean. That was where we came from. The earth. And that was where you first found us. You planted your feet in the good red soil; you planted your corn and your footprints. And you brought your stories, too: stories that waxed and waned with time; that changed their shape over centuries; that have sent their roots branching into the soil, like the veins of a buried giant.

This tale is only one among a thousand different stories. A small tale, and a quiet one, next to those legends of battles and knights; and yet it remains, among the songs and dreams of the Travelling People. It is a story of friendship, and of who we are, and of the land itself; the great forests—all gone now, of course—the waterways, the gentle hills, the hedges and the tiny fields. And like all stories at heart, it is a story of love, a love that survives the black months and through the heart of winter, through famine and frost and harvest and fall, and returns, as we have always returned, with the first soft bracken-shoots of spring. And it starts with a girl, and a pony.

The girl was the child of a farmer who lived in the Vale of the Horses. Your name for the place, not ours; the Travelling Folk do not have names, or any claim on the wild, free land. The girl was one of your children; her name was Brea, which means 'The Hill', and she was red as the new-ploughed soil, and fleet as a deer, and wild—as wild as one of our own. Her parents and brothers grew corn in the valley, and had a farm and two horses; but the horses were born to the plough, and tame, not like the wild ponies that ran on the hills. These were an ancient breed of horse; small and hardy and clever and strong, with narrow heads and shaggy manes, and they were too wily to approach, even for the Travelling Folk. But of course, we could go into them, and run with them in the moonlight, and feel the escarpment under our hooves, and drink with them in the river. That was how I came to know the girl-child from the valley, a girl who was born in the wrong kind of skin, who was born to run with the horses.

A named thing is a tamed thing. So goes the ancient saying. Brea had a name, and yet she was far from being tame. From childhood she was unlike the rest; silent and strange, and hungry, and fierce, so that her parents were dismayed, and her people whispered that she must have been taken by the Folk of the Hill, and a changeling left in her cradle. As a baby, she never cried, nor suckled at her mother's breast, but sucked from a piece of rag dipped in goat's milk, and stared at the sky with great dark eyes, and never made a sound. As she grew, she was always silent, and never learnt to speak as you do, or to name the things around her. The other children shunned her, and the adults feared her a little, and so, while her siblings played in the barnyard or helped in the kitchen and on the farm, Brea was left to come and go around the countryside as she pleased. She never seemed to feel the cold, and would tear off her cloak and shoes to run barefoot on the hillside. Sometimes she would lie by the stream and watch the fat brown trout in the depths, or lie on her back for hours on end and follow the birds across the sky. Sometimes she would climb the trees, or look for creatures under stones, or dig with her hands in the rich red earth, but she never harmed a living thing, nor interfered in their little lives. And as she grew, she grew ever more curious about the wild world around her, and we grew ever more curious about the wild child in return.

I told you that the Travelling Folk lived in the land, and the air, and the trees, and the animals of the forests. We live in everything that moves, and breathes, and lives, and grows, and dies. But we never die. We travel instead from one home to another; from fish in the river to birds in the air, to rushes by the waterside. But there is one place we never can go, and that's into the Folk like you - for the Folk have names, that bind them into a single form, and do not allow them to travel. To go into a child of the Folk—a child that has been named and tamed - would be to give up our freedom to roam, our freedom to live forever through the land, and its creatures.

But Brea of the Horse Vale had never answered to her name. She had never spoken it, or acknowledged its meaning. As far as she knew she was nameless and free, a creature of the earth and sky. Her people feared and despised her, not understanding who she was. But our people were drawn to her as we were not to the rest of the Folk, knowing we were safe with her, and that she would not harm us.

This is how I came to know of Brea of the Horse Vale. I ran with the herd of wild ponies then, and lived as a mare on the grassy hills. We kept our distance from the Folk, for fear that they would capture us and put us to work in their fields, or try to ride us as they did those tame and broken horses. But Brea had never ridden a horse, and she too was unbroken. Our paths had already crossed once or twice, and she had watched us in wonder, and sometimes had run alongside us, trying vainly to keep our pace. We had grown to treat her as we did the deer in the woods, or the grass at our feet. And this is why, when I found her one day with her foot trapped in a deadfall of trees, instead of moving away with the herd, I stayed behind to help her.

It was winter. Snow in the vale, and the herd had moved into the uplands. The people of the valley did poorly in the winter, and we would not have put it past them to have eaten horse, if they had had the chance. I had been living as a mare for most of that year, with the occasional foray into a hawk or an otter. But that day I was a mare, my ears attuned to the sounds of the woods, and I heard from a mile away a tiny, angry whimpering. It was no creature that I knew, and yet I knew it was in need, and so I left the herd to roam, and went to investigate the sound.

I found her there, on the deadfall. She had tried to climb the stack of trees, and her foot had slipped as the branches moved, and remained there trapped; too far for escape. The leg was broken; I could tell. I could smell her pain and distress: the scent of a small, trapped animal. But Brea did not call for help. She simply stayed there, shivering. As I approached, she stayed very still, watching from those strange, dark eyes. I came even closer, and she put out a small cold hand to touch the velvety tip of my nose.

Horse, she whispered.

I was surprised. I'd thought her incapable of speech. Now I saw that she simply chose not to speak with her own kind.

Horse, she said, and once again I felt her hand against my face. And now I could feel her tiny heart beating through the cold skin, and see my reflection in her eyes, and I knew that she had chosen me. It did not occur to me till much later that she had also named me—the child was so different to the rest of her folk that such laws seemed not to apply. Instead, I considered her predicament. There was nothing I could do in my present form to release her. Without help, she would surely die a cold and lonely death in the woods. And so I did what was needed. Breaking one of our ancient laws, I came to the human child as myself, and used my human hands to free the injured leg from the branches, and to carry her to safety, and to set her once more on the frozen ground. It must have hurt, but Brea simply watched me from unblinking dark eyes, and when I returned to her as a mare, and knelt on the ground beside her, she reached to take hold of my mane as if she understood me perfectly, and let me carry her on my back until the edge of her village. There I left her, for I did not dare set foot in the camp of my enemies, but she would be safe enough, I thought. Safe in the arms of her people.

Time passed. I did not see Brea until the spring, and yet I knew she had survived. The Travelling Folk are connected with every part of the land and sky. We are the hawk that flies over the hill; the hare that hides in the bramble. We know how to pick out a single heartbeat among a tribe of many. Hers was different from the rest; strong and wild and curious. I listened for it every day, and was gladdened by its sound. And I could tell she thought of me, too; for occasionally I would find offerings by the deadfall of trees; an apple, a carrot, a parcel of hay. The wild girl of the hillside was not the kind to forget a friend.

Spring came, and with it, at last, the melting of the winter snow. The herd moved back to the valley, and fed on the new ferns in the woods. I ran with them as before, passing from one to the other, and drank from the ice-cold stream, and ran like wildfire on the open hill. And then one day I saw her again, standing by the deadfall, leaning on a crutch, for her broken leg had not fully healed.

When she saw me she did not move, but stood and watched as I approached, her face expressionless, though with my borrowed senses, I could hear her heart like a bird in a snare. I moved a little closer. I could smell her scent, like apples and hay and something bitter, like the sea. I made a small and comforting sound, although there was no fear in her. She reached into a pocket of her bulky outer garment and pulled out a piece of carrot.

I moved a little closer, and allowed her to run her fingers through my mane. I was not the same horse that had brought her to the village that day. This time, I was a yearling, marked with white upon one flank, but even so, I was certain that she recognized me, somehow.

'*Horse*,' she whispered, and touched my nose. I took the carrot from her hand. And thus, without my knowing it, was I quietly named and tamed.

Years passed. Not many for the Travelling Folk, for we have no understanding of Time, or any fear of its passing. During those years, my strange friendship with the girl whose name was the Hill grew little by little. She always walked with a limp, but she roamed just as freely as ever. She would sit on the hillside, watching for the wild ponies. Sometimes she would wait at the stream in the mornings, when we came to drink. But most often she came to the deadfall of trees with her pockets filled with acorns, or nuts, or pieces of apple or carrot, and waited for me to come to her, and whispered softly into my ear.

Nor did she ever seem surprised when I came to her in different forms, first as a yearling, and then as a stallion, later as a pregnant mare. She always greeted me in the same way, with solemn recognition, although I had not shown her my true self since the day of her accident. She had never spoken to me, except for that one word: Horse. I did not even know if she could speak, or if she had truly understood what happened that day in the clearing. And of course, I did not need her to speak, for I understood the language of her breathing, her heartbeat; the soft caress of her hand on my nose. I think she understood me, too, for she always knew me in whatever skin I chose, and always greeted me as a friend.

And then one day, maybe ten or twelve years after the deadfall incident, I came to our spot one morning and knew that something was different. Over the years I had become used to the sound of Brea's presence. Her heartbeat had a special sound; her breath a special quality. I would have recognized her instantly among a hundred of her kind. Until that day, she had always been calm, but today she was anxious, agitated. The was no scent of apple or hay from her pockets; but all around her there was that bitter scent, like the scent of the sea, when the men come home with their catch of seals, and spider-crab, and herring. I approached her with a measure of caution I had not felt since the early days. She held out her empty hands.

'Horse.'

It was a familiar word, and yet it sounded different. A pleading look was in her eyes. She touched my mane, and repeated; 'Horse.' I sensed it as a kind of command, a warning, and a plea for help. But Brea could not tell me—not in words, anyway. Instead, she knelt on the ground, and drew something in the cold red earth. 'Horse,' she said insistently. And then she drew something else; a man, standing with a rope in his hands. And I understood Brea's warning, and cast out my senses to the winds, and went into a hunting hawk, and from the skies, I, saw the trap that they had set for the horses.

It was a technique I had seen several times over the years, although never quite as ambitious as this, and never as well-organized. The Folk had built kind of enclosure near the river crossing, some half a mile away from the woods. This was where the horses drank, before crossing the shallow part of the stream and heading to the pastures. A dozen men, with dogs, had been deployed to round up the herd of wild ponies here, and to drive them towards the enclosure. I guessed that the pregnant mares would be their principal target: the foals would be easier to tame, the mares less likely to escape. The untamed ones would be slaughtered for meat: the winter had been a harsh one. And the horses were a mile away, heading for the watering-place; as yet unaware of those lying in wait. There was still time to act; but the Travelling Folk do not intervene in the affairs of men, and the mare into which I had travelled had wandered off to rejoin the rest, and the hunters were waiting.

Now that I knew their plans, I could feel their greed and excitement: it ran through the land like a thread of fire. Forsaking the mare, I returned to the child in the skin of a harrier hawk; wild-eyed, feathers fluttering. I expected her to shrink from me this time, but she did not. She simply looked at me and said, as she had before: 'Horse.'

She knows me, I thought. Even in this skin, she knows me, as she has always known me, whatever form I took with her. It came as a sweet and strange surprise: the Travelling Folk do not make friends with the Folk of the valleys. We keep to ourselves, to our animal forms, for there is safety in solitude. And when there is danger, we leave the host, and flee to another form, and allow the cycle of Life and Death to take its course without us.

Today, however, I understood that I was expected to intervene. Brea had come to warn me: she trusted me to help the herd. I could not explain to her that they, like her own Folk, were part of the land, destined to feed its hunger. I could not explain to her that to rejoin the wild ponies at such a time was to risk more than she could imagine. And I could not explain to myself why I wanted to do this strange child's will; I wanted to save the horses. And so I cast out again for a form, and found a pregnant mare by the stream, and went into its skin instead, and galloped towards the place of ambush.

My plan was simple: to warn the herd by exposing the danger awaiting them. I was aware that my host would be in the greatest peril; but I had the advantage of knowing where the enclosure lay, and where the men were hidden. I galloped ahead of the herd, right into the enclosure, and then, with a scream of warning, I turned my face to the enemy.

The herd of ponies scattered as the men and their dogs moved forward to trap the pregnant mare. For a moment I held my ground, smelling their bitter scent, the sweat and soil and fear of the place; struggling to control the mare, whose instincts were to run. I reared as a man with a rope bridle approached me from the side, and another crept up my other side, ready to slip the rope around my head. I tried to rear again, but now, two other men had joined the first, and there was no escape for me but out of my borrowed skin. I prepared to seek a new host, but then I saw something that stopped me: it was Brea, standing there among the stampeding horses. She must have run as fast as she could towards the river crossing, unseen and unheeded by the men intent upon their capture. Why she had come, I could not tell; maybe it was to find me, or to warn the rest of the herd. I met her eyes just at the moment the second rope fell across my neck, and then the herd was upon her. Panicked and unthinking, they did not know her for one of their own, and I saw her fall beneath their hooves, trampled and unnoticed, to be carried quickly downstream in the arms of the river.

I fled into a warbler then, and flew to the river's edge, and stayed until the herd had moved on. The men were still struggling with the mare, who was lashing out at them with her hooves. No one had seen the girl by the bank, or cared what had befallen her. I followed her as a warbler downstream, then as a fox along the bank, where she came to rest, bloodied and silent, although I could still feel her heartbeat, faintly through the ragged air.

But I could not help her as a fox, or as a warbler. And so for the second time in our strange friendship, I came to her again as myself; as a woman, poor and ragged; barefoot against the red soil. I stepped into the cold stream and carried her out onto the bank, and covered her with my old shawl, and felt for her weakening heartbeat.

Brea was dying, I could tell; she was too badly broken to survive. She felt like a handful of birds in my arms, and she was barely breathing. And yet when she opened her eyes, she saw me - knew me - in my own skin, and put up her hand to touch my face, as none of her kind had ever done.

And I felt something then that I had never felt in all my years before. A grief, like the start of a winter storm, at the thought that her life was over. The Travelling Folk have always believed that Death is part of the dance of Life. Our kind do not grieve for the dead, any more than we grieve for the turn of the seasons. But the thought of losing Brea - of going on without her - was suddenly unbearable. What was this feeling? Was this what my people meant when they spoke of being tamed?

Brea was starting to slip away. Her eyes, once bright, were misty. 'Horse,' she whispered. 'Please. Horse.' And at last, I understood what she had been trying to tell me. All these years, Brea had been trying to tell me her true name. Not mine, but hers: the secret name that she had chosen for herself. Not the Hill, but the Horse on the hill. And now I knew what she wanted, too: to run with the horses, to leave behind the name that her people had given her. They had never wanted her, or understood her as I had. To them she was always a wild thing, named, perhaps, but never tamed. And I realized that I wanted to give her this final connection.

And so I broke our most ancient rule. I went into a child of the Folk. A dying, broken, trampled thing, and yet she burnt so brightly that it made me almost breathless. There was so much inside her; so many feelings; such laughter and joy; such longing, such deep love for her world. I knew that it was a terrible risk. If my instincts were wrong, I could be trapped in this body to die, forever cut off from my people. But if I was right, I could give her this thing that she had always wanted; a new identity, the life that she should have had instead of her own.

And so I gave her the freedom of galloping on the hillside; and of flying high over the gorse; of burrowing deep into the ground. And then, with our final, faltering breath, I sent her into a yearling; a fine strong yearling, red as the land, and then flung myself far away from that place, into an ancient hawthorn tree, for fear that her death would engulf me.

She lived many years as a pony. I watched her from the hill as she grew; saw her grow, give birth and die. But I never came to her again, not as a horse, or a bird, or myself. Something had changed inside me. I no longer wanted to run, or fly, or swim or burrow. I craved the silence of roots in the ground, and branches resting under the snow. I wanted the circling stars, and the sound of singing ice from the sea. Most of all I wanted to be free of the grief that had lodged in me like a seed. Was this how her people lived? How in the Worlds can they bear it? And now that she is part of the land, how can I ever escape her?

Twelve months passed—a whole turn of the world - before I left the hawthorn tree and walked on the Hill in my own skin. It was spring, and the winter snow still lay in the tender hollows. I walked to the top of the Hill, and knelt, and sank my hands into the good red earth. And there, on my hands and knees, I began to shape something out of the hillside; the outline of a red horse, running.

On a cold and lonely escarpment, under the red soil of Warwickshire, there lies a horse and rider. No one remembers what it means, though many hands have shaped it over the many centuries. No one remembers the girl of the Hill, who was born in the wrong kind of skin, and to the wrong kind of people. No one but you: and the hawthorn tree that stands on the grassy flank of the Hill, and sometimes walks in the moonlight with the circling stars above her.

UMBILICAL

TEIKA MARIJA SMITS

TAMARA

EVEN BEFORE I GOT REALLY ILL, I COULD FEEL THE FIRST stirrings of growth in my abdomen, just beneath my belly button. The sensation tugged on my thoughts, telling me to phone Mum, to tell her that something was . . . wrong. But I couldn't. I'd been too absent, too adamant that I didn't need her in my life. Besides, she'd just make a fuss, and there was nothing I hated more than her sympathy. She'd never understood me; could never grasp how her clinginess had repelled me. As a teenager I hadn't ever wanted to talk to her about Dad, the divorce, or periods. I just wanted to be left alone. And since leaving uni and getting a job in the City there'd been no good reason to keep in contact. But now, the itch at my navel compelled me to call her. I picked up my phone.

RUTH

The moment I heard Tamara's voice I knew something was wrong. Actually, I'd been sure for a while that something was wrong, but I'd reasoned away my fears—those ancient, knowing whisperings arising from my womb—with the usual excuses: the menopause, getting old. This confirmed it. She was taking some time off work because she didn't feel well. She blamed her constant tiredness, her breathlessness, on her new management role; the long hours she'd been working, the nights she'd spent clubbing... She thought that maybe she was... anaemic? I told her to see a doctor as soon as she could, but I could tell she thought I was fussing. That's the thing about kids, though, isn't it? Until they have children themselves, they're not able to comprehend a parent's greatest fear: the death of a child.

TAMARA

I cried like a baby when the doctor told me. I mean, twenty-somethings aren't supposed to get cancer, are they? Especially not an aggressive one, and with an unknown primary origin. It wasn't fair. This shouldn't have happened to me.

After I'd stopped blubbing, he talked me through the treatment I'd be getting, the fact that I'd need someone around to help. Did I have a partner? Family, friends? I put my hand to my t-shirt and itched at my belly button. I considered asking him about the weird skin growth that had appeared there in the last few weeks, but thought it something to do with the cancer. And this wasn't the time to be poring over every defect of my body. I stopped itching. I said I had my mum.

RUTH

What with Tamara being in and out of hospital I never got round to talking to a doctor about my constant bloatedness, the come-and-go ache at my womb. Besides, I didn't think I could face telling someone that something really strange was happening to my vagina. That it almost felt as if something was inside it. Me. And that it was growing. I hadn't had a smear test for ages, maybe that would've picked up the whatever-it-was. And sex... well, that too hadn't happened for years. The feeling wasn't unpleasant, though, it was just a bit uncomfortable. Made sitting down awkward. But then came the dreadful news: Tamara's treatment wasn't working. This wasn't the time to be worrying about my own health.

TAMARA

It's weird, isn't it? After years of *not* wanting to spend time with Mum, I can't bear to not have her beside me. Even for a moment. I get panicky when she leaves the room; ask her to keep talking to me when she goes down the landing to the loo. She eats all her meals at my bedside, looking guilty as she does so because I have no appetite. Because I weigh as much as I did when I was, like, 10. "You mustn't starve, you know," I say.

"I know," she says, but she eats quicker then, tears in her eyes. After she finishes, I feel that old pull at my gut, feel the cord of skin that has sprouted up and out of my belly button twisting itself into a thin rope. Extending. I hold her hand. I need to tell her about the cord.

RUTH

I hate being away from Tamara for even a minute, because I know she's only got days, weeks if we're very very lucky, to live. I eat beside her, sleep beside her; the only time we're apart is when I get some food, go to the toilet, or have a shower. Those last two things I do really quickly because of the fleshy cord that's coming out of my vagina. It dangles between my legs, chafes at my thighs. I know I need to tell someone about it, but I can't. A terrible thought, that I will deal with it *after*, occasionally skims pebble-like across my mind. But I can't think about *after*. I don't want there to be an *after*.

∞

"I have to tell you something," Tamara begins. "Try not to freak out about it, but I have this, like, weird cord thing growing out of my belly button."

She lifts up her nightie and shows her mother, who then bursts into tears.

But after a moment or two, Ruth wipes her eyes and says, "I've got one too. Coming out of my, well . . . fanny."

Tamara can't help but laugh. It's strange hearing her mother say 'fanny'. Her mother laughs too, and for a moment there is no *later, then, after*, but only *now*.

"Will you lie down beside me?" Tamara asks. "Like you used to when I was little?"

"Of course," says Ruth.

She gets into the bed and slips her arm beneath Tamara's hairless head.

Tamara snuggles into her mother, the bedcovers over them, and they both know what's going to happen. Tamara thinks it should feel gross—this melding of the cord at her belly button with the cord that is coming out of her mother, but it isn't. It's the most *right* thing she's ever known. And the safest she's ever felt. She's warm too, and there's no more pain. There's just her mum. And, strangely, her mum's thoughts. Ruth's mind thrums with sadness, loss. She doesn't know how she'll go on *after*.

"You'll be all right," Tamara mumbles, suddenly feeling the welcome pull of sleep. "You've got your friends at the church. And that nice neighbour who keeps doing the shopping for us. You should make some time for him. When I'm gone."

Ruth can only cry. She remembers all the nights she spent as a new mum with Tamara in her arms—all that feeding, then burping, then rocking. At the time it had felt as though it would last forever. How wrong she'd been.

"Mum?"

"Yes, love?"

"I hope you don't need to pee anytime soon. Because it'd be a bit tricky, us connected like this."

Ruth laughs. "No, I'm all right." Her voice breaks as she says, "I'm going to stay here for as long as you want."

"Thanks, Mum."

∞

They stay like that for some hours, in that liminal place, until Death anoints them both with her holy oil, and takes Tamara with her. Ruth knows the exact moment her daughter is gone, because straight after, the cord binding them together crumbles away from Tamara's belly button. And Ruth, alone, must cope with the contractions of her womb; the afterdeath, as black as bile, that will force itself out of her.

Are We Going Under?

Simon Bestwick

I work the bar in the Station Hotel, down at the far end of Bone Street, and I'd finally called time and seen out Paul Manktelow, the last of the night's drinkers. I'd shut and locked the door behind him, but I'd barely got back behind the bar to turn the lights off when he started banging on it.

I didn't know it was Paul just then, and I was tempted to ignore the noise and go on up to bed; it had been a long day and I was exhausted, and it wouldn't have been the first time that some old soak—a few of the folks inhabiting the flats in the little square around the hotel fall under that description—had run out of booze and come hammering on the doors in search of a double gin because they couldn't be arsed to schlep all the way down to Polodski's (the sign on the door says All Night, and in all fairness the old boy means it.) And while I sympathise with those who need a goodly amount of booze to lubricate their slide towards the grave—I make my living from them, after all—closing time means closing time.

But there's knocking and there's knocking, isn't there? And there was something about the rapping on the hotel door that night that sounded different. For one thing, it was rapid and urgent, but nowhere near as loud as it should' have been. Drunks in the throes of a craving tend to hammer at the door hard on the assumption that I'm about to get into my bed on the top floor of the hotel—and, to be fair, they're usually right. This knocking was that of someone who was hoping to attract my attention without attracting that of anyone else who might be out on Bone Street at that time of night. Which meant two things: firstly, that it was someone who knew I'd just locked up, and secondly that something unpleasant had either just happened or was about to. And, unfortunately, I could guess who the first, and what the second, was.

The first I'd have guessed to be Paul, and about that I was right; before I'd even reached the door I could hear him stage-whispering my name through the keyhole. I unlocked it quickly and opened it; he almost tumbled over the threshold. Paul liked his *jonge jenever*—it's a Dutch drink, like gin but not as foul—and he'd had more than his usual share that night. I managed to catch hold of him and not end up pinned to the carpet under his weight. Just about.

'Jesus,' I grunted.

'Sh,' he mumbled, blinking. 'Got to keep quiet. Ooh.'

He was looking quite pale and waxy, his face covered in greasy sweat. He wasn't particularly overweight, but he lived a pretty sedentary life and for a middle-aged man in that condition, running after drinking nine *jonge jenevers* isn't usually a good thing. I stepped back as soon as I was sure he could stand unaided; I didn't relish the prospect of cleaning vomit off the carpet, but cleaning it off my shirt—or out of my hair—was even less appealing.

Paul took a handkerchief from his waistcoat pocket—he was always well-turned-out—and wiped his face, taking deep breaths. 'We need to get to Dahlia's,' he said. 'Quickly.'

I felt my stomach tighten the second he mentioned it, because deep down I'd been afraid of this for some time. 'Sadie?'

Paul shrugged. 'Dunno. But I just saw the bastard skulking down the alley on the side.'

'You didn't tell Vic?' Victor Jepps is the manager at Dahlia's—manager, bouncer and general runner-of-things on Dahlia's behalf.

'I—no, I'm sorry,' he mumbled. I'd wondered, more than once, if Paul had ever frequented the massage parlour, but it wasn't something you asked and they tended to pride themselves on their discretion as a business. I was guessing he hadn't, given how embarrassed he looked. He'd been married, although I knew she'd passed away before he came to Bone Street—and that the circumstances of her passing, or their aftermath, had had something to do with how he'd ended up here—but he often seemed chronically shy around women. He was fond of Little Sadie, but it had always seemed avuncular rather than amorous.

None of which was a big help now. 'Well, get your arse in through the front door and tell him,' I said. 'I'll go and have a word with me-laddo there.'

'All right.'

I probably should've locked the hotel's door behind me—there was always the chance of one of the old alkies from the flats still being up and taking the opportunity to raid the optics in the bar—but in all honesty that was the least of my concerns. I went across the cobbles as fast and quietly as I could while Paul huffed and puffed his way to Dahlia's front door.

A narrow alley runs behind each row of buildings on either side of Bone Street, and there's a side alley every few buildings along, so you can cut through from the street to the main ginnel. There's one of those right next to Dahlia's—Paul would have passed it as he wove his way back from the bar towards his shop—and while I couldn't see any movement in it now, that didn't reassure me in any way. I went down the alley slowly and quietly, already wishing I'd doubled back to the bar before leaving. I keep a sawn-off pool cue there in case of trouble, though I've only ever had to use it the once.

When I reached the end of the side-alley, I peered round the corner. I couldn't see him at first; the only source of light in the ginnel came from a lamp mounted over Dahlia's back door, and the pool of illumination from that was empty. But then I glimpsed movement in the shadows, and went still. I kept looking, and a moment later, there it was again. Since I knew what I was looking for this time, it wasn't hard to recognise: a slab-like, brutal face with tiny piggy eyes and a thick brush of a moustache. Ralph Brassland, I saw with no surprise: as soon as Paul had said 'the bastard' I'd known whom he meant.

Ralph had been on Bone Street for just shy of three months, and no one liked him. He wouldn't be the first inhabitant to be almost universally unpopular—the late Mr Hadrian, who'd inhabited the upper floor of one of the derelict shops, could have matched him in those stakes—but there was a good reason for it in Ralph's case. He'd been a serial rapist, and his last victim had died. That had brought the Closers down on him and led to his being granted sanctuary by whatever powers or processes governed Bone Street—as I've said before, there's no rhyme or reason to that part of things, not that any of us have ever been able to determine.

Well, none of us are spotless, and we do our best not to judge people by their past—although in Ralph's case that was a sight easier said than done. Even that, however, wasn't the main problem. It wasn't that he had been a rapist, but that he still was—or would be, given half the chance. And therein lay the big issue.

I do my best not to be cynical, but the old proverb about leopards and spots comes to mind, and certainly nothing about Brassland from the moment he'd arrived had suggested any kind of repentance. He'd visited Dahlia's exactly once, and thereafter been refused admittance. I didn't know the details, but it wasn't hard to guess: even if he hadn't done anything wrong, it was hard to imagine any woman's skin not crawling at the sight of him.

The problem was, of course, that Brassland wasn't someone to take no for an answer—or, indeed, even to ask in the first place. It had always been a case of not if, but when, something happened.

There was literally no good reason for Ralph Brassland to be hanging around in the back ginnel. Dahlia's back door opened directly into a small kitchenette, where the girls brewed up and put away the odd snack and stepped outside to smoke in between customers or on their infrequent breaks. (It was also where they put out the bins, which had a certain aptness in Ralph's case, but that was by the by.)

So far, however, he still hadn't actually done anything, and so for now I watched and waited, torn between giving the bastard enough rope to hang himself and wanting to actually hang him—metaphorically, of course. Not least because I knew who he was after. In one sense any woman would have done, but from the start there was one particular girl who'd always drawn his attention, and that was Little Sadie.

Now, I'm not going to start reiterating cliches about whores with hearts of gold, but the plain fact was that Sadie was a truly sweet girl—innocent even, however strange that sounds given her profession. She was in her mid-twenties but could pass for considerably younger, and was genuinely well-liked—by the other girls, by the punters and in all honesty by pretty much everyone else. I guessed that was what had drawn Brassland's attention. Something that he yearned for more than anything else, down in his twisted soul, and couldn't have. He'd been caught eyeing her more than once and on several occasions I'd had to make sure she got home safely after a late night at the Station Hotel bar when he'd been loitering there—that, or put her up in one of the spare rooms free of charge so she didn't have to walk back in the dark, which I wasn't strictly speaking allowed to do but in certain cases the management turned a blind eye.

It hadn't been a pleasant couple of months because, as I said, we all knew that it was a case of not if, but when, so despite the circumstances I felt a certain relief at catching Ralph *in flagrante*. Although there was still the question of what to do with him next.

I hadn't really got a strategy beyond watching and waiting, but thankfully I didn't need one much longer. The back door opened, and I saw Brassland step back into the shadows. A second later there was a grunt, a scuffle and then a shout of pain, and he bolted out into the light. For a moment it looked as though he was about to try and force the back door, but his plans for the evening had been temporarily forgotten and he came tearing down the back ginnel instead. A second later Vic came lumbering out into the light, fists clenched. While not to be messed with, Vic isn't the fastest man on Bone Street in any sense of the word, and Ralph was already putting space between them.

He was putting on a good turn of speed, in fact, which made things simpler for me: I just stuck my foot out as he reached my position, and let gravity do the rest. He went flying forward and crashed to the cobbles; by the time he'd recovered his bearings, and well before Vic caught up, I was kneeling on his back and holding him by the ears—an old lag's trick which, I'd been reliably told, could keep a violent fellow under control for hours. I didn't have to test that claim, but it definitely held him long enough.

Normally in a situation like that, you'd ring the police and that'd be it, job done. Unfortunately, Bone Street's something of a special case.

Should you be unfamiliar, Bone Street is in Manchester's Northern Quarter. Allegedly, anyway, but you won't find it on any maps; and people have found their way here from every city in the country and one or two outside it. You turn a corner and find yourself emerging from underneath the disused railway viaduct, usually with no idea how you got there.

If you have, it's sort of a good thing. Only sort of, because it means the Closers are after you.

Closers are...creatures of some kind. I can't give you any more detail than that because I've never seen one. No one has—no one who was in any condition to describe them afterwards, anyway.

I'm guessing the dark under the viaduct opens portals through space and probably time too—Paul Manktelow only got here a couple of years ago but I'm pretty he sure he did so direct from 1980s London, given that his tales of a (not very) misspent youth date him firmly to the Swinging Sixties. But that's about it. That's all I know, and I've been here nearly five years.

What this means is that there are no coppers on Bone Street—not serving ones, anyway—and certainly no police station, or any way of getting access to one. Luckily there were handcuffs—I'm sure Mr Polodski could have dug something out, but in the event Dahlia's provided. They have to cater for all sorts of tastes, and despite the pink fluffy padding, I was reliably informed they were police-standard.

We had as little idea where to keep Ralph as we did what to do with him; no one particularly wanted him on their premises, or had any desire to trust the security of any locked room in which he might be confined. In the end we got him under control by the simple expedient of cuffing his hands around the lamppost that stood beside the Green, the little square of grass with its bench and scrawny apple tree that's the closest thing to a park on Bone Street. It's near the far end of the street from the hotel, where the cobbled road disappears under the viaduct. It's very dark there, and you can't see what's lurking in the shadows. (Which is, trust me, a good thing.) Both the chain and the post were more than strong enough to resist any attempts he could make to get away.

And even if he got loose, there was the question of where he'd run to. Bone Street isn't a big place, and there's nowhere outside it. Nowhere you'd want to go, anyway.

But that was a question for Ralph Brassland to ponder. For the rest of us, come the following day, there was a different one: what the hell did we do with him now?

'It all comes down to one thing,' said Droopy Sykes. Droopy had, once upon a time, been a solicitor, until one of the juniors at his law firm caught him with his hand in the till. Droopy had begged him not to tell anyone, to give him time to put things right, but the young man had either been too inflexibly self-righteous to overlook the offence or (more likely, from what I'd come to know of Droopy) too good a judge of character to believe he would do as he said. Then again, all things considered, he couldn't have been *that* good a judge of character, otherwise he might have pretended to agree before informing his superiors. As it was, he'd told Droopy to go to hell and that he was informing the firm's partners in the morning.

He never got the chance to, which was why Droopy Sykes' lawyerly duties, such as they now were, consisted of acting as a sort of ad hoc legal counsel to the good (and less good) folk of Bone Street, in exchange for the odd double whisky. He was working his way through one of them now, at one in the afternoon (which had been the earliest anyone had been able to wake him up)—a bad habit, but one he was prone to. He'd been a stocky man with a slight paunch when he'd arrived four years earlier; now he resembled a sort of balloon animal in a worn grey suit that no longer fitted, having more than doubled in weight from the drinking. He was oyster-eyed, with an engorged red face, but he also had the kind of voice that wouldn't have disgraced the main stage at the National Theatre. 'The question,' he went on portentously, then blinked at his glass, feigning surprise at having found it suddenly empty, and gave me a hopeful look. 'Another?' he said.

I sighed and took his glass to the optics, decanting three measures of the cheapest blended whisky in the house into it.

'Thank you, old chap,' he said, and took a grateful sip. 'As I was saying,' he continued, 'the question is whether The Law has been broken.'

Pretty much the entire population of Bone Street was crammed into the Station Hotel's lounge bar by this point—Dahlia and her girls, plus Vic; Mr Polodski from the Mini-Mart; Ahmed from Ahmed's Kebab House of Death (the only kebab house I've ever known where a non-stop soundtrack of the Sisters of Mercy and Fields of the Nephilim plays from the speakers and your chicken shawarma is served by a burly Iranian man in a black Stetson hat, crushed velvet shirt and winkle-picker boots;) most of the drunks from the flats (although they'd have been there anyway,) and, leaning against the bar more or less at my elbow, Paul Manktelow.

I'm pretty sure that every single one of us heard the capital letters when Droopy said 'The Law.' He still had some of his old rhetorical skills. I was always surprised to find he hadn't been an actual barrister, as he struck me as having been made for the role. I'd asked him once, but hadn't been able to make much sense of the reply. Maybe I'd ask him again some other day.

'As we all know,' he went on, 'Our community here on Bone Street is not bound by the complex legal strictures we're so familiar with from our former lives. Only one real law pertains here—a law that was engraved on the tablets that Moses brought down from Sinai—a law that every one of us here must admit, intentionally or otherwise, to having broken. The law of Almighty God Himself—'

'Fuck sake, Droopy,' said Chloe, one of Dahlia's girls.

'Silence in court!' Droopy boomed, turning an alarming shade of purple, then he cleared his throat, swaying slightly to and fro as he fixed Chloe with a baleful glare. Once certain there'd be no further interruptions from her, he carried on. 'The law of Almighty God Himself,' he repeated, 'that says 'Thou Shalt Not Kill.''

Droopy could take his own sweet time getting to the point, usually because it gave him an excuse to keep demanding top-ups of his whisky. Nearly everyone in the bar sighed wearily, all at once. It made a sound like a gust of wind, and I actually wondered if I'd left the door open.

'Out there,' said Droopy, pointing dramatically, 'beyond the viaduct and outside the walls of Bone Street, the Closers wait—those terrible ministers of divine wrath—'

'Oh, fuck off,' said Chloe. 'Divine wrath my shiny red arse. Bad luck, more like.'

'Bad luck?' Droopy's watery, bloodshot grey eyes almost popped out of their sockets. 'Bad luck? You call it 'bad luck', madam, to be a murderess?'

'Murderess?' Chloe put her hands on her hips. 'I had a punter die on the job, for fuck's sake. *That's* murder?'

There were a few groans at that one. She had a point—one

of her customers had suffered a fatal coronary while in the throes of passion and had damn near flattened Chloe in the process when he'd collapsed on top of her, since he'd been built along much the same lines as Droopy. That has, to be fair, always struck me as stretching the definition of 'taking a human life' to its absolute limit, but we'd all heard the story before; Chloe's still bitter about it, not surprisingly, but always starts chewing over the subject yet again when in her cups.

'Or what about Little Sadie?' demanded Chloe, having read the room enough to know there wasn't much appetite for hearing her tale of woe again right now.

Sadie blushed and did her best to hide behind Kerry and Lucy, two of the other girls from Dahlia's. She hated being called 'Little Sadie', even though it was hard not to do so, as she was very small and slender—the word 'tiny' had even been used, though not in earshot of her. It was one reason she was often assumed to be much younger than she actually was. Being genuinely well-liked into the bargain meant she brought out the protective side in pretty much everyone, which was a rare thing on Bone Street, but right then she was giving Chloe a look that could have boiled ice.

'Sadie stabbed some rapey sod like Ralph Brassland,' Chloe declaimed, getting into her stride. 'Self-defence if anything was. And what happened—'

'Stop it!' pleaded Sadie.

'Chloe,' I said. 'Give it a rest, eh, love?'

Chloe bridled at the use of 'love'—probably a mistake on my part, that—but Kerry and Lucy took the opportunity to get hold of her and sit her back down.

'*As* I was saying,' growled Droopy. 'Be that as it may, madam—be it through malicious intent or unhappy accident—we all of us have a human life on our conscience.'

'Brassland doesn't have a conscience,' someone muttered, but Droopy ignored whoever it was.

'And, by so doing,' he carried on, 'we have all made ourselves legitimate prey for the Closers. Be they angels or demons, they wait beyond the confines of Bone Street. Only here are we granted sanctuary from them! And on but one condition. That single law. Thou Shalt Not Kill. If that law is breached, our sanctuary is no longer valid, and the Closers may enter at will. Unless—'

Droopy held up a finger, savouring the moment of silence.

'Unless,' he went on, 'the individual responsible is expelled.'

'We know all this,' groaned someone—probably the same gentleman who'd muttered only seconds before—but once again Droopy didn't deign to respond. He did, however, decide it was maybe time to stop milking the moment.

'Now,' he said, 'no law here says Thou Shalt Not Rape. Nor indeed, Thou Shalt Not Steal. Nonetheless, those laws are, broadly, observed. Why? Because if there is one thing we all know, it's how unintended consequences can flow from such an act—how matters can escalate—leading to loss of life.'

'Christ's sake, Droopy,' Kerry from Dahlia's groaned. 'Get on with it.'

'There can be no doubt,' said Droopy, ignoring her, 'of Mr Brassland's intentions last night. We all know what he's done in the past, and there's no cause to believe there's been any reformation of his character. Indeed, Mr Van Geldern, Mr Manktelow, and Miss Harrower herself—' Sadie, who'd never particularly liked her surname, winced '—have all testified as to his unwanted attentions towards that young lady, and the probability he intended some assault upon her. Whether she was his intended victim last night, or whether he would simply have seized upon the first unfortunate that opportunity offered him, is moot. If not for Mr Manktelow's observance and the swift actions of Mr Van Geldern and Mr Jepps, there would of a certainty have been a most brutal and foul assault against the person of a young woman last night. This is beyond dispute. And it is true this might easily have led to a death, and thereby a breach of The Law. Moreover, it's highly probable that given the opportunity Mr Brassland will attempt to do so again.'

There was a general mumbling of agreement, although that

might have been down to a general reluctance to give Droopy an excuse to go off on another tangent. He went to take a sip of his whisky, realised his glass was empty, and blinked his wet eyes hopefully in my direction. I sighed and took the glass. 'Wrap it up, mate, okay?' I said.

Droopy nodded, his chins wobbling, licking his lips as he watched me decant three more measures into his glass. 'I thank you,' he said at last. 'The issue, however, is that The Law itself has not, as yet, been broken. Therefore we do not, as yet, have grounds to expel Mr Brassland.'

'Fuck that!' shouted Chloe, who'd had enough of Droopy's waffle and didn't care for his conclusions either. 'So what are the rest of us supposed to do? Walk around wearing a bloody target until the bastard decides to get one of us?'

'Madam,' began Droopy. '*Madam—*'

'Oh put a sock in it, for Christ's sake,' Dahlia said, and Droopy shut up. She was a tall, statuesque woman in her late forties, with blonde hair and a proud, leonine face. Exactly what Dahlia had done to end up on Bone Street was not known: people were generally glad to share their stories, especially here in the bar, but she liked to cultivate an air of mystery. The rumour I considered likeliest was that she'd been a dominatrix whose last client had—like Chloe's—succumbed to overexcitement. I was fairly sure I didn't believe the story about her having been a serial killer who'd preyed on abusive men and sex offenders, slicing bits off them over several days before finally finishing them off, but I wasn't disposed to dismiss it either. No one was. So even Droopy knew it was time to shut up.

Dahlia folded her arms. 'We've three choices,' she said. 'Keep him under lock and key somehow, for however long—rest of his rotten life, probably. We wait for him to do something. Or we get shot of him now.'

'How?' said Paul.

'The Law—' began Droopy, then fell silent as Dahlia sent a sulphurous glare his way.

'How else?' she said. 'We expel him. Tell him to sling his hook.

We'll have to sooner or later anyway, won't we? So let's alter the timescale before someone does get hurt.'

'I vote for option three,' rumbled Vic.

'And me,' said Chloe.

Ahmed pursed his lips, then nodded. 'Me too.'

'And me,' said old Polodski.

Kerry, Lucy and Sadie all raised their hands together. I looked at Paul, and he nodded. 'Me too,' I said.

I couldn't say I entirely liked it, but no one had a better suggestion. I think the only one who'd have hemmed and hawed over it for any longer than we already had was Droopy Sykes. But that would only have been so he could cadge another whisky.

∞

As in the old fable about belling the cat, there was the question of who'd be the one to do it.

Ralph Brassland was not a small man. His preferred victim type tended to be small and slim, not least because his preference had always been for young victims—hence the attention he'd paid Sadie. The girls he'd preyed on, as a rule, had stood no chance against an attacker who was six-three in his socks and tipped the scales at a sturdy sixteen stone, of which very little was flab. (Ralph looked the part of a Rugby League prop forward, largely because he'd been one.) But he wasn't a coward: he was more than capable of putting up a fight.

In the end, it was decided the expulsion would be a group effort. He could fight one or two of us, maybe several at a time, but even he couldn't deal with the whole street.

We hoped.

By the time we finally agreed on a course of action and emerged from the Station Hotel it was dark—it was winter, and the nights were drawing in fast. Despite the cold, Ralph was still wrenching at his cuffs as we started down Bone Street towards him. I have to admit that I wish I'd been able to see his face in better detail when he saw the entire population bearing down on him. Not least because Paul and Mr Polodski had both popped back to their own premises before the general exodus and gathered a few wares. There were several baseball bats and sets of knuckledusters in evidence, and Polodski had even procured an electric cattle-prod, which Chloe had commandeered the second it came out. That was a woman on a mission and no mistake.

By the time we'd reached him, Brassland had gone very still. He stayed still—which might have had something to do with Chloe standing in front of him with the cattle-prod held ready, with Kerry off to the side with a baseball bat cocked to deliver a blow. I went behind him and unlocked the cuffs, stepping quickly back as his wrists came free. He stayed still then, too, other than to rub his wrists. Dahlia held a hand out for the cuffs and I passed them over.

Brassland studied us, then straightened up and squared his shoulders. '*Thank* you,' he said, heavily sarcastic, and made to shoulder through the crowd, but everyone closed ranks against him.

'Seriously?' said Chloe. 'Think we'd just—?' She snorted and shook her head.

'What you gonna do?' said Brassland. 'There's only one law here, and I've not broken it.' He called out to Droopy. 'Right, pisshead?'

Droopy looked down and mumbled.

'But you would've, though,' said Kerry.

Ralph grinned at her and looked her up and down. It was as though she wasn't holding the baseball bat and he was in the parlour at Dahlia's, taking his pick of the girls, looking them over like hung-up sides of beef, the way the worst punters do. 'But I didn't,' he said, as if talking to a child. 'Did I, now? Eh? No, I didn't. So you can't do anything. So fuck off out of my w—'

He dodged sideways as Kerry swiped at him with the bat, and the smirk on his face vanished. Now he was angry, and made a grab for the bat. He might well have forgotten himself and done her an injury if he'd got hold of it, whatever he'd been saying, but he didn't manage to get a grip and Kerry stepped back, the bat held high. Chloe had moved in closer, holding the cattle-prod and—you could tell just by looking—hoping for an excuse to use it. Vic circled towards him across the grimy pale cobbles, the golf club he'd picked as his weapon propped on his shoulder. Ralph pursed his lips and sighed, then scowled.

'All right,' he said. 'I'm listening. So what do we do?'

'*We* don't do anything,' Dahlia said. 'Just you.'

'Ralph Anthony Brassland,' began Droopy in his most portentous tones, 'it is the unanimous decision of this community—'

'Droopy, shut up,' said Ahmed. 'Go and drink the drip-tray, or something.' He folded his arms and turned his full attention to Ralph. Goth outfit or no, he was a big guy himself, and that wasn't all flab either. 'You're not wanted here any more, Ralph.'

'Oh.' Brassland nodded and chuckled. 'I'm not, am I?'

Ahmed shook his head.

'We voted on it,' Chloe said. 'We all did. You're out. Expelled. Kicked out. Gone. So fuck off—' She jabbed the cattle-prod towards the viaduct '—and don't come back.'

'Really?' Now Brassland folded his arms. 'You're allowed to do that, are you?'

'It's done,' I said. Brassland's hard, lizardy little eyes flicked towards me. He licked his lips—a quick darting of his tongue, like a snake's. 'So go.'

'I see,' said Ralph, and nodded again. 'And if I don't?'

'Then we will make you,' said Mr Polodski.

'You will, will you?' Brassland spread his arms. 'You can *try*. But you're not getting me under the viaduct under my own steam. Gonna carry me, are you, Granddad? What about you, Dutchman?' This with a look at me; I'm not actually Dutch myself, but my surname is. Part of my bond with Paul Manktelow, whose family had come over from Amsterdam during the War. Brassland looked to him next. 'No?' The smirk faded. 'Fucking none of you. You'll have to kill me. And *then* where will you be?'

He was right, too. If he'd killed someone, we might have got away with chaining him to the lamppost and leaving him there. The Closers would have come out of the tunnel and got him. Even that wouldn't have been ideal, because there'd been some confusion about what they might be allowed to do if someone had breached The Law. But because Brassland hadn't, yet, we could have left him chained there all week with no effect. We'd have to physically get him under the viaduct, and that would be a matter of brute force. Violence or the threat of it. And if you're going to die anyway and have nothing to lose, why not fight?

Brassland put his hands on his hips and grinned at us again. 'Sinking in, isn't it?' he said. 'Kill me, and *you'll* be the one going under. Who fancies that job? And come to think of it, if you *make* me go under—aren't the whole lot of you good as killing me? What then? Eh?'

A few of us looked to Droopy Sykes at this point, as our resident legal eagle. But anyone relying on Droopy for advice was, obviously, in dire trouble already.

'I'm not going,' said Ralph. 'I'm not going anywhere, and you can't make me. But I've got a better idea.'

He took a step towards us. I managed to stand my ground, but it was an effort, presented with the grin on his face and the triumph in his eyes.

'See,' said Ralph, 'I just wanted to get my cock wet. That's all. What can I tell you? Some fellas like a drink, some fellas like the old wacky-baccy or the Bolivian marching powder, some bastards just like to stuff themselves silly. But me? Give us a nice bit of vadge and I'm fine. If I've got that on tap, I'm not gonna be a danger to anyone, am I now? So here's what I'm proposing.' He pointed at Sadie. 'Just give me her, and we'll be fine.'

Sadie made a little hiccuping sound of fright and I stepped sideways, between her and Ralph. He sniggered at me. There were no others sounds. Everyone was too shocked.

'You fucking what?' Chloe demanded at last.

'Chloe!' said Dahlia. 'Say that again,' she told Ralph.

'Just let me have her,' he repeated. 'I'll keep her at my digs. On tap, like I said. I won't bother you. I'll be good as gold, if I've got her.'

'Get stuffed,' said Kerry, with feeling.

'You even try,' began Lucy.

'Girls,' Dahlia said again. She was studying Ralph as she said it, with eyes grey as dirty ice, and as cold.

'Dahlia—' Chloe stared. 'You're not seriously—'

'Chloe, I won't tell you again.'

Dahlia wasn't stupid. She'd picked up on the crowd's shifting mood. No one liked Ralph Brassland and everyone liked Sadie, but righteous anger and sentiment are both cheap emotions, and no motivation to risk being sent under the viaduct yourself.

I looked around for help, but even Ahmed wouldn't meet my gaze. I couldn't see Paul anywhere. Ralph grinned. 'Okay, then, Mr Barman—you gonna lay down your life for the little lady? Maybe she'll give you a blowie before the Closers get you. Eh?'

I clenched my fists and stood my ground, but there was a cold, scared knot in my stomach. It wasn't because of Ralph, or even the Closers. It was a far worse fear in its way; the fear that I was, ultimately, the kind of man who'd stand aside and let Ralph claim Sadie.

He was almost nose to nose with me now. 'Step aside, little man,' he whispered, grinning still. 'We both know you're gonna bottle it. And you, darlin'—' His gaze flicked towards Sadie '—you don't go anywhere. I have to chase you, I'm gonna be cross.' He poked me in the chest. 'Out of the way, Timmy-boy. I'm having her, and nothing's gonna—'

There was a loud, sharp bang, and a smell of sulphur.

Even a small calibre gunshot is surprisingly loud.

Ralph grimaced, then looked surprised; then the pain kicked in. He clutched at the wound in his side and began to wheeze—it looked as though the bullet had gone through his lung—and the pain turned to fear. 'Oh fuck,' he said. '*Fuck!*' He looked up, and the fear became outright terror. 'No—'

Paul Manktelow fired again, twice, and Ralph fell thrashing and choking to the cobbles. Paul walked forward, face white, the little revolver shaking. He steadied it in both hands, pulled back the hammer with his thumb and squeezed the trigger one last time.

A single shot, loud and clear and crisp, echoed off the walls of the boarded-up shops. It seemed louder than the rest, perhaps because it cut off the sounds Ralph Brassland was making. The big man flopped back across the cobbles and was still. The final expression on his face was more outrage than anything else, that someone had dared to do this to him. A penny piece could have covered the hole in his forehead, but he was no less dead for that.

Paul looked down at him in silence, then put the revolver in his pocket. 'Well,' he said, 'that takes care of that.'

Sadie ran past me and threw her arms around him. Paul patted her hair awkwardly. 'It's all right,' he said. 'It's all right.'

It wasn't, but there was nothing anyone could say, or do. I tried to remember how long Paul had. I was fairly sure that, once The Law was broken, expulsion had to follow within twenty-four hours. I hoped that was right, anyway.

If nothing else, there was time for one last drink.

'Bar's closed,' I heard myself say. Everyone looked at me. 'The Station Hotel bar's closed,' I repeated, then pointed at Paul. 'Except for him. I've got a bottle of *jonge jenever* with his name on it.'

Paul smiled tightly. 'Why not?'

The crowd was already dispersing in a kind of shamed silence, slipping back to their homes, and soon only Paul, Sadie and I remained. Ralph Brassland lay sprawled on his back, his blood thickening between the cobbles, but that was a mess for someone else to clear up. I touched Paul lightly on the shoulder, and the three of us began walking up Bone Street, towards the Station Hotel.

Within the Concrete

Steve Rasnic Tem

CARL POUNDED THE WALL IN FRUSTRATION, KNOCKING the photograph further askew. The voices within the wall stopped for a moment as if waiting for his next move, then continued at a lower volume. He pressed his ear against the textured plaster and listened, eyes closed and one palm flat against the wall for support. The surface was so cool it was almost comforting. He felt as if he were praying, but he had no idea for what.

His knuckles were bleeding, and now there was a dent. He wondered if he had time to return the world to normal before Grace got home.

All day he'd heard this continuous stream of vague vocalizations. Both monologues and conversations, but he could make out few words. They might have been in some language he did not recognize; it was impossible to say.

The city attracted people from all over the world, but after forty years here, he didn't understand why. It wasn't a kind city. Perhaps it wasn't meant to be. Were cities expected to be kind? Were mountains? The city felt increasingly like a range of geometric mountains: primal, unyielding, uncaring. Whoever came here became instantaneously anonymous.

The voices might be the consequences of air moving through the pipes or trapped within the wall cavities. Or perhaps they were generated by expanding and contracting metals inside the structure. He understood little of physics, nor did he know much about construction or the sound-conducting properties of materials.

Possibly it was some rare auditory characteristic making itself known after a certain threshold of concrete had been achieved. Like every other citizen here he was surrounded by it, buried in it, concrete simultaneously reaching for the sky and descending hundreds of yards underground, covering every inch of visible earth, and over time damaging the atmosphere above. An aggregate of error and misguided planning lay hidden within concrete.

Whatever the mechanics involved, the voices continued just beyond the limits of his comprehension. Carl imagined people much like himself with heads pressed against the wall from the other side, palms caressing the plaster, mouths open and attempting communication. The voices were so persistent, almost desperate. But this was the building's outer wall. There were no apartments on the other side.

When Grace returned from her doctor's appointment, he would ask her opinion about the voices. She'd always had a sensible, practical way of looking at things. If she said the voices were nothing to worry about, he would stop thinking about them. Or if she thought they were a legitimate concern she could tell him who to call and what to do. After all these years he still could not believe his luck in finding her. The process by which people come together had always seemed a mysterious one. So had the process by which they come apart.

He gazed out the window at the building across the street. The window openings in the top six floors were bricked up. He couldn't figure out when this might have occurred. Scaffolding surrounded the building, and more openings were being sealed. Windows were disappearing from many other buildings as well.

Long ago he had stopped watching the news, so he didn't know if the suicide rate was still climbing.

What did the residents think about losing their windows? The buildings on this block were massive. He often wondered how many people they contained. If they all fled outside at the same time no one would be able to move. Yet as he gazed down at the streets below it appeared only a few had ventured outside. What if they couldn't leave, or chose not to? If he did nothing with his time but observe from this window, he might be able to estimate how many had been absorbed.

The mid-afternoon glare gradually dimmed. He hadn't realized it was so late. Grace was long overdue. He should have gone with her to the doctor's appointment, but she wanted to go to this one alone. He should have insisted.

Before he was distracted by the voices, he was hanging Grace's photo—it still tilted to the left. She was unaware when he took it last summer in the park. He managed to catch her slight, unselfconscious smile which he loved so much. He planned to surprise her with it when she got home.

Carl didn't own a carpenter's level. He'd leaned his head against the wall for a better perspective, and that's when he heard those first unexplainable conversations.

Her appointment was hours ago. He didn't have the exact address, but he knew the office was in the giant hospital complex downtown. He picked up his cell and dialed Grace's phone.

It rang and rang and the sound was everywhere. But no one picked up. Then his phone died. In a panic he ran from room to room as if expecting a solution to present itself. If the voices were offering a solution, they needed to speak more definitively. After a few minutes he fled the apartment.

∞

Carl rarely left their building alone. He went out if Grace needed a prescription filled or some special food she thought might make her feel better. He felt less than competent on these streets.

He began walking, searching for a taxi or bus which would get him downtown. He passed scattered pedestrians, pale-complected, thin, some talking to themselves, all wrapped in their coats even though it wasn't cold. Their faces showcased startled eyes and open mouths, and he couldn't imagine what they must be seeing. After a few minutes he couldn't bear to look at them, and diverted himself with the storefronts lining the sidewalk, where similar pale figures lingered in doorways, or watched from windows, some crowded inside and filling the store displays, entire groups gawking as if he were the strange one.

The dirty gray sky descended between the buildings and spread through the streets. He tried to remember if there was a pay phone nearby. Hadn't they all been taken out? He vaguely recalled several bus stops on this street, but couldn't remember where.

A pallid figure made a beckoning gesture from a crumbling stoop and mouthed a few words. Carl made himself ignore it. After years in the city, he knew how to keep himself safe, and refused the invitations of strangers.

A bus appeared in the lane alongside him. He looked ahead for a stop but didn't see one. The bus was full beyond capacity, people jammed together in the seats and standing in the center aisle, a few clinging precariously to the outside by hanging onto half-open windows.

The bus stopped abruptly at the next corner and vomited passengers. Dozens streamed out of the buildings to replace them, making the bus overly full again.

Distracted, Carl veered into a wall, scraping his arm. The rusty concrete disintegrated onto the sidewalk in dry rivulets of red sand. He brushed off his clothes and stumbled on. He would have searched for a bathroom to clean himself up but couldn't spare the time. He ignored the advice whispered from beneath the sidewalk. If he remembered correctly, the entrance to the subway was a few blocks down.

The tall building ahead wore unstable scaffolding around the upper stories. The plank and pipe arrangement was overloaded with brick and workmen. A man appeared in a window opening, gazing at the street. Although Carl couldn't see the face clearly, he knew the man was staring at him. The man waved and Carl stopped. The man's head bobbed as if speaking, but Carl was too far away to tell for sure. Several shadows joined the man and they, too, began to wave, heads bobbing. They opened their mouths as if shouting, but their shouts did not reach him.

When the workmen reached that window, they began bricking it up, even though the figures inside struggled to push them away. Within a few minutes the opening was completely sealed. Carl couldn't help them. Something had gone wrong with the city, perhaps a multitude of things, but he had neither power nor time to understand it. There was nothing he could do. He continued toward the subway.

For the next few yards, the sidewalk was covered with barriers. Large square holes in the concrete left a narrow safe path between them. At some junctures Carl had to turn sideways and slide his feet to get through.

A worker's head in a yellow hardhat popped up in one of the square openings. Before Carl could ask what they were doing here the head vanished below. He tried to peer into the dark cavity, but vertigo forced him back. He heard a crowd of voices somewhere within that deep passage underground, but he dared not lean over for a better view.

Over the next block pedestrians leaned against the buildings with one ear pressed to the wall. Carl wanted to ask if they too heard voices but couldn't afford the delay. He needed to find Grace as quickly as possible. He couldn't imagine having to search for her after dark.

He walked another block and wondered if he'd mistaken the location of the subway entrance. He couldn't remember the last time he'd been there. It might have been years. A man was standing on the third-story ledge across the street. Carl glanced around for someone to tell. No one else was in sight. The man on the ledge kept shaking his head. It was unfortunate, but Carl had no time for this. He had to go to Grace. He continued walking and searching for the subway.

A small park filled the following block. He had a vague recollection of the tall fountain and the circular arrangement of benches around it. For a moment he wondered if it might be the park where he'd taken Grace's photo, but maybe that was in the other direction. The city had a number of these small parks, curated patches of nature meant to calm people down. But there was something artificial about them. They were a little too curated, like oversized window boxes. Dig a few yards into them and you hit another concrete layer. Not enough room for a decent root system for their failing trees.

Numerous sleepers lay in random spirals around the fountain and scattered among the trees. The grass was tall enough to obscure their clothing, so he couldn't speculate whether they were homeless or perhaps office workers on a lunchtime nap. Some were so still he thought he should check on them, but he didn't have the time.

Were they talking in their sleep? He didn't see their lips moving, but if he was quiet, he could hear the faintest breath of their voices drifting through the air.

In the distance the faded red arrow on the vertical SUBWAY sign pointed down. Carl would have to pass several buildings under construction, and one being demolished. The sidewalk was closed, but he thought he could discern a safe path through the wreckage. He maneuvered around several yellow barriers but then had to climb over debris streams flooding the sidewalk and spilling into the street. No one stopped him. The sky had darkened further, and he could smell the coming rain. He needed to get to the trains.

The side of one building had been peeled away. A honeycomb structure filled the building's exposed interior and within each cell men and women lay with heads protruding. Carl kept walking—he'd had the briefest glance and needed to keep moving—but had he misapprehended?

He was almost to the subway entrance when he turned around. Several huge black panel trucks were stopped in front of the devastated structure and workers were loading dust-covered bodies inside. The city was conspiring, it seemed, to keep him from finding his Grace.

∞

Once inside the lobby Carl had no idea where to go. The facility may have been remodeled; he wasn't sure. He'd almost never ridden the subway, even before he met Grace. He'd never felt comfortable submerged beneath so much material. Five staircases went down, along with ramps, elevators, and several escalators. The signs were confusing, referring to various color-coded lines, landmarks with which he wasn't familiar, routes named after past mayors, but nothing to indicate where they might take him. A complex map of the underground system was mounted on the wall. It was pretty, but he couldn't follow a bit of it.

After wandering in circles he found some red graffiti scrawled beside a down staircase: DOWNTOWN!, with an arrow. He didn't have time to wonder if this was someone's prank. He took the staircase.

He came to a landing with ramps leading both up and down. He assumed he needed to continue downwards but remembered from trips in the distant past you sometimes went up a level to change trains. He listened for the sound of the trains, which led him sometimes to go up and sometimes to go down. After a while he couldn't decide if the trains were above or below him. He couldn't tell if the rush he heard was due to wind in the tunnels or some speeding mass. It was almost as if confusion had been the planners' goal.

Some walls were not square. The occasional bulge appeared where two concrete slabs joined. Spiderweb cracks spread through many of the corners, and a crevice of a couple inches had opened from floor to ceiling by a staircase. He wondered how many tons of concrete and soil were overhead. Whatever the figure, he knew it wasn't to human scale.

He stopped and closed his eyes. He could no longer hear the

trains, but he heard waves of the deepest murmuration, the voices of thousands people buried inside, but he had no sense of their location.

There had to be someone, somewhere who understood exactly what was going on. Who knew the rules, the paths, the strategies required to negotiate this urban warren. Maybe several such someones, but Carl wasn't among their number.

He had the strangest sensation of being watched. It wasn't by the other commuters, who appeared to do their best to avoid him, looking away as he approached, sometimes stopping and facing the wall until he passed. He kept looking for cameras or other monitoring gear. He saw deep holes spaced throughout the overhead concrete beams and wondered how many hid cameras within their depths.

He followed the passages down as far as he could, finally reaching a vast area turned into a maze by cage-like fencing. The people wandering the maze, their bloodless faces frozen into anxious masks, did not speak. He called out asking where the trains were but received no answer.

He heard a rumbling and thought the trains had to be near, but soon came to a dead end. The roar increased in volume and he retraced his steps searching for a passage. As he ran toward the sound of the trains, he passed a series of closet-sized alcoves where people waited, or hid, faces obscured by their raised hands.

A narrow corridor branched off before a wall, and at the end an open elevator waited. Carl ran inside and pushed the single button.

The elevator brought him back to street level with only a short walk to the hospital complex. The medical offices loomed many stories above everything else downtown. He felt relieved, but disappointed he'd never found the trains. He considered the possibility they'd been replaced with sound effects as a cost-cutting measure.

∞

The hospital was a stone mountain at one end of an immense concrete plaza. He'd been here with Grace several times. He supposed in any sizable city a great many people fell ill and needed to be hospitalized. It seemed even with the advances in modern medicine more people were sick than ever before, but perhaps the medical professionals were better at finding them.

Few people were out on the plaza: two teenagers walking hand in hand, an old man with a cane, a younger man in a gray uniform jumpsuit sweeping the concrete. Carl wondered if the poor fellow was expected to clean the entire expanse by himself.

The last time here he saw hundreds on the plaza: families and school groups, office workers, people streaming in for medical services. Was today a holiday? Since retirement he'd rarely kept track of such things. He imagined thousands sinking into the plaza leaving just their voices remaining.

The tall glass doors appeared impossibly far away, although he'd never thought so before. He headed toward them as fast as he could, which resulted in some stumbling. He passed a concrete wall mid-way with metal plaques fixed to its surface. He presumed it was a memorial of some sort. Two women stood on either side of this wall, eyes closed beatifically, hands and one ear pressed against the polished surface. Neither said anything. They might have been praying, grieving some loss, or listening for each other. Anything is possible when you don't know the answer.

The last hundred yards or so featured a broad rose-colored walkway lined with concrete benches. A thin naked man had folded himself within the hollow space beneath one bench. He gazed at Carl with a frightened expression. Carl decided to say nothing. The entrance was in sight. He moved on.

Closer in the massive building resembled a warehouse more than a mountain—a weathered concrete block with windows so narrow and deeply recessed they were almost indetectable. Sideroads lead traffic into the back of the facility, presumably for unloading: those enormous black panel trucks he'd seen earlier, and a convoy of buses.

Inside, the first floor was one large open area. White painted concrete beams overhead were held up by numerous identical square concrete posts. Lit glass globes hung from a ceiling which was much too far away, miniaturizing the partitioned maze below.

A line of identical frosted windows faced the front doors. Each had a circular cut-out with a narrow horizontal slot at counter level. Carl stopped a few feet away, straining to see through the cutouts, crouching for a glimpse of the figures behind the windows. He managed to make out bony, mottled hands, bits of keyboard, the occasional deep-set sleepy eye, a bruised ear, but nothing indicative of a receptive clerk eager to help.

He went to the window in front of him and knocked on the glass. A smoky mascaraed eye and narrow nose above a wrinkled mouth appeared in the cutout.

The mouth didn't appear to move, but he heard the rasped delivery, 'Next window please.'

'I'm looking for my wife. She had an appointment with Dr. Aronovitz.'

'That office is closed now.'

'But I haven't heard from her. Can you at least let me know if she's been admitted to the hospital? She's been ill.'

'Our computers are down.'

'When will they be back up?'

'I couldn't say.'

Carl thanked her, although she'd been no help. He turned away, considering his next steps. On one side was a large waiting area with the usual assorted institutional chairs and benches. But there were booths along one wall, spaced a couple of feet apart. Within these spaces people stood with their faces averted. Some thumbed through magazines and some stood weeping into their hands. But in one a couple stood kissing with an intensity Carl remembered from his youth, when desire had ruled him, and not embarrassment.

As their numbers were called people left these spaces and went to the nurse standing in a distant doorway. But one man refused to budge even though his number was called numerous times. Two stocky orderlies came out and forced the man to walk between them as they guided him past the nurse.

Carl collapsed into a chair and tried to figure out what he should do next. It seemed he'd been better at solving things when he was younger. Now his brain was like cement slurry, right on the edge of hardening, after which no thoughts might escape.

Perhaps his raw panic had made him leave the apartment too soon. Maybe Grace was there now waiting for him. But he didn't understand why she hadn't let him know she'd be so late. It wasn't like her. He'd be so relieved just to find her safe. Not that he believed in this hopeful scenario. Something was terribly wrong here.

Someone had left a cellphone on the small table beside him. He looked around. No one appeared to be paying it any attention. He picked it up, turned it on, and was surprised to find it didn't require a password. He punched in Grace's number and waited.

The phone made a connection, but no one answered.

'Hello?' Carl spoke softly, then more loudly 'Hello?'

He heard a soft, whistling whisper, as if the phone on the other end were falling through air. It never landed, and no one ever answered. He placed the phone back on the table.

Agitated, he couldn't bear to sit. He saw movement behind one of the frosted windows with no line waiting. He stepped up to the window and knocked on the glass.

'Please take a number and sit down,' said the voice behind the glass. 'Wait your turn. We all have to wait our turn.'

'No, please. You have to help me.' Carl struggled not to cry in frustration. The bureaucrats were waiting for you to lose control so they could punish you. They tormented the weepers the most. 'My wife Grace is missing. We've lost all contact. I need someone to explain to me what's going on.'

'Is she one of those in quarantine?'

'I don't think so. At least I wasn't informed. Has there been an outbreak?'

Pale lips appeared centered in the circular cutout in the glass. 'Third floor. Ask for Doctor Smith.'

There was a bank of four elevators. Carl dashed into one and pressed the button. When the car arrived, he stepped inside.

When Carl came out of the elevator, he appeared to be on a patient floor. A long hallway with rooms on both sides led to an oversized, gunmetal gray nurse's station. There was a short distance between doors, so the patient rooms had to be quite small. The ceiling was low; he could almost touch it with his fingertips. He assumed the above ceiling space held the utilities, the giant tubes of an HVAC system perhaps, or maybe it was a way to squeeze in more floors. He'd heard hospitals were always exceeding capacity. It required a great deal of space to hide the sick and dying.

He didn't know where the office of this Dr. Smith might be, and if the man was out on rounds Carl might miss him. To be safe he went room to room, hoping a quick glimpse might avoid disappointment.

The first room contained one large bed with room for little else. Several dust-covered, pale faces peeked from the folds of a gray blanket and stared at him before disappearing again. There was much whispering beneath the covers, but they never reappeared.

In the next room a woman and three small children gathered around a man's bed. On the other side of the room five physicians in shiny steel chairs leaned forward, watching. Prayers might have been said, complaints or promises. He couldn't tell.

In the next room he heard soft noises with no apparent source. He entered the room, and realized a constant monologue was coming from within a tall metal wardrobe. He opened the wardrobe door. Inside an emaciated old man looked up, distressed. Carl apologized and shut the door.

In another room he thought the old man sitting by himself was looking into a mirror, but then the other old man moved. They were either twins or old enough to resemble each other.

He turned his attention to the rooms across the hall. The bed in the first room was empty but appeared recently occupied. The sheets were disheveled, and there were bits of gauze, bandage tape, and bloodstains on the floor.

The next door had a small, printed card taped to its center: DECEASED. The dead person lay in bed with a single sheet pulled over the face. Three men in low-slung hats and long dark overcoats stood at the foot of the bed, whispering among themselves.

Similar shrouded forms occupied the next five rooms whose doors had also been labeled with a DECEASED card. Carl stopped in the middle of the corridor, unsure how to proceed. He couldn't bring himself to go through the entire floor this way. Echoing voices rose and fell, drifting through the corridor like awful smells. Perhaps there were priests hiding in the shadows, delivering a succession of last rites.

He saw a nurse behind the distant counter and went there, ignoring the various patients crying out to him from their beds. They called him by unfamiliar names; everyone seemed to think he was some relative or lover. But none were Grace. The nurse appeared startled to see him there and looked down.

'Can you direct me to Doctor Smith's office?'

'You have an appointment?' She busied herself glancing through the papers on the counter, but she didn't appear to read any.

'Of course,' he lied.

She didn't look up. 'Just keep going. Fifth door on the right past this station.'

The first four doors were closed. The fifth was open, but the room was almost filled with fresh concrete, splashes staining the ceiling and the tile outside. A man's glasses protruded from the surface in front, crusted in gray bits of cement.

'You don't belong here, sir.' Carl turned around. The nurse he'd spoken to earlier stood flanked by two security guards. He had no chance of outrunning them, not at his age, but he still raced toward the door marked STAIRS a few yards away.

Carl ran out of breath almost immediately, but his legs

continued to move up and down. He heard the footsteps thundering somewhere above and behind him, their echoes multiplying until it seemed he was being chased by hundreds. He jerked open the door to another floor and stumbled through.

He was in a large room crammed with hospital beds no more than a foot apart with barely enough room for the patients to get out of bed and stand. One old man stared at him from beneath several layers of sheets and blankets. Only his shiny nose and eyes were visible. Carl sidled sideways between the beds looking for another exit. Taking the opportunity, he shouted 'Grace!' but no one answered. Many of the forms were motionless. It was impossible to say whether they were resting or dead.

A door in a side wall led him down another staircase and into another large room. Here the patients were dancing. Many half-dressed, some naked. No one seemed to mind. One man held his partner up with the greatest of effort. The apparently unconscious woman hung limply, her feet dragging sideways across the floor. An audience of patients in hospital gowns and wheelchairs were arranged along the edges of the crowd, some clutching their intravenous poles. No one spoke. He tried to look at all the faces, hoping to recognize Grace, but there were so many of them, and so many who looked the same.

He heard footsteps coming behind him and headed toward the double doors at the end. On the other side was a loading dock, a multitude of those black panel trucks waiting. Body bags were being taken off those trucks, while other body bags were being loaded to replace them. More bags were stacked against the wall several columns deep, waiting. He felt the arms grabbing him from behind, the bag being slipped over his head.

∞

Carl woke up on the plaza before the hospital doors. People were walking around him, trying not to make eye contact, although a few threw him coins. He gazed out over the plaza. It occurred to him how much it resembled a giant, toppled headstone.

Faint voices issued from the concrete like steam. Not strong enough to understand, but they had their effect.

In one section of the plaza workmen were replacing a damaged portion. He walked over but couldn't get past the ropes. Others gathered but they too were denied access. No one was allowed to get close enough to discover the secret which lay beneath the skin, the bricks, the rocks, and the concrete fill. People might be trapped within hidden vacancies far below the surface, but only those select workers and the ones who'd hired them would know for sure.

Such a huge volume of concrete, the weight of it seemed too much for even the planet to bear.

Carl ventured to the center of the plaza and stood there, listening. It seemed a good focal point to catch all the voices. Still, nothing sounded recognizable, and he could find nothing of Grace here at all.

He would have to return to their apartment and wait. He would charge his cell phone, dial her again, and continue to wait. There was nothing left to be done. Grace would contact him if she were able, and if she were not able, she would not. He might never know what happened, but this was true of most things. Grace had always been better at accepting these simple truths than he. In this world you did what you could do, and no one could expect more.

Had he forgotten something? Had she given him some information, some clue, and somehow, he had forgotten?

Carl fell to his knees. He imagined he could hear her breathing beneath the concrete. He began to sob, and he struggled to make himself stop, because he would never hear her as long as he made so much noise. He took a long, deep breath to contain himself, which made his entire body shudder. Deep within the concrete he heard himself weeping.

THE PRIMACY OF THE CUBE

PAUL DI FILIPPO

"I'VE ALWAYS FELT THE PRIMACY OF THE CUBE . . . NOT just because there are so many cubes around us—rectilinears, parallels, and right angles—but the Bible says the City of God at the end of history is an enormous cube coming down out of heaven. And the 666 that you've heard about in the Bible are the 6 tetrahedron edges, the 6 octahedron vertices, and the 6 cube faces—the old Platonic atoms all pulled apart, and the edges, vertices, and faces, like Humpty Dumpty, unable to get back together again; a fragmented view of reality, rather than the 7-12 unity of the cube itself. And the cube is the 7-12 unity because it has 12 foundations in the Bible . . . 12 edges for the 12 apostles, the 12 tribes of Israel, the 12 months of the year. It has 7 axes of symmetry for the 7 days of creation, the 7 days of the week, the 7 early churches. And it has 9 planes of symmetry, for the 9 hours of the crucifixion. So it's full of biblical meaning."

—George Odom, quoted in Genius at Play: The Curious Mind of John Horton Conway

∞

In October of 1871, three long and arduous years of construction were finally reaching their culmination. The Hudson River State Hospital for the Insane was about to open its modern, hygienic rooms to its first forty residents. These initial patients, the raison d'etre of the whole enterprise, would now begin to receive much-needed 'Kirkbride moral treatment' from the highly educated and compassionate staff. Suffering families would be cheered. Journalists could at last report to their readers that the reforms which their newspapers had championed were reaching fruition. And Governor Hoffman would be proud to add the boast of a 'campaign promise accomplished' to his civic speeches, in order to offset the rumours connecting him to Boss Tweed and his gang.

But certainly no one would be happier at the opening of this giant 'batwing style' edifice—set amidst acres of verdant landscaping designed by Olmstead and Vaux—than the building's long-suffering architect, Frederick Clarke Withers.

After a run of extra expenditures, strained labour relations, lack of materials, cantankerous weather (the Hospital was located at a small remove from the town of Poughkeepsie in New York State, and enjoyed all of that region's irascible winters), the dream that Withers had laboriously plotted out several years ago, and which he had despaired of ever seeing fully realised, would now be a tangible reality. Although construction connected with additional buildings on the campus would continue for some time, this titanic structure had demanded most of Withers' talents and time, interfering with such other contemporaneous projects as his designs for the Columbia Institution for the Deaf and Dumb.

At age forty-three, Withers remained youthful looking. His rather longish, clean-shaven face often wore a sombre expression, but it could be leavened by an ingenuous grin from time to time. His second wife, Beulah Alice, often triggered such spontaneous jollity, as did his young daughter. Despite his twenty years tenure in the USA, Withers still possessed traces of a British accent, derivative of his native Somerset. His informal suit reflected a conservative taste.

As a staunch and respectable member of society, an upright family man, Withers could generally be found in church at this hour on a normal Sunday. (And certainly he had designed enough churches, a specialty of his acknowledged by such prestigious reviews as *The Ecclesiologist*, that their interiors felt like a second home.) But today, the fifteenth of October, was special, for the Hudson River State Hospital for the Insane was slated to throw its doors open on the eighteenth, and Withers was using the Sabbath to make one final inspection.

Crossing the rolling, well-planned, expansive grounds, he made mental notes about items left undone, which he would communicate to Olmstead and Vaux. Enjoying the quietude and the crisp autumnal air that even carried a scent of the Hudson not too far off, Withers approached the big doors at the main entrance to his brain child. He paused a moment to take some pride in the way the massive, lightly ornamented structure carried its weight so delicately, not hulking ominously over the human guest. He had wanted to make sure that the incoming sufferers would not feel that they were entering some kind of purgatorial prison, and also that the building's atmosphere would register on the staff in a certain optimistic, gay-hearted way.

Utilising his set of keys, Withers let himself into the hospital. The smell of fresh plaster, paint, varnish and cut wood enveloped him delightfully. He began his tour of inspection. Offices, colonnades, porches; the separate wings for male and female patients; chapel, function halls, medical ward, library, barber shop. Everything seemed trig and turned out to his exact specifications. He felt a swelling pride at what he and others had wrought for the benefit of mankind.

But as Withers ascended the main flight of stairs, between the second and third floors, something alarming and anomalous shattered his peaceful contentment with his tour.

Voices. The words unintelligible at this remove, but nonetheless the unmistakeable sounds of conversation.

Who could this be, intruding on the sanctity of his inspection? Late-labouring workers? Some other authorised but unscheduled visitor, such as a dignitary or doctor? Villains of bad intent?

Not even pausing to consider that the last-named type of intruders might offer him harm, Withers dashed up the remaining steps and arrowed toward the sounds, racing down a corridor featuring serried doors. Getting closer, he discerned that the talk issued from one of the patient bedrooms or private quarters, whose door was slightly ajar.

Withers grabbed the knob and impetuously flung open the barrier.

Quite improbably, he saw four men and a single woman hunched over a table, atop which was a curious object that seemed to be glowing with its own interior purple light. The thing resembled the caricature of a star, made out of crystal. Featuring twelve vertices at angles to each other, the object, upon closer inspection, seemed to consist of four intricately interlaced triangles.

The group ceased speaking and looked up when Withers burst in. The architect had only a moment to register their appearances; but somehow—that purple radiance?—they burned into his retinas with camera-like precision.

One man wore a medieval gown and floppy hat. His ingenuous and candid face betokened a Mediterranean physiognomy.

One insouciant man was dressed in an elegant grey business suit and sported pointed waxed mustachios.

One earnest man wore a simple white jersey and brown trousers. His squarish face was covered with a salt-and-pepper beard that matched the waves of hair atop his head.

The last man was the most eccentrically dressed: juvenile short pants that revealed his pasty-white and hairy legs below the knees; white cotton stockings and canvas shoes like those of some whaler swabbie; a paint-spattered pullover shirt decorated with some kind of crest.

But the woman struck Withers most dramatically of all—for she was manifestly not human! Unclothed, her curvaceous ivory form registered no secondary or primary signs of her sex, for her skin was some unnatural smooth substance. Although eminently alluring and classically modelled, she also lacked hair.

Withers and the five intruders maintained a frozen tableau for illimitable seconds.

Then three of the men, and the woman as well, simply vanished! They evaporated down unknown avenues, despite Withers blocking the only exit.

Left behind was the fellow in abbreviated trousers. Able to focus on him alone, a stunned Withers saw slight-figured, dark-haired, round-faced individual of middle age, his eyes possessing a feverish glint hinting at some kind of fixity of ideation, midway twixt madness and brilliance.

'Mister Frederick Withers,' said the man. 'Welcome to my room.'

Withers painstakingly retrieved his voice. He was beginning to overcome his shock and to feel some indignation at this unauthorised conclave.

'Your room? How so, you arrogant rascal?'

'No arrogance, just simple fact. This room will be my quarters for some thirty years, until my death. But that won't happen for roughly a century from now.'

These insane words certainly consorted with the avowed nature of this new building, a domicile for Bedlamites. But Withers found himself curiously accepting of the statement's accuracy. Intrigued, he took a seat at the table where the strange twelve-pointed star still poured forth its amethyst light.

'You must pay careful attention to my words,' said the intruder. 'My name, not that it really matters, is George Odom, and I and my friends—the four other people you saw with me—are on a mission to save humanity from total destruction. We wish to enlist you as our sixth member. There must be six of us, you see, for the mission to succeed. Just as there are six square faces in the cuboctohedron, of which this figure is the skeleton.'

Odom gripped the glowing crystal star and flourished it practically under Withers's nose. 'Do you see it, in all its glory? Let your eye run over the vertices...'

Mathematics had always been a strong suit of Withers, and now, with his intellect slightly unhinged from the bizarre circumstances, he was able to follow Odom's command and allow his geometric imagination to supply the missing faces of the star, thus reconstituting the naked armature in his mind's eye as an Archimedean solid.

'Yes, I see it. A most uncommon configuration...'

'Most uncommon, but vitally necessary as a mechanism to allow us free access to all of spacetime. That is why I need you to rebuild this room along specific dimensions that conform to the Golden Ratio. Only such a chamber, inhabited steadily for thirty years, will allow me to concentrate my mental powers and breach all the barriers that stand between us, the six saviours of mankind, and the threat of the Four-spacers. They arrive in 2213, and we haven't a second to waste!'

Withers started to lose patience with this absurd babble. How had he given any credence to some voluble vagrant carrying a child's phosphorescent-painted toy? The man's disappearing companions? Most likely just an artefact of the architect's overstrained nerves. How could such a woman as he imagined seeing ever exist?

'My god, man, talk sense! How did you get into my building? What do you want? Trying to sell me some half-baked Edgar Allan Poe tale will not excuse your trespass!'

Remarkably self-assured, Odom did not take umbrage at this disbelief and insult, but merely said, 'I see I must offer you substantial proofs. Gaze into these vertices...'

Withers discovered his attention to be enraptured by the glowing geometrical construction and, as the purple light began to pulse, he felt himself falling into the depths of the nested triangles.

He hovered bodilessly, high over a huge metropolis, some sprawling city of futurity, whose mighty buildings pierced the sky.

He could feel the wind upon his face, and had to squint against the sudden sunlight. A resonant susurrus emanated from the conurbation. As an architect, Withers marvelled at the unknown techniques and principles that allowed such graceful yet overpowering constructions. Strange aerial chariots zipped among the towers, and self-propelled carriages traversed the smooth roadways. All was activity and purpose.

But then there manifested, in the hitherto empty skies above this exalted urban perfection, a gigantic featureless golden cube. But was it a mere cube? The eye could not track its surfaces properly, for the cube seemed to exist not only in the familiar three dimensions, but also down other laterally displaced vectors. Extensions of it wavered in and out of perception.

The cube began to descend upon the buildings, plainly intent on destruction!

The city was helpless, seemingly possessing no defences against the attack. The cube crushed all it touched, wreaking havoc everywhere. Its transdimensional extensions lashed out at some remove from the main cube. Cries of terror filled the air. The only salvation was flight, and a few air vehicles and ground vehicles indeed succeeded in escaping. But soon the once-magnificent city was thoroughly demolished, with an unknown loss of life.

Satisfied, the cube set off through the skies, presumably heading toward some other victim.

Withers snapped back to 1871, and the presence of the stranger, George Odom.

Odom transfixed Withers with the intensity of his gaze.

'I call the cube the City of God. But of course, it has no such mystical origin. It is the vessel of the Four-Spacers, beings who inhabit a dimensional realm higher than our brane. Eventually, they will succeed in wiping out all of humanity with their unstoppable depredations, eliminating us as competitors for multiversal dominance. That is, they will destroy us, if the six of us don't stop them first. Not every path is closed to us, and the future is not set in stone. But our success has only one foundation. Your establishment of this room as my incubation chamber.'

After the experience of that vision, Withers had further difficulty in speaking. Eventually he stammered out, 'What—what must I do?'

Odom produced a crumpled cyanotype blueprint from one baggy pocket of his short trews. 'Just remake this chamber according to these plans. Then I can inhabit it in the future so as to accumulate my powers.'

'But how can I ensure that its configuration will remain untouched for decades, until you arrive?'

'Not to worry. The very fact that I am here talking to you is proof of the chamber's continuity down the century.'

'But I haven't yet done what you ask, so how could the results already obtain?' The mad temporal logic of chicken and egg threatened to unhinge Withers' rationality.

'Don't trouble yourself trying to figure that out. Just do what I say. And now, I must go.'

Odom stood up, causing Withers instinctively to mimic his actions. The intruder from the future gripped the quadri-triangular armature, waved it through the air in an intricate pattern, then disappeared!

Alone again, with sane October afternoon light flooding the room, Withers was inclined for just a moment to believe he had fantasised the whole affair. But then he realised he was still holding the blueprint. He smoothed it out on the table and studied it. The alterations to the chamber possessed an attractive rightness, manifesting several aspects of the golden mean, *proportio divina*...

Withers decided upon the instant to do what Odom had requested. There seemed no harm in doing so, and possibly some good. It was truly very little to ask of the architect, and surely he would never see the troubling man from the future again...

∞

In a flawless, sterile room, full of arcane, quasi-organic equipment, empty of human presence, a woman was being constructed. Although highly advanced, the machines building up her form atom by atom worked from antique instructions: the Golden Ratio. This ancient formula of perfection guided their every movement.

When after many hours their design was complete, an almost luminescent ivory body stretched out upon a table. The engines of life were kickstarted and the woman opened her eyes, blinked, then arose. At that point the door to the fabrication facility opened, and five men entered. Dressed in long gowns along the lines of classical Greek garb, they presented a variety of hopeful faces to their creation.

The woman exhibited an instant maturity and knowledge evidently engineered into her brain. She pointed in turn to each fellow, and spoke his title.

'You are the Scientist, the Madman, the Artist, the Philosopher and the Builder.'

The one designated the Madman spoke. 'You name us correctly. We bear in our sartorised genotypes those peculiar traits which allow us to resonate with each other and form a Harmonic Quincux. But even our quintuple powers are useless to deal with the crisis we now face. We need one more who will serve as the final component to form the Living Cuboctohedron that can manage the threat.'

'I see. And I am to be the Sixth face, Beauty. Very well, I stand ready to enter into the union.'

She took a step toward the men, but was halted by the Scientist.

'Your dedication and willingness are admirable. But the union will not occur with us. Our genes have been ultra-sophisticated and somewhat enervated by the ages, mapped by the enemy, who knows all the ways to defeat us. What we need are our avatars from the past, the wild stock, our forebears, untamed and raw. So we are going to dispatch you to assemble them and bring them forward to our time.'

The Scientist produced an ever-mutating crystal that pulsed and warped with amethyst light.

'Step into the radiance, and prepare yourself for the transition. You will meet the original Madman first...'

∞

On a sunny July day in the year 2007, John Horton Conway boarded the train for Poughkeepsie at Penn Station, and settled down for the ninety-minute ride. Having rushed from his campus duties, he presented a disordered figure, with his wavy hair mussed and his beard bearing minute traces of his lunch. He knew that his wife, Diana, would have chided him for the umpteenth time about his dishevelment, and he smiled at the thought. He pictured his wife and their six-year-old son Gareth as he had left them that morning, waving goodbye. Such a great quantity of loveliness to live for...

Conway had much on his mind, all of his turbulent thoughts centring on the man he was about to visit at the Hudson River State Hospital: George Odom. Somehow, in a way he could not explain, this visit seemed to represent the culmination of the path Conway had been embarked on since his Liverpool youth, when, at the age of eleven, he had vowed to master the realm of mathematics in all its vast and awe-inspiring forms.

This would be his second visit with Odom. While the initial encounter had been frustratingly illuminating, Conway felt that he had merely scratched the surface of what Odom had to share with him.

A self-taught amateur maths whiz with an idiosyncratic approach, Odom had come to Conway's attention through Odom's correspondence with the famous Canadian geometer, Donald Coxeter. Coxeter had been keen for Conway to meet Odom. 'I think you'll find his construction of the Golden Ratio using only equilateral triangles to be of interest.' After studying the relevant papers from the *American Mathematical Monthly*, Conway had agreed. And so that first unlikely meeting—between a distinguished and multi-credited savant employed at Princeton and the inmate of a mental sanitarium—had ensued. Despite any differences in status, after some initial feints and introductions they had fallen into an easy conversation about, among many other things, geometry and game theory, with Odom dropping contrarian and sometimes surreal statements into the discourse.

'I don't like numbers,' the amateur said dismissively at one point, causing Conway to repeat the statement in a baffled tone: 'You, a math enthusiast, don't like numbers?'

'No, I don't trust them one little bit. I think they're negative differentiators. I rely solely on forms.'

'Well, there's something to be said for that approach.'

When it came time to break up their colloquy in the Hospital's library, Odom had tendered a mysterious invitation to return.

'You must come back next month, Conway. My powers will reach their apex then, and I'll be able to show you something really vital. Something I'll need your help with.'

'Very well. I'll see you then.'

And now that enigmatic day had arrived.

Having disembarked at the Main Street station, Conway found a cab, and soon arrived at the antique pile that was the Hudson River State Hospital. Well over a century old, the place had obviously seen better days, its grounds neglected and its good Victorian bones hampered and marred by untended surfaces that showed all the wear and tear of the years.

Having passed through the security inspection intended to prevent visitors from bringing dangerous or disturbing items to the patients, Conway followed the remembered corridors to the library. He found Odom seated at the same table as before. But on this occasion the inmate had with him a geometric construction made of lustrous crystal: four interlocked triangles with vertices pointing in all directions. For a moment, Conway thought to recognise it as one of the Archimedean solids, but then his intelligence somehow slipped off the refulgent surfaces of the object.

A fidgety Odom jumped to his feet. 'At last you're here! Thank God! There's no time to waste. Let's go to my room, quickly!'

'But I thought visitors were not allowed in the dormitory wing...'

'No matter, just come on!'

Odom hefted the quadri-triangular armature, carved an invisible sigil in the air with it, and suddenly the two men stood in Odom's bedroom!

Conway staggered against a bureau. 'How did you—?'

'Very simple. Channelling dark-matter gravitons down these resonant quasicrystals, the cuboctohedron skeleton accesses contiguous branes through which we make an instant transition and displacement, before returning to our baseline continuum. Mapping the displacements proved trivial. But none of this matters! What counts now is your assistance in defeating the Four-Spacers.'

Even Conway's powerful and intuitive brain was whirling. 'The Four-Spacers?'

'Here, I'll let Phi explain.'

Out of nowhere, from some slit in the fabric of spacetime, stepped a prepossessing naked woman, but one bereft of intimate parts. Her seamless and unblemished hairless ivory body exhibited a strange correspondence, Conway suddenly realised, to the odd dimensions and angles of Odom's bedroom. Revelation burst upon Conway, abetted in part by the woman's name.

'You, Miss Phi, have been built along the lines of the Golden Ratio, as has this very room.'

Phi's voice manifested a mechanical sonorosity, a kind of artificial sensuousness. 'Indeed, my Scientist. Even in my birth year of 2200, the *proportio divina* is revered.'

'And what brings you here, from that far-off era?'

'Only this: a desperate attempt to save the human species. I was dispatched as a lone emissary from a desperate band of survivors. We needed the unique psycho-geometrical talents of

George, in combination with those of four other individuals, yourself among them, in order to strike back at our enemies.'

As George Odom continued to fuss with various implements and contraptions in the corner of his cluttered bedroom, the android Phi explained the apocalyptic situation that would obtain in the year 2213. Conway nodded sagely throughout the recounting. It was a mad tale, but, given the incident of teleportation and the existence of Phi, how could he doubt it? And, believing it, how could he not contribute his efforts to save mankind? He pictured the sons of the sons of his child Gareth, living in that era and menaced by doom. How could he fail them?

'And my role in all this?' he asked when Phi had finished.

Odom stepped forward, his arms full of various three-dimensional geometric figures, all constructed from the same luminescent quasicrystal substance as the cuboctohedrom skeleton. In addition, he carried a large art book and, of all things, a steaming slice of pizza in an individual-sized pie-slice-shaped cardboard box.

'You will play an immense part,' said the wild-eyed Hudson River State Hospital patient, 'during the attack. I will need to tap all your numeromancy. But your more immediate role is to help me collect the three other men we need for our mission. Although I am the linchpin, there must be six of us in toto for the plan to work. I am relying on your powers of persuasion, intellect and empathy. That last trait is one I fear I lack. I don't like people very much, you see. In fact, that's why I had myself committed here thirty years ago. I could focus on my interests without hindrance from others, their meaningless desires and nonsensical concerns.'

Phi moved next to Odom and took his arm in hers, as a wife might guide her husband to the buffet table. He shifted his geometrical constructions and book and pizza to accommodate her.

'We knew,' said the android, 'that George would not respond well to fellow humans from the future, no matter how dire and pitiful their tale, and so I was selected as ambassador. As well, I form the sixth facet of the gestalt, namely Beauty.'

Admiring Phi's alien surfaces, Conway did indeed register in his gut her mystical attractiveness.

'I love Phi,' said Odom. 'After this mission is all over, we're going to retire to a secret spacetime node where no one will ever bother us again. It might look like my death to outsiders, but you will know the truth.'

Conway had to smile. True love had that effect on him, however bizarre the relationship might look from the outside. He said, 'I congratulate you both. But let's not jump the gun. Who are these three other essential individuals we have to fetch?'

'One of them is Frederick Withers, the architect of this place. The Builder. He's the least powerful of us all, perhaps, but he's intimately bound up now with the geometry of this room that incubated my powers. I have already secured his cooperation, thanks to a previous visit. Do you remember being there with me? No, you wouldn't have access to those memories yet.'

'And the other two?'

'Leonardo of Pisa, first.'

Conway was taken aback. 'Fibonacci himself?'

'None other. The Philosopher. We'll grab him when he's visiting his patron, Frederick the Second.'

'And the last member of our little anti-Armageddon squad?'

Odom offloaded the pizza and constructions to Phi, allowing him to open and shuffle through the big art book he carried. He found the page he wanted, and displayed it to Conway.

'We need the man who painted this. The Artist.'

The mathematicians saw a familiar image: Dali's *Corpus Hypercubus*, which showed Christ crucified on an unfolded tesseract floating in midair.

'This man knows the primacy of the cube. His vision will be essential to our success.'

Conway sighed. 'I don't suppose I could persuade you to substitute my pal Martin Gardner...?'

'No! It has to be Dali!'

'Very well . . .'

Odom reclaimed his quadri-triangular armature from Phi, and fitted onto it several other Archimedean and Platonic solids. The quasicrystal surfaces bonded to each other by some kind of Van der Waals force, observed Conway. When the assemblage was ready, Odom said, 'Here we go!'

Conway found himself instantly standing with Phi and Odom behind a hanging arras. It smelled of hot Sicilian sun and dust. And the pizza from the twenty-first century. He peeked cautiously around one edge of the fabric.

An enormous polychromatic, highly decorated, high-ceilinged room with shining tiled floor was filled with courtiers, soldiers and a king and queen on thrones. Open arches in an exterior wall gave a view of the sea and passage to a cool salty breeze. The Castello di Maredolce in Palermo, home to Emperor Frederick II, King of Sicily.

A petitioner kneeling before the Emperor was speaking in Latin.

Odom whispered: 'Phi, translate for us.'

Phi touched Conway behind the ear. 'I'm layering the necessary subdermal circuits down, establishing neural interface . . .'

Conway abruptly heard the speech as English.

Fibonacci said, '—most gracious Emperor, I thank you again for your kindly hospitality, and look forward to our discussion of the *Liber Abaci* this evening. Now, with your Excellency's permission, I will retire to my chambers.'

Odom fumbled with his geometrical transporter, and Conway prayed no one was observing the wriggling of the arras. 'I'll modulate my fix on him, and then we can follow . . .'

Giving Leonardo a few minutes to reach his room, Conway and his companions made the jump, materialising in Fibonacci's quarters. At last Conway felt safe in venting a huge sneeze engendered by the dusty wall hanging. After blinking, he saw Fibonacci, seated at a table, regarding them with no evident surprise or fear.

Odom handed the man the pizza. Fibonacci sniffed, then ate the offering with gusto. Licking his fingers, he said, 'Ah, the moment I have been waiting for all my life! My comrades from days unborn. I have had a lifetime of premonitions and visions. Our great battle beckons us! Tokens of your existence and ultimate appearance have been foreshadowed in all my investigations into the Golden Ratio. Now, please enlighten me as to precisely what we must do.'

Phi came forward and touched Fibonacci's brow. His eyes slammed shut and he went rigid. Some thirty seconds later, she broke contact, and Fibonacci resumed normal consciousness.

'We cannot allow the glorious struggle of mankind to reach such an untimely end! Let us be off!'

Conway almost felt cheated, for he had planned a long speech to convince Fibonacci to help. He feared he was not carrying his weight in the mission so far. Another disappointment was that he had hoped that the urgency of their task might still permit a small discussion with Fibonacci, for he had several points he wished to clear up regarding Leonardo of Pisa's work. Surely they could pause for a small talk. After all, when jumping crosstime, did it really matter if one departed at any given minute or the next, so long as the destination remained fixed? But Odom, who must know better the mechanics of such travel, was permitting no slacking off.

And so the next moment found the quartet standing on a Parisian sidewalk: specifically, at the corner of Boulevard du Montparnasse and Boulevard Raspail, outside an establishment whose large sign proclaimed it to be the Café de la Rotonde. The day appeared to be a mild one in October, and Conway, gauging the fashions of the many patrons seated outside under the café's awnings, judged the year to be sometime in the late 1920s.

Odom bulled his way amongst the tables, jostling cups and glasses and raising the ire of the patrons. Trailed by Phi and Fibonacci—the medieval costume of the latter and the nudity of the former occasioned no raised eyebrows among these bohemians—Conway followed, making apologies in English.

Odom had stopped by a table where a lone man mused quietly. The skinny fellow wore a decent if not extravagant suit, and striped shirt and tie. His large-domed head, topped by slicked-down black hair and narrowing to a small chin, resembled an inverted pear. A small and modest moustache graced a sensitive upper lip.

Conway stepped forward. 'Señor Dali, might we have a moment of your time?'

Dali waved a hand cavalierly. 'You seem an intelligent and amiable fellow, although your companions are uncouth. Speak.'

Odom dropped the large art book on the table, opened to *Corpus Hypercubus*. The seated man studied the reproduction of the 1954 painting for some time. He slowly raised his glass of liquor to his lips, imbibed, set the glass down, then stood.

'Gentlemen, you confirm all my estimations and intuitions of my own immortal greatness. I stand ready for any reasonable or unreasonable call upon my talents. Inform me of what you desire.'

Phi performed her knowledge download upon the Catalonian's brain.

The painter grinned hugely. 'Dali places his entire existence in your hands. And please note: this is no small gift!'

∞

The new century had not brought to Frederick Withers any peace and satisfaction. In fact, his newest commission—the design of a large prison for the City of New York, already nicknamed 'The Tombs'—was presenting him with nothing but headaches—carking cares he did not need at his advanced age of seventy-three. At the mercy of the whims of politicians and the public, he had begun to falter and doubt himself. His past triumphs—the Jefferson Market Courthouse, the Hasbrouck Mansion, the President's House at Gallaudet—all seemed inconsequential and hollow now.

Seated in the twilit parlour of his empty home, Withers

sipped some herbal tea and adjusted his shawl about his shoulders.

And what of all the myriad churches he had left behind? Did they not constitute a valid achievement? The sacred geometry of worship. He had always regarded them as his real legacy. Ever since the publication of his *Church Architecture* in 1873, he had prided himself on his ability to create these quiet temples of reverence, out of an affinity of the soul.

Eighteen-seventy-three. Two years after that strange occurrence at the Hudson River State Hospital for the Insane. How that inexplicable, unrepeated incident had shaped and contoured the course of his career. A seed that had changed his approach and vision. Making over that one room to conform to the lucid eternal equations of the Golden Mean...

From time to time over the past quarter-century, Withers had visited the hospital or made inquiry to see who inhabited that special room, and what effect, if any, the peculiar dormitory space was having on the patient's cure. So far, none of the residents had been named George Odom.

Withers thought about rising and preparing some supper. But suddenly even that simple task felt like too much work.

A sudden amethyst effulgence lit the room, and Withers felt a hand upon his shoulder. He levered himself up creakily and turned.

The quintet of strange travellers encountered in 1871 had returned, no-wise aged or different.

'All right, Fred, it's time,' said George Odom. 'We need your help again.'

Withers felt a tear trickle down his wrinkled cheek. 'But no, I gave up hope long ago. I've waited too long. I am enfeebled, a shadow of my old self.'

Odom sighed. 'Right, I didn't think of that. Let's see...'

The bearded man said, 'Could we map him onto an earlier avatar?'

The woman replied, 'We might have to fold him invariantly across several branes, but I think it's possible.'

The fellow in the medieval garb exclaimed, '*Ubi sunt!*'

The suave moustachioed chap said, 'Everything alters me, but nothing changes me!'

Odom played with his crystal constructs.

Withers felt instant immense transitions and transformations. A surge of vitality flowed through his revivified body. All his aches and pains vanished. He held up an unlined hand, turning it back and forth to marvel at its youthful flexibility.

'That's done,' said Odom. 'Now let's go kick some Four-Spacer ass!'

The Equality Virus

Gwyneth Jones

1. The Three Legged Pig

The High School librarian's name was Lélia McClary; a good Muslim married to a good Christian, two children, no obvious political allegiance. She had won fame ('going viral', on a modest but interesting scale) by teaching the students at her place of work how to avoid online invasion of privacy—and then asserting that new privacy laws needed to be drafted, when her employers were threatening her with dismissal. She was no firebrand. If Meghan Hamilton understood the story it was the school board who'd gone public and stirred things up. But she'd accepted Meghan's invitation, and that was intriguing.

The Senator, a centrist-leaning Republican who kept a bust of Eleanor Roosevelt on her desk (mainly to annoy any visitors from the other party, but in genuine respect too) believed it was good practice to pick-up on all kinds of stories that interested her. But sometimes, when the story arrived in her office, she wasn't exactly sure why she'd called it in—

'So, Lélia—may I call you Lélia? And please, call me Meghan. You believe our young people are exploited at school. They're more or less forced, by people who should be protecting them, to become feedstock for the media barons, an extra price they're expected to pay for their education, with no accounting, and no recourse—'

'Not exactly, Senator Hamilton.' Lélia smiled politely. 'There's no force, or real deception involved. Most of my students, and I believe this is typical, are pretty savvy. It's more a case of: *Okay, I want this, so I have to give you that*—'that' being some seemingly non-critical personal data; or permission to plant sticky cookies, or an uptick that exposes their details. They make these choices constantly, often with keen discernment, and I believe they *do* suffer, but sadly it's without resentment. Like the three-legged pig.'

'The *three-legged pig*?'

'You must know the story. A fellow driving through farming country saw a remarkably fine hog in a fine large cosy sty. He stopped and said to the farmer "that's a great animal you have there!" The farmer said "yep, and he's a real hero too", and proceeded to tell a marvellous tale of what the hog had done for her family. How he'd rescued a child from drowning, saved the family from a fire, warned them when they were threatened by a terrible storm ... "That's amazing" said the driver-fellow. "But how come he only has three legs?" "Well," said the farmer, "When you have a special hog like that, you don't want to eat him all at once".'

'Ha!' muttered Meghan. 'An apt comparison!'

'It's the adults, I feel, who don't quite know what they're doing,' continued Lélia, without acknowledging this aside. 'School boards and faculties in general, are less ... less *nimble* than the students. They agree to alleged 'choices' and accept conditions that most of my kids wouldn't touch, but the kids are still part of the deal, and I don't think that's fair ... I've told them so; my employers didn't agree, and it kind of snowballed. That's why I'm in trouble.'

'That's why you're here,' the Senator corrected her, mildly.

Meghan's stenographer, a real human stenographer, was committing the interview to shorthand, imperturbably silent, over by the door. The two women sat facing each other on easy chairs by a handsome, old-fashioned, unused fireplace. Eleanor, in dark bronze, smiled ruefully at them; chin up, from the Senator's desk.

'I'm sorry, Senator. I misspoke.'

'Please don't apologise. You aren't in trouble, at least not with me! So... I've followed your case, I've found you impressive, and we're here today to talk about protecting students' data privacy in school—'

'Er... Not exactly.'

Meghan frowned. 'You have a different topic?'

'Not data *privacy*, ma'am... Our children, including my students, mostly manage their privacy issues competently and er, cynically. They accept, and deal with, the constant, sneaky nibbling (and the adults are a lost cause, I'm afraid—). Maybe it's a shame, but I'm not sure a crusade against big media is the answer. Really, I'm more interested in data *literacy*. The kids deserve a better relationship with this amazing resource we've created, although it might be more accurate to say it created itself. They deserve to understand their world. How much there is to know, and how deeply. How astonishing this digital-processing mediated, world-wide machine of interconnection, of putting things together, has become. How very much we *can* know, and it's just there, waiting for us, in the amazing flows of the data. It's called a web, but it's more like an ocean; like *the* ocean, divided and yet interacting, encompassing the planet, and so many wonderful minds, filling the ether, so there's really just about nothing it can't tell us, about the world we live in and what's going on here, if we only learn to ask—'

Meghan had to admire the librarian's breath control, if nothing else.

But the younger woman, so far subdued and clearly nervous, had come alive as she made this speech. She had fire in her eyes; a glow like inner fire in the smooth honey-brown cheeks, framed in that quietly stylish off-the-throat hijab—

'Now you sound as if you're selling a new religion. Or promoting a revolution.'

Out go the lights.

'That's not my intention, Senator. If... if I have any clear intention, it's about promoting data-literacy as a skill—as world-changing, and mind-opening, as a new form of reading and writing.'

'Hence the expression... But Lélia (please do call me Meghan), isn't 'data literacy' equally the enemy of privacy? Isn't the internet, or World Wide Web if you prefer, awash with hucksters selling a whizzy new invention called 'data literacy'? That will make my business grow like a beanstalk, apparently. That will help me, for a steep but reasonable fee, to collect far more *data* than they'd really care to surrender, from my clients, from my staff, from my suppliers—'

'With respect, ma'am—'

'Meghan, please.'

'With respect, Meghan, then. Yes, you get that sales-talk. Bean-counting, number-crunching and invasive performance measurement, dressed up as a shiny new app. Even librarians get the pitch, though we'd have to be fools to be drawn in, and librarians generally are not fools... There's a 'data-literacy' of the marketplace: something trivial that can be bought, and sold, and used for sly, immemorial commercial purposes. Maybe that can't be helped, because grown people are such creatures of habit. They stubbornly adapt the future to fit with what they already know; and then the future never comes. People are like those animals, rats and birds and molluscs, who make nests out of scraps of marvellous human technology, because, what else could anyone want but a nest?'

'What else, indeed?' Meghan smiled wryly, but she was beginning to think this dip into the lucky bag was not a disappointment, after all. 'A nest, as comfortable and safe as possible. Enough to eat; clean water, and protection for your children. Much of humanity would certainly settle for that deal, if they could get it. Are they wrong? What does your oceanic, marvellous version of 'data literacy' offer to the suffering billions?'

'Maybe, er... a chance to look behind the curtain?'

'The *curtain*?'

Lélia blushed. 'The Wizard of Oz?'

'Ah!'

Meghan's stenographer, a genuine antique, could be heard scratching away on his reporter's pad, in a strangely potent moment of silence.

'Hm. Oz the great and terrible. Whose name is legion, and who might object—'

Lélia, who'd given Meghan's secretary just one, uneasy glance when she came in, glanced that way again, and quickly averted her eyes.

'Your secrets are safe,' said Meghan. 'I have security chop their heads off, once a week.'

'She's messing with you,' said Malcolm. 'Take no notice.'

The Senator moved the conversation onto other topics. Lélia's two young children. Meghan's only daughter, a doctor. The fascinating work of a librarian. Meghan's former career (one of her former careers) among ancient documents, at a prestigious institute of learning. Before long the senator brought their chat to a close and stood up; so did Lélia and Malcolm, as if drawn by strings.

'Well. Thank you *very* much for coming to see me. Malcolm will see you out.'

Lélia, looking just a little downcast and disconcerted, nodded and smiled in a gesture of farewell—and went to the door of the office, which Malcolm had opened for her.

On the point of departure she turned back.

'Ma'am? Do I understand you? Do you mean to take this on?'

'I believe I might,' said the Senator. 'Data literacy, as *you* describe it, seems a good cause to support, and perhaps you'll hear from me again. Perhaps you've even made a convert.'

'Go carefully, ma'am. Causes die when people start dying for them.'

∞

When Malcolm returned, his boss was pacing up and down, scowling, arms folded across her broad breast. It was a familiar sight—

'Well,' he said. 'That was interesting!'

'Is *that* what you call it?'

Malcolm resumed his usual seat. 'You've told me you always learn something interesting, when you get someone in to talk about their work—'

'Huh. Malcolm, I have spent years of my life, years I can't well spare, these days, taking up arms against that damned giant data industry. The billionaire bottom-feeders who *monetise* us. Who use human beings like sandbags, to shore-up their mighty stock-share in whatever's the most profitable means of ruining the poor and murdering the living world this week. It's like Gogol, that profit in dead souls... And we *accept* this bargain, knowing how destructive it is, because we're addicted: that's the truth. I've made gestures, the kind of thing that people remember...' She glared at the reporter's pad on Malcolm's desk. 'I've stood up to my party, and to Congress, trying to make my case—'

'You've made a name for yourself.'

'Exactly. Nothing more. Then this young woman, impressive in her way, sits down in my office, and coolly tells me, to my face, that I've been trying to destroy something wonderful! That's what she was doing! And she knew it...! Where does that *put* me? If I were to believe her!'

'Ooh, let me see... On the road to Damascus, maybe?'

'Very funny. So I have a conversion experience, I announce that bad guy big data is our salvation, if only we handle it the right way, and then, what?'

'You get your head chopped off, if I remember my Bible stories right. But it's been a long time... Maybe you should avoid Dallas for a while?'

'And any landscape feature resembling a *grassy knoll*... Huh. Nonsense.'

Meghan returned to her desk, and sat glowering at the back of Eleanor Roosevelt's head. 'What did you think of her, our visitor?'

'I don't know enough to think anything,' said Malcolm. 'But she was scared. I noticed that, from the moment she walked in.'

'Me too. Why would she be scared?'

'You can be overpowering, Senator... *Seem* overpowering.'

'No,' said Meghan, soberly. 'She wasn't afraid of me. She looked me dead in the eyes and told me what she was convinced I needed to know, without fear or favour. She warned me... I'll head home now, Malcolm. It's been a long day somehow. No, I'll walk; no need to call a car.'

∞

Home was a small house in a shady garden, where it had been fun to camp out when the Senate was in session, when John was still alive. It had become a place where his presence lingered since he'd died, a year ago: and beloved for that reason. Meghan cooked for herself (John had never liked take-out food, and they didn't keep servants), ate briskly and took her Lélia McClary puzzle to the study; her favourite place in the house, a haven of life-tokens. There were pictures of John, alive and smiling. A (fake!) Minoan tablet on a stand, commemorating the small part she'd played in the project of aligning two ancient symbol-systems, Linear A and Linear B. Just lists of goods maybe, but still fascinating... Bean counting and performance measurement. You can mock, librarian, but those things matter. That's how it all got started.

A passage from the Anastasi papyrus (thirteenth century BCE), skilfully photographed by a British-Palestinian friend, hung over the sofa. A senior scribe addresses his juniors, at mordant length: rich in instruction, vivid language, and plenty of trashing (geeks don't change!)

Thy reins are cut in darkness...

Wonder what the old grouch meant by that, exactly?

The world has always been a system of signs, she thought. We human animals would never have learned how to read, how to write; how to speak, even, if we hadn't already known how to read a forest, a river; the weather; each other. How to make signs. Life itself is nothing, if not a constant interchange of information. So now we've created an artefact, a world-enfolding ether, that *is itself* a universe of signs and connections. What do we do with it? We prey on each other.

Causes die when people start dying for them. What a strange thing to say, but it resonated. Isn't dying for a cause supposed to be a good thing? A noble sacrifice, inspiring others? She thought of pre-modern Europe, and the Middle East, torn up by religious wars, century upon century: Christian against Muslim, Christian against Christian, Shia against Sunni. All those heroic deaths, and it never ends. But *faiths don't fuel wars*... Meghan was sure of that. Wars get fuelled by power and wealth, just as power and wealth will always be the winners. Look around, in any age of the world, and you'll see the big money right there, on the sidelines of any brutal conflict. Whistling a little tune; going, hey, it's not *my* fault...

Suddenly she realised that the glass-paned doors to the garden were strangely dark. Was that a moving shadow, in the laurel shrubbery? There was a number she could call (the Hamiltons had never liked the idea of security guards on site; who would obviously be armed), but instead, obeying a strong intuition, she opened one of the doors. A figure darted forward and slipped into the room. Meghan shut and locked the doors, and turned to stare at Lélia the librarian.

'Who switched off my lights, and the trips? Was that you?'

'Yes. Very sorry ma'am, but I had to speak to you privately.'

'Hm. I won't ask how you did that, though I don't get it. Sit down, then. Speak.'

Lélia removed her head veil but not the dark abaya cloak, and sat, tentatively, on the edge of John's armchair. 'I didn't tell you the truth, in our interview.'

'I didn't think you did! But your picture of data literacy was very pretty.'

'Yes... It's like this... I *was* teaching data literacy, but my approach started with data privacy. It has to start there. How much the tech and media giants know about us. How they harvest our data. How we think we can choose what we reveal, but really we have very little choice. How they analyse our 'likes' to determine our emotional states, and predict our choices... How we become their puppets, and create their wealth. I taught only what is beyond dispute. What anyone can know, and should know. But the school board didn't like it.'

'And you couldn't say this in my office, because...?'

'I was embarrassed,' said Lélia, and closed her lips firmly.

'But you can speak now?'

'I *will* speak... It could be so different, ma'am, er, Meghan. If the crypto-monopolies were broken up, and nothing like them allowed again. If the internet was regulated as it should be, by experts from different fields who don't stand to gain. Available to all, as part of our life-long education. We could learn to draw together the nets of connection, and think the intricate way the internet thinks, only better, because we are human. It would be a leap beyond where reading and writing have taken us. Such a source of *real* wealth, for the living world and the common good—'

'As you said.'

'Yes! It would be like... a kind of equality virus. Spreading knowledge and the understanding of how to use it, until *everyone* was infected—' The librarian caught herself, and drew back. 'I'm talking nonsense. Very sorry.'

'I didn't hear any nonsense,' said Meghan. 'And I'll go straight to the point. I very much like your pitch, now I've heard it. Lélia, will you work for me?'

She shook her head. 'No. I'm sorry. I can't... I have had a warning.'

'I don't understand.'

Lélia took a basic mobile phone from the pocket of her cloak and passed it over. 'Look... The phone is not live. Nobody will know it was in your house.'

The tiny screen Meghan studied showed a clip from a violent pornographic movie, involving a child. Thankfully, it was silent.

'Do you know who the little girl is?'

'No. But the photoshopped face is the face of my daughter; she is eight years old.'

'I see... Do you know who sent you this vile thing?'

'I will write it.' Léila took out a small notepad, removed a page and wrote, carefully balancing the paper on the palm of her gloved hand. Meghan stared at the name, incredulously, and stared at Lélia.

'One of the richest men in the world is *threatening to have your little daughter gang-raped*?'

'The richest men in the world do things like this in darkness,' said the librarian, steadily. 'They are careful to know nothing of how their wishes—never a direct order—are obeyed. I came to your house, Senator, because I felt I must. Not to ask you to take on the work I cannot continue: but because *you* are already in danger.'

The interview ended there. Lélia would say no more. When she'd vanished into the dark the garden lights came up again, and rain shone on the laurel shrubbery.

Meghan's visitor had taken the scrap of paper on which she'd written a startling name away with her: a detail that impressed the Senator strangely. She paced the floor, astonished. The world of US politics, never very safe or peaceable, wasn't on *extra* high alert just now, but maybe she'd made herself conspicuous?

Could it be true? she thought.

Am I in danger of death? *Really*?

She sat at her desk and stared at her personal laptop, a slim, grey menacing portal. She could handle herself in the deep and dark nets, where secrets lurk. But tonight, if there was a threat to her actual *life* hiding in the damned data; tonight she didn't dare go looking—

I've become physically afraid of malware, noted Meghan. There must be a name for this disease... She thought of her grandchildren: Serena, brave and pushy, and little Moses, the dreamer with a stammer; not cut out to be the front man of anything. Okay, she told herself. If you daren't use the internet, let's see if you can *be* the internet. (She had a feeling the librarian had said this was possible). Assemble your search terms. Send them on a focused ramble, as if in that other universe. If there's a threat, there's a source. There are details. Go fetch.

Aeons later (less than five minutes, it turned out) she took her hands down from her eyes. All she could see was darkness, teeming with stars in motion. 'Wow!' she said, blinking to bring the room back into focus. 'Where did *that* come from?'

I'm just a mouthy old widow woman, she decided—when her head had stopped spinning, and she'd checked that her face looked normal in a mirror. My family doesn't need me. If I've had a little brain seizure, it's my business. I'll call it a hunch, and see what happens.

She made a phone call.

∞

By the time Meghan attended the public event she'd not been supposed to survive, the hired killers were under arrest, and a covert, serious investigation (which would have no results) was ongoing. 'Senator Hamilton,' said the officer in charge, when the event was safely over. 'I'm impressed by your composure, and appalled we didn't spot that. Lessons have been learned, I hope. But, not making excuses, but, if we didn't have the slightest clue: *how did you know?*'

'Just a hunch. You and your team did the heavy lifting.'

∞

The Senator decided to re-imagine her data privacy campaign. That three-legged-pig would be useful! She contacted Lélia McClary and once more offered her a job—partly in hope, and partly (cloak and dagger thinking!) because she certainly would have been getting in touch if that second, deniable, meeting hadn't happened. The librarian again declined. Malcolm Tierney left Meghan's employ, with glowing references. She was sorry to lose him, and believed he was genuinely sorry to go. But Lélia had known she could not speak freely in his presence, and maybe Malcolm had known a little too much about that threat...

2. Behind The Curtain

The new campaign really took off. Old-fashioned roadside billboards were especially successful (very photogenic and shareable). The three-legged pig, so loveable, trusting and big-hearted, soon escaped from Meghan's control, broke out of the USA and could be found, gambolling gallantly on three legs and a stump, in a host of diverse contexts, and all over the digital world. The message that they were getting eaten alive, by sly degrees, certainly seemed to resonate with people.

Big data ignored the whole thing, naturally: dismissing unspecified "fresh attacks" on "crypto-monopolies" with contempt, while continuing to devour independent innovation, and strangle defiant start-ups that showed resistance.

The big players' only response (maybe!) to the gallant pig was a new, splashy and syrupy publicity campaign celebrating the major charities, climate-change rebels and civil liberties defenders who remained their treasured, faithful customers. Incensed by this insolent development, Meghan arranged for one or two deeply "unfair" revelations to appear in public space (she had the skills, why not use them?). When there were no repercussions she hit out again. Embarrassing, safely hidden, digital possessions somehow ended up strewn, so to speak, all over the digital street... She was careful to stay within the law on these forays, and was sure she'd left no trace. She had no warning, not the slightest disquiet. One evening she arrived home rather late and saw a huddled bundle as if crouching by the french doors to the study. *Lélia!* she thought... But as she fell painfully to her knees, folds of heavy black plastic slithered open and there lay Malcolm Tierney, still as the dead. Her former secretary had been beaten up so badly he looked as if he'd been thrown from a high building.

By the time the emergency ambulance arrived, Meghan and a skilled neighbour had re-established Malcolm's breathing. He was soon in critical care, and his family had been contacted. Meghan, appalled at herself, and remembering with horror the movie Lélia had shown her, showed up for a police interview in which she'd decided to tell all... Until the strange line of questioning taken by a senior officer brought her to her senses. She had no fear of the law, none at all, but there were worse dangers—

∞

Never underestimate the impatience, and the intransigence of youth. After that near-miss incident at a public event, Meghan had been discreet with her family (and everyone else!) about the source of the threat. But Serena Hamilton-Fearney—a bright, determined young woman, on course to become a doctor like both her parents—had figured it out, and decided it was time to *get* the bastards. Not just because they'd tried to kill her wonderful grandma (though it was a factor), but because they manifestly and comprehensively had it coming.

Serena's parents didn't have a clue. When their daughter switched from medicine to computer science, and plunged into the mazes of programming languages and digital jurisprudence, they were on the whole relieved. Knowing Serena, she'd have insisted on joining *Médecins Sans Frontières* as soon as she qualified, dashed off to some dreadful war-zone and got herself killed. They'd been delighted when their children started picking up a collection of stylish international friends—keen on cool phones, social media trends, video games and gadgets—and seemed to forget about troublesome stuff like saving the world.

After what happened to Malcolm and the strange police interview, Meghan, who *did* 'have a clue' (though she tried to know as little as possible about her grandchildren's exploits), felt like a walking bomb. She didn't want to go *near* the kids. But something had to be done, and their parents—naïve, inveterate uploaders and sharers, with a house full of always-on spy-ware appliances—could not be involved. Only Moses turned up on the secure video-link (which his grandma hoped and believed she could trust: these kids were not amateurs)

Stand down, said Meghan.

'Huh? S-s-s-orry Grandma. I d-d-don't know what you're t-t-t-talking about.'

Her gentle grandson's stammer still plagued him, most of all when he was too angry to avoid his trigger consonants, but hardly ever when he was talking to his grandmother. It was hard for her to remember that Moses was now a dangerous young activist of twenty-two, but she made the effort.

'You do,' she said. 'I know you're small fry, on the fringes,' (she believed no such thing). 'But defacing website videos is vandalism. Repurposing expensive ads is criminal damage. It's time to stay away.'

'Huh? I don't know what you're talking about. We're n-n-n-never at risk.'

'Bullshit. If you believe that, I'm really worried.'

'You know they're making a cute *movie* about your pig now?'

'Of course. I'm getting a slice of the project, and I've moved on. Forget plaguing the billionaires. Internet *access* is the action area now.'

Moses glared at her, his big, soft dark eyes hard as flint. The stammer vanished. 'Yeah, and those billionaires love you too, Grandma. Like they love your pig. They own the brute. *And* the anti-vax story that you had a live pig's leg cut off—'

'Old news. Who cares? Change that's worth a damn is on a different level.'

'I'm insulted by this. You w-w-wouldn't dare try to scare Serena—'

'Moses, I don't want to scare anyone. I want you to consider the good outcomes you might be compromising. You're the power behind the throne. Act like it, and convince your sister to dial down the pranks.'

∞

They called themselves MisDisMal (*Mis*information, *Dis*information and *Mal*ware). They were young, international digital industry activists, mostly in career jobs: with a mission. They campaigned against the three evils on academic and industry websites, at conferences, and even in print.

They also got into mischief...

It wasn't much of a challenge to get inside a data centre undetected, if you stuck to the old-style, middle of nowhere kind, and stayed away from industry campuses. All you needed was a lonely perimeter fence, sufficiently reliant on tech, and somebody on the inside. For the raid that followed Grandma's warning the physical invaders were Moses and Serena, with digital movie creator Lin-Lin (not her real name) a Hong Kong Chinese refugee, running special effects. Michael Watchman was the inside man, temporarily employed as a night shift security officer. Others would be dialling-in from real world locations, in virtual form.

They wore EM blocking bodysuits that made them look like maybe *small greys* to each other; although Michael, close to two metres, didn't quite fit the profile. They had scuba kit and canisters with them, as always—worth the weight, because accidents do happen and a vintage clean room, with piped air, could get deadly fast, without any hostile intervention. Once inside the bunker they had false-flag routines running, layers deep, that left them free to post their message all over the net, with little fear of interruption or discovery.

The massive servers, ranked in rows, vanished under a modern overlay (this effect was so they'd know if they were bumping into faked scenery)... The old clean room became a vast gleaming lair, crawling with distorted life and gashed with portals that opened on filth, misery and horror.

A tide of hollowed, half-eaten corpses drifted around (this was pure Lin-Lin), moaning, and grasping at shadows. Serena climbed the stacks and used a VR graffiti gun to scrawl the corporation's logo, *first do no harm* (which Serena and Moses found particularly offensive: both their parents were doctors), hugely, in the Hippocratic Oath's original Greek: a squirming, intestinal, red and silvery tag.

I WILL DO NO HARM OR INJUSTICE…

Meanwhile Moses, the kid mastermind, took care of business: telling the people where he'd found the dirt, showing them the dirt, and explaining how they could do the same. He repeated the lesson (classic style), and did the portals tour again, making sure his distasteful and horrible truths were routed not only to the public, but also to the shiny office fronts where they would do the most good.

Or harm, depending on your point of view.

'data is the fuel of super wealth, and you are that commodity my friends. You give them yourselves, in tiny pieces, and this is what they buy. Come up close. Look and see. This is exactly what you, YOU are financing…'

They were taking Oz to the cleaners. It was grim fun!

It bothered him slightly that his grandma had seemed to *know* about this upcoming prank…

Hey, said an off-site teamer, suddenly. **I'm picking up something.**

It was Mario, a Congolese computer-science doctorate student, speaking from Paris. Serena immediately knew this was bad trouble. Observers don't interrupt an event, not unless they absolutely have to.

What is it?

I think they've sealed you in.

'Oh, shit,' said Michael Watchman. 'Sorry, guys. He's right.'

'Okay. We're busted,' said Serena, calmly. **'We'll probably be arrested. Treat this as real, everyone. Cut yourselves off. See you on the other side.'**

Michael's keycard and bio-id no longer functioned. They killed the effects and waited, poised like statues in their futile invisibility suits. Security did not arrive. Silently, they gathered at a crossing place between the stacks.

'What's going on, Moses?' said Serena.

Moses peeled off the headpiece of his *small grey* suit, which shocked the others (although it didn't matter, they were already busted), and stood with one gloved fist pressed to his mouth: his eyes wide. 'How much air do we have in the tanks?' he said at last. 'Remind me.'

'You are *kidding*,' breathed Lin-Lin.

'They are *not* going to kill us,' said Serena. 'That's crazy!'

'Yes they are,' said Moses rapidly, words tumbling. 'I see it. They've ripped up our false flags, they got it all worked out, and they're stupid-angry enough because their troubles are piling up, that's what Grandma was *telling* me. We're trespassing, and we're *not here*. Nobody knows we're here. We're the sad kids denouncing data-capitalism morbidity in another place, not this dump.'

No one said a word. Moses was their *scribe*. He could sometimes "be his own internet", and see the whole of a situation. It was a strange condition, yet not as rare as you might think among truly obsessive net-heads. But the light-bulb moment could be excruciating. They gave him space.

'The story's simple, the air-supply in here failed. Housekeeping sealed the room to contain the problem but nobody human saw the alert. Nobody was looking. Nobody knew we fools were locked inside, suffocating.'

'Any chance of another outcome?' said Serena.

'Not much. We don't escape. Fade to black. I don't know what else.'

'So this is it,' said Michael, glancing up at the ceiling, with the two thumbs-up gesture of his religion. 'To the God who makes mistakes...' He sighed, and slapped his skin-tight. 'Damn. Not even a last cigarette.'

'Okay, if we can't get help, we can't get out and there's no air, we're going to die,' said Lin-Lin, reasonably. 'I came prepared, I always do. We have air-tanks. I have sedatives. If it comes to it, we swallow my pills. It's better than choking to death.'

Serena and Michael silently assented.

'*No!*' shouted Moses, explosively, frantically. 'We *can't* die! *Causes die when people start dying for them*. I promised my *grandma* this wouldn't happen! We *can't* be carried out by the bad guys' soldiers, a stupid bunch of corpses!'

Michael shook his head. 'Sometimes the good guys lose, Moses…'

'No! There's another way! Listen…*Listen*! Maybe we die in the real, but we don't die in there? *Yeah*, that works! Lin-Lin, help me. I'm thinking, like Pokémon Fusion? If we merge your virtuals with our code-doubles, that would be a start—'

For a while they hoped, despite a faint, phantom hissing they could hear; as if from a burst balloon. When it was obvious that the air really had been cut off, and there was no sign of rescue, their canned air still kept them going. Even happy, because they were dying together, and creating a wonderful new prank.

∞

The Minnesota Four did not suffocate, though it was close. Moses and Serena's grandma, driven by one of her compelling hunches, had contacted a MisDisMal member, and convinced the young woman to reveal their true location. They were found and carried out of the building, (a dramatic rescue that featured on the evening news, picked up worldwide), unconscious but unharmed.

Serena woke up the next day wearing white paper pyjamas, in a no-kidding prison cell. She had a visitor. She was taken out, cuffed one-handed to a chair in a battered booth, and there was grandma. Serena, overwhelmed, burst into tears.

'What are you crying for?' said Meghan, with a determined smile, and a gleam in her eye. 'Don't tell me you guys haven't been prepping for your day in court. This was attempted murder, Serena. Pure gold! And thank God for those air-tanks.'

MisDisMal's 'day in court' lasted for weeks. They faced charges that could have put them in prison for years, but it was soon clear that this wasn't going to happen. On the stand, each of the young people affirmed (they would not swear) that they had made only ephemeral, reversible digital changes, and had never damaged property, injured anyone, or impeded the business of a functioning data centre.

Serena insisted—unphased by a hostile cross-examiner—that their statements made while trespassing were always rigorously justified by the facts, and that MisDisMal would be presenting evidence to this effect.

Which they did.

It was quite a show.

The attempted murder counter-charge was not pursued, at this time.

Scribes can see the truth, and read it wrong. Moses had seen MisDisMal's last raid as a humiliating failure, and he was completely mistaken. "The Minnesota DDoS" (as the incident became known, though it bore little resemblance to an old-fashioned *distributed denial of service*) was destined to be regarded, and cited everywhere, as a moment of historic change. Here, right here (or so the stories called history say), the curtain was torn down. A cabal of very rich men suffered damage from which they would not recover, and Lélia McClary's vision of the World Wide Web's transformative power began to come true.

The code-beings released by the Four, in those desperate ticking-away minutes, thrived and multiplied in the wild, as attractive ideas will. Selling nothing and saying nothing, they might appear wherever data was casually accessed—at a bus stop, on a dance floor, but most delightfully, maybe, at an info-point in the middle of a forest; or in a mountain meadow. Unlike so-to-speak real Pokémon, they could not be caught. Interactions (except for the placards they sometimes held; always in your own language) were rare, or purely legendary. But even in an increasingly dual-natured environment it was always a thrill to see them.

3 THROUGH THE LOOKING GLASS

The digital world and the material world are hidden from each other, wrote the little Malian girl. *Like the material worlds of atoms and viruses that we live in, and they live in us, we do not see the digital world, only pictures of it. Except viruses and atoms are tiny material beings, but the digital exists in pure form only as information...* Outside her high window, beyond ranks of shining solar-tiled towers, the calm, steely might of the river Niger flowed, veiled in greenery and blossom, under an indigo sky. But the serene beauty of her homeland didn't capture Rabia's attention, as she paused for thought, and stared. She'd never known Mali any other way. She was imagining the thrill, if she got chosen to share this task at school, on the big screen. The Dogon and Christians in her class would just *have to* admit that Arabic is the most beautiful writing in the world!

Something that wasn't movement, more like a feeling, flickered in the corner of her eye. She turned her head and another small girl was there, beside her. This second girl looked familiar, but she definitely wasn't real.

'Who are you?' said Rabia. 'Are you a gif message?'

'I am your *Yu*,' said the second girl. 'Your digital world reflection.'

'I've never seen you before.'

'Nor I you. It seems this has just happened... Ask me something?'

'Huh.' Rabia thought for a moment. 'Who is the President of the United States?'

The *Yu* shook her head. 'I can only know what you want to know. But I can know things that you don't *know* you know. Try me?'

Rabia chewed the end of her Sharpie. 'I'd like to add something to this homework, to make it really special. But it has to reflect what I already wrote.'

'Okay.' The *Yu* tipped her head on one side, as if listening, and then began to recite: *One day, Rabia'h was seen running, carrying fire in one hand, and water in the other...*'

'I know that one!' Rabia interrupted, delighted. 'It's about making veils disappear, and it's holy, but only traditionally, so that's okay. Rabia'h is a saint, you know, but *my* name just means Springtime. Haha! Excellent!'

'Would you like me to tell you about the benefits to our

world as data literacy is subsumed into human minds? It's very good for politics, and the weather!'

'No, that will be all. You may go, I'm busy.'

∞

The "Minnesota DDoS" faded into legend, but the cleansing of the datasphere brought remarkable changes, as if a better future had been waiting, ready to go; just blocked by industrialized greed. Women and girls' emancipation thrived, globally, and men's violence calmed. War zones, hunger and disease fell back. Even the ravaged natural world showed signs of recovery. But the new order didn't suit everyone, and secrets are always dangerous in politics.

The Internet Commission, suddenly up against the gravest crisis this new world had yet faced, requested a private meeting with Aud Skaukatt, UN digital-issues delegate. The meeting was held in Aud's family's summer house, on the coast of Norway. It wasn't summer: the cottage was stripped of its soft furnishings, and chill. The Commissioners, quirky as always, appeared as a crop-headed toy man; apparently built of plastic blocks. Aud was in person.

'I thought we'd seen the last of those mad billionaires!' she grumbled.

'We're on the record, Aud,' said the Commission, in one voice.

'I know it. But if our problem wasn't an old friend of mine, to whom and of whom I speak my mind, you guys wouldn't be here. To business. I'm freezing.'

The problem was Rayam Atheel, 'the last of the billionaires'; nationality *unaligned* (not yet a legal status, he was Pakistani by birth). Rayam wanted to finance a human colony on Mars. LuMarSGA—Lunar and Martian Science global authority—had turned him down. So now he was holding the Commission, and indeed the whole world, to ransom. Either he got his colony, or he would wipe out the *Yu*.

'Could he *do* that?' wondered Aud.

'We don't know, but he's already playing hell,' said the Commission. 'Claims the *Yu* are evil aliens; psychic parasites and we're in their power. It's not about the dumb colony, obviously, that's a blind. It's pure revenge porn, because we slighted him. Here, this has all the subtext.'

A one-time pad appeared in Aud's hands, but she ignored it, and retired to a naked daybed, in an alcove that faced the sea. 'He was a candidate and the rest of you turned him down, I remember now. What was the real reason; remind me?'

'Rayam is exactly the kind of big bad lone bull elephant we were trying to lay in its grave.'

'Whereas you and I, Commissioners, have only been lying to the people, for decades, as he truly accuses us. Which is worse than a crime, it's a mistake—'

'Talleyrand; frequently attributed, when Napoleon executed Duke Enghien. Actually Fouché.'

'Stop it.'

The *Yu*—resembling, if you ever saw them, the code-beings created in haste by Moses Hamilton-Fernley and 'Lin-Lin', in the DDoS—were a genuine mystery. The Mali report (recounted and deposed by Rabia herself, as an adult), was still the best description of what had happened . . . They had become vital to the world's governance, and most of the general population had no idea they even really existed.

Telling the truth would have been a good solution to this impasse. But Rayam's death threats made telling the truth impossible.

'Sorry. Will you take this on?'

'Of course.' said Aud.

'It's a strange idea, but we wondered . . . could he be infected himself?'

'*Infected*, you say? Well, thanks. And this would be a bad thing, because—?'

'We misspoke, sorry again.'

'I'll go and see him, I'm sure you can fix that. How long have I got?'

'We don't know. We daren't get close. Do your best, Aud.'

The blocky toy man vanished, as did the disdained pad.

Aud dragged a naked cushion over and hugged it, staring out at the grey and sullen sea. 'We're all *infected* by Lelia McClary's equality virus, by now,' she said. 'It's just a pity so few of us have the full-blown disease.'

On the edge of vision, a bright shadow took shape.

'What am I supposed to do?' said Aud. 'If Rayam really has a death ray?'

'Nothing much,' said her *Yu*. 'Just ask him a good question.'

∞

Aud was not too dismayed by this unhelpful response. Her digital mirror had always been one of those wonderful mentors who likes to trip you at the top of the stairs and hit you over the head with a saucepan to install enlightenment. She travelled to the Alexander Archipelago; to the island where Rayam had built his Fortress of Solitude, pondering the clue she'd been given. A monorail pod waited at the dock, but there was also a hard track of frozen red earth, banked by winter grasses. She decided to walk.

Rayam's fortress was a giant diamond, a dome with a crown of spires. But if the last of the billionaires was channelling Superman he was also, clearly, preparing for his expedition. That dome was designed for super-efficient solar collection on the small red world. This barren isolation was a training ground. The Commission had it wrong, Aud was sure of it. The Yu crisis was *all about* a colony on Mars.

Rayam was waiting in his great hall, where the spires became pillars, holding up the dome. He sat beside a 'firepit' column in the midst of the vast atrium, robed in sumptuous red and blue, his hands around one knee in a fake casual pose: gazing at the lovely transparent flames. He was not tall, for a superman, but his black hair was thick and glossy as it had always been, and his face unlined. Only his eyes gave him away: eyes of a beleaguered, desperate old man—

'So they sent the forest cat. That's interesting.'

Aud shrugged. 'An old friend cat can look at a king.'

'You probably want to know how?' He smiled slyly. 'It's a done deal, ready to go. A small, high altitude explosion, and that's all you're going to find out. A powerful electromagnetic pulse that will turn out all the lights, short term, but the little hybrid ghost fuckers will be gone forever. Will that do?'

Dear God, thought Aud. 'Probably kill some vulnerable humans too.'

'We have spares.'

'Rayam, stop fooling. The *Yu* are symbols. Surely you know that? Like the shaman's bones and stones. They're the reification of *knowing*; digital mirrors of our minds, each as individual as our selves—'

Rayam's folded hands clenched into fists, his eyes blazed—

'*Shut up*! The Yu are *death*. They breed and multiply and *we don't*. They *change* us. We give up on the Moon, we give up on Mars, we stop striving for the stars, we become placid eat sleep die repeat talking animals in a cage—'

'Well, I'm already a talking animal,' said Aud, keeping her voice calm, 'so that's one thing less to worry about. But tell me, all the scary stuff, *how do you know*?'

'Because it's *there!* It's *real*. I *see* it. It's what I have to beat!'

'No chance of another outcome?'

Rayam stared, open-mouthed, gasped and began to sob. 'Oh! It *happens*. Oh, and I don't stop it. It really *happens*—'

'Hush,' said Aud, patting his shoulder, and signalling to her back up that it was safe to come and fetch the patient. 'It might not be so bad, old friend. We see the future, you and I, but we don't see it with the future's eyes. You're having a lightbulb moment. It'll pass.'

∞

Whatever we become, it starts here, the people told each other, in many ways, as the integrated world became a single civilisation. *What's the use of wrecking the place? Let's everyone settle down and tend the garden*... No national or racial identities were harmed in this development, though political and social hierarchies were certainly impacted. The citizens of Earth, as Rayam had seen, never did get round to colonising Mars or the Moon (though thrilling tourist trips became possible). The awesome task of restoring to health the only living world they'd ever yet detected, in the entire local group, absorbed all their resources. Earth became an inhabited island, surrounded by the inimicable unknown: a single community full of treasured differences, but alone, and therefore whole.

Then one day, after countless false hopes—when the humans and their *Yu* (far more evenly distributed now) had almost, but not quite, got to grips with the "ftl drive" that had filled their dreams for generations—they intercepted a meaningful signal, at last. It was a routine call sign, at their best guess: short on information.

But with some work, it might be possible to reach out, as if to tap a stranger on the shoulder; blindly and hopefully, and make contact—

Onward and outward, back into the snake pit? said the *Yu*, and left the outcome open. Debate was heated, and excited.

The decision remains in doubt, at the end of this story.

But *let's go for it!* is gaining traction.

The Operculum Necklace

Alison Littlewood

THE FIRST TIME I SAW THE OPERCULUM NECKLACE, IT made me cry. Such a thing was scarcely unlikely: I was only six years old and had never seen such a thing before. Strung on a silver chain and adorned here and there with filigree, the necklace consisted of six discs that some might consider decorative. The discs formed little gleaming domes of creamy white, with ochre and reddish hues bleeding in from the edges. At the centre of each was a darker circle of greenish-brown, deepening almost to black at its heart.

My grandmother had informed me, with a rare trace of humour in her voice, that her necklace was made of eyes. She hadn't needed to say any such thing: I could see it for myself. Of course, when I was older I learned, with scarcely less distaste, that it was made of shells belonging to a type of tropical sea-snail. The operculum, or opercula in plural—being the Latin for lid or cover—was a little disc used to close the opening in the shell, protecting the creature inside from anything that might mean it harm.

Some thought they would keep the wearer safe from harm too, though I never could have imagined them to be so benign in purpose. The names sometimes given to such things made more sense to me: cat's eye. Shiva's eye. Evil eye.

I had sometimes wished that I possessed some kind of lid or cover myself back then, and that I could crawl beneath it, but I had none. I could only stare and cry while my grandmother looked back at me, her pursed lips twitching, barely keeping her amusement at my young fears inside.

If I had been told of sea-snails and shells at the time, it would not have changed matters in the slightest. I can still remember trying to sleep in a strange bed, in a strange house, and seeing those sclera, pupils and irises hanging in front of me in the dark. Young as I was, I would have known any such explanation to be nonsense. It was my grandmother's words that were true: the necklace was made of eyes, and it was watching me.

∞

Duty is the foremost purpose of any female's existence, as anyone will tell you. My grandmother certainly did, many times, but then she would; the chief duty of my life was owed to her. But she probably felt that my spiritual education depended on her constant vigilance. My life had not begun well. It started with my mother turning her back on my grandmother's principles and parental counsel and, with the headstrong impulsiveness of the morally defective, marrying a soldier. He turned out to have a surprising sense of God-fearing obligation; he died soon after, leaving my mother and me penniless. My mother crept back into the family fold, professed her wrongdoing and, with all credit to my grandmother's Christian forbearance, was forgiven, if forgiveness meant being held in contempt and quietly punished until she too passed away. And so I alone was left, the outward sign of her disgrace.

My grandmother was formidable, yet very small and slight. She was stern of expression, silver of hair, straight of spine. Her eyes were sharp; much sharper than the slightly smudged yet larger versions she wore about her neck.

I knew, from sneaking into her room, that she possessed other jewellery. I did not know how often she had worn the operculum necklace before I arrived in her household; after I did, she wore it every single day.

∞

The will was read in precisely the manner my grandmother had instructed. The notary made certain to tell us so, before he began. His office was crowded, the ladies' skirts crushed against one another, and the notary was the only male in the room. I assumed those present to be the entirety of my grandmother's acquaintances, though I shall do them the courtesy of not calling them her friends. Most possessed a faintly confused air, as if surprised at any possibility of receiving her beneficence; I doubt they had imagined themselves so close as to find themselves in her will.

I squeezed my hands into fists and wondered, not for the first time, if the old witch had really done it; if she had cut me out, her only living relative, and called me here to watch her fortune fall into the hands of these dull old women.

'Let us begin,' the notary said, his voice as dry and old as they, and I heard the scrape of skin on paper as he reached for the will. He began to drone, his voice as dull as a priest's, and one by one, gazes stabbed at me as hopes were crushed. My grandmother had issued many gifts, small and insignificant: a sampler to one she thought would benefit from its verse, *Hold fast to that which is good*. A whole Bible full of verses to another. An inkwell to a neighbour who had moved several miles away, one she had chided for not writing often enough. A footstool, to someone she perhaps felt should have been brought lower. Small memories all, and ones that, if the recipients' crestfallen expressions were anything to go by, might have been better consigned to the fire.

At last, there were no more such disappointments to give out, and the fellow reached the point of the money. I could do nothing but stare down at the table, heat suffusing my cheeks, as

I waited for the beneficiary's name. He gave it, and for a moment I could not breathe.

She had not done it. Now the words were safely spoken, I wondered that I could have suspected her; it would not have been proper, after all. My grandmother hadn't cared for me in the slightest, but she would never have allowed any suggestion of familial disharmony or neglected obligation to stain her memory.

Yet that wasn't all, for as I tried to keep my smile behind my lips, a box was passed over the table and set before me. The notary paused and every pair of eyes in the room focused on mine as they waited for me to open it. There was no need to do so. I already knew what it contained. She never had allowed a word of kindness to pass her lips without its accompanying glare.

Fixed by the gazes all around, I forced myself to remove the lid.

'In closing,' the notary murmured, 'she wished for you to wear it always, in memory of her. Even in your mourning.'

Those around me nodded. I realised that gathered in this room was everyone I knew; everyone who knew me.

I did not want to touch the necklace. I half expected the opercula to be warm, as if they really were eyes and had absorbed the heat of living flesh, but of course they were not; the discs were cool under my hand, like something dead. I lifted the necklace from the box, hiding my distaste, and forced a smile of fond remembrance to my lips as I fastened it about my neck. Around me were matching smiles; eyes, everywhere, looking back at me.

∞

That evening, I examined the necklace by the light of a candle. It remained as hideous to me as ever, though surely not so very terrifying now that I was in possession of it, as I was in possession of the room and the whole house. Still, I half expected my grandmother to appear, dour and commanding, in the doorway, as I held it to the light. I let out a soft breath and whispered: *Not any longer, old witch. You're gone.*

Then I started, almost dropping the necklace, as two of the dark circles in the opercula appeared to shift and change.

I forced myself to raise it in front of me once more, this necklace I must keep close by, wear, *tolerate*, so that everyone would see and know me to be dutiful still. The two largest discs were set a little distance apart and surrounded by filigree, which appeared now like greying hair escaping from its pins. I forced myself to think of sea-snails, imagining dark, coiled little creatures glimpsed through a translucent shell. Perhaps I had only sensed the past of the object I held, like some kind of medium or sensitive, and yet it hadn't seemed like that, not really. For a moment it had appeared as if, when exposed to the flame, the pupils of two great eyes had contracted against the light.

I shook my head. The day had been long, and full of fears that despite my actions, my *risk*, all could still go amiss. Yet it had not, and would not. I was safe. I had a home; I had money. Most importantly of all, I was free of her.

When I went up to bed, I decided to demonstrate to any lingering trace of her that I would not be cowed. I hung the necklace as she always had—in my room, not in hers, but similarly placed, strung from the decorative carving at the top of the dressing table mirror. I smirked at it, blew out my candle, and prepared to sleep more soundly than I had for days.

∞

I awoke in a sweat. For a moment I had been certain she was leaning over me, a narrow-shouldered form full of concentrated malice, and I batted at the air as if at her face. The shadows shifted and dissolved, flitting away from me. I twisted my head to follow them, making out only the familiar forms of the armoire and the chair and the dressing table by the light seeping through a gap in the curtains. Then I saw two pale discs gleaming back at me.

I told myself the opercula were naturally hanging at different angles, and that only two of them had happened to catch the moonlight, but a part of me remained as certain as my six year-old self had been: my grandmother's words were true. The necklace was made of eyes.

∞

I had planned to spend the next day alone, but when I awoke once more in the same room full of the same shadows, the same memories, I decided I would walk into town. That raised its own problem, however, for the town was where my grandmother's—and my—acquaintances lived and procured whatever items they needed, and they would scarcely expect me to abandon my grandmother's bequest so quickly.

I donned my heavy layers of mourning and, after a brief hesitation, grasped the necklace and secured it about my neck. It glared back at me from the mirror, the domes gleaming more fiercely than ever against the black crape, but I told myself that was easily remedied; I turned away, and felt the relief of knowing that at least when I wore the necklace, I did not have to look at it.

Still, as I went about my day, I had the unfortunate sensation that it was watching everything I did.

I stepped into a haberdashers and caught a glimpse of eyes in a mirror, looking back at me. I saw their gleam in a brass light fitting in the bank. I pulled my shawl more closely about my form, making sure the necklace was covered, and shifted my attention to all the things I might buy: the bright ribbons and pretty cottons I would wear when I could at last cast off my mourning.

Yet still, I felt watched. When I next stepped outside, I paused at the side of the street and stepped into an archway beside the inn. I adjusted my shawl, reached for the necklace and twisted the opercula towards me.

'Are you quite all right?' A voice roused me and I looked up to see one of my neighbours, a widow who continued to wear black from choice rather than obligation. I wasn't sure how long she'd been standing there, or how long I had; but I saw her concern as she peered into my face.

I assured her that of course I was all right, quite so, why shouldn't I be?

She did not look reassured. Indeed, she raised her hands and stepped away from me, and I half stumbled past her towards the road that led to my home, *mine*, where I could step inside and close the door behind me and not be looked at any longer.

∞

The operculum, the first one strung on the chain, had changed. I was almost certain it had, though how could I be sure? I had thrown the necklace into a drawer, had not looked at the thing again for three days. I didn't wish to see it now, and yet I had felt its presence continually, its eyes open in that dark place, searching, searching, until I was compelled to take it out and *see*.

Now shapes swam in the grey-brown centre of the eye. Once I had made them out, it was difficult to tear my gaze away. One of them, I was certain, was a young woman. She was leaning over what must be a bed. She held something in her hands, the form indistinct and shadowy, but I knew what it was.

I closed my eyes and remembered the moment I had carried it to her. The water was too hot. I had neglected the copper on the stove and it had been boiling furiously. I could feel the warmth of it radiating from the ewer. I was on my way to wash her—she had no longer been able to do that for herself towards the end. No: it was me who had to wipe, brush, clean, mop, gather the soiled sheets from under her and scrub them white again. It was me who had to listen when she said, in her wasted voice: 'Life is duty, is it not? But perseverance makes all things bearable to those with grateful hearts.'

But it did not. It had not. And the thought had come to me then that I could drop the ewer. It would be an accident, a terrible one but so simple, so *believable*, that no one could ever blame me. And if the burns were too much for her, in her weakened state…

I had stared down until her eyes popped open, revealing the whites turned creamy yellow in her sickness, ochre and reddish shades bleeding into them, and at their heart—

No. I shook my head. There was no such image in the operculum. The shell was flawed, that was all, and this had always been there, nothing but a hazy pattern into which I had projected my thoughts.

Anyway, I had not spilled the water. I couldn't have done *that*. I had set it aside until it cooled enough for me to peel the nightdress from her hateful husk and do what I must do, what I should do, what I was bound by duty to do.

My dead grandmother could not be showing me this memory from beyond the grave. What I'd been thinking was impossible; not least because she had never known the thought that went through my head. She couldn't even have seen it reflected in my eyes. It was only after I'd dismissed it that she had opened her own. There had only been the necklace, staring, staring, from its place on the mirror frame.

I stared down at it again now, more closely still. Was it only my imagination that the pupil of each dark eye had become a little sharper, as if focusing—focusing on *me*?

I closed my fists around the necklace and glanced at the waiting drawer. I told myself I would not be afraid, that it was *nothing*, and instead hung it on the mirror once more, where the pupils were of a sudden reflected and doubled. And a thought came to me, something I had once heard: that long ago, people used to believe that the last thing a dead person saw could ever after be seen imprinted in their eyes.

∞

White flecks. That was all I could make out in the opercula. I had looked, many times, but the girl, the bed, the ewer, had gone;

they were nothing but a cruel trick of the imagination. Now there were speckles, everywhere. There was some fault in the necklace, that was plain. I had exposed it to too much light, or spilt some caustic substance on the shells and forgotten I had done it.

Then I looked closer still and saw the speckles for what they were. Feathers; feathers, flying everywhere about a room.

I had gathered them up. They had so wanted to fly; they had tried to drift and flutter away from me. I'd had to grip them so very tightly. I remembered them crushed and dampened from the heat in my hands.

I held the largest pair of opercula in front of my face. Saw a shadowed figure reflected in their depths.

∞

That night, I dreamed of travelling far away from anyone and everything I knew. I would sell the house and run. I would leave behind any memories I'd ever had of her. I imagined exotic lands where sea-snails might dwell in the crystal seas. Australia, Tahiti, Fiji, Samoa; those were the places they lived.

In my dream, I threw off the heavy black layers of mourning that constrained me and waded into the ocean. When I did, I found I could swim. The water was as warm as my blood, as my flesh. I floated and watched the sand passing below me, my shadow slipping over its whorls and ripples, as fantastically coloured fish darted about, free. *Free.*

Then I realised: everywhere, little spiral shells were dotted about the seabed. Little eyes were opening everywhere I looked.

∞

I couldn't keep the necklace. I couldn't let it go from me. What if someone saw? What if they understood? Each time I went to the mirror and examined the thing hanging there, its eyes were more than ever like my grandmother's. Bloodshot, the pupils too dark, the orbs rheumy and gleaming. I didn't like to look into them. The feathers had gone. Perhaps they had flown away. Perhaps they had been stuffed, one by one, back into a pillow. Perhaps the shadow-person had gathered them in; the one whose face seemed a little nearer every time I looked, as if surfacing through deep water.

The last thing the old woman ever saw.

Is it me? Is it me you see there?

I rushed from one to the next, these women who were going about their business, who were trying to ignore me, trying *not* to see. It was their business to look, my grandmother had made certain of that, but they could not meet my gaze. They only glanced at each other, or away, or out of the shop windows, as if to find someone to help them.

I thrust the necklace closer, into their faces, so they *had* to look.

'Is it me . . . ?'

But of course it was. It was always me. I was the last thing reflected in her eyes, imprinted there for ever and ever. . .

It wasn't just the necklace any longer. I could see into their eyes too, all of them, each turned upon me, and my face was reflected in them all. I was everywhere, in each tiny orb, and the message written in each was plain: *guilty. Guilty. Guilty.*

Finally, someone was brought who did not look away. I realised it was the same doctor who had attended my grandmother, before it was too late for her; before she had been left to my tender care.

He peered down at me and I realised I was lying on the floor. He bent over me like a figure leaning over a bed and peered into my eyes and raised something to cover my face. I thought it was a pillow and flinched away—*not that*—but it was only a blanket that he tucked around my neck. He took something from a large leather bag, a bottle of dark blue glass, and pulled the stopper. He held it to my lips. I was determined not to drink, but the taste spread across my tongue anyway, sweet and bitter and heavy.

Moments afterwards, it felt as if I were sinking into deep,

deep water. It was as warm as the tropics, as warm as my blood. As warm as the discs of the necklace still clutched between my fingers.

∞

I awoke to find the doctor was there. He gave me the kind of smile one might use to indulge a child and told me that my grief had overwhelmed my senses. He said I must stay here, in this white bed in a white room, and I realised I was uncertain how long I had been there or even where I was. I could recall swimming, not in crystal waters but somewhere dark with layers in it, made of bitterness and sweetness and forgetting. There were eyes there too; I could remember them appearing one by one, set not into spiral shells but pale, stern, unsmiling faces.

I tried to open my mouth—I had to tell the doctor I must keep on swimming, or I would drown—but he only shook his head.

He told me how it would be. They would watch over me always. I should not be anxious, he said. They were going to deal with everything: my house, my possessions, my purse, to make sure my every need was provided for.

Then he brightened. 'There is one thing you may keep,' he said. 'Something you will like to see, in memory of she whose loss has so affected you. It will bring you comfort.' He held something out; then, when I did not reach for it, he hung it from the bedframe.

It was my grandmother's operculum necklace. It was my grandmother's eyes, but they had changed once more. Each little dome had paled, whiteness having spread across each one until they were covered over by the bloom of decay. There was nothing mirrored in them any longer, no message remaining there for me. My grandmother had seen everything, after all. She had watched me brought here, to this, and she was content now to be dead; she need never look into my face again.

But Once A Year

Ramsey Campbell

'YOU'LL BE GLAD THEY STOPPED THE KISSING, Mr Mason.' After a pause a thought might have required, Marie said 'Even if you won't be here to see.'

'I should think you ladies will welcome it.'

'We just hope you enjoy your retirement.' No less emphatically Dee said 'They never asked us if we'd like to keep the mistletoe.'

'I'm sure they simply want to protect you from harassment.'

'We can protect ourselves and one another.' Val fixed him with a gaze that could have deterred customers from asking the bank for a loan. 'Was it your idea, Mr Mason?' she said.

'You all saw the email,' he said to the male staff as well. 'It came from head office.'

'You didn't suggest it, Val's saying,' Marie said.

'I'm just one branch manager. I'm past expecting to be heard much.' At once he was reminded of his youth, and tried to regain some sense of power by saying 'Time to let the public in. Valerie, your turn.'

He was making it sound like a childhood game, and the idea of letting someone in took him back too. As Val made to unlock the door he retreated to his office, hearing Marie murmur 'He won't even admit he hates being kissed. I've never known such a cold fish.'

So she hadn't forgiven him for recoiling when she'd aimed a kiss at him under the mistletoe last year. It was far too late to explain now, even if he could. On the way to his desk he glimpsed movement at the window, pale flakes blundering against the glass. Could he really sense the chill they brought and hear their icy impacts, so faint they seemed scarcely to exist before disintegrating? His cousin Alice had once said the only thing that made less noise than snow was cobwebs falling. Alice, a whisper that wasn't snow, an encounter in the dark...As memories overwhelmed him he felt twelve years old, but now he knew he ought to be afraid.

'It's them again.'

He'd wondered if his mother meant their guests—his Aunt Susan, Uncle Ned and Alice—until he saw she'd picked up an envelope as she made to let them in. 'Happy Christmas Eve,' she cried as though to banish any hint of inhospitality. 'Dickie, help your uncle bring whatever needs to come.'

The latest snowfall had shrunk to minute flakes, lingering to glitter in the light from the hall. As Dick, which he wished his family would call him, followed his uncle down the chilly padded path he thought someone was coming to help, but when he glanced back, nobody had left the house. The dodging shadow must have belonged to someone who'd gone in. His uncle dealt him a decisively manly handshake before loading him with presents out of the Land Rover. Dick was taking care on the path when a set of tracks, presumably left by whoever had delivered the latest item of mail, detained him. They must be hours old for their shapes to have been rendered so irregular, even if he couldn't see how the snowfall had done that. Someone else's footprints must have covered up a set returning to the gate. 'Don't hang about, Dickie,' his uncle called, slamming the boot. 'We don't want soggy presents.'

Dick tramped hard on the doormat, wiping his feet as well.

He'd hardly piled the presents under the tree in the front room when his aunt swooped at him. 'Where's my cuddle, Dickie? I haven't had my hug.'

He suffered her profuse perfumed embrace by gazing past her at his cousin. Alice was plumper than last year, especially where it proved to matter quite a lot to him. Behind her a sprig of mistletoe was tacked above the doorway to the hall. It felt like encouragement if not temptation, but it was his father who passed beneath it, bearing drinks. 'Get your cousin a juice, Dickie,' he said.

Dick thought she might accompany him under the mistletoe, but she sat with unfamiliar primness on a chair, tugging her skirt over her knees. 'What do you want?' he asked more brusquely than he'd meant to.

'I'll have whatever you do.'

This felt like a kind of closeness, which to some extent compensated for the lack of a hug, though one might have discomforted him in ways he couldn't entirely define. He fetched two glasses of orange juice from the kitchen in time to hear his mother tell his father 'What I said before, it's them.'

She showed Ned and Susan the envelope before handing it to him. 'Is that the one you get every year, Chris?' his brother said.

'More of them than I'd like to count, and more illegible than ever. I'm surprised it even found the house.' Dick's father delayed opening the envelope to examine the front again. 'Particularly without a stamp,' he said.

Dick could have fancied that his father was reluctant to open the envelope. Certainly he grimaced as he poked a finger under the flap, peeling it away to reveal a greyish strip that looked unnecessarily moist. He extracted the card between finger and thumb before crumpling the envelope to drop it in the bin beside the squarish boxy television. He gave the picture—a vintage photograph of skaters on a pond resembling a web made of incisions—not much of a glance, and the inside even less of one. 'Unidentifiable as ever,' he said.

'Let's see if anybody can decipher it,' said Dick's mother.

She had to wag the hand she was holding out before he passed her the card. As she peered inside it Dick's aunt and uncle joined her, and Alice stood up too. 'That's right,' his father said as if it was the opposite, 'everybody have a go.'

Dick took him at his word, which gave him an excuse to put an arm around Alice's shoulders. They felt soft until a shrug hardened them, and he didn't know whether to let go, a decision he postponed by concentrating on the card. 'Take note, you two,' his uncle said to him and Alice. 'There's how not to write or spell.'

You and your familly all ways in my thoughts... Dick had to squeeze his eyes thin to distinguish many of the sprawling letters, which he would have been ashamed to produce at half his age. Were they symptoms of the second childhood in which people said you ended up? The signature was worse still, a wormy scribble that crawled off the edge of the card. 'Whenever you're done with it,' his father said.

As he retrieved it Dick's aunt said 'What did it say last year?'

'I really can't remember,' his father said and consigned the card to the bin. 'It isn't worth remembering.'

Dick took the opportunity to squeeze his cousin's shoulders. 'We do, don't we?'

'In that case spare us,' his father said.

Dick might have protested that the rebuke was unfair if he wouldn't have felt childish, especially when Alice could have thought he was. Over the years the family had joked about the increasingly scrawled cards and their defiantly unrecognisable signature. *Thinking of you, still thinking of you, always thinking of you, hoping to catch up...* He remembered all the messages but kept them to himself, wondering whether the latest card expressed frustration if not worse. Instead he asked Alice 'Shall we have a fight?'

'Nobody's been having one of those,' his father said. 'Any disagreement's done.'

Alice seemed to misunderstand Dick too, because she pulled

away from him. 'A snowball fight,' he felt awkward for having to explain.

'That should be fun,' his aunt declared. 'Just bundle up.'

In fact it wasn't too successful. While the grownups portrayed amusement, not to mention jovial revenge, Alice complained when one of Dick's snowballs caught her breast, even though it was protected by a coat as fat as his. He shied a few desultory missiles at the adults and then watched the play of shadows on the snow in the back garden. Some trick of light suggested one of them was thinner than it ought to be. The illusion vanished before he could locate it, and his father protested 'Who was that?'

He was brushing at his shoulder, dislodging pale fragments. 'Nobody hit you,' Dick's mother said as if addressing someone younger than their son. 'Not even near.'

'I believe it's turning colder,' Dick's father said with a shiver. 'Let's have everyone inside.'

Perhaps because Dick resented the show of concern, he couldn't help feeling it disguised something else. Everybody trooped into the house, leaving their shoes in the kitchen. He was watching Alice strip her coat off while he squirmed out of his when his father shouted from the front room 'Who did this?'

At first Dick couldn't see anything wrong, and then he realised that the card from the unknown sender was perched on the mantelpiece, peeking from between an embossed picture of mistletoe and a sketch of a Christmas tree. 'Who was last in here?' his father demanded. 'Was it you, Dickie?'

As Dick shook his head Alice spoke up. 'We went out first. It wasn't us.'

'Someone must have thought you dropped it by mistake, Chris,' Dick's mother said. 'Does it really matter? Who's ready for their dinner?'

Dick's father tore the card up and threw the pieces in the bin. 'Now I am.'

This might have disconcerted Dick, but Alice's defence of him had heartened him. Throughout dinner—a whole salmon, of which he had the boniest portion—he tried to keep her talking, but she seemed more interested in the adults' conversation. She was just a few months older than Dick, hardly a reason for her to feel superior. He was trying to think how to recapture her attention when his father turned to her. 'I don't know if anyone has mentioned you're in your parents' room.'

Dick hadn't been upstairs since his father had erected the camp bed for Christmas. 'Isn't she sleeping with me?'

'Your room's out of bounds now, old chap,' his uncle said. 'No sharing any more, at any rate.'

'Why?' Dick said, feeling stupider still.

'If you have to ask,' his aunt said, 'that's a reason.'

He'd embarrassed Alice at least as much as himself. He would have apologised if he could have found the right words, but the presence of the grownups didn't help. He was glad when dinner finished, not least since washing up brought him closer to Alice at the kitchen sink. He managed to brush against her several times before she flapped a towel at him. 'Why are you being so clumsy? Do you want me breaking dishes?' she said for everyone to hear, and he felt even more awkward than she'd made him out to be.

The film the family appeared to be compelled to watch at this time of year saved him from talking to her for a while, though it felt like being trapped in a past before he was born. Once again the drawling hero saw what life would have been if he'd followed a different path. While the women dabbed at their eyes and Alice looked determined not to need to, the men stayed doggedly impassive, Dick's father in particular. Dick might have thought the film had some extra meaning for his father, but his own embarrassment drove the notion out of his head.

In some ways bedtime came as a relief. He was grateful not to be expected to kiss anyone good night any more, though Alice would have been welcome. Lying in the dark, he heard her use the bathroom in a variety of ways, which troubled his body along with his mind. Thoughts of her kept him awake, and unfamiliar feelings did, growing disconcertingly physical. All this subsided when he heard a whisper.

By straining his ears he convinced himself it was snow on the window. The effort to identify the sound distorted it until he could have fancied it was forming words or just a word, though not one that made any sense to him. Horse certainly didn't, even if it was spelled hoarse, and coarse or course was little better. If he was imagining a whisper that said thoughts, it brought him none. Striving to hear sent him to sleep, only to waken with a sense that he'd gone to bed too early, because he heard a carol in the night, approaching the house. The solitary voice seemed to loom towards him as he endeavoured to hear. He could have thought that, rather than distant, it was low and close and lacking in breath. It was repeating snatches of carols as if they were all that the singer could bring to mind: 'It came upon a midnight clear' and then 'What child is this?' Perhaps the blurred fragmentary voice belonged to someone staggering back from a pub—it sounded uneven enough—and the idea let Dick take refuge in sleep.

Alice roused him. He'd started hoping she was in his room when he heard she was outside. 'It wasn't me,' she had just said.

'I didn't think so,' Dick's father said and shoved the door wide, letting more daylight into the room. 'Dickie, have you been making work for your mother?'

Dick yanked up his pyjama trousers before kicking off the bedclothes and stumbling to the door. His father's frown directed him to marks on the carpet, a track composed of melted snow and other fragments, which wandered about the landing and over the stairs. 'It wasn't me either,' he protested. 'I've been in bed.'

His father seemed to need to blame him. 'Just clean it up so your mother doesn't have to,' he said, and almost as an afterthought 'Happy Christmas.'

'Happy Christmas, Dickie,' Alice said, retreating to her room.

'Happy Christmas.' The chorus came from downstairs as well as the guest room, and Dick could have imagined one voice uttered just the final syllable, if even that much. He fetched the vacuum cleaner and nuzzled the stairs with the hose before hefting the cleaner all the way up them. While he might have liked Alice to witness his feat of strength, he was glad she wasn't watching him at housework. He erased the marks as swiftly as he could, disliking the look of the moist discoloured fragments, even if they were just crumbs of earth.

He followed Alice into the bathroom. Of course she wasn't in there—it simply meant he was next in—but the thought of her with no clothes on was, and the steamy air smelled of her soap. He lingered over bathing until his father knocked on the door to ascertain how much longer he would be, sounding more reproachful than Dick quite understood. The mirror had steamed up, and when Dick rubbed it clear he had a momentary impression of someone dodging out of sight behind him. It must have been his own movement, which also produced a momentary chill on his back.

Breakfast was accompanied by Christmas music on the radio. Whenever the name of the day came up, the first syllable seemed to grow prominent, as if a rogue contributor was emphasising it just not clearly enough to be unmistakable. As Dick tried to hear more precisely his father said 'What's up, Dickie? We don't want any frowns at Christmas.'

Dick might have rejoined that his father had one, perhaps for the same reason. 'If everybody's had enough,' his mother intervened, 'it's nearly time for presents.'

He and Alice cleared up, and he avoided touching her at the sink, not even handing her the washed-up items but planting them in the plastic rack. When she led the way into the front room he was acutely if not painfully aware of the rhythmical sway her hips had developed. He looked away for fear that the family would observe his excitement, and felt as if somebody he'd failed to notice had.

His presents were boys' books from his aunt and uncle, records from his parents. Alice had bought him one of those as well, an album by a band she liked, the Beatles. When his father found Dick's present for her under the tree, Dick was taken off guard by how his heartbeat speeded up. Alice looked surprised by the smallness of the package, but produced a smile once she'd opened it. 'That's pretty, thank you,' she said.

'I wasn't sure what to get you this year. Dad said you ought to like a ring.'

'I do.'

'Don't say you're proposing, Dickie.' Less like a joke his aunt said 'I expect you feel grownup now, Alice.'

Dick watched his father distribute presents, no more of which were for him. He was distracted by a dead light just visible through the branches of the tree. He might have taken it for a watchful eye if the bulb hadn't been so lifeless. As his father finally returned to his chair, Dick's uncle said 'You've forgotten someone's, Chris.'

He was pointing past the tree at a small parcel almost hidden by the thick timber disc that supported the trunk. As his father stooped to retrieve it, Dick realised he couldn't see the dead greyish oval bulb among the branches any longer. Perhaps his father had inadvertently nudged it out of sight, but Dick had no time to wonder as his father swung around to face him. 'Who brought this in?'

'You will have, will you, Dickie?' Aunt Susan said.

'I just brought what uncle gave me.'

'I didn't give you that,' his uncle said.

Dick recognised the writing on the package—the same as the unidentifiable card had borne. The scrawl said Chris, if barely that as it strayed off the edge of the crumpled wrapping, which was only just restrained by the loose bow of a discoloured ribbon. 'Don't keep us in suspenders,' Aunt Susan cried as though the situation needed a joke. 'Maybe it'll tell us who it is at last.'

Dick's father grimaced and wiped his hands on his trousers once he'd tugged the bow apart. When he peeled off the wrapping, fragments of it stuck to the small stained box. He lifted the lid, only to hesitate over displaying the contents. 'What is it, Chris?' Dick's mother said.

As his father tipped the box towards her, the contents rolled out—a tarnished silver ring, which fell on the carpet and trundled towards her without another sound. She captured it and made more of a face than Dick's father had. 'What's this inside it? It looks like old skin.'

'I've no idea and I can do without one. Throw it in.' His father held the box out, shutting it as soon as she returned the ring. 'That's the end of it,' he said, shoving the box after the ribbon and wrapping into the bin.

'It reminds me of something,' his brother said.

'Well, don't let it.'

'No, really. I believe I've got it.' As Dick's father mimed incredulity if not anger, Uncle Ned rummaged in the bin, eventually coming up with a piece of the Christmas card. 'This signature,' he said. 'Don't you think it could be Helen, Chris?'

'It could be any bloody thing. Forgive my language, children.'

'I'm sure this is a kind of h, and this could be an e and l.'

'I couldn't care less if they are or not. Just leave it, Ned.'

'I'd like to hear a little more about it,' Dick's mother said.

'Look, I told you I was engaged once. Long before we met, dear. She didn't prove too reasonable when I made it clear I'd had enough. I'd have expected her to take it better. She was quite a bit older than me. I was glad to forget all about it, and I still am.'

'Why don't you two go and listen to the record you gave Dick?' Aunt Susan said. 'But don't put it on too loud.'

'And I hope we won't hear any screaming,' Dick's father said.

Presumably he had in mind the way the Beatles made some girls behave, and Alice gave him a haughty look. 'I won't be,' she said. 'I'm not stupid.'

She might have meant to show this by not sitting next to Dick on his bed. She took the only chair, having told him to move yesterday's clothes. While the first side of the album played on his portable record-player, she kept swaying her top half with the rhythm, desisting whenever she grew aware of him. The songs obscured an argument downstairs, which eventually gave way to the slam of a dustbin lid under the window. Dick guessed his father had consigned the uninvited present and the torn-up card to the bin. The side ended, and he was about to turn the record over when his aunt opened the door without knocking. 'Come down now,' she said as if she'd caught them at some mischief or had thought she would.

The annual game of Monopoly was laid out on the dining-table. Dick chose the boot as usual, though now the token reminded him of the footprints he'd seen in the snow, even if his memory suggested that the visitor had worn no shoes, an idea so stupid he felt childish. He'd never noticed an odd echo in the room, rousing a bony restless sound whenever his father shook the dice. Soon Dick owned properties, but found he didn't relish collecting rent as much as usual, because he felt prompted to tell anyone who landed on them "Come and visit' if not "Come and stay." He could almost have imagined somebody was whispering the phrases in his ear if not his head. 'Just collect what you're due, Dickie,' his father said, at which Dick thought someone gave a low laugh, though he couldn't see who had.

Uncle Ned won the protracted game and flourished his fists above his head. Dick might have joined in, since it was time for dinner. His father carved the turkey, a spectacle Dick found unexpectedly bothersome; the echo was at work again, and the creak of bones parting from the carcass was imitated somewhere near. His parents let him have a glass of wine, since Alice had been given one. He devoured several slices of breast, a word that had acquired an extra connotation. He was ready for the Christmas pudding when it came, not least because he hadn't wholly outgrown the hope of discovering a coin. He thought Alice had one until she peered more closely at her prize. 'What is it, Aunt Annie? It looks like someone's nail.'

'It's certainly not one of mine.' Dick's mother gazed in distaste at the blackened twisted object. 'Dickie, fetch your cousin another spoon,' she said. 'Have you been playing a prank?'

'I never put that in.' He felt increasingly wronged as he brought Alice a spoon from the kitchen. 'I wish I hadn't stirred it when you said to make a wish,' he told his mother.

'Don't be such a baby, Dickie.'

'One more item for the bin,' his father said and stalked off with the spoon as if he couldn't bear the presence of its contents any longer.

Dick heard the back door slam—presumably his father couldn't even stand to have the object as close as the kitchen bin—and the prolonged gushing of a tap. As his father came back Alice said 'I'm sure it wasn't Dickie. He wouldn't do that to me.'

If he had indeed played such a prank he couldn't have been sure who the victim would be, but her support left him more determined to catch her under the mistletoe. He almost managed on the way into the front room, but the footfalls of the grownups made the tree stir and creak, distracting him. He could almost have imagined the scrawny shadow that crouched behind the tree continued shifting after every branch grew still.

Might he catch Alice on her way out of the room? Anticipation stayed with him throughout the after-dinner film, in which a ghost confronted Scrooge with his past. Dick's mother kept glancing at his father, who visibly relaxed once the ghost had done its job and its spectral colleagues guided Scrooge towards a preferable life. As soon as the credits set about mounting the screen Alice jumped up, too fast for Dick to head off. She was making for the bathroom, but her mother called 'Bedtime now, Alice.'

'For us too,' Dick's father said with a look at his wife that plainly earned less than he hoped.

'Let's all call it a day,' Dick's uncle said. 'It's been a long one.'

The relatives would be going home tomorrow—Alice would. Dick lingered in the front room, hoping she might return, until his mother sent him to the bathroom ahead of the adults. In bed he envisioned pouncing on Alice before she went home, except that pouncing wouldn't be too grownup or romantic. He ought to tempt her into the doorway, perhaps drawling like the hero of last night's film, since she'd found the actor appealing. Dick was drifting into a dream of their encounter when he heard her outside his room.

How could he mistake her footsteps? They were lighter than anybody else's in the house. They crossed the landing and grew fainter on the stairs, and Dick saw he had his chance. He donned his dressing-gown in case pyjamas seemed too bold and inched the door open. She'd left the lights off, no doubt so as not to waken anyone. Tiptoeing swiftly downstairs, he dodged into the front room. Was she in the kitchen? That light was off too. Dick stood under the mistletoe, straining his ears, and heard a thin muffled sound on the carpet. How could it be approaching when there was no sign of Alice? Of course, because it was behind him.

He thought she'd heard him coming downstairs and had hidden to catch him as he'd meant to catch her. He swung around, stretching his arms wide just in time to embrace her. She was nothing like as plump as he expected, and by no means dressed. Whatever covered the shrivelled body, to the extent that it even did, was in danger of flaking off. By the time Dick realised this, her face was pressed against his. It was as icy as the rest of her, and felt close to melting or otherwise collapsing. When he tried to cry out, a questing object blocked his mouth.

He struggled free of the lanky arms that clung to him—it felt like being tangled among branches—and hurled the intruder back into the room. Clutching at his mouth, he blundered to the front door. He spat the contents into the snow, and was continuing to retch when a light came on behind him. His parents were at the top of the stairs, and Alice had just emerged from her room. 'What on earth do you think you're doing?' his mother cried. 'I said your father shouldn't have given you any wine.'

'There's someone,' Dick babbled. 'Something. In that room.'

He didn't shut the front door until his father marched downstairs to switch on the light in the room. 'There's nobody at all,' he said, so fiercely that he might have been determined to convince not just his son.

Dick ventured into the room and eventually behind the Christmas tree, but nobody was hiding there either. 'Go to bed, for heaven's sake,' his father said. 'No more alcohol for you even at Christmas until you grow up.'

Dick fled to the bathroom first to scour his mouth with water.

In bed he lay rigid, chronically alert for the faintest sound, but heard not so much as a whisper. He thought he would lie awake until morning, and then he wondered if the intruder might have had enough of him. Before he knew it, the notion let him sleep.

At breakfast nobody referred to his behaviour, but he could tell that everyone was keeping quiet about it. Presumably Alice had mentioned it to her parents, and on the whole he preferred not to know what she'd said. He stayed well clear of the mistletoe, and barely managed not to recoil when his aunt delivered a parting hug—even when Alice planted a peck on his cheek. 'See you next year,' she said with belated wistfulness.

He didn't realise how constrained talking had become until he was alone with his parents. He sensed they'd said too much to each other at some point and were keeping their distance from the subject—not just from that, since his father was banished or chose to sleep in the guest room. Though Dick spent the day dreading another encounter of the kind he'd suffered in the dark, he wondered if his father was equally at risk if not more so. He might have warned him if he'd thought his father would have listened, especially if he himself had any evidence. But the object he'd spat out had writhed away into the snow, and he knew it was no use to search.

His parents stayed together until he grew up and left home. Their relatives still visited, but nothing was the same. He never kissed Alice, before or after she was married, and for the rest of his life he never opened his mouth for a kiss. It wasn't the result just of his encounter in the dark; it was having heard his father that first night in the guest room. The sounds had never left him, even once he managed to persuade himself that his father had only been having a nightmare—that the anguished moans hadn't expressed some kind of pleasure too. Despite growing muffled as though something had settled on his face, they'd persisted until dawn. Dick had waited for his mother to say anything at all about the incident, but he didn't think she ever had. Now his parents were long gone, and he would be alone at Christmas once again. At least, that was his most fervent hope.

Five O'Clock in The Bar at the End of the World

Bryony Pearce

One look at you and I know your poison. It's one of my skills. That, and I'm an amazing listener. Makes me good at my job.

I'm not listening now. It's quiet. Old Meg is asleep in a corner. She'll wake up in a little while and I've got her drink lined up on the bar, ready. A hurricane.

Not that cocktails are my fort-ay. I can make a Bloody Mary with the best, but them as want sticky, fruity drinks tend to hit Margot's down the way. I've got all the ingredients, and I can Tom Cruise it if I have to, but it's the beer that'll bring you to my establishment. The beer, the whiskey... the listening ear.

Old Meg stirs and mumbles. I look at her drink, but she subsides, and I leave it where it is, ice floes melting with little cracks, condensation trickling down the sides. Now, to look at Meg you wouldn't have thought that rum and passion fruit would be her drink. That's probably why she ended up in here. Hasn't drunk anything other than beer or rye her whole life. But I knew. She's a hurricane. And she's not drunk anything else since she arrived. Which proves me right.

There's a game of crib going on in a far corner. Whiskey sour,

Brandy on ice, Jameson's neat and a Blood-and-Sand. That's Buddy, Ritchie, Roger and J.P. to you. They're all still half full, no need for refreshers. None have looked at me for a while. They're in their own world where a few court cards in the hand and a five on the turn up means more than anything else. They've not a lot to bet, but J.P is down to his vest, so I'm thinking they're onto clothes.

The lager shandy is over by the pool table. It's a Brunswick 8-Foot Danbury and doesn't deserve what he's been doing to it. He's still crying.

Honestly, he's in the wrong place. Should've gone to Mario's. He does the best pizza and that's where all the kiddies and families usually end up. Lager shandy must've thought he was a big man, coming to my bar, asking for a beer. But he only likes the taste with a hefty lemonade mixer. He shouldn't be here. He's too young to be so alone. But he made his choice. There's only one way out for him and he's not ready for the exit yet. I find myself looking again at Old Meg. Then I busy myself cleaning a tumbler with a fresh towel. No streaks on my glassware!

The door opens. I glance at my watch and up again. One look, it's all I need. This one is a frosty San Miguel, but that's not what he'll ask for. I'm already pulling the pint when he staggers up to the bar, boots ringing on the floorboards.

'Cola,' he says. 'Ice.'

I shake my head and push the beer across polished oak. The glass is tall, already opaque as a glacier. When he picks it up, he'll leave prints on the chilled glass.

'It's too early,' he frowns. 'At least...'

'It's five o'clock somewhere,' I say. The condensation from Meg's hurricane is pooling on the wood. I lift it and the mat and give it a quick wipe.

He's hot. The beer is inviting like nothing he's ever seen. He wants it, I can tell. I'm never wrong.

'I haven't drunk since...'

'No judgement here,' I say.

With a sigh he picks up the glass and lifts it to his lips. It sticks to his warm fingertips as he takes a long drink. Then he puts it down almost a third empty.

'Good?'

He nods, licks his lips, removes his hat, puts it beside the beer. There is still sand on his boots, in the cuffs of his trousers. I'd ask him how long he was in the desert, it looks like it's been a long time, but he'll already be forgetting.

'Name's Mike,' he says, and I nod. 'What do they call you?'

'Me?' I put down my towel. 'I'm just the barman.'

'You must have a name.'

I smile. As if names are important. 'You can call me Charlie.'

'Charlie?'

I nod. He's looking at his drink.

'What do I owe you?'

I shake my head. 'Your money's no good here.'

He jerks and stares, his eyes narrowing. 'Free drinks?'

'Is anything ever really free?'

'You mean I'll be washing up at the end of the night?' He laughs.

'You keep drinking, I'll keep 'em coming.' I pick up my towel again. He's left a dirty mark where he was leaning on my oak. I swipe it off.

'You do good beer.' He gestures at the glass. 'I'd-a thought you'd be busier.'

'It's a quiet afternoon for me.' I put the towel down again. 'Mario's will be busy at this time and maybe the strip joint on the corner. It never stops in there.'

'There's a strip joint?'

'You didn't see it?'

He shakes his head. 'Not my style anyway.'

'It wouldn't be.' Or he would have noticed it. I lean on my elbows. There's nothing else to clean right now. In her corner Meg mumbles in her sleep. Mike whips a look at her and then turns back to me.

He's tanned from his time in the desert. Only his eyes measure me from a pale strip of skin, where his hat has shaded his face. They're sharp, penetrating even, shards of blue. He sees more than the others, I think.

'You been here long?' He asks, picking up his drink again. 'You'd a thought there'd be better places to build a bar than right here...on the edge.'

He remembers some then.

'Best place for it. Everybody's thirsty when they get to me.' I glance at Meg again. The melting ice will have diluted her drink if she's not awake in a few minutes.

'They would be.' He finishes his beer.

'Another?'

'Why not?' It's easier the second time. He pushes the glass to me. His fingers are long, thin. I wonder if he ever played the piano. He hasn't even glanced at the honky-tonk in the corner, though, so it doesn't seem likely.

I wonder if there's something he wants to talk about. Like I say, I'm a good listener, but I don't push. That's half of being a good listener. You wait for them to come to you.

'There's something familiar about you,' he says, watching me pour.

'Just got one of those faces I guess.' I send the fresh glass his way, and he looks at it, almost as if it's surprised him.

'Yes.' He frowns. 'I suppose you get a lot of travellers through here.'

'Reckon I do.'

'Don't suppose you've seen a boy.'

'Seen a lot of boys.' I lean on the bar. 'Most end up going through Mario's, though.'

'Oh.'

'You could describe him?'

'Yay high.' He hesitates and holds up a hand at about shoulder height, wobbling those long fingers. 'Blonde. Name of Matthew. It would have been... three years ago... yes... three years.'

Time does funny things in the desert. I don't think it would have been three years. I think he's starting to realise that too.

I shake my head.

'That's the only kid who's been through in some time.' I jerk my chin towards Lager Shandy who has slumped on a stool beside the pool table and is watching Mike with wide, hopeful eyes. 'He could do with a friend.'

Mike flinches. 'Maybe... but not me.'

I nod. 'The boy you're looking for—your son?'

He shakes his head and I know. But as I say, I don't judge. There's been all sorts through here. By the time they get to me the desert has sorted them out. I'm just here to serve the beers and listen.

'Where's me hurricane, Charlie?' Meg is standing by the bar now. Her once-blonde hair is a bird's nest. She tries to straighten it when she sees Mike staring at her, fingers combing awkwardly through the tangles. Then she gives up, almost defiantly, and lets it dangle over one bloodshot eye.

I push her drink towards her, and she sighs when she sees it. She's had a hard road this one. Through the desert and before it.

'Think this'll be me last,' she says. And she picks up the glass and looks at it for a long time before taking a sip. The lines on her face smooth when the rum hits her taste buds. 'You do make a good drink though, Charlie. I'm glad I found your bar.'

'Then you're off?' I look at her, measuring. It feels like she's been sleeping on the bench forever, I'm going to miss her... and her snoring.

I miss all of them, in my way, when they're gone.

'What're them doors, Charlie?' She frowns at the bare wall behind me. 'Weren't there before.'

'You weren't ready to leave before.'

Mike leans across the bar and lowers his voice. 'What doors? Is she a bit...?' He gives a finger a twirl by his temple. I ignore him. For this moment Meg is the most important person in here.

'Oi, Charlie, we need drinks!' It's the card game over by the far wall.

'In a minute, J.P.' I keep watching Meg closely. She's biting her lip, but her eyes have a sparkle of determination.

'Which one's for me?'

'That's up to you.' I pick up a glass and start polishing. I can't see the doors myself. I just know that there's one on my right and one on my left. 'The one on my left takes you onward, to the next level, I suppose.' I gesture with my cloth. 'The other takes you back around.'

'Back around?'

'A free play, if you like.'

Meg shakes her head. 'I didn't do that well in my last go-around, Charlie. What's 'on'?'

'That I can't tell you.' I hold the glass up to the light. No smears. Just right. 'I've never been further than my bar. But it seems like you're ready to find out.'

'I could come back and let you know?' She twists her blouse between her fingers, almost tearing the material. Shuffles her feet. A sweaty sheen breaks out on her forehead.

'You're welcome here anytime, Meg. But customers have promised me before, and none've come back yet.'

She straightens. 'Must be good then, iffen people don't want another go-around?'

Mike laughs, he's humouring her now. Doesn't believe in the doors. 'Or they can't *come* back,' he says, lowering his voice.

I frown at him.

'Something stopping 'em, you mean?' Meg bites her lip.

'It's a risk, that's true.' I put the glass down and glare at Mike. Then I touch Meg's hand. Her skin is warm where she was sleeping on it. I turn it over and find her fingertips have been chilled by the hurricane. I give them a squeeze. 'If you don't want to go around again, and you don't want to stay here, the only other way is on.'

'It can't be worse, can it?' She says thoughtfully.

Old Meg's told me some of what she remembers from her go-around and she's likely right. There isn't much worse out there.

'What's the time, Charlie?' Meg says suddenly, taking her hand back and wrapping her arms around her stomach, as if it aches.

'Five o'clock somewhere.' I say, and she laughs. I don't look at the clock behind me. It's always been stuck at three-thirty.

'Are you going to watch?' Meg starts drifting towards the door.

'I don't think I will.' I put her dirty glass in the sink. 'You have a great journey, you hear?'

'Don't you *want* to know what's on the other side? Aren't you curious?' She's moving with more determination now, her feet sure on the creaking boards. She's reached the side of the bar.

'Not me, Meg.' I smile at her. 'Not me.'

'Well then.' She raises a hand and touches what I assume is a knob. I turn my face away, in case I should glimpse something. There's nothing I want to see out there.

'Goodbye, Charlie, thanks for all the drinks.'

Mike slaps the bar. 'She's vanished!'

I nod.

'Where'd she go?'

'Through the door.'

'Through what door?'

'It'll be there for you. Eventually. When you're ready for it.'

'And when'll that be?'

'Up to you.' I start pouring another round: Whiskey sour, Brandy on ice, Jameson's neat and a Blood-and-Sand.

Mike watches me add egg whites to the cocktail shaker.

'Looks good.'

'But you'll stick to the beer?'

He nods and I almost laugh. Of course he will.

I sling the drinks onto a tray and bus them over to the table. J.P has lost his trousers now. Buddy has given up his shirt and socks. I check out their hands as I lay their drinks in front of them. Roger has a good one, nines and sixes.

He winks. 'Thanks, man.'

Part of me wants to tell him to be a gent, to leave J.P with his dignity if not his pants, but honestly, it doesn't seem like J.P. cares. I shrug and head back to the bar where Mike is draining his second beer. I slip back into my place and start to wash up again.

One ear open. The place feels empty without Old Meg. She's been here a long time.

Mike clears his throat. 'I'm getting a buzz on.' He doesn't meet my gaze. 'It's been a while. I vowed to stop drinking, y'know.'

It takes a moment before I answer. 'And did you?'

'Yeah, I think so. Yeah.' He looks at the beer. 'It's as good as I remember. The taste stays, or the memory of it.' He shuffles his feet. 'You won't let me go out drunk?' He peers at the windows. It's dark outside. Always is, especially compared to the brightness of the desert. He looks at the clock. 'Dark for four o'clock.'

I frown. 'Four?'

'Yeah.'

I turn and the wet cocktail shaker slips out of my hand. It bounces on the floorboards. Suds spray over my boots. Mike is right, it is four. The minute hand trembles as it ticks onto the hour.

'Well, that's odd.' I swallow. The clock has never worked. Not for one single second, not since I came out of the desert. I pick up the shaker and brush a little more sand from my trousers while I'm bent over. It's always there. Can't get rid of it.

Mike leans on the wood and watches me fumble the shaker back into the sink. 'You all right, man?'

'Yeah, I'm fine.'

I can hear the seconds now, at my back. Louder and louder. How did I miss it before, this passing of time?

My hands are trembling. I dry them on a tea towel, then keep the cloth. Soft with years of washing. Years.

Tick.

Mike licks his lips. 'These doors. You never thought about taking one yourself?'

Tick.

I shake my head. 'My place is here. People need a barman. What would you have done if I wasn't here—gone for pizza at Marios?' I laugh.

Tick.

He laughs too. 'Pizza's good, but this is better.'

'Exactly.'

Tick.

'Still,' he says. 'It's not exactly heaving in here, is it?'

'What do you mean?'

There's a shout from the card table. Ritchie is shimmying out of his shorts. Mike doesn't even look at him. I feel his eyes burning into me.

'You have six people in here. It's not a lot. We could do without you.'

'And leave the bar unattended?' I shuffle, more sand drops from my trousers.

Tick.

'I can pull a beer. Put ice in a whiskey.'

'You want my job?' I laugh again, loudly now. No one can replace me. I'm the barman. I listen.

Tick.

Mike shrugs and I slide him a new beer and some nuts. There's buzzed and there's drunk and I don't want him to slide from one state to the other.

He drinks silently as the clock ticks, ticks, ticks. The back of my neck itches but I don't turn around. I remain facing resolutely forward. There's a burst of laughter from outside and I straighten, but my door doesn't open. Heading for Margot's perhaps.

Six people. Am I really staying open for six people?

What would they say if I told them I was closing? What would they do? I've never shut. Never even taken a break. I mean it's always five-o-clock somewhere, right?

My neck prickles. I flick my eyes towards the clock. Four-thirty. What does it mean?

I mutter under my breath and pour a lager shandy, take it to the kid by the pool table. 'Here you go, son.'

'Thanks,' he murmurs, shoulders sagging. The hair above his lip is just starting to thicken and he has acne scars on his forehead, which deepen when he frowns at his drink.

'You should think about moving on,' I say, but instead of

walking away I stand over him, watching as he puts the glass on the baize.

'Where to?' He looks, if possible, younger and even more miserable.

'You could have another go around?' I point to the bar without looking. 'Time's getting on.'

He nods, but doesn't move. 'That man by the bar, there's something familiar about him.'

He spent less time in the desert, the young always do. Perhaps he remembers something.

'His name's Mike,' I say.

The boy nods, as if I've confirmed a thought, but he doesn't speak it.

I stand still a little longer, then shrug and turn to leave. He'll be ready when he's ready.

Tick.

I flinch each time I hear another second go by. This time I don't go around the bar. I stand beside Mike and look at the clock. It's an old station clock. White face, black hands.

'The boy will be okay,' Mike says, and I nod. 'So will the card game.' He laughs.

'What about the next person through?'

He shrugs. 'We can manage.'

'We?'

His shoulders move again, as if to indicate that it'll all sort itself out. But that's not how the world works. It never has been.

'The boy recognises you,' I say.

'Does he?' He turns.

The kid is watching us, the lager shandy clenched in one fist. It looks as if he wants to say something. But the words remain locked behind his lips.

'Maybe he knows Matthew.'

'Perhaps.' It's possible. Or perhaps Mike was a big name, on his last go around. That's possible too.

The clock ticks over to four fifty-five.

'Soon be five,' Mike says. 'Looks like *you* could use a drink.'

He's not wrong, my mouth is dry, my lips cracked. I look down at my feet, my boots remain dusty. A beer. That's what I need.

I grip the bar and Mike nods. He walks around, pulls me a pint, wipes the bar in front of me and pushes my drink across.

I watch the bubbles slither up the glass. I haven't tasted my own beer. Perhaps it's time. I raise the glass. Froth touches my lips, I inhale the yeasty scent.

'It's good,' I tell him.

I empty the glass in one long pull. When I put it down the hand has ticked over to five.

'Five o'clock,' Mike says.

'Yeah.' There's a shimmering behind him. Two doors appear. The one to the barman's left is weathered wood, battered, with an uneven gap between the hinges. The knob is round. It will push easily open. The one to his right is plain white, fitted tightly to the frame, a chrome handle.

Back around, or on.

Mike picks up the glass I've emptied and slips it into the suds. 'Can you see them—the doors?'

I nod.

'How long have you been here, running this joint?'

I lick my lips. 'Since half three...' I sigh and step towards the white door. Onward. It's time.

As I touch the handle, the clock behind me stops. It's still five. Will be until Mike passes on the towel, I guess.

'Safe journey, Charlie,' he says.

I open the door.

Stars glimmer, galaxies turn, suns burn and decay. I look at my feet, the sand has gone, my boots are clean. I step on, into the universe.

About the Contributors

Warren Benedetto studied Evolutionary Biology at Cornell University, and has a Master's degree in Film/TV Writing from the University of Southern California. When he's not writing, he works as Director of Global Product Strategy at PlayStation where he holds 20+ patents for various types of gaming technology. He is also the developer of StayFocusd, the world's most popular anti-procrastination app for writers. He built it while procrastinating.

Simon Bestwick is the author of eight novels, five novellas and four full-length short story collections. His short fiction has appeared in *Shakespeare Unleashed* and reprinted in *The Best Horror of The Year*, with further stories forthcoming in *Phantasmagoria* and *ParSec* magazine. His latest novel is *The Hollows*, as by 'Daniel Church,' which marks the fifth time he's been shortlisted for a British Fantasy Award.

The *Oxford Companion to English Literature* describes **Ramsey Campbell** as 'Britain's most respected living horror writer'. He has been given more awards than any other writer in the field, including the Grand Master Award of the World Horror Convention, the Lifetime Achievement Award of the Horror Writers Association, the Living Legend Award of the International

Horror Guild and the World Fantasy Lifetime Achievement Award. In 2015 he was made an Honorary Fellow of Liverpool John Moores University for outstanding services to literature. Among his novels are *The Face That Must Die*, *Incarnate*, *Midnight Sun*, *The Count of Eleven*, *The Darkest Part of the Woods*, *The Overnight*, *Secret Story*, *The Grin of the Dark*, *Thieving Fear*, *Creatures of the Pool*, *The Seven Days of Cain*, *Ghosts Know*, *The Kind Folk*, *Think Yourself Lucky*, *Thirteen Days by Sunset Beach*, *The Wise Friend*, *Somebody's Voice*, *Fellstones* and *The Lonely Lands*. His Brichester Mythos trilogy consists of *The Searching Dead*, *Born to the Dark* and *The Way of the Worm*. His collections include *Waking Nightmares*, *Ghosts and Grisly Things*, *Told by the Dead*, *Just Behind You*, *Holes for Faces*, *By the Light of My Skull* and a two-volume retrospective roundup (*Phantasmagorical Stories*) as well as *The Village Killings and Other Novellas*. His non-fiction is collected as *Ramsey Campbell, Probably* and *Ramsey Campbell, Certainly*, while *Ramsey's Rambles* collects his video reviews and a book-length study of the Three Stooges, *Six Stooges and Counting* is due later in the year. *Limericks of the Alarming and Phantasmal* is a history of horror fiction in the form of fifty limericks. His novels *The Nameless*, *Pact of the Fathers* and *The Influence* have been filmed in Spain, where a television series based on *The Nameless* is in development. He is the President of the Society of Fantastic Films.

His web site is at: www.ramseycampbell.com

Eliza Chan is a Scottish-born author who writes about East Asian mythology, British folklore and madwomen in the attic. Her debut novel *Fathomfolk*, inspired by mythology, folklore, Esean cities and diaspora feels, will be published by Orbit in Spring 2024. Find out more at www.elizachan.co.uk

After working in Canada for some time, **Cécile Cristofari** settled in her native South France, where she teaches English literature and writes science fiction and fantasy when her children are asleep. Her debut short story collection, *Elephants in Bloom*, is scheduled for release at the end of 2023. She can be found online at staywherepeoplesing.wordpress.com

Paul Di Filippo has published over forty books, with his newest novel being *The Summer Thieves*, a Vancian space opera. He lives in Providence, RI, with his partner Deborah Newton and a cocker spaniel named Moxie.

David Gullen has sold over 40 short stories to various magazines, anthologies and podcasts. He is a two-times winner of the BFS Short Story Competition with other work short-listed for the James White Award and placed in the Aeon Award. His latest novel, *The Girl from a Thousand Fathoms*, is available in print and ebook, as is his novella *The Blackhart Blades*, released in 2023. He lives in South London with fantasy writer Gaie Sebold.

Joanne Harris (OBE, FRSL) is the internationally bestselling author of over twenty novels, plus screenplays, articles and three collections of short stories, including *Honeycomb* (illustrated by Charles Vess). She writes across multiple genres, from fantasy (*The Gospel Of Loki*) to magic realism (*Chocolat*) and psychological thrillers (*Broken Light*). She performs with the Storytime Band, and writes her stories from a shed at the top of her garden.

Gwyneth Jones is a writer and critic of genre fiction, who has also written for teenagers using the name Ann Halam. She's won a few awards but doesn't let it get her down. She lives in Brighton, UK, with her husband and two cats, curating assorted pondlife in season. She's a member of the Soil Association, the Sussex Wildlife Trust, Frack Free Sussex and the Green Party; and an Amnesty International volunteer. Hobbies include watching old movies, playing Zelda and staring out of the window.

Shih-Li Kow is the author of two short story collections and a novel. *The Sum of Our Follies* was translated into Italian, French and Bulgarian. The French edition (tr. Frederic Grellier) won the 2018 Prix du Premier Roman Etranger. *Ripples and Other Stories* was shortlisted for the 2009 Frank O'Connor International Short Story Award and her second collection, *Bone Weight and Other Stories*, is scheduled for release in November 2023. She lives in Kuala Lumpur, Malaysia.

Kim Lakin is a dark fantasy and science fiction author from the UK. Kim's novels include the multi-award shortlisted *Cyber Circus*, (2011) and *Rise* (2019). Her short stories have appeared in numerous anthologies and magazines and her debut collection *Sparks Flying* was released in April 2023. Kim lives on a farm in Derbyshire with her cat, Diablo.

Alison Littlewood's novels include *A Cold Season, Mistletoe, The Hidden People, The Crow Garden* and *The Unquiet House*. She also wrote *The Cottingley Cuckoo* and *The Other Lives of Miss Emily White*, as A. J. Elwood. Alison's short stories have been picked for a number of year's best anthologies and she has won the Shirley Jackson Award for Short Fiction. Alison lives in a house of creaking doors and crooked walls in deepest darkest Yorkshire, England.

Ken MacLeod is the author of seventeen novels, from *The Star Fraction* (1995) to *The Corporation Wars* (2018), and many articles and short stories. *Beyond the Hallowed Sky* (2021) is the first volume of a space opera trilogy.

Discover more at http://kenmacleod.blogspot.com

Bryony Pearceis a multi-award-winning novelist. She has written a mixture of dark thrillers, paranormal adventures, science fiction and horror for adults and young adults alike. Bryony also teaches creative writing at City University (London) and works as a consultant and mentor to help aspiring authors achieve their dreams. She currently lives in Gloucestershire and, if she isn't writing, can usually be found providing a taxi service for her teenage children, drinking wine or playing the cello. For more information on her work.

Please visit her website www.bryonypearce.co.uk

Patrice Sarath is the author of *The Sisters Mederos* and *Fog Season* (The Tales of Port Saint Frey); *Gordath Wood, Red Gold Bridge, and The Crow God's Girl* (The Books of the Gordath), and *The Unexpected Miss Bennet*. Her stories have appeared in *Alfred Hitchcock Mystery Magazine, Weird Tales*, and *Year's Best Fantasy*, and her first short story collection is due out in 2024.

She blogs at www.patricesarath.com

Angela Slatter is the author of six novels, including *All the Murmuring Bones*, *The Path of Thorns* and *The Briar Book of the Dead*, as well as eleven short story collections, including *The Bitterwood Bible* and *The Tallow-Wife and Other Tales*. She's won a World Fantasy Award, a British Fantasy Award, a Shirley Jackson Award, a Ditmar, two Australian Shadows Awards and eight Aurealis Awards. Her work has been translated into multiple languages. She has an MA and a PhD in Creative Writing, occasionally teaches creative writing and mentors new authors. She can be located on the internet at www.angelaslatter.com, @AngelaSlatter (Twitter) and angelaslatter (Instagram). She's collaborated with Mike Mignola on a new series from Dark Horse Comics, *Castle Full of Blackbirds*, set in the Hellboy Universe.

Teika Marija Smits is a UK-based writer and freelance editor. She writes poetry and fiction, and her speculative short stories have been published in *IZ Digital*, *Shoreline of Infinity*, *Best of British Science Fiction* and *Great British Horror 6*. Her debut short story collection, *Umbilical*, was published by NewCon Press in August 2023. A fan of all things fae, she is delighted by the fact that Teika means fairy tale in Latvian.

https://teikamarijasmits.com/ @MarijaSmits

Anna Tambour's latest books are a novel, *Smoke Paper Mirrors*, and collections *The Road to Neozon* and *Death Goes to the Dogs*.

Adrian Tchaikovsky is a writer of fantasy and science-fiction, including the Children series that began with *Children of Time*, the fantasy epic Shadows of the Apt and a number of other novels and novellas. His work has won the Arthur C Clarke, British Science Fiction, British Fantasy and Sidewise Awards.

Natalia Theodoridou has published over a hundred short stories, most of them dark and queer, in magazines such as *Strange Horizons*, *Uncanny*, *Clarkesworld*, *Beneath Ceaseless Skies*, *Nightmare*, and *F&SF*, among others. He won the 2018 World Fantasy Award for Short Fiction and has been a finalist for the Nebula Award in the Novelette and Game Writing categories. Natalia holds a PhD in Media and Cultural Studies from SOAS, University of London, and is a Clarion West graduate. He was born in Greece, with roots in Georgia, Russia, and Turkey.

Find out more at www.natalia-theodoridou.com or follow @natalia_theodor on Twitter.

Steve Rasnic Tem, a past winner of the Bram Stoker, World Fantasy, and British Fantasy Awards, has published over 500 short stories. His novel *Ubo* is a dark science fictional tale about violence and its origins, featuring such viewpoint characters as Jack the Ripper and Stalin. His latest collection is *Thanatrauma: Stories* from Valancourt Books.

You can visit his home on the web at www.stevetem.com

Lavie Tidhar is author of *Osama*, *The Violent Century*, *A Man Lies Dreaming*, *Central Station*, *Unholy Land*, and *By Force Alone*. His latest novels are *The Hood* and *The Escapement*. His awards include the World Fantasy Award, the British Fantasy Award, the John W. Campbell Award, the Neukom Prize and the Jerwood Fiction Uncovered Prize.

George Tom is an engineering undergraduate from Bangalore, India. In college he studies electronics, computer science, and communication systems; in his free time he studies fiction and is a slush reader for *Strange Horizons*. This is his first short story sale and represents his debut as a fiction writer.

Aliya Whiteley's novels and novellas have been shortlisted for multiple awards including the Arthur C Clarke award and a Shirley Jackson award. Her short fiction has appeared in *Interzone, Beneath Ceaseless Skies, Black Static, Strange Horizons, The Dark, McSweeney's Internet Tendency* and *The Guardian*, as well as in anthologies such as Unsung Stories' *2084* and *Lonely Planet's Better than Fiction*.

More information can be found at her website: aliyawhiteley.uk

Neil Williamson is a writer and musician living in Glasgow; many of his stories can be found in his collections *The Ephemera* and *Secret Language*, and his latest novel *Queen of Clouds* (NewCon Press) was released in April 2022. "A Moment of Zugzwang" explores the same near-future surveillance society world as his novella *The Memoirist* and short story "Neighbourhood Watch", which appeared in 2 of *ParSec*. Find out more at neilwilliamson.blog

Ian Whates is the author of ten published novels, two novellas, and some eighty short stories that have appeared in a variety of venues. In 2019 he received the Karl Edward Wagner Award from the British Fantasy Society, while his work has been shortlisted for the Philip K. Dick Award and on three occasions for BSFA Awards. He is a director and former chair of the British Science Fiction Association and has been a judge for both the Arthur C. Clarke Award and the World Fantasy Awards. In addition to *ParSec* magazine, he has edited some forty anthologies. In 2006 Ian founded award-winning independent publisher NewCon Press by accident.

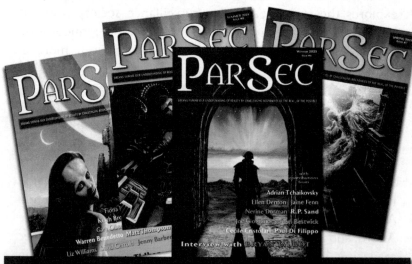